THE
CALLERS

Michael McDonnell

Special thanks to:

Tatiana Wilde: Editor
Bookfly Design: Book Cover Design
Petya Tsankova: Book Interior Design

ISBN paperback: 978-1-736465-0-1
ISBN ebook: 978-1-7363465-1-8

Entanglement Press

CONTENTS

To my family

CHAPTER 1

Ben Stern woke up depressed. Still, he liked his morning routine: the daily three-mile run, ample newspaper availability, even dressing in his business-casual clothing, plus lots of coffee – beginning after his run and continuing at an addictive pace throughout the day. Ben liked this early morning circuit. The activities were directed and generally comforting. Their anodyne effect usually worked. On waking this morning, however, something in his mind produced a kind of acid reflux, prompting him to think about his current status, or situation, or both. He was alone, so he coped with it. The pleasing morning routine helped. Ben stood still for moment, his jaw slack and his lips slightly parted. He quickly parsed out for himself his different circumstances. I'm a nice guy, he thought, interested in many things. Ben felt he had become an accomplished person. Green eyes blinked and he found himself standing in front of his apartment building in Arlington. Must begin my run. His hand idly rubbed at the top of his cropped head, and he began trotting, then allowing the pace to pick up.

As he ran at his usual clip past the Ballston metro stop, some mental modality in his head conjuring the image of a kind, but always fretful grandparent – his dad's mom. Smiling Mae superseded that image, then vanished from his mind, as she had vanished physically from him to reside now back in Manhattan. Ben volunteered a kindly thought for the pretty Mae and felt nostalgia, followed by a dissonant tug. Well, it had been eight months, not quite three quarters of a year, and therefore not an entire year, so Ben drew a fine point on it.

By this time, Ben had already turned around and launched into the backstretch, his clip comfortable and hopefully producing the desired endorphins so helpful for the day's activities. He pulled toward his apartment building on the upcoming corner, making his approach as a renter – not an owner yet. He had the resources, he often mused. He would be ready, sure, to get on track again. He, Ben, would be a provider. Enough with the stages of adjustment, I'm done. I'm fine. Work has been great! I'm sure I'll meet somebody and that will be that, he thought.

Somehow, he navigated himself through his building lobby, up the elevator, and into the foyer of his one-bedroom apartment. Ben made a verbal click to himself, quickly shed his running gear, and took a quick shower. He moved efficiently, wanting to be, like always, at the center by 7:30am.

—

Jim Casey sat at his desk, softly rubbing the bristle cut on the back of his head. He leaned back in his chair, then ran his two hands quickly over his face, as if to snap himself out of a shallow fugue state. He enjoyed seeing his feet propped on his desk, a privilege he enjoyed since he had no boss or any real level of bureaucratic authority to report to. He hadn't really had one for some time, almost since the beginning. Jim stretched his back and yawned. No one was going to come by and tell him to take his feet down. He liked that, when thinking about it. Casey absently glanced around his office, which was ample, and set up with reproduction Federal-style furniture, with prints on the walls and photos festooned on flat surfaces. He looked at the picture of Margery on his desk, she smiled back. There she was, silver-haired and pretty, his wife of forty years plus, now dead these past two. Jim turned to pay attention to the photos at the end table by his desk, where his three daughters presided, with children and husbands completing the retinue. Jim smiled and sighed.

The inert Xeroxed Federal style of his office satisfied his disinterest about such things. It worked just fine for him. Still, his own affects and personality insinuated themselves. There, on his desk and end table, even more family pictures, revealing a menagerie of smiles and poses. A framed Sierra Club award was mounted over the couch. Audubon prints flanked the award in deference. Looking again at the whole of his desk surface, Jim glanced absently at the picture of him and his "fellow conspirator", Harold Oberkotter. There, in that picture, they were much younger. Both sporting fu manchus. He was looking in one direction, eyes open, maybe a little vacant. Jim winced, then shrugged at the thought. Oberkotter was plainly looking in another direction and showed a similarly vacant stare. Jim studied himself in the photo, witnessed his younger self, examined for a moment his long brown hair from that time and his unlined face. He took in the image of his partner, Oberkotter, who was staring off in a different direction from his. Eyes clear, vacant and slightly magnified behind eyeglass lenses. Yep, we were there at the beginning, Jim thought. He cracked his knuckles.

—

Ben was in his head, but stepped out of the elevator as it disgorged him at his floor, where he was greeted by the wry and slight Jim Casey – he with the enviable office suite. Jim stood there, surveying Ben and grinning.

"Ben, my man, thanks for coming in today…"

Ben smiled and relaxed. He liked Jim, liked being joshed by him. He looked to Ben a bit like a cagey, grizzled Bob Newhart character, with Icelandic sweater vest.

"Hey Jim, how's that Pentagon Papers thing going? Oh, better get a haircut," Ben beamed back.

"Trust your eyes, son. I'm neat and tidy these days," Jim grinned.

Ben winked and resumed his route, heading directly to the open-floor office, wending his way to his desk, depositing layers and briefcase, then angling over to the coffee station.

_ CHAPTER 2

President-elect Steve Rasmussen stood still on the dais and placed his left hand on the dark, substantial Bible that had trotted out from the Library of Congress for such meaningful occasions. Rasmussen raised his right hand, whereupon the Chief Justice began administering the oath of office. Though only marginally comfortable in a suit, no matter how well tailored, Rasmussen looked loose and at ease to the crowd assembled below, at street level. It was an especially cold January morning for Washington, a city otherwise often humid, even tropical. The soon-to-be-bona-fide President observed the puffs of air the Chief Justice emitted while delivering the oath. Rasmussen looked toward the assembled crowd below the podium. He smiled at the sampling of his electors, broadly speaking. The Rasmussen full-on smile came across as warm and inviting, despite the lantern jaw and slightly prognathous chin. When at rest, his face appeared impassive and yes, stony. But, broken into a grin, it – and its owner – conveyed warmth and likeability. His campaign managers marveled at the phenomenon, and were thankful.

–

"Truly, truly, the American public has seen an astounding re-emergence of Whiggish Republican politics, never more so than in the triumph of the Rasmussen-McLearned ticket," intoned George Will, conservative opinion maker and friend to the recording camera.

Mark Shields, a center-left newspaperman managed to just shake his head.

"The Republican Party had, with Steve Rasmussen, 'seen its opportunities and took 'em,' as an old Tammany boss might say.

4

Rasmussen was, for the Republicans, the only way," here, Shields scrunched his shoulders and put his hands together for emphasis, "that they could have conceivably squared that electoral circle, which they did!"

"What was interesting throughout the primaries and the presidential campaign was Steve Rasmussen's ability to make his very public gay identity such a non-issue for many rank and file Republican voters and even for the extremely conservative wings of the Republican Party," observed the manicured commentator, Sandra Bream.

"Rasmussen was able to do this, while also benefitting from a broad outpouring of support from gay Americans and a bewildering range of support across the political spectrum."

Shields nodded glumly, "Yeah, you could see in President Steve what you wanted to see in him."

George Will nodded at Shields and then at the camera, "His message on effective, limited and pragmatic government," Will paused to lightly hold his chin, "resonated and captured a broad plurality of the American public."

A moment of silence ensued, then a Dodge Ram pickup rushed across the screen for viewers at home, who quickly became acquainted with the vehicle's pulling power and torque. Those watching were then met with Sandra Bream's steady gaze.

"Mark, you've been through many electoral cycles. This one must be the most unorthodox, the weirdest? Certainly for the Republican far right."

"Sandra, definitely out of the ordinary, but also a little bit of the Nixon-goes-to-China thing," Shields replied, leaning forward, towards the camera, for emphasis.

"Rasmussen was and is a successful software entrepreneur, a notable Silicon Valley figure," Shields began gesticulating, surprising himself, "He is a self-made business-builder, a guy who has successfully developed a large software analytics firm –

well-run, well-respected... For our viewers, I would say – look at the whole package."

Here Shields began enumerating with his fingers on one hand.

"Rasmussen's a techie, out-of-the-ballpark success. He's a believer in markets, but also in 'human capital development', as he puts it. He's a self-described Christian, dual confessional Lutheran-Catholic. He's gay," Shields continued enumerating, "he's a big guy, was a phenomenal college ball player at Minnesota, and he lives in California – and they love him there."

Shields was shaking his head, some weariness evident, "Did I leave anything out? Some say he's stiff but, then, before the voters he's not. The guy is an electoral force of nature, Sandra, and this election is the culmination of that."

Shields closed his mouth firmly, signaling that he was done talking.

"Thank you, Mark Shields, for those insightful comments," Sandra Bream said to the camera.

–

Meanwhile, Steve Rasmussen, President-elect, scanned the friendly, jubilant – but well-ordered – assembly of people gathered below the outdoor presidential podium. Before him were the media, dignitaries, some citizens of different strips, all bundled up against the January frigidity. And there, too, was his family, drawn from the different reaches of Minnesota and Wisconsin. As he looked out, Rasmussen re-animated and cracked a broad grin, his white teeth even and visible. He waved shyly, discreetly, and mid-ceremony. The crowd erupted into scattered hoots and cheers directed at their new President. His eyes moved lazily from left to right, taking in the scene. He could actually take in a lot – his vision being very good, both forward and peripheral, a great football asset, allowing him to take in "keys" on the playing field. Steve

Rasmussen looked out at the many members of the extended Rasmussen-Dirnbauer-Kadrowsky kin. He nodded toward his three sisters, all still living in Minnesota, all (magically, he thought) with agreeable spouses.

The Washington winter sun, not lambent, still showed itself for the inaugural, unobstructed among a few gray-white clouds. Rasmussen felt as if he were standing outside of himself, viewing the proceedings. His niece Tammy, his sister Jill's girl, stood beside him holding the Smithsonian Bible. A U of M volleyball player, she was nearly as tall as he was. Mom couldn't be here; he blinked, seeing her for second, her soft, warm brown eyes and generally serious gaze. Decades of smoking Parliaments while sipping Folger's coffee had conspired to afflict her with a case of fast-acting pancreatic cancer. His partner Ralph – also gone, he thought, also victim to the big C. Steve really missed Ralph's erudition. Such a smart, knowledgeable guy. His missed his small neat Ralph, who always met his sometimes-absent gaze with smiling blue eyes and an even wider grin. He would always grin back.

As his niece held the Bible, his left hand placed upon it, his right hand raised, the Chief Justice reciting, he saw himself listening. Rasmussen stiffened appropriately, held himself straighter as he responded to the prompts of his oath. He glanced across at President Obama and his family, who seemed happy for him, and also somewhat relieved. The two daughters looked bored and detached. The President and the First Lady did indeed look a bit relieved, happier to be moving on. He felt a sudden urge to make a small wave to them, something he quickly suppressed.

The brief, solemn recitation concluded and President Rasmussen promptly received an animated hug from his niece. The Obamas smiled in unison. Rasmussen grinned, feeling a bit giddy himself. He surveyed the crowd, who were happy for him, strangely partial to him, given what can be a Democratic town. The large-framed Republican Silicon Valley business-builder, gay linebacker, cerebral engineer, widower, and now self-described "confirmed bachelor" lifted his right arm in a full-bodied wave, and delivered a few hoped-for inspirational words about the providential role of his country, which he believed, he really did. The crowd emitted more cheering. President Obama, two-time veteran of this protocol, raised his chin slightly, while looking at Rasmussen to signal the coming exit from the podium. With this stage in the formalities concluding, the new President started to feel a little looser as he and others began shuffling down the Capitol steps. The security detachment roused themselves and hastened to his side. Feeling someone tug at his elbow, Rasmussen turned slightly.

"Congratulations Steve, or rather, Mr. President," the now-citizen Obama grinned. President Steve returned the smile, "Gosh, thanks Barack, never thought I'd be doing this..."

"No worries, you'll be great." The former President was being sincere, but cursory, given what he wanted to say.

"I'd like to block just a bit of your time, actually as soon as possible, practically speaking."

Rasmussen fully turned toward his petitioner and focused on him, "Mr. President, sir, that's no problem. We're still getting organized a bit, but sure. Early tomorrow in that fancy office you and the electors are letting me occupy for a while?"

Obama tugged again at Rasmussen's coat sleeve, as if to acknowledge, "That's great, then I'll come by at 8:30 am or so."

"No problem, that sounds great."

"Perfect," Obama clapped the top of Rasmussen's shoulder, and allowed the new President to flow forward toward the rest of the inaugural activities.

_ CHAPTER 3

As always, Steve Rasmussen showed up early for work. His admin, Lindy, whom he'd brought over from Sybylline, was there to meet him, ensuring the requisite amounts of hot black coffee were on hand for the both of them. Coffee was Rasmussen's only remaining vice, now that he had sworn off gluten, thereby alleviating a clinging sinus inflammation that had plagued him most of his adult life.

The new President sat in the Oval Office in and reflected on his agenda for the day, which loomed before him. A proverbial boatload. Wiley, his Chief of Staff, had compiled it. There was the congressional menagerie, the bureaucratic menagerie, public relations stuff, some foreign policy things. He glanced at his watch. Obama should be on deck. As if on cue and at the door, Lindy appeared, hazel eyes open and smiling; following her was the now-refreshed former President, winsome from seeing someone else now shouldering the load. Obama turned to thank Lindy for an earlier offer on coffee, joking that he wanted to be as fully awake and as helpful as he could be.

"Mr. President?"

"Oh, uh, thanks Lindy, I'll take one as well, just black, as always."

"Steve," Obama declared the name, and stood for a moment before sitting in the blue chaise opposite the Resolute desk at which Rasmussen sat. "I'm really glad you're able to set aside some time to talk. I promise I won't be too long. I know how busy this all gets." The former President drew a wide semi-circle in the air for emphasis. Hearing this, Rasmussen rested his large frame more deeply into his chair, and smiled thinly.

"Barack, Mr. President, it's a pleasure. I definitely need all the good advice I can get, and I value the mileage you've recorded here." Rasmussen paused and relaxed his shoulders. "I also want to say how grateful I am for the openness that your team has demonstrated. Our guys are commenting on how great the collaboration has been. The working groups have been great..."

Obama smiled and looked down at his lap for a moment, "Steve, I'm glad, and please don't hesitate to let me know if you need anything, or if I can help you get at a few corners or move any unanticipated things, at least by me, let me know."

"Well, that's great, Barack, and really very appreciated," Rasmussen's smile was broad and even, conveying sincerity.

"Wonderful." The former President paused, and then leaned forward. "Steve, I don't want to weigh on your time here, and I guess I called the meeting, so I should make it a bit quicker and get to the point."

The new President's expression was now stony and attentive, as the former President continued, "I want to emphasize to you a very important meeting you should schedule at the earliest convenient time, I think."

"Sure, who should I be seeing?"

President Obama seemed visibly heartened just then by Rasmussen's simple agreement.

"Steve, again, to cut to the chase a bit, I'm here today and I'm glad we can talk a bit. That is, confidentially." Obama paused, and registered an expression unlike any that Rasmussen or the literal billions of people in the world had probably ever seen or associated with the former President. Obama's expression was sheepish, freighted, almost quizzical. The kind of expression, it occurred to Rasmussen, that one might have from holding a secret, while wondering and waiting for the other shoe to drop. He had a seen a similar expression on Hilary Clinton's face, when she strode across a television network stage to congratulate him on his electoral victory. What is on that collective administration's mind? Steve wondered. He thought about Clinton. She had been confident and intelligent, sometimes courtly, sometimes brassy, a little out of it sometimes – thankfully, Rasmussen thought. But then, he saw the same expression on her face that one time. A concerned, veiled look. What was that about?

Obama caught himself and continued, dislodging Rasmussen from his own reverie. "I think it's important, Steve, that you set up a meeting with a man named Jim Casey. He's a very sharp guy. He'll be able to brief you on some subject matter that is very sensitive."

"Okay..." The new President now began shifting his own large body around in his seat behind the Resolute desk, as if trying to gain traction.

"No worries, nothing's boiling over," Obama leveled his gaze for emphasis.

"But this meeting, I would say, is very important for you, very fundamental, and you should have the meeting soon." Obama paused and relaxed for moment.

"Casey has 9-D security clearance, the absolute highest level. He's old, but very alert. You'll like him. A bit of an odd bird, though. Exotic holdover from the Nixon administration."

Now, it was Rasmussen who gazed levelly at Obama.

"As I said, you should meet Casey soon," Obama continued, "at least some time in the next few weeks. Please include your Secretary of State designate. Levchin, isn't it? And don't worry, she'll get confirmed." Obama's grin was mischievous.

"That's no problem," Rasmussen answered blankly. "I'll make sure Irena's there."

"Good, I'd also like to be at that meeting, and I'll facilitate it as well. I'll contact Casey and we'll work with your office to schedule it."

"Um, Barack, this man Casey, he must be in his mid-eighties, right? That's a pretty senior civil servant." President Rasmussen rested his elbows on his desk, and cupped his chin in his palms.

"Yeah, I know, but believe me, he's very vigorous, a very spry guy. You'll see." Obama eased himself out of his chair, extending his hand to the President, who enveloped it with his own large hand.

"We'll see each other again soon. I'm looking forward to your meeting with Casey." Obama started to direct himself toward the Oval Office door. "Don't worry about me, I know my way out."

Rasmussen laughed, and swung himself deftly around the presidential desk. "Barack, I know I'll need your advice, party bickering notwithstanding. Thanks very much for sharing this, uh, directly. I look forward to meeting with Casey. Sounds interesting, a bit enigmatic."

Grinning, Obama turned closer toward Rasmussen, "Yeah, you'll see."

"Right, well, let's set this up, when you're ready. I'll be on standby," Rasmussen loosened his lantern jaw, and placed his hand on Obama's shoulder, ushering the former President toward the Oval Office vestibule, while offering an additional thank you. The two men wished each other well. At the door, President Rasmussen looked on as his predecessor became convivial again, chatting briefly with Rhonda, Rasmussen's official minder and schedule-keeper. The new President stepped back and closed the door behind him. He stood still for a moment, looking across the room at his desk and the chair where President Obama had been sitting. President Rasmussen gazed past the large federal window behind his desk, then turned his head to look past the window framed on the adjoining wall. The Presidential jaw loosened again. "What the fuck?"

_ CHAPTER 4

Some weeks earlier, Ben Stern's boss had perched himself, or rather his left haunch, on the far corner and open space of Ben's desk. Holding a jacketed coffee in one hand while propping his late thirties, mildly soft frame up with the other, Timmy Ramirez was, at least at this point, a calm and non-intense person.

"Brosef, can you drop into my office for just a little bit. Won't be too long."

Ben dutifully got up and followed Timmy, heading into one of the hallways running from the open plan office space.

"I came by your office earlier to see if you wanted a Starbuck's hit, but you weren't there. You hadn't come in yet – unusual for you – or you were in the can, or some other shit."

Ben grimaced, "Yeah, I was late for me. Metro was stalled for a while, we were stuck at Foggy Bottom."

He and Timmy ducked into Timmy's hallway office. Timmy managed Ben's group, the Applied Topical Analysis unit, so enjoyed the privilege of a little executive seclusion. Ben sat down in the blond wood chair opposite Timmy's desk, and placed one foot across the opposite knee. He generally felt comfortable with his boss, as did the rest of the ATA team. Direction from Timmy was clear, critical remarks relevant. Ben liked Timmy and the feeling was reciprocated. Timmy liked team cohesion, hence frequent Thursday (though not every Thursday) sessions of non-sexist and non-biased team bonding at McHerlihy's over a few beers. Ben appreciated those evenings.

Ramirez smiled a bit, and nodded slowly for effect. He leveled his limpid brown eyes at Ben, "You know, you are being noticed..."

"Okay..." Ben suddenly felt nervous, despite the warm glow emanating from Timmy. Feeling compelled to do something, anything, Ben started to scan Timmy's office, adding to his own furtive mien, while taking in short glances at the photo of Timmy's wife, Carole, and the twins, and the doctoral diploma from Cornell, framed and hung on the adjoining wall, and positioned just above the ficus plant. Ramirez let out an exaggerated sigh and folded his hands behind his head. Timmy smiled more broadly, but kept his eyes level with Ben.

"Last week, Mr. Sierra Club-vest popped into my office. Very nice guy! I really don't know the man, maybe say hello to him in the lobby sometimes. That's about it. But here he was last week, and he's pretty nice dude – this old Berkeley hippy, Jim Casey, yeah I found out more about him.

"Do you know why he was here?" Timmy's intonation ended on a high note, his smile became broader.

"Uh, no, why?"

"He was here about you." Timmy was now pointing his index finger at Ben, for singular emphasis. "Casey was curious about you, why do you think that is?"

Ben was sheepish, "I know the guy casually, I don't know. I get his humor, I guess. He's from the Bay Area..."

"Well, I'm from the Bay Area, too – with of course, an extended artic stay in Ithaca punctuating things..." Ramirez was shaking his head from side to side, but still smiling.

"Do you know what Casey does?"

"No."

"Neither do I."

Timmy sucked in his breath, as if he were taking a drag off a cigarette, "He's been around for a long time with the department, or so I should say, with his department within the department. Been in this building since we moved to K-Street nine years ago. Has been working independently I wanna say, since forever, for all intents and purposes. So, I was able to find out some things.

"The guy has complete freedom. I don't think you'll find him on an org chart. I mean, we're kinda covert, or I guess, low profile.

This frail old man's off the grid," Timmy took another virtual cigarette drag, the breath sucked in between his lips.

"Whatever it is, he's not blending in somewhere, say in suburban Iran, or he's not snappin' necks and cashin' checks. He's an analyst. Somebody mentioned to me some kind of "global anthropology" remit. He's actually an anthropologist, or had been at Cal, so that makes sense," Timmy shrugged and concluded.

"Uh, yeah, well... I like Casey, he's a good guy. As I said, we seem to have some sympatico...," Ben was trying to be helpful, at least toward the flow of the conversation.

"Well, as my dad, Mr. Ramirez, used to say, 'be that as it may.'" Timmy straightened his posture and spine, and held a pencil directly up in one of his fists.

"Casey wants to bring you on board. He flew it by me as a professional courtesy."

Timmy rubbed his hands together, waiting to see any reaction from Ben, then continued, "I let him know you're a decent guy, a very sharp analyst, reasonably together – which is saying a lot, given the emotional development issues we sometimes see with people drawn to this business. Make no mistake, you pass muster – for the most part," Timmy grinned at Ben.

Ben looked back at Timmy in his sterile but cheerful office. The photos indicated a warm family life. He thought of his own relative autonomy, and of Timmy's decency as a boss. He liked what he was doing and he liked his colleagues, all decent people. That was something to the risk-averse Ben, who instinctively appreciated nice situations. Ben knew he had a good gig and it provided grounding for him, especially given his life's derailment when Mae decided to leave him. A German term suddenly popped into Ben's head, *langweilig*, boring. Yes boring, maybe I'm too boring.

"So waddya think?" Timmy was staring and smiling.

"Not sure," Ben wasn't. "It's great here with you guys and the work, the projects. It's all good, why leave?"

15

Timmy nodded slightly, but was a little nonplussed. He rallied on behalf of the offer, and was surprised at himself. He didn't really want to lose Ben to Casey, but some part of him sensed it would be good for his friend. In spite of his own logistical needs, he started to make the case for Ben's transition into the new, albeit vague role, which again surprised Timmy. To his confusion, he was actually acting the part of the ethical and supportive manager.

"Casey has definite need of support. He's only one guy. And, he's carrying a God-knows-what coverage mandate, if he's indeed got 9-D clearance. Someone told me he has," Timmy stifled an involuntary yawn.

"I do like Casey," Ben mused. "A weathered, old California duck – by way of Omaha

..." Ben seemed amused at the thought.

"That's right! He's from Nebraska, that's where he grew up, in Omaha." Timmy also seemed taken by this biographical detail.

"Then, long period at the academic labor camp in Hyde Park, followed by escape to the mind-altering expanses of the Berkeley campus. And he's been around, intermittently, since Nixon, with us... Apparently teaching, writing, but always with the program... always with us." Timmy smiled even more broadly and scratched his chin. Then the expressiveness in Timmy's face suddenly left, his eyes became vacant, he disappeared into thought, then re-emerged.

"Look, I don't think it would hurt if you sat down with Casey and did a little exploratory analysis. Find out what he wants, see if it might be interesting for you."

Timmy shrugged his shoulders forward, yawned, then looked up and smiled at Ben, "I'll call Casey and set up a meeting between you two – he doesn't have an admin. Anyway, I'm sure you guys will meet for a discussion in the next couple weeks. It'll be fun – and weird!" Timmy smiled again.

"Okay, great," Ben grinned back in the affirmative, placing

his hands in his knees, then unconsciously doing another quick scan of the office and its memorabilia – the pictures of the twins, Carole, the diplomas and awards, the standard issue furniture.

"Meeting over?"

"Yeah, chief." Timmy rubbed at the side of his face. "Oh, another thing, Carole wants you to come by sometime for pizza night. We should set that up."

"That'd be nice," Ben replied on his way out. He left the office door open, as Timmy requested.

_ CHAPTER 5

For some reason, the mystery of what the work with Jim Casey would be was actually appealing, Ben thought, while sitting on the metro on his way home. Ben rested his back against the orange plastic bench and leaned against the berm of the metro car's entry door. His face assumed that engrossed expression one finds among analysts along the Bos-Wash, whether the expression conveys efforts toward assessing nuclear throughput rates, copula modeling, or the granular detail of Medicare claim filings. Whatever Ben was considering, he never grew tired of it, but enjoyed turning whatever it was over in his head, thinking about the different facets and angles, nuances and things that couldn't be easily parsed. It was a professional asset, something in his personal T-account that compensated for spells of social awkwardness.

Was this just a lateral move? Ben turned it over in his head. He stretched his legs out in the metro car and allowed other thoughts to appear and subside. Jim Casey's cheerful face sailed, moon-like, across his mind. Casey was like so many people he – and his parents – knew in the Bay Area. Those old Northern California people, who were wiry, fit, lucid, kitted out in natural fibers. With their bright eyes and hollowed-out faces, they were indistinguishable from each other – the men and the women. For a moment, Ben indulged himself with more daydreaming, picturing himself on a flat raft being carried down a wide and calm river. By then, the metro car had eased into the Ballston stop, rousing Ben from of his reverie and onto the metro platform. He stopped for a moment to collect himself, picked up his loose cloth satchel (from an old conference) and began walking toward the escalator. The cavernous matrix and cubed design of the tunnel chamber reminded him of the math textbook covers from junior high. He passed through the different channels and up onto street level.

As he walked along Alexandria Avenue toward his apartment, Ben marshalled the experience of his conversation and mulled over it. I could work with Jim Casey, or I guess, *for* Jim Casey, he thought. Ben was literal and specific. He's a pretty small operation, but that 9-D status, Ben reminded himself, that's intense – and interesting. Ben continued his pace toward his apartment, pausing and breaking as needed, but lost in thought. I like Casey – from what I know about him, which isn't really much... An attentive expression spread across Ben's face, an expression much like the one his mother, a former litigator now avid gardener, would form. Processing things silently, Ben's face relaxed again as he entered his apartment and laid his satchel on the marble-top kitchen counter. He checked his answering service and listened to the friendly, sonorous, slightly absent voice of Timmy reminding him about pizza. Ben should come by that Saturday, Ben should come by and meet someone Carole thinks is interesting...Very cute, you will like her! Ben sighed, although he *was* interested. He was Carole's charity case; it chapped his ass, as much as he appreciated and liked Carole's efforts. But he would be there. Why not?

Ben wasn't really hungry and didn't feel like going out or making something for himself. So, he sat in his living room and spooned some granola from a small bowl, washing it down with Diet Coke. There was reading material, so he began to read. This was tranquility.

–

As on many a 5:30am morning, President Rasmussen was moving his big frame from the gym end-line to center court, glancing his hand at the center line, then sprinting back to end-court, then moving with dispatch to the three-quarter line, then sprinting – and wheezing – back to the end-line.

"Mr. President, Steve, sorry, just one second..." his assistant and crucial aide-de-camp, Rhonda, attempted to intervene. Rasmussen gave a final wheeze, broke his work-out trance and smiled at Rhonda, although he was a little irritated, "Yeah Rhonda, what is it?"

"Sir, it's President Obama. He called and was a little vexed," Rhonda said, registering some discomfort. "He wondered why you hadn't scheduled that meeting you had both discussed."

"Um..." Rasmussen shook his head to calibrate. "I thought that he would be sorting that, arranging with you, etc." The President seemed bemused as he dried the back of his neck with a small towel. Rhonda gave a puzzled expression, then looked down at the varnished basketball court floor.

"Fine, fine," Rasmussen conceded. "Can you block him in for an early appointment? See if there's a 7am slot for some day over the next few weeks. That would be good."

Rasmussen straightened himself up and wiped the sweat that had beaded on his face.

"Already done, Steve, I've put them in for three weeks from this Tuesday," Rhonda practiced the alert-but-informal style that the President preferred. "Oh, and President Obama is bringing someone named Jim Casey, along with someone from Mr. Casey's team," she continued.

"Okay, fine." Rasmussen now appeared distracted, since the task of setting an appointment and mollifying his predecessor had been completed. Then thoughts began to germinate in the presidential frontal lobes. What was Obama so concerned about? Or not? Why so cryptic? Rasmussen looked down-court at the other basket, where the former President had enjoyed playing pickup games with his security detail.

"Steve," Rhonda snapped the President from his momentary

fugue. "Some good news, Sybylline closed at 121 yesterday. Results were good and analysts expect strong performance on the year." Rhonda smiled and nodded at the President.

"No surprise there. Zhou is doing a good job running the show. But anyway, I'm legally not supposed to care about that now," Rasmussen winked at his assistant. His interest indeed was stopped at the doorstep of a blind trust, where several billion dollars of his equity participation currently slept.

"Mr. Zhou is so sharp and such a nice guy," Rhonda concurred with the President. Her expression then changed, aware of a more pressing issue.

"President Obama is on hold, Steve. I have to get back to him. He had been so insistent about setting this up..."

"No worries, we haven't been talking too long. Anything else I need to do?" Rasmussen playfully queried.

"No, Steve, thanks," Rhonda chuckled, and made a fast exit out of the White House gym to assuage the former President. Rasmussen absently watched her leave and then squared himself on the end-line again. He placed his hands on his hips and then launched his entire 250 pounds – thirty pounds lighter than his college playing weight – as high as he could. He landed, sunk his rear end, and sprang back up again. These consistent squat jumps, part of his circuit training since his playing days, were practiced. Rasmussen was a self-confessed creature of habit – fortifying his routines and processes. Calculation, repetitive exercises and prescribed steps always exerted a calming effect on him. Repetitive activity, practice – Rasmussen had relished these habits since he was a boy – they offered a contrast to what other children would usually do. Steve's well-read social worker mother noticed that in her child as well. Mrs. Rasmussen was a keen autodidact, as pointed out by friends and family (though not using that specific term). She noted how her son was, endeavored to read relevant literature, but kept her thoughts to herself. And over the course of things, her son grew toward a time and place where he was exercising vigorously in the White House gym.

President Rasmussen continued to fold his frame and spring, still showing some of the force he had as a Minnesota Gopher, decades earlier. His muscles, bone and joints remained responsive. Everything still worked, even with his "abashed knee", an abstruse clinical term meant to indicate some disability. Rasmussen severely strained his knee in the first half of the Rose Bowl during his senior year. His injury didn't require corrective surgery – that is directly, the consulting doctors and orthopedic specialists concluded. The knee was technically "fine", but nevertheless enervated. It was as if his knee had had something like a cardiac infarction, something like a damaging and weakening heart event, precluding any further extraordinary stress on it. That was Rasmussen's knee. Any additional shot to it could undo the whole thing. The doctors were intrigued. The pro scouts were sobered. Rasmussen had been highly touted. His ability to read keys and developing offenses, his weirdly abundant physical force and speed, drew franchise attention. But the "abashed knee" was off-putting. Pro interest faded. Rasmussen, engrossed in his studies, merely shrugged his large body. Stanford University had accepted him for its dual-masters in operational research and electrical engineering. He enrolled that fall. His mom was happier about it.

_ CHAPTER 6

Ben only had to walk about ten minutes to get to Timmy's apartment. His boss lived just a bit further out and frequently took the same Ballston metro, if he opted not to drive on that specific day. The Washington weather was much colder than usual for February, but Ben enjoyed the near Artic chill and had kitted himself out with gloves, beanie, scarf and earmuffs. He preferred the traditional over-the-head vs the back-of-the-head wrap around kind of earmuff. Ben walked briskly through the cold and darkness. The steel and glass apartment complexes and restaurants along the way conveyed the comfort and social certainty that young graduates and older technocrats seemed to like. Always easy to grab a coffee, get your dry-cleaning done; opt for Chinese, Thai or good Mexican if you didn't want to make something; there were other choices too. Ben liked his neighborhood, it was soothing. He liked Washington in general and frequented the bookstores and museums, also attending presentations of one sort or another that were open to the public. He was not alone, there were others who could transfix themselves over newsprint and monographs. The Washington environment was nutrient-rich for these folks. On job and locale, Ben felt content. No reason to change out of Timmy's team, he idly thought. Ben was still thinking on it, turning its facets again over in his head, as he took a left and then down the side street where Timmy's apartment was.

Ben cradled a bottle of Montepulciano under his arm, which seemed to be the right gesture for the promised deep-dish pizza. Arriving in front of Timmy's building, Ben stopped and took a quick intake of breath. The purpose of his visit resurfaced in the front part of his brain. Timmy, or rather Carole, had a mission for him – to be open, fun and positive with someone she wanted him to meet. Ben was not shy or discomfited by this imminent task.

He liked Carole and felt happy to oblige, plus he enjoyed meeting people. Even though introverted, he enjoyed the bonhomie of socializing and the analytical aspects to it. He copped to his introverted default state, but also enjoyed people – he just made sure to allow himself time to recharge. Some people thrive on encounters and interactions – the greater the magnitude, the more energized. Ben was far from that end of the spectrum. He enjoyed people, but also could find himself feeling drained and lackadaisical if he felt immersed in the social pool for too long. Every now and then he needed to hoist himself out, drip dry, and then mentally and emotionally stretch out on some cool even strand of the mind. A little down time to read, drift, that's what the doctor would order.

Of course, Ben's low resonance state proved to be incompatible for him and his former wife, Mae. Ben's basic passivity, somehow artfully masked because of his own penchant for hard work and a non-stop curiosity, was nevertheless there, and eventually quite evident to his social, active spouse. She grew to believe that Ben's basic nature was in fact toxic and needed to be wholly modified or expunged. Ben's social energy was always, always finite; his being requiring breaks from activity and the steady replenishment that solitude and peace provided. Just the opposite, Mae was tireless. They had met at Stanford, with its many tireless people. He, the lingering (but dedicated) graduate student in political science; she, the self-directed gimlet-eyed MBA. Post marriage, Ben would marvel and reflect on how odd it was that the two of them had been actually paired together. But, then again, not so hard to fathom. Ben looked great on paper.

At some point during Mae's first year at Stanford, she had taken the initiative and reached out to Ben, who responded obligingly in a friendly, conscious yet almost plant-like way – the way a plant tracks the sun, or the way the body metabolizes – very naturally and automatically. Mae's dad had known Ben's father through litigation work Stern senior had done for the Sprinkel real estate business. Both older men spoke often on the phone and considered each other as friends. They compared notes on their children, as people do. Pere Sprinkel passed on relevant information to his clear-eyed daughter. Mae considered the particulars and moved on it, giving Ben a winsome (and to the point) phone call. They met for a coffee and then quickly afterwards for dinner. Mae's beauty and self-confidence, her warmth (at this point), and interest (in Ben!) were cogent, and enveloping, and made it feel natural that he should be with her, that he should follow her direction.

It was a stroke of romantic luck at the time that Ben was, at least culturally, Jewish. Ben's parents, Ken and Mary Stern – both litigators, also kept a secular home, but had an abiding respect for the world's variety of faith traditions. Mary (nee Halloran) would attend mass and temple, although both fitfully. High holidays and Catholic Eucharistic seasons were observed, even if just for the social pleasures they brought. Religious instruction was a potpourri, also fitful, but also following the doctrinal sheet music. The Sterns emphasized faith and did a certain amount of shoulder shrugging. Nobody cared too much, the grandparents had gotten agnostic about the whole thing.

To Mae and the Sprinkel family, this was, in any event, perfect. Mae duly noted to herself and others that Ben was "cute" and "so sharp"; he was also "funny", she confirmed to her circle. And Ben actually was funny. He could be funny and diverting, many people thought that. Ben was funny the way people who are prodigious readers can be, making brief asides and off-beat associations that people liked. This helped Ben, it helped him a lot, providing cover for sometimes lengthy periods when he was just oblique. Meanwhile, he floated happily along on the tide that was Mae's charisma, being drawn closer in. That such an attractive, magnetic and goal-oriented woman (with such exacting standards) could be bonding with Ben defied credulity – as much for Ben, when he sat back and thought about it, as it did for his friends, department colleagues and research library companions. His monk-like peers were a little envious, but still happy for him. They would ask about Mae's female friends, but to little effect. Ben was lucky and he knew it.

At Stanford, and with Mae in mind, he picked up his academic pace, and was able to muster a defense of his dissertation just as Mae was finishing her MBA in marketing. The Stanford network is broad and deep and Ben found direction toward the archipelago of intelligence agencies in Washington. His analytical skills and curiosity would do nicely there. For Mae, this was again perfect. She loved the idea of combining interests in policy and business and threw herself into landing something with a top-notch public relations or lobbying firm, which she was able to do in short order. All was possible.

Following their move to Washington, Mae ably adapted and sought to shepherd her and Ben's progress in the capital. Quiet and generous Sprinkel money subsidized, or rather bought, a nice apartment in the District, and marriage plans were being drafted. Ben loved his new life, like a fish in highly oxygenated water; he felt so nice and at home with everything. He proposed in a way that Mae tacitly scripted...

That was just over four years ago, Ben blankly reflected, standing in front of the twin glass door to Timmy and Carole's apartment building. He looked at the metallic buzzers and name tags on the brick wall perpendicular to the entrance. Scanning, he found the desired button "Keller-Ramirez" and pushed, tripping an off-key buzzer sound.

"Homes, that you?" Timmy's voice sounded through the intercom.

"Yeah, it's me, with an offering: cheap red wine, but chosen with care."

"Excellent, come on up," the door clicked while emitting an

even higher off-key buzzer. Ben entered and passed through the lobby, which was well-maintained with a décor oddly torn between modern minimal and the District's omnipresent federal style.

Ben took the elevator to the third floor, then walked down a well-lit hallway, which was punctuated with framed soothing pictures of nature and pastoral sketches. The patterned floor runners were clean and unblemished. This is a place where adults live, Ben thought quickly to himself. He came upon apartment 3D, where Carole opened the door just as he was about to knock.

"Ben!" Carole gave Ben an enthusiastic hug and took his coat and the bottle of wine. The twins, roughly waist high to Carole, bobbed beside their mom and Ben, giggling.

"Girls, we're gonna get pizza real soon and you guys are staying up soooo late!" Carole was bent at the waist, making an exaggerated expression for her daughters.

"Hi girls, I'm Ben," Ben smiled, and put his hand out in a limp splayed way so the little girls could grab it easily. Both laughed at Ben's proffered hand and scooted behind their mom, peeking and giggling at him. Carole put her arms akimbo and crooked her head sideways, giving a mock glare at the twins.

"Well, Ben, as you can see, the girls are a little skittish this evening." Carole lowered her head a little more in mock emphasis, and the little girls laughed more.

"This one is Rosemary, but we call her Rosey." She raised her tiny hand in a wave.

"And this one, her sister," Carole was leaning now toward the adjacent little blond child, "is Constance. She goes by Connie."

Ben smiled again, even more broadly, at the twins and nodded, a little dazed by the identical image before him.

"Girls," Carole cupped her hands to her knees and crouched down a bit before the twins, "why don't you go to the DVD room." Turning, Carole whispered to Ben, "That's what we call it."

Carole continued to the twins, "and tell pretty Brenda that Ben is here..."

As ordered, the twins started to scamper toward the living room, laughing and yelling, "Ben is here! Ben is here!"

One of the girls stopped then at mid-step, and went back to pull Ben by the wrist toward where he was supposed to go. In tow, he entered the Ikea-inflected living room dominated by a wall-mounted wide-screen TV which, even in its slumbering state, focused the attention of the twins. In the room stood Timmy, looking a little sheepish, with his hands tucked into his pockets. He stepped off the throw rug and walked over smiling and clapping Ben's shoulder, "Hey man, welcome to chez Carole and, of course, me." Timmy then turned to look into a figurative side camera. "The trap has now been sprung – per Carole's evil machinations." Hearing that, Carole sauntered quickly forward, past Ben's side, while turning toward him, showing Ben a small smile.

"Yes Ben, my evil plan, I'd like to introduce you to our friend Brenda. Tim and I thought – well, you're both so bright and nice – that you guys would probably enjoy meeting each other."

"Wow, cool, really!" Ben enthused, and he meant it. The social kabuki continued. Ben looked over at the expanse of leather couch and saw a young woman sitting at one end, nodding her head and smiling, chuckling a bit. He noticed how cute she was and felt a little disoriented not having noticed her sitting there when he had entered the room.

Timmy stood between them, pointing to Brenda, who was now standing, then to Ben, "Ben, Brenda Donovan. Brenda, Ben Stern."

"I'm so glad to finally meet you, Ben. These two were always saying these great things about you."

"Likewise, Brenda, it's really a pleasure," Ben tried to maintain the amiable good-guy level gaze, but couldn't keep his eyes from darting up and down quickly over Brenda's form. She was wearing a casual light blue patterned Liz Claiborne dress, which the two women in the room knew and the two men did not. The dress emphasized Brenda's figure but in an indirect, even demure way. She had an oval, even face, which was slightly flush. Her light, clear blue eyes met Ben's green ones, and held his gaze. She had an ease about her and stood noticeably taller than Ben, even with her flats on. Her strawberry, reddish blond hair was pulled back into a ponytail, which emphasized her conventionally pretty features. Ben liked what he saw. There was a certain fullness to Brenda, which contrasted with Mae's fine-boned delicacy.

"Hi, Ben?"

Ben blinked. Oh, man, he had been lost in thought. Carole, Timmy and Brenda stood in a semi-circle in front of him. Beyond the semi-circle and stationed below the wall-mounted TV, the twins were sitting Indian-style, engrossed in some six-year old twin girl activity. This is not a good first-draft impression, Ben acknowledged, but Brenda was smiling at him anyway. Her eyes registered amusement at Ben's flat footedness. Carole leaned forward and added in an exaggerated whisper, "He's shy." Ben winced, and smiled.

"Okay then," Timmy began officiating, "enough with the introductions. Let's decamp for drinks to the kitchen, for kitchen cabinet talks a la Roosevelt, or maybe Stalin."

"Just don't say Hitler," Carole reproved her husband for the glib referencing.

"Beautiful wife, I know you would like a glass of red wine, what would you two like?" Timmy resumed his role as host.

"Beer sounds fine for me," Brenda responded, as she took a half-step closer to Ben.

"Yeah, I'll take a beer, too, please. That sounds good," Ben nodded.

"What'll it be? We've got Becks or Rolling Rock," Timmy offered.

"Becks is fine for me, thanks."

"I'll have a Becks as well, please."

"Great," Timmy satisfied the orders, "then one for the dealer. A Rolling Rock for myself," which he set aside. He then opened Ben's bottle of red wine and decanted a glass for Carole. The four sat around the white kitchen table, the kind with a lacquered surface for fast and easy clean ups. From the living room, the twins' chatter sounded at a lower but still happy buzz, as they traded stories. The pizzas soon arrived.

—

Ben glanced through the kitchen doorway into the living room where Timmy stood in front of the twins, who were attentively listening. The girls peered up at their father, who was making the kind of sweeping exaggerated gestures which parents allow themselves to do when instructing their small children. Timmy was pointing and nodding at the sippy-cups and paper plates carrying slices of pizza. The little girls were listening, with their little necks crooked to see their father better and their mouths slightly ajar. Timmy clicked one of several remotes and started their movie; their small heads shifted toward the large TV screen and Timmy made his way back to kitchen, pausing at the doorway to make a small entreaty for good behavior. Ben saw the girls nod faintly, their eyes never leaving the screen.

"Wow, Carole, the kids are just so cute!" Ben declared, as Timmy sat down at the kitchen table.

"Very good, Ben, you're doing a nice job buttering up your hostess, which you should do – given your introduction to lovely Brenda," Timmy batted his eyes, eliciting laughter from the women and from Ben, who felt the heat gather in his face.

"Don't listen to him, Ben." Brenda made a clown-like grimace. "In fact, I'm pretty assertive – so, I wanted to meet you! These guys talk about you all the time. I said to myself, 'I've gotta meet this guy.'"

"Well, thanks Brenda, that's so nice – I don't see it," Ben was smiling, taking a stab at self-deprecation and levity. "And these guys," he continued, pointing to Carole and Timmy, "they're the greatest. Carole has been my sponsor, my patron saint, for all things requiring human social interaction." What am I saying? Ben asked himself. He thought he was being funny, but feared he was blowing it, quickly.

"Ohhhh..." Brenda raised her eyebrows a bit and broke into a broader grin, she turned a quick beseeching glance toward Carole, who smiled at both of them.

Ben continued smiling and chuckling, he would not be stopped. "And, of course, Timmy, or Tim. Carole always calls him Tim," which prompted Timmy to nod sagely.

"I hate that he calls himself Timmy," Carole carped to the rest of the table. "Tim is so much nicer."

Timmy remained mute, but was again grinning, nodding and holding up his hands in sympathy to Carole, conveying a silent agreement. "What should we do with this goofball?"

"Anyways," Ben continued, "Tim – that's in deference to you Carole – is super sharp. Granted, a little weird, but definitely stand-up. He's a great friend, and the best boss, as much as anyone can define such a concept."

"Well thank you, direct report," Timmy's voice took on a resonant baritone. "Ben's a sensitive, insightful, responsible young man, and very handsome." Timmy sidled his chair closer to Ben and put his arm protectively around his shoulder, then mugged as if for the camera.

"Alright you two," Brenda was laughing and shaking her head, "enough with the bromance, I get it. Anyways Ben, you definitely get points for having these two guys as friends, and in your corner."

Noting that he had managed to gain some points made Ben blush again. Timmy and Carole looked a little sheepish, but were happy with Brenda's comment.

"So, Carole, are you thinking about maybe going back to the lab, with the twins now a little bit older?" Brenda thought to re-steer the conversation, departing from the Ben and bromance theme.

"Ah, not really, I love being with the girls, and just having more time with them. We don't need me to go back, at this stage. Timmy's doing fine with work, and I just want to be with my girls," Carole smiled and shrugged. "Maybe sometime later, I'll try for an adjunct at GW. They're always looking for people to teach organic chem. Doing a class or two would be fun, and wouldn't dominate my time either."

"Definitely, you should pursue it with them, when it's right for you, Carole. I think it sounds like a great option," Brenda was encouraging.

"Thanks, yeah, well maybe soon, when the kids are a bit older. Anyway, I really don't want to go back to the lab. The work's interesting, but the corporate crap..."

"That's my girl." Timmy chimed in, was jovial, "Anyone want another beer? A soda?"

"Actually, I'll take a Coke-light, or just any diet, if you have some," Brenda responded, then leaned forward to take another slice of Hawaiian. Hmm, there is a shapely girl with a healthy appetite, Ben idly thought. For an often highly-abstracted, bookish person, his libidinal current ran deep. Ben straightened himself in his chair and turned his head to capture in view both Brenda and Carole.

"So, how did you two guys meet? Not you and Carole, Timmy," Ben raised his hand in a playful mock defensive gesture toward Timmy to preempt any comic riff on romantic coincidences and relationships. "I've heard the Cornell University saga," Ben declared and winked at Carole.

Carole laughed, as Timmy raised an index finger as if poised to add something to the official record. Carole, grinning, jerked her thumb toward Brenda and tilted her head, "We met at yoga class. They have great daycare on the floor just below the studio, so I would take the girls there and have an hour for the session," Carole began explaining. "Brenda was there for a lot of those workouts, so we got to know each other."

"Yeah," Brenda added, "we really liked each from the get-go. I was inspired by Carole's flexibility – I mean *real* flexibility, that stuff is hard!" Both women laughed at the remark. Brenda became a little embarrassed, but was still smiling, while looking down a little and rubbing the bridge of her nose. Brenda looked up again to give an even fuller smile to the group.

"I mean, I would check to see if her teeth were stained red from chewing on coca leaves or something. She had all this energy in this chemist-mom package! I mean, I wanted to learn which co-op I could get that stuff from!" Brenda began to giggle, which tripped giggling in Carole, and a bemused look from Timmy. Carole playfully cocked back her fist and gave a love tap on Brenda's shoulder.

"You mean *gat*."

The two women stopped frolicking and stared at Ben. Brenda leaned toward Ben, with a smile on her face and eyebrows raised in mock emphasis.

"What?"

"Umm, *gat. Gat* is what'll give your teeth the red wine stain look. It's a stimulant, like caffeine, maybe addictive. People in Yemen like to chew it," Ben elaborated.

The two women looked at him for a moment, then burst out laughing. Ben felt Timmy's arm come around his shoulder and squeeze him in a hug, "Didn't I tell you? Knowledgeable. The man is knowledgeable."

Carole tilted her head and was solicitous. "Oh, Ben, we love you and you're so cute. And so smart! It's so nice having such a smart friend," said the PhD holder in biochemistry. Ben, still blushing, could only laugh at himself, just as the others were laughing at him – and with him.

With most of the pizza consumed, along with some beer and a number of carbonated drinks, Carole and Timmy's stratagem to introduce Ben and Brenda began to unwind and conclude. The twins were dozing in the living room, while a default screen for a Sponge Bob video showed pixelated on the TV. Soundless, Sponge Bob alternately pointed to segments, editor's choice and voice over cuts. Timmy walked softly from the kitchen into the living room and scooped each girl with a corresponding arm, so they rested on his chest and each shoulder. He walked slowly to the foyer, as each cradled twin continued to snooze, out for the count. Carole, Ben and Brenda stood by each other in the foyer, while Timmy approached them, holding the girls.

"They're so cute!" Brenda whispered in a hushed, excited way.

"Well, cute now..." Timmy raised his eyebrows and grinned, "Feel free to take 'em for a weekend, if you're a thrill-seeker."

Brenda laughed and Timmy continued, "Ben, buddy, maybe you? Carole and I could use the break and you could tag team with Brenda." At this, Timmy leaned from his waist, bringing the sleeping toddlers closer to Ben, who smiled and backed away reflexively, while giggling as well. (Girlishly? He wondered).

Smiling again and recovering, Ben began, "Guys, this was great. Fantastic to come over and see the twins. They're getting so big!" Timmy hoisted the girls higher on his shoulders as if to emphasize and winked.

"Our pleasure, Ben. So great to catch up with you away from the office! You're on our short list of favorite people – and folks tagged to look after the girls," Carole added, teasing Ben. She took a half-step toward Ben to give him a quick hug.

Ben nodded and shook a little for Carole's affectionate hug, "Really so great to see you guys – and of course, thanks for introducing me to Brenda." He smiled genuinely.

At that, Brenda widened her eyes playfully, "My pleasure as well, Ben. You are such a gentleman!" Brenda kept her eyes wide, and lifted her eyebrows further as she exchanged a glance with Carole. Both women suppressed some laughter. Everyone started to chuckle involuntarily, as they exchanged hugs and pats on the back and shoulders. And, then, summarily, he and Brenda were out the door and walking toward the elevator, passing the tasteful prints along the hallway, as they went. Ben glanced sideways at Brenda, while she kept her head tilted forward almost demurely away, he thought. Brenda reached the elevator first and tapped the button to the lobby. The door promptly opened and Ben stepped politely aside to allow Brenda to enter first. They descended in silence, with Ben shifting slightly on his feet, while Brenda stood serenely and perfectly still.

As the elevator settled, and door started to open in the lobby, Ben stole another sideways glance at Brenda, who just continued to gaze in front of her. Ben liked her, instinctively. She was funny, Ben thought – parsing quickly and she didn't take herself too seriously. She also exuded confidence. She was very self-possessed, as Ben's mother would say. Such even white teeth, too. She smiled when listening to you, or when she laughed and showed those wonderful teeth. Her laugh was mezzo-soprano, Ben thought, full and very throaty. Weird that I'm describing it like a wine bouquet, he reflected further. Yeah, the laugh, it came out like a sharp "ha!" signaling she caught you or caught something, then descending into full peals. He really did like her, Ben thought. I should say something, he decided. Be steady, he self-admonished.

"You know, I really liked hearing about your journalism work, Bloomberg, your views on things. Very cool," with that, Ben broke what had been a lengthening spell of silence.

Brenda shifted herself toward Ben, as the two walked into the lobby. She amiably tugged at his upper arm and smiled. "Thanks, that's nice of you to say. I definitely like my job. I like the investigative aspect of it. The need to tease things out and then to be able to back them up. It can be amazing what you can learn."

It seemed that Brenda had somehow halted their progress towards the front door and Ben found himself standing still in the lobby while she subtly retracted her hand from Ben's arm. Brenda looked directly now at Ben, while she squared herself. Her eyes were clear and she lowered her chin just slightly, so her gaze met Ben's more evenly. Her mouth formed a closed but warm smile, concealing the telegenic teeth.

"You know," she wanted to share more with Ben, "I really like my work because I like the detail part of it – the digging, the research, the analysis. I like getting out and finding the story, but the analytical part – the puzzling out of things, would be fine for me. I love that part anywhere – in an open plan office, in a cave..."

Ben chuckled at her assessment and nodded, understanding, "Yeah, I love the analysis, which a lot of people might find pretty dry. I like to stitch together something from all of the different points, and see if it really coheres." Ben suddenly felt a little diffident and looked down at his shoes for a moment, "I also, in a weird way, like the frequent frustration and futility of the process. The work can be a fitful thing. It's hard for us to filter out our cognitive biases, we're inclined to see patterns where none exist. At the same time, it's easy to overlook what's hiding in plain sight – given specification or conceptual error. Scylla and Charybdis. Anyway, I like my job, I like getting paid for it."

"That's what I like about you, Ben." Brenda's smile widened and opened up more, "You love what you do, and you love your job. It's enough for you."

"Well, uh, thanks, I do really like what I do. I feel very lucky to have the job that I have," Ben paused and looked down, feeling a little diffident.

Brenda smiled at him, "Cicero once said gratitude was the greatest of all the virtues." She lightly touched the top of Ben's shoulder again. Smiling, Brenda leaned slightly at the waist and planted on a small kiss on Ben's cheek. Ben crimsoned.

"You are so cute!" Brenda offered. For Ben Stern, that, like the kiss, was unexpected and very agreeable. "I think we're hitting it off. We've got to continue our mutual admiration society!"

Ben felt warm elation gather in his stomach and into his chest. He felt happy with the impression that she liked him. He was being engaging – or she seemed to react to him that way. For Ben, being engaging was possible, but its manifestations were unstable and ephemeral, like quicksilver. For him, charisma was some unknown or rare earth element. He really did appreciate this moment of affection, right then and there. Certainly, Mae had concluded after their trial marriage period that he was not engaging or charismatic. The somber thought pierced his good feelings.

Brenda's smiling face materialized, "Man, you were drifting there for a second. Normally, I'd be a little pissed off, but you're cute and adorable, kind of like a sleepy puppy just now, just for a second." Brenda raised her hand to cover her smile. "You just seemed to go blank, for a tiny bit," Brenda scrunched her expression and held up her hand, showing a small space between thumb and index finger. "Just for a few seconds," She emphasized, giggling. "Anyway I agree, Ben, we should continue to be mutually admiring," Brenda reached into her bag, and grabbed a post-it note, which she supported against the bag, and began jotting down her cell phone number and email.

"Here's my contact info, give me a call when you have some time." She handed the small piece of paper to Ben, who took it and folded it into his billfold.

"Brenda, fantastic, I really can't wait to get together soon. I'll ping you with some ideas," Ben reached over and gave Brenda a hug and slight squeeze, a practice the methodical Ben had internalized from watching television and growing up in California. His parents were always affectionate with him, too. A positive card dealt by fate. Brenda stiffened, though, taken aback but still chuckling lightly at Ben's formal gesture.

"Great, Ben, call me, I wanna hear from you, soon!" Brenda was smiling and encouraging, while taking a step or two backward.

"Thanks so much, have a great evening. We'll talk soon," Ben replied, smiling. Brenda smiled and waved one last time before opening the door and climbing into the cab outside that Carole had arranged. Ben stood there for a moment and then walked toward the building's glass doors. He felt happy and enthused about his new friend.

—

Timmy emerged from the twins' bedroom, with the girls now arranged in their tiny adjacent beds. Outside the door, he took a quick step back to and cocked an ear to listen. After being nestled in, the girls' breathing became steady and light, as they descended into dream land.

Timmy walked into the kitchen and saw Carole still sitting at the table, sipping from a mug of coffee. He slipped into the banquette and bumped playfully against her shoulder. She winked back at him, content with her good works, satisfied with the spectacle of seeing two dissimilar people – the open, magnetic Brenda and the thoughtful, gentle Ben – apparently hitting it off. That's what Carole told herself. Brenda seemed to like him. And, there was enough commonality there. They were both so nice, and with Ben...Was it just a dusting of social autism, or just simple shyness? It didn't seem to faze Brenda... Anyway, he could be funny. Funny! And what's not to like there, Carole mused. Timmy shifted in his seat and shot a comical look to push Carole out of her head. She smiled at him, but continued to ponder. And Ben... well, she was surmising, that was easier. The man was captivated, she could tell. Ben's emotions were translucent and he was plainly attracted. Brenda is gorgeous and vital, just right for her wounded-duck Ben. Carole took another sip of coffee and put her mug down on the table. She rested her chin on clasped and folded hands and allowed herself a brief pause. Then she leaned in to Timmy and rested her shoulder against him.

"So, whaddya think? A successful mission? Is my intuitive sense about Brenda and Ben right?"

Timmy sighed and looked sideways at Carole, "Ah, yes, another chapter in Carole's nerd pair-bonding efforts. Very good, I think it went well." Timmy shrugged, as if to say why bother? The evening's good deed and entertainment had concluded. Carole nevertheless pressed on, knowing she had to tease out precious details from her grouchy but observant husband. So, she continued to press, and they bantered and dissected over another cup of coffee.

CHAPTER 7

To his surprise, Ben found himself emerging from a light emotional fugue, something he had accommodated for some time. Slowly, to be sure, but a kind of low-res blue feeling that had surrounded him now seemed to be ebbing, or slipping away. He had managed to bustle along during the past two years, engrossed in his work, his interests, reasonable sociability and a sense of humor that passed general muster with work colleagues, with friends, with technocratic Washington. The love and the occasional spells of creature comforts that he experienced with his parents and their affluence also worked like a numbing balm. Ben's folks – both litigators, with his mom later opting for gardening and home design – had tried to coax and encourage him to let up a little, to relax a bit and to not be too focused, too hard on himself – to look up once in a while and to enjoy himself. But Ben saw that his parents misunderstood. He loved his work and his interests in what shaped people and history and in why things turned out the way they did, to the extent anyone could parse such a thing. Ben embraced one's inability to really understand the present and having only an incomplete view of the past; he didn't even try to divine and peer into the complex future. He loved the visceral contingency and the variety of history – from earliest Harappan civilization, to Viking settlements in Newfoundland, to assortative mating in test-based meritocratic America. To engross himself in the macro and the micro – that desire was his character feature that helped him steadily move through coursework, graduate work, seminar papers, presentation decks, oral presentations, oral defenses, some lecturing responsibilities, exam grading, ramen noodles and other stuff at Stanford for close to a decade.

Of course, Mae had tired of Ben's proclivities and interests soon enough. While Ben was amenable to attending the different gatherings and events Mae organized, he wasn't flourishing in Mae's world. Ben was always nice. Mae's friends even said so, sometimes in a commiserating way, as in, "He's such a *nice* guy..." but Washington friends of the Sprinkel-Stern pair began to think of Ben as the dimmer, slower half of that partnership. Mae was charismatic, a lambent personality, drawing in friends, colleagues and connected acquaintances. Where she seemed to purr with life-force, fully self-actualizing, Ben appeared to be lagging, maybe even wheezing, to keep up with their tandem effort. He was irretrievably a reader and a thinker, preferring ample amounts of time to himself, at times resembling a small woodland mammal, who secures – as it can and when it can – crucial resources, which for Ben were quiet and solitude, resources sheltered from Mae's glowing bank of social energy. Ben's inner monk bothered the shit out of Mae. It was something she hadn't fully apprehended before they got married.

Ben's inability to keep up, to make progress, was chaffing for Mae. Things had to change. So, she began to work on him. Short captious remarks and inflexible instructions started to come through, as a way to steer Ben and as an outlet for Mae's own executive dissatisfaction. Ben was the proverbial cathode television with rabbit ears being adjusted, getting tapped and knocked on the side for better reception. He became a bit confused, and hurt, but he complied. He was a pleaser, irrespective of any of his own needs.

Ben thought Mae's carping was just a natural part of their marriage, and accepted it as such. Because she had focused on him so much during their courtship and early marriage and because of Mae's magnetism – her star quality – Ben was smitten, in some ways like anyone suffering from Stockholm syndrome might be. In the context of Mae's encouraging, her showing concern for friends and social causes, the small mendacities registered in his mind as some kind of cosmic background radiation. Not so noticeable in the immediate sense. He continued to love and admire, he loved to gaze upon her clear, symmetrical face, especially when she was quiet and sleeping.

Unlike so many people in so many places, during so many times, Ben had been the fortunate recipient of a wonderful childhood. In fact, he still benefited from two competent and kind parents who had always sought to provide guidance and shelter for their son. He had a teasing but devoted kid sister. Ben's adolescence had been untroubled and he had sailed through it, ironically cushioned and buffered by a slight social aphasia which presented its own problems. He was an omnivorous reader, a pleasant person, a slight but capable athlete, popular with his fellows and without guile, comfortable in the abstract. He was a duly recognized meritocrat ready for a budding technocratic career.

Going to Stanford, therefore, proved to be a natural fit. There, Ben's mind-meld with the subject matter would trip no stigmatizing responses from the other over-achievers. And, like a car fitted with accessories, Ben had a dry wit, was an apt mimic and was also self-deprecating – as many pleasers are – in a way that could often be disarming. He managed steady progress through the Stanford campus over ten years, with some breaks for study abroad and research fellowships. And, everything being equal, someone who has honed research and analytical skills over such a stretch of time seeks to use them in a rentable way. Government and intelligence work rolled his way as if by conveyor belt.

In Washington, Ben was more of the focused hedgehog to Mae's engaging and networking fox. He burrowed into his work, while Mae worked on the social alchemy which was a more natural endeavor for her and which captured her native energy. On one level, the agreeable Ben was easy material to shape and knead. He was passive to Mae's plans and the social commitments she made for them. But Mae began to equate Ben's simpler tastes with a sort of complacency; in his quieter nature, she started to perceive dimness. In this relationship, Mae had directed her own vast energy to organize it, structure and catalyze it, with results that were marginally better to diminishing, as she began to judge. Aside from the persiflage from his coaching and directing wife, Ben was content, even happy, but Mae began to reassess. Ben seemingly responded to her prompts, which was satisfying, but then would return to a state of rest that was his more natural way. This was wearing on Mae. Ben was cute, he was credentialed! He was, or seemed to be, the right one – the right guy. She nevertheless began to review, to become self-critical over her own choices. As months sped by, the evidence against Ben was accumulating. He was inert social material, lumpen and indelible. She knew he loved her and sensed he was growing to love her more, like a pet might, perhaps, but this now began to make her feel a bit guilty. She also saw the reality of the "mis-hire" she had made. Ben was simply not right with this situation. Mae drew on third-party advice, talking to select friends about her frustration with him and her waxing ambivalence about him. Her friends were supportive, seeing Ben as such a sweet guy, but so passive, such a stone – maybe he was phobic, some wondered. And Ben was not going to change, so her friends counseled. Despite so many agreeable things about him, his core was immovably there. Ben was pleasant, could be fun, could be funny, but the quiet reader was like another piece of immobile furniture in Mae's life, upon further thinking, downgraded from bright accessory.

Ben had his habits; he flossed, he exercised, he liked to run. All of this was done predictably, dependably. He was neat, fastidious really. They did things together – he loved their trips, how discursive he could be on this or that subject, but patient, too. So knowledgeable, but not overweening. Mae, though, found Ben to be too much of an observer. He was warm and he was loving. He was good in so many ways, great with his family – even with her family! – But, and here Mae's brow would not so much furrow as straighten and her thoughts would turn, Ben wasn't that great in other ways. So, she continued her mental calculus, weighing the pros and cons of her putative life partner. The man has no energy. He is so content, she winced at the thought. Images of Ben reading, sipping a coffee, literally poring over the spread-out pages of the Sunday New York Times and Washington Post on the kitchen table, would sail across her mind and her jaw would tighten just a little. Where is he going? What will he do? Mae thought of her own family, its spirit, its energy and enterprise. Her men, the Sprinkels, they were movers, they were owners, they *do* things. The Sprinkel men were real estate kings! She hated how they were patronizing to Ben, without even intending to be mean, but they loved Ben, he was almost a *chotchka*. With that thought, Mae's eyes would shut tighter, while she gripped, with thumb and index finger, the thin bridge of her nose.

CHAPTER 8

Ben had known for several months that something was wrong. He had at times even tried to talk to Mae about it, but she was either distracted and vaguely reassuring, or captious and dismissive and would simply cut him off. Sometimes, she would appear to be trying to say something, but some underlying emotion, some grimacing would percolate through and catch her throat, stifling anything she might have wanted to express. She'd shrug, or wave her hand, saying "it's fine", and then she would brighten and smile and her naturally cheerful manner would return. She would suggest to Ben that they go out, maybe for a stroll or coffee, perhaps to a movie, or for lunch or dinner, simply to get out of the place where her emotions nearly crested. Anything to be outside and to expend some energy. Ben would again be won over, and, in fact, reassured. He'd feel fine again, and any misgivings he had would be quickly pushed aside to some quiet cache in his brain.

One Friday, Ben had gotten back home from work at a reasonable time, feeling good about the week and ready for a soothing evening. Much anticipated recovery or *erholung* as the Germans would say, who were the current subject of his intensive agency-related study, or at least the radical fringe ones were. Thinking about it, he would confirm again to himself, BND really blew it in Hamburg, then shake his head.

He placed the key in his apartment door lock to find the door quickly opening from the inside. Mae was standing in the foyer, ready for him. Her eyes were a brighter blue than usual, wide open, cobalt. She grabbed Ben by his two upper arms and gave him a quick mechanical kiss on the cheek, pronounced and wet. Mae then stood and smoothed the shoulder of Ben's jacket, staring absently past him. He was surprised by Mae's forward greeting at the doorway; she was home relatively early, too. For some time now, Mae usually had business functions or social-cum-business functions after work on Friday. She usually showed up later in the evening where Ben, book in hand, was there to greet her. She would set herself down at the kitchen table and at first stare at Ben, as he, with book still in hand, would sit down at the table, always opposite her gaze. His movements were unconscious and slower than natural, moving as a small prey object might, undetected. Placing his book on the table, he would begin amiably – asking about her day, noting that the coffee was still hot. Are you hungry? Should we go out for something? What about a movie at the Multiview? There's still time... Do you feel like Thai? And Mae would revive herself, blinking a few times and give Ben a small indulgent smile... Sure, why not? And so they would do something on a given Friday evening. Maybe it would be a combination of the above, a variation on a theme, sometimes they would stay at home. Mae always had Saturdays booked for them – a dinner at someone's home, meeting friends at a restaurant, an occasional play, a Washington event, some conclave with her Stanford and Harvard friends, a get together with Sprinkel family friends. Saturdays were orchestrated.

Ben remembered when there was less pump-priming on Friday evenings. They used to surprise each other with quick weekend trips and getaways. She of course had more money, so she'd surprise him more often. It was all very well understood that it was *their* money, but Ben felt a little shy about the use of what amounted to a massive dowry from the Sprinkel clan, who were doting and very happy to have Ben in the family fold. Mae was effervescent and off-the-cuff. Ben would deliberate more on the chance-like adventures he might spring. But he loved it, loved it! Mae's energy and optimism would pour over him and the whole coterie of her friends, male and female, large and small. She remained always "together", *bien dans sa peau*, confident but not off-putting, sharp, funny, but not sadistic, so it seemed. She could dish with the best of them, but would generally practice catch and release, allowing her unfortunate prey of the moment to wriggle free. Unconsciously among her aspirational peers, this counted as a gentle nature. To these qualities, not unusual for such ferocious competitors, Ben would turn an at times bemused and at other times blind eye.

So there she was, standing in the apartment foyer; her hands still grasping Ben. She pulled him in for a tight hug. "Oh Ben, the weekend! Thank God!"

Mae loosened her hug, and separated her body from his, "Ben, why don't you get cleaned up and relaxed. Take a shower and wash away the week. I'll be in the kitchen, I'll pour us some coffee."

"Thanks hon, sure. That sounds great!" Ben blinked and felt bemused.

She was relaxed and welcoming, albeit in a little detached way. Again, Ben was wondering why she was home that early. Strange developments. Mae usually had to detox and idle – not to be questioned or chatted with until some 15 to 20 minutes had passed after landing back at the apartment. Systems had to cool. This friendly, albeit clinical, Mae was agreeable. He preferred this novel situation.

Showered, towel-dried and refreshed, Ben stepped through the living room – a space reflecting the reach of the Sprinkel Upper East Side aesthetic, and resplendent with Sprinkel family antiques and fine art objects, including a beautiful mounted and encased silk screen which was positioned above the couch. Through the living room, he passed the kitchen entrance, maybe we'll catch a movie tonight, Ben thought. Mae was sitting at their round kitchen table.

"Here Ben, I've already poured you a coffee..." She gestured to him to sit opposite her at the table. Ben felt relaxed even though Mae had departed from the usual routine. She hadn't called him at work to say that she'd be home early, which was strange since that was exactly what Mae would do in such a situation, at least that was what Ben was thinking. For Mae, it was about thorough execution. No detail left alone and to itself, the woman executed.

Mae peered across the table at Ben who was sipping his coffee, and thinking about possible movie choices for the evening.

"Ben, how do you think things are going?" she lobbed.

Ben handled the beveled surface of his coffee cup and smiled openly. "Pretty good."

There followed a pause between the two. Still smiling, Ben felt he should offer something else, "It's just great to see you home early!" he enthused. "It's a treat!"

Mae continued to peer at Ben, then pursed her lips, "But Ben, do you really think things are going well? Are you happy?"

"Yeah, I mean, sure. I'm happy, I think things are good."

Somewhere along Ben's spinal cord, some ancient sensory organ began to signal caution. But he persisted.

"Why? Is there something wrong?"

He sank toward the back of his chair and folded his arms, hunkering down for some sort of onslaught. He knew something, some diatribe, was coming, but couldn't predict the theme. Mae's repertoire had been growing over the past several months. First small, it continued to accumulate.

Mae sighed, straightened in her chair and rested both hands on the table, spreading out her fingers.

"No, Ben, I don't think things are good, nor are they working. They're not working anymore." The last phrase had caught in Mae's throat, maybe from some deep feeling, traces of deep feeling, maybe just from frustration. She was, at that moment, a manager dealing proactively with a problem.

Mae shook her head, "No Ben, this is not working for us, not for me, not for you." She stared very hard at him now, her eyes more deeply cobalt, in Ben's mind. Yes, unwavering. He felt a sadness envelope, a life defeat. He loved Mae, so he told himself... But then, the trickle of an endorphin flow began to irrigate. He loved Mae, yes. Yet, in parts of him, in parts of his brain, there was relief. He blinked and saw Mae staring still intently at him, her mouth set, she was motionless. He loved Mae he said to himself. But he also felt calm. There was no use, not at this point.

"I'm sorry," Ben finally said. He looked down into his half empty coffee cup.

–

And so Ben and Mae concluded. Ben felt the first rushes of displacement, embarrassment, as he explained to his family and then to friends that his marriage to Mae was over. His parents had grown accustomed to Mae, but were instinctively a little wary of her, despite the Stern-Sprinkel sympatico. They still tried to comfort their first child. Ben's sister, too, was supportive, emotional, crying a bit for Ben and giving him tight hugs when she saw him. Most of Ben's friends at the Hoover Institute and sprinkled along Bos-Wash were, however, more clinical. They felt bad for Ben, did want to ease whatever pain they could and support him. But, they were analytical types, like he was. They were deliberative, weighing the evidence they saw, making attempts at hale and even ribald humor to cheer their friend, drawing helpful inferences as they could from the eliding Ben on personal matters. And Ben, like his friends, puzzled over developments. He felt sad, but also ambivalent about the break. He was alone and missed the good times with Mae, but he did feel relief as well. Amounts of cortisol, like battery acid, were no longer flowing so amply through his body. He was alone, but he was tranquil. His boss-friend Timmy grabbed him by the shoulders one day and told Ben that he was standing taller, walking straighter and that his ass was no longer in such a sling. Timmy and Carol had met Mae and had formed their opinions. Ben gave a spontaneous and high-pitched laugh at Timmy's remark. He was right. Ben felt better.

The separation was amicable and methodical. Pre-nuptial terms clarified everything, and the Sprinkels, as a collective, liked Ben. It was just one of those situations that didn't work out. Mae, with her limpid blue eyes fixed on New York, was no longer interested in keeping their large Washington apartment, when a simpler pied-a-terre would be fine. Her fledging but thriving public relations firm would be expanding. New York was the next stop, her time and attention would be needed there. She, with Ben's deference and compliance, sold their large Washington place, and with the Sprinkels' blessing, ceded half of the proceeds to Ben. Ben, in turn, moved into his comfortable and comforting small apartment near the Ballston metro stop. Everything about the divorce just went nicely and smoothly, paced and punctuated by electronic signature signings and exchanges of emails, law office meetings, conference calls, and the receipt and dispatch of notarized documentation. Ben felt as if he had been moved conveyor-like through the process, coming out clean, sorted, with only traces of vertigo.

_ CHAPTER 9

Ben was feeling loose. He had gone one late Sunday afternoon to the Pipeline, a California-style burger place not far from the Ballston stop. He sat down at a booth and savored the idea of an early dinner on a lazy Sunday; he was relaxed, with the single aspect of linear productive thinking on him being the stapled white monograph he had brought to peruse over a burger. Ben's waitress approached his table. She was pretty, he noticed (discretely, he hoped). Whether or not she had, she was friendly and open, responding to Ben, making a cheerful observation or two. Her warmth didn't seem to abate, as Ben later asked for the check, which was heartening to him. She left to make an accounting of his early dinner, returned with the bill, then abruptly left again. Ben handled the serrated paper slip, scanning down the column of figures to the total and a brief penned message from his waitress, which read: *"Thank you! Sarah."* And, next to Sarah's name, she had sketched a kind of smiley face – not one which had a drawn circle and abstracted dots and curve for eyes and a smile, but a lively, thoroughly sketched face. It was a face Sarah sketched with cherubic cheekbones and a small merry pointed chin. The grin was closed but broad, with articulation showing how it pushed against the winsome cheeks and merry chin. The eyes were drawn to imply light and attention, the eyebrows were raised. This required effort, Ben thought. Such a nice thank you note. As he laid money on top of the bill, then placing a salt shaker on top of that, Ben then paused and took the pen he had brought with him – he had been reading and adding marginalia to the monograph copy. Ben crafted a brief note under Sarah's smiley face:

"Hi Sarah – Thank you so much for dinner this evening. I thought you were really nice, and I was wondering if you'd

*like to go with me to a show at the Kennedy Center. I have two
tickets to a show appearing a week from next Friday. Here's
my number... It would be great if you can go!" And then Ben
paused, and signed,*

"All the best – Ben."

Ben put his pen away, took monograph in hand and pushed
himself away and up from the table. As he walked by, a little
embarrassed and even giddy from penning his message, Ben
glanced to his side at Sarah, who was then intently taking orders
from a yuppie couple, who were barely able to contain their moving
and exploring two-year old. Ben exited from the restaurant and
raised his hands upward with fingers crossed. He had seen Yul
Brynner do it once in a movie. Brynner was a Tsarist cavalry officer
who in one scene recounted that when the infantry marched by,
the formed cavalry would let go of their reins and hold up their
hands, fingers crossed. The Brynner character pulled off this *esprit
de corps* with elan. Ben liked the historical sense of it, he liked that.

—

Monday came and Ben resumed his work routine. Through the
week, endless cups of coffee fueled his analysis. Discussions
with co-workers, grad school chum emails during down time, the
lunches in and lunches out. He thought about the waitress and
hoped she would match his daring and call the number he'd left.
Ben waited and sensed that a call would happen. He reasoned
that the chemistry would catalyze, and the attractive waitress
would call him. Her reaction would be positive, supported by her
instinct and intuition. But the week progressed and no voicemail
from the waitress was received. Mulling over a Peet's coffee during
a mid-afternoon break on Wednesday, Ben began to re-calibrate

some daydreaming and his expectations. He would see this young woman again, but only at the Pipeline, and only if he were seated in her coverage area. She would be nice to him, because she was a nice person. Ben would be friendly and courteous, because he was a naturally considerate person. Lightly transfixed, he reasoned through this and arrived at its analytical finality. Ben accepted this.

—

Thursday came and went, again with no message from the pretty waitress. This evidence further supported Ben's fresh assessment that the call would not come. There was no oddly hoped-for *kismet*.

Ben now scanned more actively through German language material, as he continued to work on a briefing paper meant to travel through the "higher channel" rather than the "lower channel" at State, as Timmy had said. Ben would provide a concise summary of any fissile heat which German fringe politics, right and left, may be generating these days. The Germans, with their thinking, their compounding words, their abundant consonants, could be stymieing for US policymakers. Someone, somewhere at State wanted to have a better handle on this. Timmy detailed to Ben. Ben liked the project, starting his new analytical quest, reading, synthesizing, mulling and thinking about the information he was gathering. For Ben, the findings should not be declared just from the gut, but should instead reveal themselves following questions posed and laid against the information on hand. Then, to reconsider, were they the right questions? What might be other questions? What, then, did they reveal? And so forth, in a kind of iterative fashion, skepticism entailing each stage, ideally. Of course, the demand for bullet points or the urgent need for a few slides could radically compress the analysis and expedite things.

Ben, in a distracted analytical fugue, reached absently for his phone, and chirped "Stern" into the mouthpiece.

"Hi, it's me." It was Timmy.

"What's up?"

"Well, again hi, I've got Carole on the other line, and she wants to talk to you. You are her current project and so she really wants to pitch you to Brenda," Timmy sounded a bit exasperated and promptly transferred Carole.

"Hiya Ben, Carol here. Do you have a minute?"

A positive, awakening, neuronal stream began flowing in Ben's brain. It's Carole and she's calling about Brenda. Why have I been such a dick? I spaced about getting in touch with Brenda.

"Hi Carole, how are ya?"

Intuiting the nature of the call, Ben was genial, but a little embarrassed.

"Hey Ben, good, really good. Anyway, I'm calling because I've seen Brenda a few times since we all last met, and she mentioned to me that you haven't yet called her. That's really surprising. I kinda had the feeling that you guys were hitting it off?"

Foregoing any pause, Ben belted righted in, "Carole, um, I do. I mean, yes, I liked her. I would love to follow up with her."

"That's what I thought," Carole seemed pleased, "but you're just like Tim." Here, Carole sounded amused, but a little exasperated.

"The personal relations stuff just goes out the window sometimes with you guys."

Ben pictured Carole throwing up her hands and Timmy raising his eyebrows and shrugging.

"I know Carole, I know," Ben chuckled and tried to sound embarrassed, because he actually was embarrassed.

"So, call her then."

"I will, Carole. Definitely will."

"Do you have her number?"

"Uhmmm..." Ben pretended to fumble at his desk for Brenda's number.

Carole audibly grimaced, "Here, I'm going to send her number to you now at your work email. It'll be easier that way. You are 'Benjamin' or 'Ben'?"

"Um, yeah. I'm 'Ben'."

"Okay, good, I'll send this right off," Carole's voice brightened. "Now really call, Ben. She likes you."

"Thanks Carole, definitely will do. I really appreciate the intro to Brenda. She's pretty cool."

"Alright Ben," Carole laughed. "You do that! Get to it!"

Carole was still chuckling into the receiver, but feeling at the same time somewhat self-conscious for being a little domineering and maternal.

—

A few weeks later, Ben Stern found himself standing in the middle of the Kennedy Center vestibule. There he stood, not far from an elegant refreshment bar. He looked presentable but felt a bit nervous. His awakened enthusiasm and the need to act on an almost contractual obligation with Carole, had moved Ben to call Brenda – to call, not to email, not to DM. Brenda was as good as Carol's assurances. She waxed enthusiastic and said that of course it would be great to get together, let's do it and, sure, she'd love to see the revival of "Nixon in China" at the Kennedy. Ben stood in a slight daze, daydreaming and pairing loose associations. A Nixonian quote came to mind: "Everyone, listen, just let me say one thing. I opposed China, I was wrong." Ben shrugged, bemused at the quote that had bubbled up in his mind. Must be because of the opera tonight, he thought.

Ben stirred himself and peered across the carpeted expanse. He saw Brenda approaching and waving at him. Ben smiled, and waved back. He roused himself further and rolled back and forth on his heels. Brenda had on a warm carmine coat, but Ben could also see a form fitting dress beneath, a moving image conveying a pheromone luster. Brenda's thick hair, clear, even face and blue eyes completed the tractor beam effect. Ben realized he owed Carole a lot.

Brenda stopped in a playful jack-knife way just in front of Ben, "Hello, sir! I do believe this evening shall be a monstrous fine one." Whereupon she made a slight bow and then began to giggle. Ben reacted with a small, shy smile at seeing Brenda cavort, pleased but a little abashed from his compelling date's free-form greeting. Brenda relaxed her posture and stared, smiling and gimlet-eyed, at Ben. She leaned slightly over and gave him a hug.

"Ben, thanks so much for this invitation. I think the show will be really interesting and I love the Kennedy Center."

Brenda took Ben's arm, and the two walked toward the main entrance to the theater auditorium, and the ticket usher. Ben fumbled in one of his pockets for the show tickets, which placed the couple in two nice center mezzanine seats so they could clearly see the dramatized meeting between Mao and Richard Nixon. Ben managed to collect himself and sought to rally, as he and Brenda made their way to their seats. It wasn't just that he was nervous, it was that he was just so attracted to her. Plus, she was such an alpha, he thought, then quickly castigated himself for being crass and shallow. He was an omega, he concluded, while smiling at Brenda as they both sat down. Brenda was grinning, then leaned in toward Ben, giving him a mock-serious frown, "This is going to be fun." She patted his arm.

The theatre darkened and became quiet and the curtain rose for the first act. The orchestral score began and a large structure came slowly to light on the stage. The shape encompassed the nose, cockpit exterior and doorway of a 747 aircraft, the "Spirit of '76", providing a dramatic background for the unfolding scene. On the stage in front of it the players were arrayed. On the tarmac stood the Chinese delegation and, adjacent to them, Richard and Pat Nixon. President Nixon made an open-hand wave to China and, by extension, the audience in the theater. Secretary Kissinger also stood there, at a respectful distance, beside the leader of the Free World. The President smiled broadly at the Chinese representatives and then turned to the audience, before singing in a clear baritone, as if only to himself:

"News, news has a kind of mystery...."

Brenda leaned in her chair toward Ben to whisper in his ear, "This is really great, thanks so much!"

Ben nodded agreeing and smiled back at Brenda. He had invited her but, as always, he seemed to be following someone else's lead. Ben leaned closer to Brenda and whispered, "That's awesome, I'm glad you like it."

The John Adams opera continued as the players moved, accompanied by the score, from the airport tarmac to Mao's private office, then to the Great Hall. Each actor declaimed for the nation, sometimes vividly, sometimes sotto voce, their own thoughts about things. Ben peered over at Brenda from time to time. She stayed quiet and virtually motionless, her eyes wide and fixed on the stage, plainly enjoying the event. A musical piece and its related portion of the story ended. The audience, a little late following the cued silence, looked at each other and then began clapping their applause. The ceiling lights flashed twice and then stayed lit, while people shifted in their seats, inuring themselves to the new brightness. Ben turned toward his date, "Should we grab something?"

"Well, since you put it that way, why not?" Brenda laughed and tilted her head toward Ben. She rose from her seat to follow.

The two managed their way through the theater crowd, which was laced with women in vintage designer ware and balding men in heavy dark-framed glasses. Ben casually surveyed the group, concluding that it must be a very well-read bunch. Entering the vestibule, Brenda and Ben quickly seized one of the coveted round tables. Being a cordial date, Ben fetched Diet Cokes from the bar for Brenda and himself. He set the drinks on the small table, feeling thankful and a bit venal that they were able to snatch one of the few places to sit. Ben was quiet for a brief moment, again surveying the crowd. People seemed to be having a good time and sharp laughter tore through the air occasionally. There were people showing intense expressions and engaged in intense conversations. Others were just chatting and casually looking over shoulders, while a few were drawing on lit cigarettes, which they weren't supposed to be doing. Ben gazed at this sample of the Washington cognoscenti, sighing a little while smiling. He turned to Brenda.

"So, you like it, huh?"

"Definitely Ben, thanks so much for inviting me. I'm really enjoying it," Brenda enthused, smiling and blue eyes sparkling toward him.

"Well, excellent, super!"

Brenda's natural charisma had washed over him again. He found himself bonding once again with what was for him a naturally magnetic woman. He was hoping it would work well.

"Yeah," Ben awakened from his momentary distraction, "I really like John Adams' stuff. I had seen this once before at BAM in Brooklyn a few years ago," he added, failing to mention that that was with Mae and while in New York, he and Mae had stayed with her parents in their 60s cross street Fifth Avenue apartment, on the same floor, across from the Lauders.

"It's very cool, I think – taking a seminal policy development, a change in worldview, and turning it into high drama, an opera," Ben observed.

"Exactly!" Brenda now looking very intent on making a point. "And I like the character and psychological insights into Nixon, into the people in his life," she continued slowly, nodding thoughtfully, "but in this bizarre non-Western context. Wow, Nixon. What a complex character." Brenda was shaking her head.

"He certainly was," Ben could only agree.

"You know," Ben took a sip from his Diet Coke, "they all kinda knew each other."

"Um, yeah. I guess so, I mean, who exactly? The characters?" Ben's observation was cryptic to Brenda.

Ben began fingering his Coke glass, and bent his head forward a little, "Well, didn't really 'know' each other, but were connected. Kind of a six-degrees-of-separation thing."

Brenda tilted her head to one side, smiling, "Well, I mean, history, and the libretto, have all the characters actually meeting, so I guess they do all get to know each other." she chuckled.

"I mean, yeah, that's right. The characters and the real people do. They do meet each other."

Ben looked up and more directly at Brenda. His posture had been more slumped, draped a bit over the little round table and his glass of soda, but he then straightened himself, thinking to explain.

"The thing is," Ben's tone was pellucid, "All of these guys, or men, they were mostly men, maybe assholes is close to the mark," he grinned, but fanned his hands out to convey meaning, "They all sort of knew each other, or were connected to each other... It seems like an obvious thing, but it's interesting to take into account as well." Ben paused for a second and continued. "I mean, think about it for a second. Both Mao and Chou traveled during the Fifties to Moscow to meet and negotiate with Stalin. Through Stalin, the Chinese leaders got to know, of course, Stalin's prime diplomat, Molotov. And so, through Molotov, the Chinese leaders would have been connected personally, had he survived, to Von Ribbentrop, Hitler's foreign policy architect and with Molotov the creator of the Molotov-Ribbentrop pact..."

By this time, Brenda was resting her chin on an open palm. The elbow of her supporting arm was pinioned on the table surface. She was nevertheless listening, a small smile making a slight curve across her face. Her eyes wandered and she glanced absently at her wrist watch strapped below her crooked hand but she actually didn't convey boredom. Brenda kept looking and smiling at Ben. Maybe she was interested in what he was saying, or nonplussed, or both.

"I know what happened to the other guys – Mao, Chou, Gang of Four, Hitler – the bunker, Stalin... I like reading history as much as the average dweeb in DC does. But, I wonder what happened to the other two? Molotov? Ribbentrop?"

"Oh yeah," Ben was nodding. "Ribbentrop, they – the Allies – they hanged him after the war. A definite unreconstructed Nazi. He was accomplished, a linguist, an actual aristocrat, married to a wealthy woman, even some business sense – had been a successful wine merchant before joining the Nazi party." Ben paused and shook his head. "He had had a number of Jewish business contacts. Maybe many considered him to be a friend, maybe he thought of himself as a friend. Anyway, they were pretty shocked to see him become a rabid National Socialist. People can really be fucked up and strange!"

"Yeah, that's true..." Brenda nodded and pursed her lips, still maintaining a small smile. "I'm impressed, Ben, you know so much. An arch history nerd... And Molotov, what happened to him?"

"Another nice guy, yeah. He lived for a long time, all the way into the mid-1980s. A Stalin protégé and true believer, like Ribbentrop I guess in some ways. Extremely capable, he helped his benefactor implement the 'Great Purge' during the late thirties, and let's not forget, had a hand in the 'Holodomor' mass punishment starvation Ukraine experienced during the Thirties. Funny thing, though, during some stages of his personal time, he wrote a book called, *In Praise of Learning*. That was Molotov..."

"Well," Brenda breathed in, "that was informative."

A tonal scale sounded in the vestibule and the lights flickered on and off to indicate the end of intermission. Brenda gamely took

Ben's arm and clasped her own to it while they walked toward their seats. Brenda leaned into him in a faux-serious way, as they approached their row.

"And, so the connection is, I guess, Hitler met Molotov who knew Stalin, who worked with Mao and Chou, who then took meetings with Nixon and Kissinger. It's a Hitler-Nixon thing. There are a lot of people who would subscribe to that," Brenda laughed at her own comment.

"I guess you could say that," Ben chuckled and smiled appreciatively. "I know it's a bullshit exercise, but it's still interesting..." Ben seemed shy now, as he was explaining "... the way people – these people – sort of tie into each other."

"Yeah now I see it..." The two of them were now seated and Brenda leaned forward in her seat to raise an index finger. "So, you have meetings running from the People's Great Hall in Beijing, connecting to the recesses of the Kremlin, then running through the Reich Chancellery, somehow tying in with a small home and kitchen and a lemon grove in Yorba Linda, California, where Nixon grew up, if I remember it right. I see it!" Brenda's smile was wide-open and indulgent.

"Yeah, I know, it's a patchwork," Ben smiled and shrugged. "Thanks for listening..." he whispered, smiling and touching Brenda's shoulder, as the lights dimmed for the second half of the performance.

The opera resumed with different players arrayed on the stage, each alone and lying in bed, each reflecting over the paths each had followed in life. Dick and Pat Nixon remember together their early struggles. Nixon recalls the war, his times in the Pacific, poker games played there, the strangeness. Mao and Chiang Ching remember dancing together, he is nostalgic for "the tasty little starlet" who showed up to his revolutionary camp during those early days. Kissinger recalls. The libretto turns to Chou who is thoughtful, while lying awake. He is fitful and cannot sleep, wondering, "How much of what we did was good?" Yet, Chou still begins to rouse himself, as the early light is simulated across the stage. He starts his day, continuing his efforts and life's work. The musical score sounds an elegiac but hopeful and optimistic note, as the opera concludes.

Blinking against the undimmed theater lights, Brenda turned toward Ben, reaching across her seat to place her hand on his wrist.

"Now, that was so good! Thank you again."

Ben felt even more relaxed around her. Some of the reserve and shyness he had shown around her at Timmy and Carole's and even a little bit that evening while waiting for her, had ebbed away.

"I'm glad you liked it, and I'm glad you decided to come out this evening."

–

The two exited the Kennedy Center together, with Brenda insisting that she would be perfectly fine taking the metro home. It's no problem, she insists. After a little polite imploring, Ben managed to dissuade her, while also hailing a taxi. After the cab pulled up, he opened the side door and leaned forward toward the driver, giving Brenda's address and more than enough to cover the fare. Brenda entered the passenger side of the cab, but stopped herself before sliding into her seat. She looked toward Ben, and raised herself from the back of the cab. With some acrobatic effort, she held herself up by grabbing his two spare shoulders, smiling directly at him and saying again what a good time she had before planting a nice full kiss on his cheek, then settled back in the cab and closed the door to go home.

CHAPTER 10

The following Monday morning, after two cups of coffee, Ben leaned back from his desk, spread his arms out, arched his back and stretched the length of his spine, letting out a small, semi-stifled yawn. Ben scratched the back of his neck and glanced around the analyst bull-pen. There, around him, were his colleagues. There they sat, staring intently at screens, sipping from cups of tea and coffee. Good eggs, Ben thought to himself. They numbered only a few, just four altogether and including Ben, so the bull-pen was capacious, which helped the cognitive current flow. Each was working on one or several applied analysis projects, "AA" work. Each of the team had his or her bailiwick and Timmy was an able impresario, channeling work and projects that meshed with the different skills of the team. There was some chit chat, but not a lot. They'd take lunch together, but not all the time. It was a good group. Ben, like the rest of the team, was content to burrow and beaver away at his work. He liked this small group, his colleagues. They were a nice bunch, and he was happy. Timmy had his analytical and bureaucratic back and he had Timmy's confidence. When it came down to it, it would be hard to leave.

The phone sounded on Ben's desk and he reached for it perfunctorily, shifting aside some piled monographs.

"Hey chief!" it was Timmy. "I've got your project manager on the line."

"Uh, yeah..." Ben was focusing.

"Hey, I've got Carole, she's trying to cultivate you for better things..." Timmy gave a long sigh over the phone receiver.

"She's wants to give you some feedback on your date with Brenda last Saturday. So, umm, yup, here she is..." Ben heard the transfer click.

"Ben!" Carole's cheerful voice chimed over the line. "So, how did it go Saturday? Did you guys have a good time?"

"Yeah, great, uh, I think we had a really good time." Ben found himself feeling strangely anxious, knowing he wanted to please Carole, wanting to provide a report that would be satisfactory. He grimaced for a moment, holding the phone to his ear.

"Well, good, nice job then, Ben!" Carole was solicitous. "Anyway, I wanted to call to check-in, and to let you know I spoke to Brenda a little while ago, too."

"Uh huh..."

"Yes, well, I think Brenda also had a good time," Carole was curating the encounter and her work. Ben also noted in Carole's voice the steady tone of the empiricist, the chemist, which she was, gathering information and monitoring the experiment as it was unfolding.

"I'm glad. She's fun and very cute," Ben gasped playfully. "I think she's great, Carole. And, I mean, really fun, and she can put up with me when I'm making an obscure reference and on a verbal jag." Ben then listened, it was like a sonar ping.

"Oh that..." Carole was laughing, "Yeah, she mentioned that, ummm."

Ben sensed the deliberative pause.

"Brenda really thought you were knowledgeable," Brenda resumed.

"Yeah?"

"Yup, that's what she mentioned to me. She had mentioned that also right after you guys came over for pizza that one time."

"Okay, well, that's good," Ben's tone was a half note higher, hoping to foster a positive trend in Brenda's reporting.

"Yeah, yeah, that's right... She thinks you're really bright – and interesting!"

"Uh, that's cool, great. Ummm, I'm glad she was able to meet me for the show."

"Yeah, she loved the show."

"Surprised, though, that she was ready to leave just after the show. I thought we could've grabbed a drink or a small bite to eat."

"Well, she was probably a little tired." Ben could almost see Carole's small smile over the phone. "But she really had a good time, Ben."

"But..." Carole now wanted to elaborate, "you should have asked Brenda a little bit more about her, about herself. You didn't have that many questions for her, Ben." Carole was mildly admonishing. "I mean..." she started to giggle lightly, "you guys talked a lot about Stalin and Mao, Hitler too, apparently. That's a pretty heavy first date..."

"Yeah, uh, I know, I get it," Ben was fiddling with the receiver, "I just thought some of the comparisons, I guess, would be interesting..."

"Yeah, well actually, she did – she thought your talk was pretty interesting." Carole wanted him to rally. "But Ben, lighten up. Maybe ask more questions she can run with about who she is. Less stuff about the planet, global shifts in power, that sort of thing." Carole was beginning to conclude, "Ben, she's pretty neat. And I think both of you guys are really nice and super bright. That's why I'm so glad that you are starting to connect..."

"Gosh, that's really nice, Carole. I know, and I really appreciate it."

"Good, because you need to be sure to call her again, and pick up your game a little bit," Carole chuckled at her own remark.

"Yes, yes, definitely wanna do that."

"Okay?" Carole was effectively wingman-cum-minder.

"Alright, then," now Carole had concluded.

The two ended their call, with Ben asking after the twins and whether she was thinking about additional teaching options. Carole enjoined Ben to keep an eye on Timmy and prevent him from doing any unnecessary bureaucratic heavy lifting – and, not to get stuck at the office so much. Ben said he would. Then, chuckling, Carole confided to Ben that it was doubly hard to ride herd on the twins *and* Timmy. Ben laughed and said he would.

—

That evening, Timmy and Carole were in their kitchen doing their recap of the day. The twins had been fed and neither of the two adults had much of an appetite for dinner. Carole sat at the kitchen table, sipping from a coffee mug, while Timmy leaned against their silver Miele refrigerator. He took sips from a coffee mug, too, almost in a parasympathetic response.

"So, how is the Bloomberg-Stern experiment doing?" Timmy laughed at the moniker he had given to Carole's interest and ongoing maneuvering in fixing up Ben and Brenda. Timmy thought tagging together Brenda's employer and Ben's last name made for some funny ersatz scientific project, like the Heisenberg uncertainty principle or something. This amused him.

Shooting a reproving glance at her husband, Carole wrinkled her brow, thinking of the difficulty in attending what should be a clear straightforward biochemical process, not one fraught with behavioral checks and miscues.

"You know, Tim, Ben is a wonderful guy – such a smart, nice person. He's cute, too. And the way Mae defenestrated him..." Carole narrowed her eyes and grimaced.

"Yeah, that's one way to put it. Defenestrated."

"Or, whatever." Carole was peeved, and found herself rallying again to Ben's cause. "Anyway, the way she kicked him to the curb."

"He did end up with a free apartment, or at least the money for it." Timmy's grin was impish. He did want the best for his friend, though.

"But really, do you think he might be viable? I mean, with Brenda?"

"Yeah, I do. She says that she knows he's a little weird. She gets that, but he's interesting."

"Uh-huh..."

Carole felt prompted and began to elaborate, "Well, Brenda said that Ben knows so much." Timmy was nodding, but with the same impish grin back in place.

"But..." Carole now seemed to be reaching for words and cogent phrasing, "he shares that information and all those insights..." Carole emphasized the sharing. "...and he doesn't have to talk right at you, trying to show he's the smartest person in the room. Brenda really liked him for that. Very interesting. 'Learned', she said, which I think is so quaint!" Carole giggled and smiled at the recollection. "I think she's definitely interested," Carole concluded.

Timmy straightened from his slouch against the refrigerator, smiling broadly happy for his friend, "Wow, well that's great!"

"She's impressed with him, so well read! And she loved the show he took her to, too."

Timmy was nodding slowly, the grin now more puckish, "That's great, babe. So, you think you've engineered some kismet between them?"

"Yeah, Brenda's bright, such a neat person. She's got a little more... life force, I guess – which would be good for Ben... Anyway, she likes him. He's cute. The chemistry's there. I also gave him a little coaching today. We'll see..." Carole nodded to herself, as if acknowledging her own observations.

Timmy topped off their coffees and looked in on the twins, who were giggling and perambulating in the adjoining living room. They had emerged from that state of "parallel play", when playing very small children are completely independent – and oblivious – to those around them. Timmy watched as the two little girls meandered through the living room, laughing and apparently tracking one another. All was safe, since all was child-protected. The twins ambled, sat for a moment, then got back up and maneuvered in a basic tandem with one another. Like two dolphins attempting to school, Timmy thought. The twins soon recognized that daddy had been watching them. One of the girls shrieked and giggled and ran toward Timmy. The other quickly followed.

_ CHAPTER 11

The President was engaged. A large, fluid person, he moved from an early morning meeting with his Chief of Staff, through some choreographed telephone calls with specific voters and "folks", for whom he had manifested convincing empathy and feeling. He, in fact, did actually "feel" for these people. But, he had his own parallel processing underway, which in his habitual form meant weighing and arraying different matters in a kind of steady state cognitive sense. It was a useful personal faculty, had helped him code and develop products which had made him very rich. But, it was a strange sort of thing. Mom had noticed how he was able to do that. He kept it to himself.

Part of him was certainly focusing on his imminent meeting with Irena Levchin. It was now mid-morning and she had made her dutiful appearance at the Oval Office. Rasmussen, though, had decided that a more sequestered setting would be better for the pending discussion with his new, and confirmed, Secretary of State.

Rasmussen and Levchin were now coursing through one of the office hallways in the innards of the West Wing of the White House. The President was moving quickly, while his chief diplomat quickened her pace to keep up. Rasmussen glanced down at the top of Levchin's sprayed and styled red hair and made some small talk about the Washington weather and whether traffic had been bad or not during her secured trip to the White House. The mass of carefully sculpted red hair then tilted to yield a fine, pretty, almost porcelain face, which looked up at the President quizzically. The pair arrived at their interior conference room, with the President making a graceful gesture to hold open the gray door. The Secretary marched under his extended arm into the room and Rasmussen directed her to take a seat at the near end of the large, dark wood conference table. He followed her into the room and seated himself at the adjoining side of the table, but just adjacent to the new Secretary of State. Irena Levchin sat straight-backed, her hands folded in front of her, resting on the table's polished dark surface. With the door closed, it was quiet and gave Levchin the impression of being sealed in. In the middle of the rectangular table sat a black, generic-looking spider phone. Different shades of gray and other earthy tones adorned the conference room. All presumably meant to soothe the apoplectic. Federal conference rooms usually had pictures of notable historical figures, distinctive monument photos, but this conference room had no such artwork and there were also no windows, which was characteristic of an interior room like this one. There were only the emollient earth tones.

A beamer screen cartridge was mounted on the ceiling just above one end of the table. The light coming from the ceiling fixtures was pale and fluorescent, and could be moderated by the wall control inset next to the conference room door. The room seemed intentionally soporific and Levchin felt herself relax and de-clench. An idle thought crossed her mind. This would be ideal for a movie marathon with her two teenage nephews. The President settled in his chair adjacent to Levchin and spread his hands wide – roughly the dimension of dinner plates, Levchin thought – on the dark polished table surface. His expression was genial and he was poised to make some initial remarks, when a quick knock on the door diverted his attention. A White House support staff member wheeled in a small tea and coffee service, laden as well with a small tray of muffins and pastries. The President was distracted but amiable, greeting and thanking the team member for the refreshments. His smile, broad and open, loosened the adamantine contours of his otherwise severe face. His open friendly expression was inviting, as he bantered for a bit with the staff member. Watching the exchange, the Secretary of State found herself feeling even more relaxed, which was unusual for her. For Levchin, any repose was usually for deep thinking or for a kind of idling watchfulness. She had in fact been very busy before this meeting, and had been seeing to the different points on the foreign policy agenda… was already active and on deck, making the political television circuit, speaking, writing, and when necessary, jabbing her index finger at things. This impromptu meeting in private was interesting but stimulated reserves of natural paranoia. What was going on?

"Dr, Levchin…" the President began. He spoke in an expansive, smiling, but looming way, leaning the bulk of his upper frame on his table resting forearm.

"Oh, sir, Mr. President, please call me Rose."

The small request appeared to stop the President in mid-stream, "Ah, okay, Rose then. But why not Irena? That's your name, isn't it?"

"Yes, of course, but I prefer Rose, my family and friends call me Rose. I prefer it."

"Hmmm…" Rasmussen was blankly nodding.

"My father was a bit of an Anglophile, he started it," Levchin explained, smiling broadly, but demurely. Rasmussen studied his subject, or rather object, since she would be an important tool for him. The hair arranged on her head was styled, but thick and straight, highlighting the mechanical care that had gone into its presentation. The President gawked at that crafted head for a moment and then sat back in his chair, presenting a relaxed posture.

"Well, Rose, I'm glad you were able to come in today and meet for a little bit in private." Here, the President began to smile more broadly and, he hoped, warmly. "I'm glad you decided to become part of this administration, part of my team."

"It's been an honor, Mr. President. I've enjoyed our earlier discussions, and look forward to getting to work." Levchin's tone was respectful.

"Just Steve." Rasmussen waved his hand slightly.

"Steve."

"I've been reading your work, which I like, and I also enjoyed the early conversations we've had. As I've said before, Dov and Enzo really speak highly of you, and they are, in some ways, a little responsible for me being here." With that, Rasmussen leaned back further and opened his arms, turning his head quickly in both directions, as if signaling astonishment at finding himself in the White House, in the bowels of the West Wing. "And so, here I am."

"Yes, Mr. President, I mean Steve. I see that," Levchin responded, almost seeming to deadpan. Rasmussen chuckled.

"We've spoken about relevant items before... key foreign policy issues, themes my administration should articulate, which ones we should prioritize," Rasmussen began with context. Levchin straightened further in her chair. "But, what I would like to hear more about, what I would like to hear you elaborate more on... is your 'meta' view..."

"That *is* interesting," Levchin interjected, emphasizing the transitive verb.

"Tell me more on what you see to be the underlying – and overarching – things that figure into the global climate, into world affairs?" Rasmussen then leaned in, again resting his elbows on the conference table, his former linebacker bulk acting as an actual sounding board for the Secretary.

"Mr. President, Steve, people are assholes. Quite simply, they are assholes." Levchin was declarative, emphatic.

The President showed a small grin, processed the Secretary's response.

"Okay, please go on."

"As a nation, and an international actor, one among many, we must acknowledge the venality of those around us, and even our own, as we discern it. Being self-serving can be good…" Levchin was absorbed in her explanation. Rasmussen nodded, continuing to parse and assess the small, vigorous presence seated next to him. Levchin's voice compelled attention as well. It could bemuse. He could hear the Russian accent, but there was outer borough, too, plus a mid-Atlantic tinge as well? That seemed to wax and wane, depending upon the speaker's emotional tempo.

"I appreciate your emphasis on general guilt, so to speak," the President said, rubbing his chin.

Levchin laughed, trying to be agreeable to her new boss.

"Well sir, I mean Steve, as you know from other discussions we have had together, and with your developing team. I am formally, or one could say categorically, a realist. We must gauge what is in our national interest and act accordingly. We must also accept that our international friends, such as they are, can be feckless, while some we may not like as much, may be at times vital to our interests."

Still smiling, Rasmussen scratched again at his chin, "Well, I have to say, I largely agree with your broad-brush narrative…" He then fell silent, and seemed to be collecting his thoughts. Levchin stared at the President, wondering if he had somehow gotten stuck. Then he began talking again, which startled Levchin.

"Like I said, Rose… your cynicism is, sad to say, something I largely share…"

"Well, Mr. President, as Palmerston once observed, 'Britain has no permanent friends, only permanent interests…'" Rose averred, nodding to emphasize the point, her voice thoroughly mid-Atlantic.

"But there," Rasmussen raised an index finger, "I draw a small distinction with your friend – what was his name again? Our country does have interests. We have an instinct for self-preservation. We even have values that we hew to." The President's face was incredulous. He grimaced and continued, "But I look to the data, to testing conditions and our assumptions. We should vet our interests all the time to ascertain what they really are, and why. How we relate to the rest of the world and why." He rubbed at his temple, then added, "I think we will have to be deliberative. Sometimes we will have to rewrite, edit our code, sometimes not. We'll have to be comfortable with uncertainty, at least some of the time."

"Very thoughtful, Steve," Levchin replied, staring directly at the President, who grimaced and shrugged his shoulders in response. He gazed down at the table and fingered open a black folio with notepad to consult sundry notes he'd written to himself. He looked up to see Levchin taking a drag on a cigarette, its blue gray smoke curling toward the conference room ceiling.

"So, enough of the meta discussion, at least for now. I'd like now to address with you some different issues I've been thinking about and I would like to get your feedback."

"Yes, Mr. President, if I can help."

"Great, more coffee?" the President offered hospitably, feeling the need for more himself now.

"No sir, I'm fine," Levchin waved her hand over her cup to indicate as much. The two then spoke further about state matters, allowing Rasmussen to run a line over the Levchin meeting item on his to-do list, which was satisfying to the methodical, newly-elected President.

_ CHAPTER 12

From the open-floor office bullpen, Ben crossed and entered one of the private office hallways. He carried with him a notepad and pen and toted a necessary coffee that lapped against the sides of the cup as he walked. He glanced down at the industrial gray carpet, indifferent and impermeable to any spilled coffee, maybe even to acid. This reassured Ben. He was totally relaxed, even though he was heading effectively for a job interview. But was it really an interview, since both Timmy and Casey were totally behind it? It was more or less a lateral move – a re-assignment – but with an office of his own, true, and better pay, although how much was still to be disclosed. Since he wouldn't be moving, literally, that far, Ben had gotten more comfortable with the idea. Timmy also seemed energized by the whole thing. But what was Jim Casey's remit, his brief? They both, he and Timmy, pondered over it. He seemed to be a general utility player among the agencies and with great clearance, and with a lot of latitude. He couldn't be bothered, he seemed completely unfazed. A very amiable person, decked in the odd Sierra Club virtue-signaling item. That was Casey.

Ben approached Casey's office and rapped softly at the ajar door, then peered respectfully inside. Casey was sitting silently at his desk with his head bowed. Maybe he was thinking, or reading something. Maybe it was an aneurysm. Ben's eyes widened at the random thought. The room was quiet, but then Casey raised his head suddenly and smiled, looking directly at him. "Ben!"

"Hi Jim, is now still a good time?"

"Perfect time, Ben, perfect. Come on in!"

With that, Casey rose and sailed around his desk to shake Ben's hand and close the office door. He clasped Ben's shoulder and motioned him to take one of the two chairs in front of Jim's desk. Ben was taking in the scene before him: the standard bureaucratic white walls, the odd mix of federal and miscellaneous things that adorned Casey's office. Those miscellaneous things – the prints, the pictures – communicated a kind of evergreen leitmotif, showing a love of Northern California and the Pacific Northwest. And, there was the energetic and amiable man himself – the blinking, small but warm light blue eyes; the thin, cropped white hair and matching stubble registering over his cheeks and chin; the small, wiry, fit frame and – to Ben's surprise – no sweater vest today! Casey was wearing what looked to be a still-new Nordstrom's "smart care" print dress shirt and pressed slacks. Ben's prospective new boss was effusive, "Ben, it's great that you've come by!"

"Well, um, yeah, your work…" Ben suddenly felt oddly shy, "your work, Jim, is very interesting…Timmy's a big fan."

"It *is* interesting! And Tim is a wonderful guy, very collegial," Casey confirmed.

The two fell silent. Casey, still smiling, stared across at Ben, who, while very interested at least to know more about him and the whys and wherefores of such a high security clearance, stumbled into an almost anaphylactic shock. Why? Ben asked himself. As an interview situation, it was not ideal. Casey rallied for them both.

"Ben, I just want to put you at ease – about me, about the role you'll play, the remit our team follows. Look, I know Timmy is fascinated about what we do at this end of the floor. And he more or less intuited correctly, I guess, the security clearance I have – and by extension, what the team has." Casey stopped briefly to gauge Ben's reaction, whether the message was seeping through. "Timmy, of course, has made it a small hobby to think about and speculate what I and nameless others may be up to." Casey shook and scratched his head absently, but kept grinning. "Anyway, no harm, no foul. All is peaceable here and Timmy's neither here nor there regarding the mandate I follow." Casey reached across his desk for a pencil, which he began manipulating with one hand.

"I've already shared with you one part of what we do here, my security clearance. That's something I generally do not do."

Ben started to emerge from his fugue and met Casey's bright, pebbly gaze. "Jim, I know you, have enjoyed our impromptu talks, and definitely am curious. I am fascinated with the prospect of being part of your team."

Ben winced, he hoped imperceptibly. Maybe some of his internal rhythms were off, he didn't know. His declaration to Casey was pat – honest but pat. Ben felt rueful. He marshalled his cognitive and social capacities. His expression to Casey, he hoped, was confident and engaged – not totally disassociated.

"Ben, I'm glad you said that, expressing your thoughts plainly. In my mind, this is really a formality." Leaning forward to emphasize, Casey added, "Your current boss is your biggest fan, has nothing but good to say about you. You're lucky to have that guy in your corner. Timmy's shared with me different examples of your work – each of which I've read. It's all very good. And, I have to say, you are prolific without being tedious. That is a remarkable gift."

Ben felt flattered, and now a bit shy – so much for self-possession. "Um, thanks Dr. Casey."

"Jim, call me Jim."

"Yes sir, sure, Jim. Thanks Jim."

"Look, as I mentioned, today's conversation," Casey opened his arms, then brought his hands together to crack his knuckles, "is a formality."

Any remnant of Ben's strange aphasia was passing – was it some form of self-indulgence? Was it some kind of instinctive protective measure? He didn't know. He liked Casey – had liked and had felt comfortable around him since they first met. And he did like the idea of the job, even though he really didn't know anything about the particulars of it.

"I am completely comfortable with you, Ben, and certainly

confident in your abilities. Moreover, you check out – your personal history and general conduct have all been vetted by folks who know how to do such things... They've given you a thumbs up," Casey's face and eyes cooperated into a warm, even mirthful, smile. He bowed his head, then, and became sheepish. "I'm sorry for what was – no need to say otherwise – a violation of your privacy."

"Jim, uhh... that's fine. No need. That was okay – certainly, given the sensitivity of the role. A close check was unavoidable..."

Grinning, Casey leaned back in his chair and with both hands slapped the surface of his desk, "Well, good. That's great Ben. I knew you'd understand. The nature of the role we're discussing is indeed sensitive."

Casey leaned forward again, still smiling, and held Ben's gaze, "You got any additional questions, comments?"

Ben felt a spontaneous desire at this time to please and didn't want to jostle. From his limbic system and into the higher quarters of his mind, the prospect of working for Casey and the mystery of it all resonated as appealing.

"Jim, I'm good. This sounds exciting!"

"Great!"

"So...I'm hired, then?"

"You are!" Casey rubbed his hands together, while continuing to smile at Ben. "So good, I'll take care of the details. While you haven't asked, which, I guess, is refreshing, you're going up a few notches pay-grade wise automatically... One of the bennies."

"Sounds fantastic!" Ben was enthusiastic, there was endorphin flow now.

"And... I'll get you accustomed to your new assignments gradually. But, first things first, you'll be diving in and hitting the ground running," Casey was now leaning slightly back and holding both armrests.

Ben was leaning forward from his chair, squaring himself

before Casey's desk, genuinely feeling interest and hoping to convey as much, "Jim, that's great!"

"Good," Casey approved, scratching at the side of his own head momentarily. "I think that, umm, not this Friday, but a week from Friday, I mean, that Friday...we will have a meeting at the White House, West Wing, at 7:30am. Of course, please keep this confidential." Casey absently began rubbing his hands together again. "For the time being," he continued, "you'll be pinch hitting with Timmy's unit, working on assignments he allocates; but now, you're part of my team. Very small, just you and me."

Ben was feeling optimistic now and sort of light in his body. Casey's own direct quirkiness was exerting a bonding effect, "Jim, I'm really looking forward to getting going with this, well, mysterious mandate that we're following."

"I had a strong sense you would and I'm glad. There'll be some paperwork for you to sign, general bureaucratic formalities. And, you'll stay in Timmy's area, where you're now sitting. You'll eventually move into an office, just two down from mine."

"Yeah, that sounds good. Let me know if you need me for anything else. Thanks for including me in the West Wing meeting."

"Super. Now, your security clearance, everything, will be processed and active definitely before the White House date. Umm, the Friday following this Friday, remember," Carey emphasized.

"Okay, yes sir," Ben respected the authority of it.

"So, I'll leave you a message and send you a quick text anyways, beforehand. But just show up at the West Wing entrance by 7:15 am. You'll be directed to the meeting. I'll see you then."

"Looking forward to it!"

_ CHAPTER 13

Ben was happy. He was on his way to see an attractive woman who actually might want to canoodle with him, but he felt a bit disoriented. He was happy with the transition to Casey's team, even though, of course, it would be just him and Casey. Ben's current colleagues were happy for him, too – mystified by Casey, but glad for Ben in his new role as a kind of utility player in this new area. Timmy and his colleagues believed Casey's remit dealt with a kind of "global anthropology" cut on world developments. Ben wasn't an anthropologist, but that didn't seem to matter. They would all have time to muse about it over a few beers at Shenanigan's, a favored venue for the group. As for that disorientation he was feeling, Ben felt he was riding along on a current of some kind, a sensation stemming from the oddness of his inexplicable bout of near aphasia during the interview and Casey's Teflon congeniality. He, Ben, was hired there, on the spot. Of course, Casey had decided on the hire earlier, Ben reflected. It was like a done deal that Ben was not permitted to fuck up. Still, weird. Ben was mum about the clearance level he was receiving – and the big salary boost. No reason to be so conspicuous among colleagues and friends, he thought. And of course, his new boss told him to be discrete.

Ben stopped himself in mid-reverie to find that he was coming up to Brenda's apartment building, a low-slung building with a Second Empire façade. He arrived at the building's entrance, and pressed the buzzer under the laminated name "Donovan". A mezzo voice responded, "Hello?"

"Hey, it's Ben."

"Come on up, golden boy!"

Ben took the stairs up two flights where Brenda was on the landing waiting for him. She gave a welcoming hug and peck on the cheek.

"My sources tell me you got a promotion. You should have told me!" She put on mock frown. "It would have been my scoop then..." For some reason, she curtsied and laughed.

Ben smiled, but felt self-conscious and dipped his head, a little embarrassed. "Wow, news travels fast."

"Yeah, I talked to Carole today, she told me about it. Timmy thinks it will be a good move for you." Brenda placed both arms on the top of Ben's shoulders, straightened herself and put on a ceremonial expression. She toggled closer to him, and gave him a few quick kisses on both sides of his face, before laughing again.

"Wow... uh..." Ben blushed. He liked her close proximity, though. Brenda pulled herself away and motioned for him to come into the apartment.

"Come on in, and sit awhile. Still a little bit of prep work to do."

Brenda began striding toward the kitchen and pointed to the couch in the small, neat apartment, "Oh, do you want anything?"

"Sparkling water?" Brenda queried.

"No, I'm cool, thanks," he said, sitting down and smiling.

"Okay, fine."

Brenda smiled back and tacked, turning and gliding down the hallway toward her bedroom. Ben sat back and glanced at the wall-mounted TV screen opposite him. The sound was low, the screen streaming an old Star Trek episode. The dialogue was barely audible but Ben settled in to watch. It was from the original series, one of his favorite episodes. It was actually toward the end. Ben watched as Dr. Spock was claiming his right for final oral testimony before certain execution on a Romulan starship. The elegant and powerful female Romulan captain – edgy, but smitten with Spock – was viewing the scene with grim satisfaction. As Spock was declaiming, his form appeared to begin emulsifying, looking like shaken sparkling water, and the familiar whirring sound began rising in pitch. Unsettled by all the whirring and sparkling, the Romulan captain ran to Spock, embracing him, trying to hold him in place, to express maybe something else...?

"Well, I'm ready," Brenda said, breezing back in.

Ben smiled and couldn't believe how lucky he was. The smooth, firm curves, shining hair, the iridescent light eyes. Her face was beautiful, maybe a little hard... Ben edited, but corrected again. She was a knockout! This is callow and childish, I know. She's a little out of my league, Ben thought.

"Let's go, handsome," Brenda smiled. "We can get there early and grab some popcorn."

"I'm with you, beautiful," Ben exclaimed, and then stopped himself. She had exercised some poetic license to call him handsome, but he wasn't sure whether dating protocol allowed him comparable bandwidth. Ben was apprehensive about these sorts of things. She was beautiful, though, Ben thought. Plainly. The two launched themselves out of the apartment to go to the multi-plex, a short walk away. As they left, Ben recognized the growing affection he had for Brenda.

–

The Chris Pine movie – Brenda's choice – left Ben feeling a little de-energized and in need of coffee. His system was immune to any caffeine-primed late-night effects and in fact required a steady dosage of coffee towards maintaining a baseline. Since Ben and Brenda had been – well, yes – dating, the couple generally liked to grab a coffee at Starbucks or at any little café nearby. Brenda on the other hand was winsome – she had liked the movie, more or less. Her store of energy prompted some jostling to their routine – she invited Ben to walk her home and instead have a coffee at her apartment. The invitation was a tonic to Ben, who happily agreed. The February evening was chilly, as the two made their way to Brenda's apartment. Both joked about the movie and its plot compilation – methodical, young, formerly-Amish, risk arbitrageur on Wall Street (Chris Pine) meets, quarrels with, and falls in love with offbeat, conflicted Orthodox Jewish performance artist (played by Katy Perry). Brenda hooked her arm under Ben's as they approached her apartment. She turned and smiled at him while opening the building door. Playfully, she beckoned and darted up the two flights, while Ben stood and gazed after her.

"Are you coming, Mr Stern?" Her voice sounded merry and oddly disembodied, coming from the apartment landing, with Brenda out of sight. Ben did a quick double-time up the stairs to join her. He entered and sat himself on the brown leather couch. Brenda was in the kitchen – really a kitchenette, standing in front of the sink with her back facing him. She was rinsing out the coffee decanter and turned her head to talk over her shoulder. "Regular coffee, right? No decaf."

Ben chuckled, and shook his head, "I free-base coffee, but it has no effect on me, other than keeping me functioning during the work day."

"Super!"

Brenda smiled over her shoulder and took a step to fill the Krupp's machine with some fresh water, then flicked it on.

"Coffee should be ready in a minute. You just take it straight black, no sugar. Right?"

"Yup, that's me."

"Me, too."

"I love it, maybe it's kismet," said Ben, raising an index finger. "I think we're coffee compatible."

Brenda rolled her eyes at Ben and gave a throaty, mezzo-soprano laugh, "If you say so."

She poured the coffee into two mugs which she slowly brought over and placed on the low coffee table in front of the leather couch. She sat down close to Ben and turned her body toward him, resting her right arm against the top of the couch cushion. Brenda sipped some coffee, while staring steadily at Ben.

"Great movie – am I right?"

Ben felt warmly and happily stuck in her lambent blue-green gaze. Unexpectedly, some faint electric current ran through the deeper sections of his brain, signaling unease. This was unexpected! The syrupy warmth of Brenda's gaze and proximity muffled that impulse.

"Yeah, umm... This coffee's pretty good," Ben's voice sounded a little hoarse.

Brenda smiled and nodded, holding her eyes with Ben's. She rolled her hips along the couch, reaching, catching and holding Ben's shoulders and torso. She first brushed her lips against Ben's neck, and then began kissing him deeply on his mouth, which was ajar. Ben smelled her tea-rose perfume and felt her hair brush his face and neck. He reached to hold her too and felt her sensuous form. His senses were magnified, yet in pleasant oblivion.

CHAPTER 14

During much of the following week, nothing had really changed. Casey had told Ben to stay in the bullpen at his old desk and to pinch hit on assignments with Timmy's team. Same fluorescent lights, same amenable colleagues, same surroundings, but Ben really didn't mind. All was apparently in order. But, as Casey had forewarned, the White House meeting was happening that week. A terse email from him indicated that Ben should show up early, at 6:30am – earlier than Casey had previously mentioned – at the north gate of the West Wing. He would be directed from there. Ben shouldn't bring anything – no notes, binders, writing paper, note pads. He should be in business attire with tie and be sure to bring a photo ID. Casey, normally easy going, underscored that Ben had to be punctual – not early and not late. And to keep the meeting confidential. Whom they would be meeting at the West Wing, Ben didn't know. Casey hadn't clarified.

That evening, at home, Ben laid out one of his business suits, his best one, along with a white oxford shirt and deep maroon tie. He then prepared a tofu stir fry with vegetables on brown rice, immersed himself in an entertaining history of the Habsburgs for a while after dinner and then settled down for some Netflix before turning in. Absent-mindedly, he'd forgotten to text or ping Brenda that evening, which he usually would have done.

In the morning, he made his way via the Metro from the Ballston stop to the Capitol, as he usually did during the work week. This time earlier than usual, with the sky still dark. Ben had been excited with the prospect of a West Wing meeting, and was also relieved for not being responsible for anything. This time, he just had to listen. The rare seat he managed to find on the train and the carriage's halting, rocking motion had made Ben groggy, but his walk from the Station onto Pennsylvania Avenue was beginning to wake him up again. He walked along the sidewalk on Pennsylvania bordering the White House grounds. He thought about some of the crazed people who would scale the wrought iron fence to 'visit' with the Obamas or previous occupants. Ben felt gratified to have a legitimate reason to enter. For what reason, and about what, he didn't know. Just there to listen, he told himself. The meeting was probably a typical working group kick-off, something reliant on subject matter expertise. Casey's cryptic manner and declarative emphasis signaled a controlling boss, Ben surmised. Something he would have to be wary of – and a bit of a surprise, given Carey's general folksiness. Ben's paranoid thoughts proved to be a tonic. He felt alert as he approached the north side gatehouse to the West Wing complex.

At the gatehouse, Ben presented his driver's license to a uniformed DC policeman. The cop looked at his clipboard, gazed at the ID, stared hard back at Ben. The only other person there, at that early time, was a US Army serviceman, leaning slightly against on the hut's walls. He was cradling a small machine pistol, and looked tired. Perfunctorily, the policeman indicated to Ben to pass through the metal detector, while calling ahead to announce Ben's presence.

"Just go to the entrance under the awning," the policeman instructed. "Right behind us, just walk in."

Ben thanked him and walked back out into the brisk air. He walked as instructed to the metal push door entrance. He had the incongruous thought of pushing the side door entrance to a strip mall or department store, but quickly purged it from his mind. Entering, he found himself in the brightly lit, federal-style lobby of the West Wing. A small, fit, well-manicured woman stood in the middle of the floor, ready to greet him. Smiling, she stuck out her hand.

"Hi, you must be Ben. I'm Rhonda Schawn, part of the White House executive team."

Ben smiled and grasped Rhonda's hand. "Ben Stern, a pleasure."

"Here, let me take your overcoat," Rhonda offered and Ben promptly obliged.

"Ben, you are responsibly on time," Rhonda was cheerful, "but, you are the last to arrive. Everyone's already here..."

Rhonda walked to one of the lobby walls, stopped and then opened a concealed side door out of the room.

"I'll take you to the meeting now."

—

Rhonda escorted at a brisk pace, guiding Ben through the hallway marked by a neutral blue gray thin floor carpet, impervious to coffee spills and dropped take-out food. The hallway was brightly lit and punctuated by the odd federal monument, which were ubiquitous. Ben kept pace with Rhonda, but was mostly silent, taking in the experience of being a working professional "going to a meeting" in the White House. He had been exposed to White House staff before, but always at other locations –conference venues, State Department settings...

"I hate how dark it stays in the morning this time of year," Rhonda said, striding and smiling at Ben. They took a left at the end of one hallway branch, and continued at a clip.

Ben saw toward the end of the hallway stretch that the wainscoting became a little more ornate and ceremonial. At the end of the stretch, there stood a door. With Ben in tow, Rhonda stopped before the door, rapped her knuckles lightly on it before opening the door half-way to lean in.

"Excuse me, Mr. President. I have Ben Stern with me, sir. He's the last of the expected participants."

"Great, bring him in."

Listening over Rhonda's shoulder, Ben heard the flat Mid-

Western tone, and felt the rush of body chemicals he usually had when faced with an unusual situation. Rhonda pulled gently at Ben's elbow to position him squarely in the room, and then closed the door behind her. He stood there for a moment, staring, until Casey, seated on a green couch and leaning forward, motioned with his hand, first toward the President and then back to Ben.

"Mr. President, this is Ben Stern, he just joined my team. He is a senior and very accomplished analyst. I thought that Ben should also be here for this kick-off meeting."

Casey was coming across as hale but respectful. To Ben, the old man seemed even more spry than previously encountered, maybe even a little more crisp. Casey was in a blue suit, like Ben's, which marked the first time he had seen him wear something other than thoroughly or roughly Sierra Club.

"Mr. President, I just want to add as well that Ben has security clearance on par with my own."

Here, Casey was taking a flyer, Ben thought.

But then, self-editing, he acknowledged that he actually did have that high level of clearance. He smiled, incredulous, and lowered his head briefly. Ben looked up and saw the administration's newly confirmed Secretary of State seated at the opposite end of the couch from Casey. She raised an inquisitive eyebrow at Ben. He nodded shyly in her direction.

Ben glanced at the matching green couch just opposite the one accommodating Casey and Secretary Levchin. Sitting weightily in the middle of it was the President. He looked at Ben, smiling widely, which seemed to brighten his still, hewn face and rose quickly from the couch, as if to intercept a pass, but shaking Ben's hand instead. The Presidential hand enveloped Ben's, but the grip was mediated, firm and congenial, without the risk of breaking any of the recipient's bones. The President stood more than a head taller than Ben and so took a tiny step back to be able to look directly at him.

"Ben, welcome, no introductions necessary, I don't think. You probably know the others here," the President winked and made a loose, small sweeping gesture.

"Thank you, sir. It's an honor to be attending," Ben responded, then sat down in one of the caramel leather federal chairs, arranged to be perpendicular to the two green couches. Seated in the chair's twin, next to Ben, President Obama leaned over and gave Ben an avuncular pat on the shoulder. Ben, a little star-struck by the assembly, smiled at the ex-President and nodded.

"Well, now, good," the President's voice was clear, slightly metallic and technical. "We're all here, and ready to go."

The President sat down on the couch again and opened the meeting.

"President Obama, do you have any initial comments? Remarks?"

"Well, first of all, I am glad we're all here to take this meeting. I want to thank you Mr. President, Steve, for setting aside time to do so," the former President replied graciously.

"I do think it's extremely important, Steve, that we're meeting right at the onset of your administration," now-citizen Obama continued, before pausing.

Obama leaned his spare frame from his chair toward the nearest green couch.

"But, that said, I think I will let Jim do the talking from the start."

The newly-elected President smiled again, brightly. He shrugged his shoulders, spaced his feet farther apart and leaned back into the couch, "Okay, that's fine. This is getting a little mysterious..."

President Obama chuckled, which drew a sympathetic chuckle from Ben. Secretary Levchin's face was impassive. Casey sat forward, at his feet a nondescript black satchel. The President's stare prompted Casey to reach down for the satchel and withdraw from it a manila folder. In a practiced way, Casey opened the folder and took from it a black and white photo matching the folder's dimensions. He reached across the small incidental table separating the two couches and proffered the photo to the President, who gamely took it. President Obama looked on, wearing a small grin. The newly-installed President held the photo now in both hands, looking bemused.

"Well, thank you, Jim. It's a nice picture – seems to be one of President Nixon, on vacation, I guess."

Rasmussen shrugged his big shoulders and smiled at the group around him.

"Sir, do you recognize each of the people in the picture?"

The President shrugged vaguely again and recited, "There's Nixon on the right, Kissinger is on the left, here, and between them..." Rasmussen shook his head, "I don't know who this man is..."

He handed the photo back to Casey, who then laid it flat on the incidental table, so everyone could lean in to see it.

"Madam Secretary," Casey motioned to Levchin, "are you familiar with who the man in the picture is, or rather, was?"

Rose Levchin stepped from her end of the couch, leaned to look at the photo, and shook her head in the negative. Ben also leaned in to see the photo more clearly. It showed three men seated in white canvas chairs. As stated, Kissinger was on the left and Nixon on the right. There was also a distinguished-looking Latin man seated in between them. The three were sitting in chairs on the deck of a small but opulent sports fishing yacht, something very upscale. In the photo, Nixon seemed plainly to be enjoying himself; he was relaxed, legs outstretched, with one ankle folded over its opposite. His expression was open and playful, as if he had just had a good laugh. The distinguished man sitting in the middle wore a mischievous, satisfied expression, but slightly muted as if by some small embarrassment. He must have been the one who had told the joke, Ben thought. Ben noted Kissinger was in a dark suit. Both Nixon and the other man looked to be wearing casual golf clothes.

President Rasmussen was smiling but growing impatient; he glanced at his Secretary of State, whose own expression was fixed but also emanating impatience. He looked at the former President, who was grinning good naturedly back at him. Casey caught this exchange and effectively shushed the former Leader of the Free World.

"Don't mind him, sir," Casey said grinning tightly, looking at President Obama, but directing his comment to the new President Rasmussen.

"President Obama has seen and heard this parlor trick before, but I use it for effect – have done so episodically for the past forty odd years."

To Ben, Jim Casey's voice seemed clearer and harder than he had heard before. The accent was dryer, consistent with an irrigation-dependent Nebraska, where he was from. The "r" in his words was hard and pronounced.

"Anyway, does anyone recognize the man seated in the middle there, between Kissinger and Nixon?"

Obligingly, Levchin leaned forward to view the photo again, "Can't say I recognize him, Dr. Casey."

"Thank you, Madam Secretary, and thank you President Obama for the forbearance," Casey responded, now chuckling a bit, to which the former President nodded amiably.

"That person in the middle is Charles Gregory 'Bebe' Rebozo. He was a successful Florida businessman and banker and an active figure in the Republican Party. Also, a very good friend and confidant to Richard Nixon."

Both Levchin and Rasmussen were impassive, radiating more impatience. Jim Casey hitched himself forward so he was sitting more on the couch's edge. He began scratching unconsciously at the back of his neck. "Now, of the three people in this picture, which one isn't human?"

Rather than displaying a warm, conspiratorial grin, the former

President now sat looking intently on at the new President, searching for any reaction, whatever it might be, on Steve Rasmussen's face. Ben blinked a few times and began shifting in his seat. Casey glanced at the President, giving him a quick nod, and then turned toward Secretary Levchin to gauge what reaction there might be. The chief diplomat's green eyes narrowed, her foundation-covered face yielding little. The baroque red hair presented a defensive front. Ben could hear Casey's breathing, which now oddly seemed labored. He looked at the white-haired, wizened man in blue suit and maroon tie sitting on the other side of the low-slung coffee table, realizing suddenly how old his new boss actually was. The room was silent. For a moment, Ben looked beyond the assembled group, to the window, where he focused on the wintry, slowly-lightening exterior, just perceptible behind the President's substantial desk and through the half-curtained windows.

Opposite Casey, the President's big frame rocked slightly as if he were trying to find a better sitting position, or was searching for a cigarette. His expression was still neutral and fixed, with no trace of his customary post-electoral warmth.

"What exactly do you mean?"

Casey returned his gaze, then nodded.

"Exactly what I just said, or asked. The person, or representation rather, that's not human was the man shown sitting between Nixon and Kissinger. The man we just talked about, Bebe Rebozo."

The President straightened and rested his hands on his knees. Secretary Levchin raised her hand to her face to suppress a grin.

"Bebe Rebozo?" the President asked, his expression glacial.

"Bebe Rebozo, yes," Casey replied, now professional. "Rebozo was a prominent Florida figure, very active and influential in Republican politics," he continued, drawing an implicit association between party politics and the non-human. "As such, Bebe had befriended Nixon and in due course had become a confidant. Nixon liked the man."

"Ummm... so, we are to understand that Rebozo wasn't human?" Levchin trilled, now engaged.

"Well..." Casey was now expansive, gesturing more with his hands "here's where it gets a little complicated."

Obama, the more experienced President, raised his hand to punctuate Casey's discourse, "Steve..."

Rasmussen turned his head mechanically toward the former President.

"Jim has been the keeper, so to speak, of this interesting relationship from the very beginning. I assure you what he is saying is true. Jim, ahh, why don't you provide more of a context first, as you did for me..."

"Of course, sir. I've been doing this for a long time, but it does get away from me a bit once in a while," Casey noted sheepishly, then rallied and recovered. Rasmussen, Levchin, Obama and Ben were all still, staring at Casey. He had the floor. Casey smiled at the small group, gathered in the Oval Office in the early morning, and began.

"You must all, I'm sure, be familiar with the television series called *Star Trek* from the mid- to late-sixties, right?"

All heads, in varying degrees, nodded mutely.

"Well, those series episodes emanated widely...simply as a by-product of the transmission for the American television viewing audience. The transmissions were in fact received by others as well... To this day, we really don't know much about them. They, though, know a lot about us...They're quick studies..."

"Why," interjected Secretary Levchin in the midst of Casey's last sentence, "did they come to us?" The accent had grown more Russian, Ben thought.

"Why? A good question," Casey replied professorially.

"The 'Callers' – Nixon's term for them, and I guess were stuck with it – were intrigued," Casey explained.

"They came because they were 'intrigued'?" Levchin drew out in her breath the descriptor, painstakingly drawing quotes in the air.

"Yes."

Levchin glared. Casey knew he was being both cryptic and glib, if such a thing were possible, in this now unprecedented meeting. He snapped out of it and continued.

"As I was saying, the Callers had intercepted transmissions, many transmissions, coming from earth. They're an advanced civilization, capable of interstellar travel. Their ships – exploratory, commercial, military, we don't know exactly – traveled frequently enough in the general vicinity of our planet to become familiar with us, at least via radio and TV." Casey leaned back and settled his rear more firmly in the couch.

"But, when they had intercepted and vetted various episodes of *Star Trek*, they became, as I said, intrigued."

"Again, why?" The response from Levchin was curt and instantaneous.

From his upholstered chair, Barack Obama looked at Levchin, then at Casey, then shifted his gaze to Rasmussen, sitting opposite. Levchin was now doing the interacting, while Rasmussen was still and quiet, a large brooding mass in the room. He was letting Levchin act, taking in the interaction and seemed to be – Obama searched for the right word – processing. Casey began making further points.

"The Callers became more intrigued as their analysts began to parse through the different episode story lines..." Casey elaborated.

"And so, they liked the show?" Levchin remained irritated, yet was more encouraging.

"That's right, they did. Very much," Casey averred. "You see, the Callers had seized upon something that's a matter of *Star Trek* lore, the 'Prime Directive'," Casey began to explain. "In the TV

94

series, the Federation and its emissaries were forbidden from impeding, abetting or distorting the development of any alien culture, whose technology was not as advanced. The Federation practiced, as envisioned by Gene Roddenberry and his script writers, a kind of salutary neglect, letting civilizations develop under their own power," Casey observed.

"Sounds eminently sensible," Levchin trilled. "But," she continued, "why did this matter so much?"

"Because," Casey's small agate eyes were now bright, "this Prime Directive, or policy of non-interference, was exactly what the Callers were practicing."

"You mean – what?" Levchin, the student, asked.

"They were fascinated that the script writers – the human beings – had come to a position that they themselves had arrived at," filled in Casey.

Now Obama was nodding, and motioning with his hand, "...which leads us back to Rebozo."

"That's right, the Callers had an interest in us, because of what they saw in us: a common sympathy for life, at least as engendered in the thinking behind a dramatic television series."

Casey continued, "They reached out to us to offer their help, more specifically, their protection. Rebozo was their way."

"You mean, Rebozo was a Caller?" Levchin queried.

"No, not exactly, the Rebozo you see in the picture was not Rebozo the human being, nor was he one of the Callers. That Rebozo in the photo was a highly-crafted, advanced holograph rendition – behind which were the Callers. The Callers had screened, I guess through Nixon's many contacts, and saw that Rebozo was due to have a cardiac infarction, which he did, and which the Callers accurately anticipated. They then replaced him, no one the wiser. In this case, they interacted with Nixon and Kissinger...through this holograph apparition. Again, nobody the wiser, until the Callers revealed themselves. The picture of Nixon,

Kissinger and the Rebozo facsimile was taken shortly before the Callers reached out through Rebozo and, effectively, unveiled themselves to the Nixon administration."

President Rasmussen began stroking his chin. "So you're saying that Rebozo was an image..."

"That's right, but a highly sophisticated one," Casey confirmed.

Rasmussen turned his body toward Obama, looking for further confirmation.

"Jim is being on the level, and he has had about 40 years of experience with this... situation," the former President asserted.

From the other end of the couch, green eyes now wide, Secretary Levchin chimed in, "But protection from what?"

"Mr. President, Madam Secretary," Casey inclined his head respectfully toward each, "the Callers took an interest in us – maybe they saw in us a little something of themselves, maybe they feel some ethical responsibility to protect a species, which can evince some respect for alien life and culture – just like the Federation in *Star Trek* does. The Callers have said this roughly, but as with other things, they remain cryptic."

"So, what is it that they do for us exactly?" the Secretary said, gazing directly at Casey.

Casey breathed in, and explained, "The Callers provide us with 'protection', I guess you could say. They have the technology to cloak our planet, shield it from outside detection. Their ships also provide a steady monitor. In that way, our planet and our species can develop under its own power – as the *Star Trek* Prime Directive would have us do and, as it so happens, the Callers' own philosophy states."

"And what," Secretary Levchin continued her line of thought, "must we do for *them*?"

Casey nodded at the question, "There's nothing we really *have* to do. If we indicate as much, we can sever our relationship with them and we'll never see them again – or rather, never see their facsimiles again, that is. They would lift the cloaking, per our direction, if we really want that."

President Obama then weighed in on the modus operandus the Callers followed.

"Steve, Rose, as Jim has been saying, they – the Callers, as President Nixon had called them – offer us protection. Their technology essentially veils the planet and protects it from those who might do us harm."

Levchin registered a grimace, "But, that I do not understand. The United States or, by extension, planet Earth, has always been open to foreign ideas, foreign ways. Why would we want to be so protected?"

Casey straightened his aged frame on the couch, shifting his body toward the newly-confirmed Secretary, "Your point, Rose, is a valid one. Why, indeed? Why shouldn't we be open? Over forty years ago, we were presented with a set of information asymmetries – of power asymmetries. We don't know anything, really, about these people and what might be out there. And that's consistent with their policy – not to intervene directly, not to influence unduly. The Prime Directive. Just like in the television show."

Casey paused, and pushed back the glasses on the bridge of his nose, "For them, so it appears, their relationship with us is perhaps an act of altruism, in a sense. Think of it along the lines of, say, a UN peacekeeping force, or Operation Care..."

"Nothing's for free, there are no free lunches, Dr. Casey," Levchin enunciated for the old Berkeley professor's benefit. Looking at Casey, she formed on her face a combination of amusement, condescension and some alarm.

"To be sure, Madam Secretary," Casey directed his stony gaze back at Rose, "but, again, we do not know. We are faced with a grab bag of 'unknown unknowns', and have been for over forty years."

Ben sat dutifully silent. He was an observer, a new hire – for this now forty-plus year-old project. He looked to his left and saw President Obama smiling ruefully and slowly shaking his head. Ben looked across at the new President Rasmussen, who sat inert but listening – not moving, but apparently thinking, musing. The room had become silent, save for the slight bronchial rasp of Casey's breathing. Rasmussen cradled his chin and then broke the conversational surface tension.

"Jim, this is all, if I may say, and pardon me – pretty fucking weird! What are next steps here?"

Casey brightened and smiled at the President, "That, sir, can follow a modus that previous administrations have followed since the beginning of our interstellar policy. I advise that we meet with the Callers on a quarterly basis – roughly every three months – to engage in informal discussions."

President Obama leant forward, "Steve, the approach seems to work, albeit it does seem one-sided. But, they seem happy with it. The Callers make their appearance in the form of their, er, facsimiles. They don't divulge much about themselves, but they are curious about us – want to have our opinion on things. Importantly, we discuss any evidence or findings of any other extraterrestrial visitations. None so far, from what we've seen."

"Yes," Casey was nodding, "that's how it ran for President Obama during his administration, and for each of the previous administrations back to Nixon's."

"Okay…" Rasmussen replied, momentarily laconic, processing. "So, this ties in with the quid-pro-quo. We have their 'protection'. They get to know us, and find out what we know re any sort of alien contact…" the President nodded, summing it up for himself.

His Secretary of State was, however, piqued, "That's all they want?" The green eyes widened, her mouth drew into a smirk.

"Yeah, Rose, that's about it," Obama confirmed.

"You see," Casey began explaining again, "for them, this is in a sense some kind of expansive foreign policy measure the US has often followed – CARE programs, nation building exercises... with the exception, the key difference, that they do not show themselves and involve themselves in any aspects of our lives. Again, what they do offer us, so they say, is protection and, in a word, privacy."

President Rasmussen straightened on the sofa, and seemed to dig his posterior into the cushion, "Sounds like we're some kind of national park."

"You could say that!" Casey warmed to the idea.

The President sighed at the imponderables, "Yeah, right, okay then. Jim, any more details on next steps?"

"Sir, as noted, the successful process to date has been for us to follow the quarterly meeting format. But, I've expedited things a little here. I can achieve contact with the Callers – simply a phone call, literally. They are amenable to an early introductory meeting in the coming weeks..."

"Great. I'll talk to my admin re my schedule and block out some time. I think an early morning time slot is best – less visible, I think," said the President, cradling his chin.

President Obama nodded, for his successor's benefit, "That's what I always thought, too. That's how we did it."

"Couple more things. Exactly who are we meeting? And, obvious question, who else knows about this?"

Casey assumed a sincere and dutiful expression.

"Sir, by my count, there are about 500 living persons on the entire planet," here, Casey gesticulated, shaping a notional globe, "who know about the Callers." He paused for a moment, then elaborated, "Of course, there are, or rather were, people now dead who knew about them. President Nixon, obviously...Presidents Ford and Reagan, Bush senior, just to cite a few other examples. It has been the accepted approach, Mr. President, that only you and your Secretary of State participate in discussions with the

Callers and know about them. This is our greatest state secret. This knowledge has only been shared with the 'Five Eyes' nations, and only at the comparable levels of government."

"Why? Why these guys?"

Casey nodded his head and closed his eyes to convey receptivity. It was a natural question. "Sir, the Callers themselves had suggested it. They do seem to know our geopolitical environment well and they felt that global coverage through this network of English-speaking countries would offer the best ongoing review of any signs of alien activity on the planet."

"Umm..." the President was cradling his chin again.

"One other thing...," Casey was still declaiming.

"Yes?"

"The Callers later insisted on the Germans being included as well in this network."

"The Germans? Why?" The President sat bemused, shifting his large torso against the back cushion of the sofa.

President Obama nodded in sympathy to the point just made, while Casey found himself both wincing and smiling.

"I mean the Callers have always been evasive on this point. In many respects, of course, German participation is not really a problem for us. Germany is after all a steadfast ally. The Callers also seem to have a high opinion of German public institutions, their objectivity, and the emphasis on empiricism..."

Ben could see the President straighten in his seat again. He was blinking and more energy seemed to be coursing through him. "Okay, the Germans – scientific empiricism – I get it. But why not the French, then, with their Cartesian logic and emphasis on rationality?"

Ben was surprised that a guy from Minnesota would make that reference.

Jim gave a noncommittal shrug, "They really weren't clear, as I said. Maybe they wanted to strike a balance of some kind.

Anyway, we roped them in during the Schmidt government. Good thing, too, that we waited, with all the leaking during the Brandt years." Casey raised an upward palm, a mollifying gesture.

Secretary Levchin was looking on as well and felt some admiration for the President; was surprised at the sudden flash of erudition. Maybe she could work more easily with this naïve American than she had even hoped. Levchin, a naturalized American, frequently thought of other Americans as "Americans". It suited her sensibility. She was irascible.

Rasmussen pondered a little bit over what had been said, looking somewhat absent, in Ben's view. "Okay!" Rasmussen stood up abruptly from his seat on the couch and physically loomed over the assembled group. The others more tentatively and meekly rose to stand.

"Great, great... Many thanks Jim and President Obama for this effective delivery on a vital topic," Rasmussen reached over to clap Obama warmly on the shoulder, who, slightly abashed, unconsciously grinned at the homely gesture.

Rasmussen turned to Jim, "Jim, I'll have my admin reach out to you about possible blocks of time for early morning availability – say 6:00am, 6:30am or so. Let's meet some time over the next few weeks, as you are recommending." Rasmussen stopped himself, appeared quizzical, "You're able to arrange something with the aliens – I mean, the Callers – on short notice, right?"

"Yes sir, that's not a problem. They, as I said earlier, want to meet with you promptly. I can facilitate..." Casey was deferential.

"Super, that's good," the President was smiling more fully, in his more usual warm canvassing way, "Rhonda will send you something."

"Thank you, sir."

President Obama began heading toward the Oval Office door, grinning at Rasmussen, "Well, this is another item on your to-do list, Steve."

"Thanks Barack, I think I might have to call for pointers on this from time to time."

"Not a problem, I'll be around," President Obama nodded again toward his successor, warm and genuine in response.

While Rasmussen continued shepherding his meeting attendees toward the office door, his Secretary of State was slowly shaking her head. Casey inferred from the irritated expression she was weighing the large number of national security issues that surely must be turning inside her mind. She seemed to be evincing more skepticism, her natural choleric state.

Before Ben actually realized it, he found himself standing again on the sidewalk along Pennsylvania Avenue, in front of the White House. Jim Casey was standing beside him, and smiling.

"I think that went well."

Pebbly, bright blue eyes shimmered but were steady, waiting for some response. Ben felt steady on his feet but vertiginous, at least a little bit. The morning was now unfolding under a feeble winter light, while Jim and Ben stood among the self-directed commuters and the more meandering early morning tourists.

CHAPTER 15

Ben decided to take Casey's advice and let things "sink in". No real need to travel back to the office. Casey said it would be fine to reflect on the meeting's discussion at home, at leisure, if Ben wanted to take a personal day. That'd be fine. Casey then left Ben standing in front of the White House, presumably so he could make his trip alone to the K-Street office. There Ben stood, rooted to that spot. He didn't stand slack-jawed, nor did he look discomfited standing there, motionless. His appearance didn't invite scrutiny from any policeman or security person. His expression was a little solemn, contemplative, like something that would manifest on the face of a young bureaucrat reviewing the day's calendar in his mind.

Eventually, Ben made his way from the White House environs and stopped at a nearby Starbucks to sit and, per Jim's advice, let things sink in. The brand-standardized design, dark wood and leather, the woven upholstery, all soothed Ben as he made his usual order – a black "medium" coffee. He departed from the Starbucks vernacular of short or tall, but confirmed always that he wanted a "medium". From his mild insistence, the barista would eventually understand and pour him a "short" one, generally "with room", as also requested. In this case, the pretty barista, with nose and lip piercings, smiled at Ben, which she called him, while handing him his coffee. Her edgy appearance belied a warm, open congeniality. Ben didn't articulate it to himself, but he became momentarily smitten, gave himself a micro-shake to bring himself back to the present, and thanked her. His mind followed that prompt and rebooted to Brenda, which occupied all his band-width capacity.

Ben took his short coffee and seated himself at the faux study carrel and dark wood table close to the serving counter. Toward the top of the wall opposite him a mounted flat screen showed images and emitted the sounds of a CNBC panel hashing out the detail on the Rasmussen administration's new proposal on corporate tax inversion. The sonorous dialogue soothed Ben and he wrapped both hands around his warm coffee cup. He started to watch the flat screen, but his gaze wandered to take in other Starbucks "guests". They seemed to be mostly GW students, reading and chatting. Working yuppies, like himself, streamed in and out of the store, ordering straight coffees or elaborate coffee constructs. Ben sipped from his own coffee and felt rueful, inexplicably, which triggered a paranoia surge. Did he look sad? Why was he looking sad? What had he to be sad about? Why so glum? Would his look invite scrutiny? Would he then spill the beans? He shook himself, then looked back at the TV screen, where CNBC had segued into another segment, and a reporter was now talking about mortgage deductibility. Ben stood up from the table, appeared to softly brush himself off and decided to head to the office, anyway.

CHAPTER 16

Ben exited the elevator and headed to his work area. He felt sheepish, wondered if he looked it. It would be hard to go unnoticed in the open-plan office area, but Ben's colleagues from the analysis team were not there. They themselves were busy maybe grabbing a coffee, busy with meetings or busy at an off-site somewhere. The exception was Timmy, who was standing not far from Ben's desk, holding a cup of coffee and grinning at Ben, "Dude, you're all suited up!"

"Hey buddy, how's it going?" Ben did sound sheepish, and appeared to shyly hunker down while settling into his desk chair. Timmy now stood over him, but was still smiling.

"Yeah, cool. I came by earlier to see if you wanted to grab a coffee, but you weren't here," Timmy made a mock-grimace.

"The guys are all out."

"Yeah, meetings, due-dil. We're pretty busy these days, as you know."

Timmy folded his arms and shifted over one of his haunches to sit at the edge of Ben's desk, "So, what are you guys up to? Did Casey have you cover some global anthropology breakfast meeting?

"Yeah, something like that," Ben gave a noncommittal shrug.

"Oh."

Timmy leaned further on Ben's desk to increase the pressure on his supporting haunch, he quickly shifted his weight to the other haunch.

"Well..." Timmy, smiling and curious, continued his line of questioning with his friend and former direct report, "Was it interesting?"

"What?"

Ben had been arranging a small stock of photocopied articles on the other side of his desk.

"The breakfast."

"Oh yeah, actually was pretty good. Sharp folks. Panel discussant covered Milanovic's work on global income inequality," Ben nodded. Sincerely, he thought.

Timmy remained perched on Ben's desk, summoning another question. Ben's extension rang though, prompting him to pick up and hunch over the phone receiver, thereby eluding Timmy's gaze.

"Stern."

"You're here!"

The voice on the phone was jovial, but with a hard, Plains accent.

"Uhhh...yeah, hey Jim,"

"I saw you come in. I was grabbing a coffee from the lobby machine. Nobody likes it, but I think it's pretty good." Casey shared his last observation in a low voice, as if sharing a confidence. "Anyway," he continued, "come by now, we can debrief."

"Will do," Ben was glad for the chance to evade Timmy.

"That Casey?"

"Yup, the boss, have to check-in. He's curious about the breakfast meeting," Ben elaborated.

"Global anthropology?"

"On rising global intra national income inequality," Ben added.

"Oh, uh, right. Hey, we should grab lunch or a beer. Maybe this Friday, would be great to catch up." Timmy wandered off, as Ben dislodged himself from his work station.

"Sounds good, let's do it," Ben offered over his shoulder, with notebook in hand, as he navigated out of the bullpen toward the adjoining hallways and Casey's office.

—

Ben leaned his body half way through the open door of Casey's office, "Jim?"

Casey had an open notebook before him and was writing something down when he looked up, smiling, and waved Ben to come in, then pointed to the chair opposite the desk.

"Ben Stern, welcome my young friend. Interesting meeting this morning, yes?"

Casey intended to be light-hearted and was, convincingly. The old man's broad toothsome smile, the open collar, the habitual sweater vest – now worn over the white business shirt Ben had seen him in this morning – contributed to Casey's mien, which was infectious and relaxing. Ben hadn't, in fact, been that nervous to meet with Casey for the de-briefing, but Casey's manner put him even more at ease. Ben was relaxed, no weighty effects from the revelation of steady US contact with an advanced alien intelligence over the past forty years.

"Yup, yes indeed," Casey waved his hand slowly across the desktop, expatiating, "I've been doing this for a long time, since Nixon. Presidents come and, every electoral cycle or two, go, making room for a successor." Casey stopped and began scratching his chin, briefly lost in thought. He pointed at a picture on his desk, "From the beginning, it was me and Oberkotter." Casey paused again, then motioned to Ben to look at the framed photo on his desk. Ben saw two young men seated on a wooden bench beside a cinder path set amidst thick solid pines. One of the figures was gazing off in another direction, the other was smiling directly at the camera and holding up one of his hands to wave. Ben recognized the pebbly blue eyes as Casey's, the shoulder length light brown hair and the Fu Manchu mustache bracketing a smile now long gone. The other young man, bespectacled and looking serious beyond the camera, sat under a dark mop top, like one of the Beatles, Ben thought. Surveying Ben reviewing the photo, Casey nodded, really talking to himself now, "Yeah, Harold Oberkotter, a very smart man, a great partner..."

Casey roused himself, again focusing on Ben. The small blue

eyes widened, the face setting into a more wistful expression, "It was Harold and me at the beginning – I should give you some historical context, just so you know what you've gotten yourself into..." The playful smile returned to Casey's lips.

"You see," he began, "for me and Harold, this all began with the Chief."

"The Chief?" Ben was quizzical, plainly Casey made use of odd nicknames and departmental lore.

Casey elaborated, "By 'the Chief', I mean J. Edgar Hoover."

Ben was intrigued, but still registered a confused look, which prompted Casey to continue, "Well, as I said, more context. You see, Harold and I were still relatively new faculty members at Cal when this all came about."

"You know Jim, I don't have too much background on you, actually," Ben volunteered. "Interesting to think about you teaching at Cal."

"Yeah, I know. Easy enough to Google me for more, for additional stuff."

Casey seemed to relax and slide back a little in his chair, "I'm Professor Emeritus at Cal now."

Ben began surveying one of the four white walls to Casey's office, which was adorned with various degrees, professional awards and other honors long accumulated. Casey noticed Ben's glance at the placarded credentials and provided color, "University of Chicago, Hyde Park – did my undergrad and all my graduate work there, which could be monastic if you let it – but, I met my wife there..."

Ben could see and study two photos on Casey's desk. One showed an attractive white-haired woman with an open smile, the other showed the same smiling woman seated on couch next to a relaxed and smiling Casey; behind the couch stood three smiling, handsome young women, varying composites of Casey and his wife. Casey was grinning at Ben's now more obvious scrutiny of the desktop and surrounding room. In a random sort of way, he laid his hands on the desk and intoned in German, "Die Zeit vergeht zu schnell vorbei...Oh brother, I'm digressing here, it's the context. Let's establish the context," Casey peered directly at Ben, smiling.

Ben pulled at the narrative thread, "Jim, you had mentioned Hoover. How again did he really figure in this?"

"Well, Hoover, I have to say, noticed our good luck, or rather his people did. Harold and I had been really lucky. We benefited from Reagan."

"From Reagan?"

Casey nodded and grinned, "Yeah, that's right. Reagan had shut down the Cal campus," explaining, while idly examining his fingernails. "Just for a little while, it was after one of the mass demos. Governor Reagan, you see, insisted on a civil containment response." Casey began nodding and grinning more notably at his arrayed fingernails, as if acknowledging their ability to help him recollect. "So, the administration tried to toe the line, then a lot of the faculty freaked out and radicalized even more. The administration got heavy and fired a lot of them. Reagan liked that. Importantly, many of the anthro folks got booted, they could do that back then." Even now, Casey marveled at the thought.

Thinking more about it, Casey shrugged. He leaned forward and rested his elbows on the desk; the grin was still on his face, as he began massaging one of his temples, "So, anthropology at the time was a pretty popular major. They needed bodies, Harold and I caught a break." Casey shrugged again.

Ben loved this back story from Casey. In Ben's mind, the decades had made Casey a kind of nesting doll presenting a fit, spare and elderly, apparent outdoors enthusiast, over a long tenured government agent and analyst, containing an itinerant Berkeley hippy scholar, by way of Hyde Park and the Great Plains.

"So, you took the offer," Ben was now grinning.

"Yup, sure did. Janet and I drove to the Bay Area that summer, as soon as I got the offer. Harold did, too, with his girlfriend – another art historian. Janet had fixed him up with her – yeah, it was good, and we were lucky."

Casey was winsome, and nostalgic.

"Okay," Ben began, opening his arms in an expansive gesture, "how did all this...?"

"You mean, the location here on K-Street?" Casey gestured to include each of the plain white walls.

"No, I mean..."

"Yeah, I know. I'm just bustin' your chops," Casey countered. "Well," he began, and Ben sensed a homily, "Harold and I were part of that generation, you know, that did a lot of experimentation... You see, not excessively so, I think. We were way too careerist, even then, too responsible really. A lot of people actually were back then, even at Cal. Anyway, we did experiment. Not so much swapping the car keys in the bowl type of thing – Janet and I were just too square for that. I'm from Omaha, and she was Lutheran, from a small Minnesota farm town. But, we were curious, adventurous and interested in expanding our horizons, like with hallucinogens. Our wives, not so much, but Harold and I were..."

Ben enjoyed Casey's unfolding story, but wanted more clear commentary, "So, the hallucinogens were important?" he prompted.

"Yes, they were, yes indeed."

"Okay..." Ben was anticipating explanation, but felt obliged to prompt again, "and...?"

"Oh, of course, yes, hallucinogens, you see, oddly – well, not really that oddly – brought us in contact with the Chief."

"You mean Hoover?"

Casey heard the question and settled back in his chair contentedly, as if to let himself and an automatic confirmation marinate. Ben was becoming surprised by his own growing impatience and by his need to coax. Plainly, the act of nostalgia put this old and otherwise vigorous Sierra Club member into a pleasant fugue state. Ben calmed himself to listen.

"Yes, Hoover, that's right," Casey resumed. "Anyway, Harold and I, probably getting the connection from another faculty member – strange, but I don't remember as to how or from whom – drove out to Orinda, which was really close by, to buy some acid. Place looked very nice, safe nice suburban house. We were outside and met the man selling, who looked like us, except a little more manicured and neater. So, we were reassured." Casey shook his head and smiled at the memory. "So, we agreed on price outside, and then go into the house. We're in the kitchen and we begin making the exchange. As soon as we start doing that, the whole place burst out into all kinds of yelling and pandemonium. I look behind me toward the front door of the house, but see two men standing in front of the door, making sure no one could bolt. Harold and I then found ourselves pinned down to the kitchen floor. Someone was reading us those very new Miranda Rights right above our heads. So, there we were, we were pretty freaked out. Man, those guys knew how to wield authority! They'd cuffed us then, hoisted us up, and brought us to sit down at the kitchen table, where we got to talk to the senior Fed there."

Ben was following the story, engrossed in Casey's drug score gone pear-shaped, "Wow, what a bad bust, was that legal? It sounds like entrapment to me?"

"Yeah, I dunno, we were set up, that's for sure. And we were freaked out."

Casey's eyes lit up, as he continued, "We just wanted to score some acid. Certainly, didn't want to hurt anybody. We were kinda blasé about it. For us, it was about self-discovery, more like a life-style choice really."

Ben was sympathetic, "You guys were shit magnets."

"You got that right. We were victims, I'd say, of Hoover's powers of observation. He believed he needed us. Since this whole thing, this mishigoss, began," Casey opened his arms to embrace the entire room, "only the Presidents and the Secretaries of State learned about the Callers, only them and a small cadre of foreign leaders. It's always been kept quiet. Hoover was the exception, though. Nixon trusted him and needed counsel for this strange new environment. And the Chief was, if anything, a problem solver. He realized and convinced Nixon that we needed to build our understanding of them, just as they were eager to know more about us. He believed that people who studied anthropology – culture, cultural formation – were the ticket. Very open-minded, I have to say. And that's where Harold and I came in..."

Casey rubbed the back of his neck, "So there we were. Hoover wanted us to be the subject matter experts on the Callers. Nixon's right-hand guys on this stuff." He stopped the rubbing then and began to unconsciously grip the back of his neck, "Hoover was definitely an interesting man – efficient, brutal, cosmopolitan, weird. He was dedicated, loved his mission, delved into the gutter. One can appreciate his cross-dressing and such." Casey grew reflective, his blue gaze steady and directed just past Ben's left shoulder. "Anyway," he snapped to and continued, "the head Fed guy at the bust sat Harold and I down at that kitchen table and laid it all out for us. This was serious. It was a serious arrest. We could do HARD time. But, the Fed guy said, we could instead help our country, and then our arrest and all those negative consequences would vanish."

Casey drew a breath through his nostrils, and exhaled. He began shaking his head again, and went on, grinning. "Harold and I studied a lot. As I said, we were basically careerists. We were not radicalized. Of course, we didn't want to narc on anybody, but working for 'our country' was not such a bad thing for us. Plus, we were scared shitless, really intimidated."

"So, what happened?" Ben was eager to hear.

Casey stretched out his back and arms to restore some blood flow, and replied, "We were told to show up that next week's Saturday afternoon at the Fairmont Hotel lobby."

"Where you'd meet Hoover," Ben had been listening and got it.

"That's right, and that's what happened. We showed up there, that Saturday, in the Fairmont lobby, and two agents were there waiting for us. They led us to the hotel room where Hoover was staying. He'd arrived the day beforehand, incognito." Casey rubbed his hands together, as if about to make the offer himself. "The Chief invited us to sit down and made his proposal. Harold and I were to help Nixon with this new situation. He wanted us – and this is important – to manage our new relationship with the Callers. We were to provide some admin, some structure, an institutional memory regarding our relationship with the new alien intelligence." Casey then leaned back in his chair and crossed his arms, appearing content with what he said, prompting Ben to respond.

"So, for all this time, for these past forty years...?"

"Yup, that's right. It was me and Harold. Still managed to hold full-time teaching roles at Cal, too – at least for most of that time." Casey stretched his arms straight above his head, grasped one of his wrists and yawned, "It's been only since my Janet died, and I've gotten Emeritus status that I've been spending more time here."

The old man moved his hand around to indicate the office to Ben, absently noting that of course there had been other physical offices. The government had moved them around the district, but this was the last stop.

The two talked more, the older man answering questions from the younger. Casey introduced Ben to the record-keeping protocol and the minutes-formatting that had been crafted over the years. Ben was shown where the "company ledger" was kept, as Casey described it, both in its secured physical form and in an encrypted version. He also related the preparations that were underway for the new President's meeting with the Callers. President Obama would not be there, as he had already facilitated the handoff to his successor. The Callers, Casey noted to Ben, would make their appearance in the form of two representatives called Jonathan Winter and Steve Allen. Casey had never met these two individuals before, so the meeting would be novel for him as well.

–

The debrief piqued both Ben's curiosity and paranoia – was this sweet old man, this reconstructed hippy, delusional? Had he been somehow able to pull the wool over successive administrations for the past few decades...? Of course, that couldn't be possible, right? There were the meetings... Somebody had to show up for those, from somewhere. And, of course, Obama had been there. Rasmussen had definitely bought it, as had Levchin. And she's quite an operator, Ben thought. What a backstory, too. With Hoover, et alia... Plus, he had this new job and, as Casey had promised, a much bigger paycheck, which was nice. Ben's baseline passivity kicked in again. He let the theories go.

It was funny, though, that none of his former team were really interested in what he was up to – except of course Timmy. Timmy was very interested. I guess people have lives and they want to get on with them, Ben surmised. This was actually good, given things were now so clandestine.

CHAPTER 17

Ben spent the rest of the day working on legacy projects that Timmy had farmed out to him, with Jim's nod. The work was satisfying, engrossing to Ben, because it was orthodox – the word came to him – it conveyed things that actually existed and were easily named. His new work with Casey invited a more primal caution in Ben. To him, there was a friendly, small, slightly wizened old man who stood opposite – and ready to channel, maybe – some indeterminate alien power. He was now, in his admittedly newly-hired way, standing beside Jim and opposite that power. Ben sipped at his ever-present cup of coffee and let his mind wander.

Later that day, he packed up a little early and wished Timmy a nice evening, who nodded, being then preoccupied with reviewing a number of urban terror scenarios. Ben waved and nodded at his workmates who were pleasant and distracted, absently bidding him a nice evening, too. He then ducked into Casey's office, but his new boss was nowhere to be seen, so he left.

–

Ben decided on dinner out just as his metro train pulled into the Ballston stop. He wanted some small distraction and was more inclined to have dinner out rather than making something for himself in the confines of his small Arlington apartment. It was his bachelor pad, but Ben, in his "young thirties" and not yet his "old thirties", didn't yet feel like a seasoned bachelor. He lacked the inclination in some sense. He did feel the id, but liked reading too much, and his technique, as well, was lacking. Ben relied on the fitful charity of acquaintances and friends for the occasional introduction of potential mates, and the lineaments of a romantic life. Could he, a well remunerated and educated urban male, actually become something akin to a New England spinster from another century? There was a certain ambient awkwardness about him, Ben had to acknowledge, before chuckling and telling himself to snap out of it. Of course, Brenda was now changing all this, he thought gratefully.

Riding up the escalator from the train platform, then arriving at the entrance of the Ballston stop, Ben opted to head straight for McGillifreddy's, a kit-pub located in the new Westin Hotel complex, just by the station. He entered the dark wood-paneled, dimly-lit interior, which was adorned with vintage advertisements, sports action pics and local pro team heraldry. The paneled walls appeared polished, embossed and fairly glowed with energy, seemingly ready to suffuse bonhomie if conversations were to ever flag among the patrons. Ben settled at a table and ordered a Diet Coke and Reuben sandwich, with gluten-free bun. Shifting in his chair, he grabbed his satchel and began rifling for some reading material, coming up with an appealing monograph. The animated image of a close-cropped blond-gray haired man was filling the wide screen TV mounted above the bar. It caught Ben's eye. Someone at the restaurant had muted the sound, so the screen was silent. Ben could only see Rasmussen's face, set above a dark suit and light tie. His eyes conveyed an earnestness, his expression was warm and the smile fluid, as Rasmussen communicated something to the American people. Whatever it was, Ben didn't know, couldn't hear. The President's face evoked carved quartz, but the overall composite of face and expression conjured reassurance and confidence, so it seemed to Ben.

Just as Ben had spread some sheets of the monograph on the table, the waiter brought his sandwich and a complimentary salad. He tucked into them and ignored the monograph.

At home that evening, Ben felt more relaxed and began seeing all of the events he had just experienced with a strange equanimity. He oddly felt at home, for now at least, with his strange new assignment and its open-ended nature. Curiosity prompted him to do what should have been obvious and more immediate: Google Jim Casey to learn more about his new boss. Ben scrolled through the links of Jim Caseys who were varied accountants, physicians, a cardiac theatre nurse, marketing people, an actuary, lawyers, a labor organizer, one Zen master, different teachers, and his Jim, an academic – true enough. On the internet profile Casey had provided the standard resume format, noting that he was emeritus faculty in anthropology at Cal and no longer advising students. Ben chuckled automatically, seeing Casey in his LinkedIn guise and given that Casey remained incognito as a long serving Nixon covert operative. Casey turned out to have been a prolific researcher and writer, too, as his LinkedIn attested. Interest piqued, Ben delved into Amazon for some of Jim's work. Two were noteworthy, both available in paperback and even hardcover. The earlier one, *War before Writing*, seemed abstruse but piqued the studious Ben – so this was Dr. Casey's bailiwick. The second one, a collaboration with Oberkotter, was entitled, *War and Mass Literacy*. Ben felt a momentary urge to click on both to add to his cart and charge the purchase. Casey would probably expense it for him through the department, or give him complimentary copies directly, even. But, he would be revealing himself, revealing himself as snooping. Really? Not really. And what would it matter? Ben made an involuntary shrug, and slumped in his chair. He then stretched the length of his body and gave an extended yawn, expanding his chest and extending his legs from his chair, his arms above head. His body sensed the filigree of tension he was carrying and broke it.

Wanting to divert himself, he accessed Amazon Prime and clicked on a second season episode of *Man in the High Castle.*

_ CHAPTER 18

The following weeks went by and were, in some sense, uneventful although Ben was now privy to the files Casey and Oberkotter had accumulated over decades. Some were more sensitive than others, with Casey insisting that Ben have access to them only in his presence in his office. These documents concerned federal efforts at detecting extra-terrestrial life – none to speak of thus far, the Feds report. Other reports reflected the thinking Jim and Harold had about the Callers – who they might be, what their origins and motivations are. It was really just conjecture, since the Callers were if anything shtum about themselves. As anthropologists, the two Berkeley professors observed that the Callers were an "open" group, or culture, seemingly pluralist in the sense that they did not aim to dominate. They allowed – so it seemed – humanity to keep doing whatever it was that humanity was doing.

The meeting notes were oddly another story. These Ben could de-encrypt with the key Jim provided – a very mundane USB-looking type of object but apparently an example of alien technology, according to Casey – and send them to a network printer. The printouts didn't excite Casey in the least. He was of the opinion that if anybody picked them up who shouldn't pick them, they would be dismissive of the copy. They might think it's somebody's amateur work of bad fiction, or even just something dry and administrative, which made sense. There were many clandestine writers among the analyst set. Nobody would take it too seriously. Yup, Ben thought, that was Casey's take. No need to worry about these documents.

Ben stacked the collected pages at his work station. He picked them up and tapped their amassed sides against his desk surface to make the pack clean and square. He then three-punched the sheets and added them to a large binder. These pages encompassed the Nixon, Ford and Carter administrations thus far. Ben wondered how the dour and scientific Carter would come across during his meetings with the Callers. Much to read. He saw that the meetings conformed to a certain rhythm and a rather limited scope, which might also explain Casey's indifference.

To anyone reading these meeting reports, whoever that reader might be, the reports would seem largely dry, since the language could be very procedural. Ben observed that the authors, meaning Casey and Harold, resorted to some informal coded language to describe sensitive things, hence the bureaucratese and the means to throw anyone off the scent. Ben though, found them to be extraordinary. Of course, as an initiate, Ben knew their real context – each document was a synopsis of *real* meetings between respective Presidents and human-like facsimiles from another world. Interestingly, the meeting meeting- minutes were accompanied with photos. They appeared, these beings, to be well groomed, conservatively dressed, curious and congenial. From the minutes, the other world beings came across as diplomatic, prone to being evasive, but eager to hear the impressions that the President of the moment and his Secretary of State had about the world and humanity. Ben read and pored over the meeting minutes, the ones which he kept in that personal binder. He highlighted comments and passages, keeping his marginalia cryptic, using different notations as code to express what he might like to follow up on with Casey. It was only right to apply some kind of veil over his own reactions, Ben believed. Nevertheless, he kept the binder in the open at the front of his desk, supported by two large reference manuals. Ben accepted the dissonance – his own reserved feelings about the notes, Casey's equanimity about them.

CHAPTER 19

Brenda was positively gleaming. They were at her apartment late that Saturday afternoon. Ben was reclining on the sheet- and duvet-strewn bed at the other end of the studio, Brenda was standing legs akimbo, naked in front of the kitchenette island. She giggled, straightened her posture and recited in a learned, reflexive way, "This is Bloomberg news, in more than 170 countries, powered by over 2500 journalists, covering the world 24 hours a day." She broke out laughing, then charged and jumped onto the bed and on top of Ben, who wheezed under the impact. Brenda, who was thoroughly beautiful in Ben's eyes, was also bigger and probably stronger. She laughed and pulled at him, tickling him under his ribcage and hard across his belly. Ben laughed and writhed, squirming hard and fell from the bed onto the floor, still laughing and wheezing.

–

That evening, the two were idle and relaxed. They enjoyed a window table at Tapas, a restaurant close to Brenda's apartment. She loved it and would often bring friends from work, yoga, or from a varied miscellany of "fob's", friends of Brenda, all within an animated orbit of the television news reporter – his girlfriend. Ben learned that Brenda's circle, or rather circles, were encompassing and elaborate, befitting a media personality and much like Mae's extensive network. Ben's own friend group, certainly not as extensive, was nice but a little more subdued. He was beginning to see a pattern here.

Ben was happy, though, and most importantly – secure. He wanted Brenda very much to like him. This in the context of Mae, who had post-divorce distanced herself from Ben in a mechanical and emotionless fashion. Ben had witnessed this – experienced this – with an insulating equanimity. He had loved Mae – he told himself that he loved Mae, but was detached, as a means of self-preservation. There was some kind of homunculus in his head that seemed to do this for him. He felt – organically? – differently about Brenda and hoped that she was somehow melding with him, too. People might say they were, but there was no way to really know.

"Hey you, earth to Ben!" Brenda was smiling at him and nudging the top of his forearm.

"Uh, sorry, I read you," Ben grinned, but felt embarrassed from being pulled from mid-reverie. He found himself blushing from being caught out.

"Ben..." Brenda drew out his name and was now coquettish, "were you thinking about me or some other female...?"

"Oh, no, no, I'm sorry..." Ben began to laugh and attempted to rally, "you are, for me, my only... lady! I'm the luckiest guy in the world." Ben surprised himself with his candor. He actually had a girlfriend. He couldn't help but be supplicating.

"Ben!" Brenda was grinning, "You're blushing again!"

She leaned over and gave him a kiss on the cheek.

"Well, yeah, umm... I guess I am."

Brenda continued smiling at Ben, her look pellucid. "Ben, I am the lucky one. You are really so sweet..." She placed her hand on his arm. "And, in your own boring way, you're not so boring, not at all..." Brenda said that in a soft tone, as she gazed across the table at Ben. She then started laughing at her own comment, "I guess that qualifies for faint praise, I can be such a dope!"

Ben cracked a broader grin and started to laugh.

Brenda nodded, giggling, "Don't agree too much..."

She cradled her chin, winked at Ben and idly scanned the other diners in the restaurant. "I wonder how many of these folks saw the movie we just watched?" The thought of the film imparted some ennui across her features. "I mean, really, it was kind of a meh film, right?"

"Umm...it was okay, I thought the actor was pretty good," Ben replied, hoping he was being objective, but he felt it was "meh" as well, even though it had a great cast. Chalk one up for experience, he thought.

Brenda had been enthusiastic about the film, though. The reviews had been upbeat, plus she seemed taken by the ad copy and the telegenic star power. Still, big box office movies were nowadays like Renaissance merchant ventures, everything had to be squared and insured. Ben liked the historic allusion that came to him. Although quiet, he brightened more so in his chair. The plotline dealt with the tension humanity experience as an advanced alien culture touches down upon earth. Who were the arrivals? How to communicate with them? Did they come in peace, or were their plans nefarious?

"I mean, jeez, if they had the ability to travel across the galaxy, I guess, from whatever to wherever... They could most likely communicate somehow with the natives, I mean, us," Brenda seemed to be admonishing the writers. Her two brows were knitted for emphasis, but she was still smiling. Ben nodded back agreeably.

"Yeah, that makes sense. Maybe they could have introduced another plot angle?" Ben offered.

Much of the film focused on the struggle, and the intended drama, of communicating with the extra-terrestrials. Long-limbed spectral shapes, technical jargon and flow charts, many cetacean sound effects. Characters talked about meaning a lot, which predominated during the first hour of the movie. In the cineplex darkness, Brenda had sighed and fidgeted next to Ben.

"No, no," Brenda was now shaking her head, while holding aloft a forkful of salad, "I really liked the idea for the film, but I think they botched it. No big deal, really." She took in the forkful and look pleased with the conclusion she had delivered.

Ben agreed, such rich subject matter after all, as he knew. Another direction would have been better.

"Yeah, I still liked it, anyway. But they could have used another plot line, maybe," Ben said for the benefit of his date.

Brenda called for the check, with their waiter duly responding. It was her idea for the movie and date night, she emphasized, so she insisted on picking up the tab. Ben felt a warm satisfaction with the evening and agreed to let her pay.

_ CHAPTER 20

Although anxious, Ben had drifted off – or rather, spaced out – but only for a moment. He was seated in the same upholstered chair he had occupied last time. This time, instead of Obama, Casey was seated on the twin chair beside him. On the couch closest to Ben, was the hulking mass of President Rasmussen, who was still but energy-laden and smiling, with his knees crooked up. At the farther end of the couch sat Secretary Levchin, a small neat figure, relaxed and watchful. Ben absently gazed at her elaborate red hair. Levchin caught his gaze and raised her eyebrows, prompting Ben to direct his glance toward the Frederick Remington painting on the opposite wall. He then turned toward Casey and smiled shyly. Casey grinned and returned a wink. They were all waiting. A second meeting with the President, again in the Oval Office, this time without the former President, who had made his handoff and now, effectively, had disappeared into the ether. Another very early morning meeting, with the large federal windows behind the President's desk revealing a still-early morning darkness. A yawn escaped from Ben, as he opened his chest and contorted his body so his arms and legs were fully extended. He corrected his posture and arranged himself compactly again in his seat.

The side door to the office space cracked open a few inches, exposing a brighter light from the adjoining foyer. Rhonda propped the door open with her body, while addressing two obscured forms accompanying her.

"Gentlemen, can I take your overcoats?" they heard her asking.

"Oh yes, thank you. Thanks very much," replied one.

"Uh thanks very much, appreciate it," intoned the other.

"No trouble at all," Rhonda was obliging, "Can I get you coffees?"

From his couch, Steve Rasmussen raised his chin slightly, "No worries on that Rhonda, we already have a set-up. We can provide something for them."

Rhonda opened the door fully and the visitors entered and stood just inside the Oval Office. They both looked at each other and then at the President, who stood and motioned to the just-arrived Callers. Casey stood up as well, his expression open, receptive at encountering old friends.

"Gentlemen," President Rasmussen exclaimed, while nodding slightly to Rhonda, who smiled and then, with the dark overcoats held over her arm, retreated, closing the door behind her.

"Gentlemen..." Rasmussen walked around the credenza and the couch opposite him to shake the hands of his visitors. He gestured for them to sit down at the nearest couch and took his seat again. Levchin was watching calmly and made no move toward anyone. Ben could see Casey's face warm with recognition, as he reached over to shake hands and then sat back down. The Callers, too, seemed at ease with Jim, they greeted him amiably. Something that of course made sense to Ben, given Casey's decades-long relationship with...them, whatever they were.

All were seated now. Casey and Ben on their respective federal chairs, the President and Secretary of State on either half of one of the crème-de-menthe couches and the two Callers opposite. Everyone was silent with anticipation, at least the humans were, Ben could sense. Then President Rasmussen leaned forward in his seat, his smile broadened, hands and arms were liberated from close proximity to his trunk, and he began making measured but sweeping gestures towards the Callers and the room around him.

"Gentlemen, welcome," the President began, "we are honored to meet with you this morning and to sustain this special relationship, a relationship that previous Presidents valued so highly, a relationship so important to our nation..."

One of the Callers then raised a hand slightly, "Mr. President, thank you and the honor is ours entirely."

"Indeed, sir, as my colleague rightly said," affirmed the other Caller.

The first one, smiling, began declaiming again, "My colleague and I would like to congratulate you on the start of your new administration and we wish you good luck on your constructive endeavors."

Ben studied the clean-shaven ebony face of the younger Caller, this being, who was entreating with the President. The first Caller was youthful and handsome, bearing, in Ben's mind, a strange resemblance to the actor Don Cheadle. The other Caller was bigger and older, broad shouldered and substantial, his complexion roseate. His graying hair was combed in a neat part. His mouth was broad and looked mobile, capable of expression. To Ben, this one seemed to evoke someone too... Ed McMahon. Yes, that completed some kind of neural pathway. He looked like Ed McMahon, but healthier, maybe.

"Mr. President," Casey broke into Ben's thoughts and into the meeting conversation, "I would like to introduce you to – if I may use the term of friendship and familiarity first used by our President Nixon – our Caller friends..."

"Certainly Jim, please do," the Don Cheadle-copy encouraged.

Casey nodded appreciatively, directing his gaze at 'Don'.

"Mr. President, to formally introduce our two Caller representatives: this – he gestured towards the gentleman at the end of the couch, closest to Levchin – is Mr. Jonathan Winter." Winter nodded and smiled.

"His colleague, this big fellow," Casey was jovial, "is Mr. Steve Allen."

"Mr. President, an honor," responded the Caller named Steve in a hearty baritone.

"Yes, very much a pleasure and honor for us as well, gentlemen," the President offered, now wanting to expedite things. "Of course, you know Jim. Next to him is a team member, Ben Stern." The

President then swiveled toward Levchin, "and to my immediate right is Dr. Rose Levchin, newly confirmed Secretary of State in my administration."

"As per tradition and practice, only she and I in this present government know of your existence; of course, Jim and his team notwithstanding."

Winter smiled and remained silent, as did Allen, shifting his weight on the couch.

Jim was solicitous, "Mr. President, I would like to suggest that we allow the Caller representatives to make their introductory remarks and pose any initial questions they may have..."

Jonathan Winter raised his right hand slightly as if to curb gently Casey's further remarks. He then posed a question, "President Rasmussen, you were a linebacker?"

"Umm, yeah – yes, I was."

This was the first time Ben had seen a confused expression on Rasmussen's face, whether in real life or on television.

"Oh yes, I see." Winter grinned and seemed pleased with the President's answer. Maybe he felt the President was being forthcoming, Ben thought. About what exactly he couldn't say. Ben looked across at Irena Levchin, who looked both perplexed and irritated at the same time. Jim seemed intent on following the conversation. Steve was looking alternately at Winter and President Rasmussen.

"Yes, a linebacker, very powerful," Jonathan elaborated. Ben listened to Winter's limpid, confident tone and assumed he was the senior Caller.

"Roughly speaking, when we were first encountering President Nixon, a valued friend, he was busy implementing with his very productive assistant Mr. Kissinger and their 'Operation Linebacker'."

Jim caught the current President's absent but stony gaze, and wondered whether the reference resonated. The Oval Office had fallen silent. Secretary Levchin intervened, "Yes, please go on." She sounded more Russian to Ben at that moment.

"Yes, right," Jonathan continued, "your President Nixon used a very forceful stratagem, his massive bombing campaign, to bring his enemies in Southeast Asia, the North Vietnamese, to the negotiating table. As a community, a society, a culture – to approximate these concepts you have – we are certainly against war and violence. What Mr. Nixon and your United States did was extremely violent. But," Winter shrugged – or seemed to – and showed the palms of his hands, "...it brought the North Vietnamese back to the negotiating table..."

Allen, almost on cue, leaned forward from the couch, "...And that did make for a peaceful settlement, albeit not a perfect one." Allen nodded, apparently to himself, seeming to acknowledge the veracity of his statement. Ben looked across the credenza at Rose Levchin, who was staring at the two Callers, her face telegraphing incredulity. The President was stony, but at equilibrium, and also scrutinizing the Callers.

"It's an interesting allusion..." Casey interjected, seeking to bind the conversation, applying unguent.

"Maybe it was a little cryptic..." Allen added, chuckling, his voice sounding avuncular to Ben.

"Mr. Winter, what are you trying to say?" This was the trenchant President Rasmussen. Ben turned toward Jim, who looked relaxed. Jonathan appeared relaxed, too. He was amiable, "Please, call me Jonathan."

Winter cupped his hands over his knees, and leaned toward the President, "President Nixon's action was forceful and directed, consequently yielding a linear result, and a desired one. Your President Nixon was a problem-solver: Vietnam was, well sort of, resolved then, following the tactical bombing and Paris – at least relative to your geopolitical concerns..."

Winter steepled his fingers and continued, "Nixon and

Kissinger were able to more fully initiate relations with China and, yes, and even with your arch-foe, the Soviet Union."

"Don't forget their proactive involvement in Chile..." Allen leaned forward again, raising an index finger.

Ben noticed that Rose appeared cheered by the course of the discussion.

"Gentlemen, I see you are true students of American foreign policy."

"Thank you, Madam Secretary," Jonathan was courtly.

Now striving for clarity, Casey interjected, "Jonathan, Steve had noted your allusion, if you could expand on that a bit..."

"Oh yes, right," Winter's body language opened up, and he leaned forward, closer to the credenza separating him from the President. For an alien life form, or whatever it was, Winter seemed very accessible, Ben observed.

"Mr. President, my dear Mr. Steve Rasmussen, we pride ourselves on doing our homework. We have learned how successful you've become in business and, in general, with your life and relationships – how, despite some slight but meaningful neural differences you have from the norm..." Winter began explaining.

Rose turned her head to look more directly at the President.

"...you were a very effective linebacker for your University of Minnesota Gophers."

"I still don't get your point." Rasmussen said, staring at Jonathan, observing the observer. Next to Winter, Allen shifted his weight from one haunch to the other on the couch, as if ready to reach toward the mint tray on the credenza.

"A Linebacker is very important to the team," Winter continued. "The linebacker must negotiate the complexity, the tension and uncertainty arising from the twin threats of pass and run, the variability of the strong and weak sides. The linebacker must assess and act. He must problem solve. Deliberately."

Winter's tone and expression became warm and confiding, "Mr. President, you are and have always been a problem solver, just like your superlative linebacking skills for your Gophers have shown. Just like Nixon's 'Operation Linebacker.'"

Rasmussen grimaced. "But, there was so much destruction..." he noted.

"Look, it's more of a metaphor," Allen responded helpfully.

"Technically, you're right," Winter now sounded clinical, "the operation indeed resulted, among other things, in much loss of life. The results of planned or unplanned human action – for that matter, the actions of all sentient life forms are non-linear, somewhat chaotic."

"But," Allen chimed in, "it drove the North Vietnamese to the peace table."

"That said, 'Linebacker' was a very muscular action," Winter conceded, his expression doleful. The alien's nuanced expressions fascinated Ben.

"At the end of the day," Allen continued, now feeling for a conclusion, "Vietnam and the United States are now great friends, right?"

"Just so," Winter added and, also seeking to conclude, "Mr. President, Mr. Nixon was a consummate problem solver, in the midst of his many personal and political problems – even choosing to resign from high office and 'face the music' as you say."

"Yes, President Nixon managed to escape criminal prosecution, which was indeed a problem solved," Rasmussen replied, not being sarcastic on the point, but clinical in his review, like Winter.

However, the current President of the United States was exasperated, despite maintaining his diplomatic demeanor. "Gentlemen, this is an interesting conversation, an interesting exchange on our foreign policy episodes, and on an important national leader."

"Yes, but..." Winter interjected, smiling, impassive.

"Who are you, really?" the President spoke calmly now, without any veiled impatience and with genuine interest. Ben looked toward the other end of the couch and saw Levchin gazing at Jonathan Winter, her green eyes open and steady.

"That's an understandable question," Winter, answered softly, still smiling.

"Mr. President," Casey sat straighter in his chair, as if to make a point of order, "it's also been a frequent question, and as Jonathan noted, an understandable one. Just as your predecessors required, you should have some tangible sign of how distinctive our two visitors are. I think now would be an appropriate time."

Casey turned toward Steve Allen, who seemed to collect himself and then stood up from his seated position. Allen looked toward Winter, who nodded at him.

"Very well," Allen said, almost to himself. "Mr. President, if we could make our way to a more open space in your office, let's say that open spot in front of your desk?"

"Alright."

The President looked game, as if expecting a magic trick. He walked across the room with Allen.

The two large men stood opposite each other in front of the embellished Resolute desk. Ben saw how big Allen was, reminiscent of the actual Ed McMahon but somehow looking more robust than the one Ben recalled from seeing on television. He stood tall and broad opposite the President, but was still not quite equal to the President's own unnervingly large stature.

"Very good, thank you sir," Allen was deferential. "Now Mr. President," he began, "I want you to make a fist and place it right where you think my solar plexus should be."

Rasmussen was bemused but agreeable; he balled a fist and placed it on the surface of Allen's red tie, which draped down his large front. The tie felt silken but the weave was rough. It reminded the President of the ties his mother habitually bought him for

Christmas. He could also feel how fleshy and deep Steve Allen's chest was, the substance of aged down lineman, to the President's mind.

"Good. Now sir, I want you to slowly, but forcefully, apply pressure and push your fist into my chest. Don't worry about me, I'm fine." Steve Allen showed a reassuring and confident face to the President, who – sufficiently reassured – began doing as he was told. The mass of Steve Allen's chest at first registered some density and resistance to the pressure from the presidential fist. Rasmussen did not increase the force he was exerting but kept it steady, yet his fist seemed to be sinking further into the Caller's chest.

"No worries, keep pushing."

Allen was cheerful, although the President had sunk his fist into his chest up to the level of his wrist. Weirdly, there was no blood, no sign of distended flesh. Rasmussen looked over at Jim Casey, who sat with arms folded and nodded back to the President, signaling him to go ahead further. Rasmussen looked for a moment at Allen's face and then continued pushing his fist through what should have been his chest cavity. The pressure Rasmussen felt against his balled fist diminished the farther he went, to the point where the resistance was slightest. The President then felt his fist exit out of Allen's back. The Presidential fingers felt unencumbered air. Then, the pressure and feel of an actual physical frame seemed to 'normalize' around Rasmussen's wrist and forearm. Caught, Rasmussen pulled back reflexively. The jerky motion elicited a chuckle from Allen, but he continued to stand relaxed and unaffected before the President.

"Hey, see, not so bad," Steve clasped Rasmussen on the shoulder, who turned to survey the Oval Office gathering. There was Jim Casey – old and confident, he had seen this all before. There was his blinking Secretary of State and there was Jim's attentive associate, Ben.

"You know," Allen began explaining cheerfully, "we've done stuff like this with some of your predecessors – not with all of them, though."

"Steve," Ben turned to hear Winter, who seemed friendly but clinical, seeking to punctuate the President's experience. "Maybe another example?" he requested.

Rasmussen suddenly felt Steve's core dematerialize – no other word – and so freed his arm.

"Mr. President, if you could, just stand straight but remain relaxed. This will not hurt at all and might be interesting," Allen instructed the President warmly.

"Uh, sure."

"Okay, sir." Allen placed the palm of his right hand on the President's chest. "Now, please stay relaxed."

Allen took a half-step to bring himself closer to the President. He took what seemed to be a breath – Ben wondered if it was for dramatic effect – then exhaled, and began lifting – hoisting – the President off the ground from his standing position. Ben watched as the presidential heft, the bulk of Steve Rasmussen, lifted upward to the full extension of Allen's raised arm, like a loaded palette from a container ship, Ben thought. President Rasmussen now hung suspended and stabilized, somehow attached to Allen's raised arm and palm. Rasmussen paid attention to the earlier guidance and was intent on staying relaxed. The President, being an analytical person, began marshalling the available evidence and impressions to give some rough credence to the Caller's capabilities.

"Okay, I think that's good," Winter broke the silence.

Allen nodded and lowered President Rasmussen to a standing position on the floor carpet, just to the side of the National Seal. The President absently began tucking in his shirt and pulling at the sleeves of his jacket.

"Sir," it was Winter again, "I think just one more visual, or rather physical example, might be helpful."

Rasmussen gazed directly at Winter and then at the others in the room. Somehow, he felt obliged to go on.

"Okay, why not? Please Mr. Winter, er... Jonathan, let's see another example, then."

"That's great, sir, thank you. I think this will be helpful and cogent. Now, Mr. President, sir," Winter began advising, "please stay relaxed. That will help the process, and we'll be able to do this safely and quickly..."

Winter then adjusted his seating so he was perched to the edge of the couch, with his knees nearly touching the credenza. Then, holding his straight posture, he began raising his right arm half way up and pointed his index finger at the President. The President suddenly felt his mid-section and upper body tighten, then finding himself floating, suspended in the air. At first held in abeyance, Rasmussen began sailing and rising in a pre-determined direction.

"Sir, please mind your head. If you could fold your body a bit, that would be helpful."

Casey, Levchin and Ben watched as the large presidential form sailed toward the upper corner of the office, to the right of the Resolute desk. Steve Rasmussen did as counselled and folded in his body, so it could accommodate the tight nesting. There, the President hung, but comfortably.

"I feel like a mounted bison head."

"I can see that," Allen offered, sounding purely observational, not being mean about it.

"Mr. President, sir, I can slowly bring you back down, just stay relaxed," Winter said.

"That would be great, thanks."

Winter motioned with this hand again, so that the President began floating back toward the throw carpet. As he approached the floor, Rasmussen unfolded his legs from a semi-crouch and touched down. He stood up fully and began brushing smooth his pant legs.

"Nifty trick."

Rasmussen resumed his seat on the couch, with Levchin touching lightly at his forearm and asking softly if he was okay. The President did seem fine and collected himself. He smoothed away any bunching in his suit and gazed thoughtfully at Jonathan Winter, who returned his gaze impassively. Ben heard Casey rustle and position himself forward toward the credenza edge.

"Mr. President, that must have been some experience, right?"

"Yes Jim, it was. Definitely unique for me."

"So, I think..." Casey went on, "you can see that the Callers have distinctive capabilities – that, for example, Jonathan and Steve are not *corporeal* in the way we generally understand it."

"Yeah, I guess I would have to concur with that."

"That's good, very good," Casey was smiling and gesturing easily with his hands. He seemed to be adopting a familiar matter of fact tone with the President. Ben looked over at Levchin, who was resting her chin on steepled fingers, listening and watching the exchange between Casey and the President. The Callers looked magnanimous.

"From everything that Jim has related, President Obama's vouchsafe, and from I've just experienced personally..." Rasmussen waved his arm around the room for emphasis, "I understand, appreciate really, that Jonathan and Steve are from another world."

"And, importantly," Casey's knees had edged closer to the credenza, "if I may, there is no there, *there*, really – to crib an expression. Jonathan and Steve are not real beings, per se, at all."

The two Callers reflexively, it seemed, shifted on the couch.

"Mr. President," Casey continued, "these two men, Jonathan Winter and Steve Allen, are holograms – very sophisticated ones. They can assume real physical characteristics, or effectively, incorporeal ones. They are there, but then again, they are not. But I want to emphasize to you, Mr. President, sir," and so Casey emphasized, "they reflect – are vehicles for, I guess – an underlying intelligence. One that is – pardon the melodrama – not of this earth."

"You know, Jim," the President had his eyes closed and was, with thumb and index finger, gripping the bridge of his nose, "I'm totally convinced, I get it."

The President looked over at his Secretary of State, who was leaning her petite frame against the opposite arm rest of the couch. She remained impassive, but did register an irritated overlay. Her green-eyed gaze was fixed on the Callers. Ben wondered if her irritation was a default mode that she couldn't completely override.

"Anyway," the President continued, "what do you gentlemen want? What is it that you guys want?"

Smiling, Winter appeared to clear his throat, "To observe, simply."

Allen piped in, "To get to know you guys, that's right." He sat more openly and took up more space, peering at each of the people assembled in the room in turn.

"The Callers are being precise and they are correct, sir," Casey added, with a nod toward the Callers. "The Callers would like to engage in regular discussions with you and Secretary Levchin. They want to hear what your observations and opinions are about this country, the world, developments of humanity in general."

Allen's mouth came slightly ajar and he sat up straighter, raising an index finger. On that apparent cue, Casey added, "And of course, Mr. President, whether or not we've had contact with or information about any other forms of extra-terrestrial intelligence."

"Okay, right," the President began rubbing the back of his neck, "I see, gentlemen," he said laconically.

"And, to state formally, and to confirm," Casey seemed to be making a point of order, "we have not had, at least per the 'Five Eyes' ongoing review, any other extra-terrestrial contact or information to date." Winter turned to Casey and made a small nod.

"You see, Mr. President," Winter said, "we have been aware of you, we do now sympathize with you and we like keeping tabs..."

Ben looked at Winter, at his handsome Don Cheadle face.

"We had been content to leave you and your world to nature and its vastness," Winter leaned forward on the couch now, his elbows on his knees, his fingers steepled, unconsciously (consciously?) mirroring Levchin's pose. "Then, as noted, we intercepted transmissions of your wonderful *Star Trek* episodes – its Prime Directive, its perspectives, its heartfelt pluralism, if I may add, much like our own. We recognized then that we should – within limits – help you or, rather, protect you, which I'm sure Jim had discussed. So, we reached out to your President Nixon, and of course soon began our friendship with Jim as well," Winter smiled at the thought.

"Well," Casey chimed in, his voice a little lower, deferential to the Caller, "it's been an honor...Now, Mr. President, as Jonathan just said, the Callers reached out to us – to establish a relationship, and yes, to offer us something valuable." Casey directed a quick glance at the Callers, who were impassive.

"In a word, protection."

Ben then saw Casey contract his frame and move his haunches closer to the edge of the federal chair.

"Sir, and Madam Secretary, what the Callers offer us and currently provide us is a form of protection."

"Please elaborate," the President's voice was terse and, to Ben's ears, metallic.

Steve Allen navigated his own heft on the opposing couch to bring himself closer toward the President, "Well you see, sir," his voice was again avuncular, "we do just that. We provide protection." Allen paused, lifted his head a little higher, and smiled to himself, possibly amused by a stray thought, "You see, Mr. President, we can – and currently do, as Jim said – provide protection. Our technology is pretty good, so we provide a kind of veil that serves to hide your planet. You know, we're doing great things with gravity these days, but enough about that. We're basically protecting your world from prying eyes."

_ CHAPTER 21

"But, Mr. Allen, surely such caution – or protection, rather – is misplaced." Levchin spoke from the other end of the presidential sofa. "Humanity has come far, especially in these last decades. We, in fact, who are enjoying the benefits of liberal, representative democracy, seek to learn more. We are an open society…"

Ben was struck by Levchin's unabashed insincerity. From his research, he knew her to be a cold warrior for the twenty-first century, never 'open' or credulous about anything. Certainly, the Callers knew this too. They had done their 'homework', as Jonathan had said.

"Well, there be dragons…" Allen remarked, looking jovial and indulgent.

Winter weighed in more formally, "Secretary Levchin, let us say that space – the atmosphere around you, around this earth – is very dynamic. It is highly interactive. In view of this, we approached President Nixon and Secretary Kissinger with a proposal – a means to allow you, effectively, to be you. Our concealing force, protecting your world, does that."

"But sir," Levchin's steady green eyes met Winter's holographic ones, "what *exactly* do we have to fear?"

Winter grimaced, "Rose Levchin, maybe nothing at all, but there could also be a great deal to fear. As I said, the situation – even just beyond the confines of your upper atmosphere – can be dynamic. One could say chaotic, even." Winter levelled his gaze at Levchin. The President was observing them both.

"Surely, then," Levchin was seeking another opening, "you could provide us with more information, more guidance, to cope with such a formidable environment."

Ben, listening intently, was startled upright by Allen's sudden laughter. The laughter didn't sound derisory, it seemed that Allen was genuinely amused.

"Rose, we don't want to 'screw the pooch'!"

Levchin looked blank.

"I mean – anyway, that's an expression your own astronauts, or maybe cosmonauts," Allen winked, "used when sticking to protocol: 'Don't screw the pooch'," he laughed again. "We want you 'people of earth'," Allen's hands made two air quotes, "to advance naturally, organically, as it really should be. Besides, we don't want to find ourselves sucked in, embroiled in any mission creep," with that, Allen reclined his Ed McMahon-like bulk into the sofa's back cushion.

Winter gave an affirming nod, "As Steve noted, our philosophy is to help you, humanity, to proceed under your own power, which is what your Prime Directive would have, as reflected in those wonderful teleplays. It is something we admire in you."

"Well, it was only a TV show," Rasmussen responded, slowly shaking his head with the incredulity of it all. He turned and gave Casey a protracted look.

Casey turned toward the Callers, "Gentlemen, I know President Rasmussen and Secretary Levchin are very appreciative of the time you've set aside to meet with us this morning," he gestured with open hands to all of the assembled in the room. "I think I share the view of the President and Secretary Levchin in saying that this introductory meeting has been a highly productive one."

The President sucked in some air, nodded and stood up, with Secretary Levchin following his cue, her small form in stark contrast to the President. Casey and Ben rose from their seats, as did the Callers. Looking pleased and even very game, Allen turned toward Casey, "Jim, as always, thanks for facilitating this. I think it went well, really well. This was a great kick-off, I think."

Winter leaned toward Casey, "Indeed, very much agree. Thanks Jim, a good meeting with the President."

Then turning toward the President, the Caller indulged an oratory tone, "Sir, it's truly been an honor, I appreciate this introduction and this opportunity you've afforded us to maintain our dialogue with you, and by extension, with the rest of humanity."

The four main interlocutors shook hands with one another and then with Casey and Ben. President Rasmussen smiled broadly at the little gathering, his features animated, displaying a warmth that was natural and inviting. It seemed, to Ben, to be the same expression the President showed in different campaign stills and often during the televised debates of the past year.

"Mr. Winter, Mr. Allen, let me say that it's been both a pleasure and, of course, highly informative. I'm looking forward to our future discussions."

President Rasmussen made a solicitous motion toward the Oval Office doorway, and escorted the two Callers out. Rhonda was on the other side of the door, holding two navy blue camel-hair overcoats, ready to meet the Callers. Rasmussen and the Callers shook hands again. Placing his hand on Winter's holographic shoulder, Rasmussen conveyed some final remarks, which Casey and Ben couldn't make out. The Callers thanked Rhonda, took their coats, and headed out toward Pennsylvania Avenue.

_ CHAPTER 22

Later that week, a large older white man stood on the sidewalk at Pennsylvania Avenue. He stood on the sidewalk, peering through the tall black wrought iron fence separating the manicured green lawn on which the White House and a connected utilitarian structure were nestled. It was mid-morning and the winter sun was still faint in the gray sky. The man continued to stand still, content on surveying the green lawn in front of the White House. He wore a serge blue overcoat, which fit nicely over his shoulders and worked to conceal his mid-section. This older man looked prosperous and content, standing there still, and inactive, blending into the urban winter scene. His graying hair was combed neatly, but bunched over his ears, affecting a style from an earlier decade. His face reflected some over-indulgence, the complexion was roseate, but he also exuded an energy and vitality. The old man focused and sharpened his view into the White House structure and the West Wing, managing to peer past the walls and supports until his gaze rested upon two figures in concert with one another in the walkway separating the White House residence from the West Wing offices. The two figures were speaking to each other. The much smaller one speaking in paragraph form, the much larger listening and responding in terse phrases.

The man on the sidewalk focused further, making out the arranged red hair of the smaller figure, a neatly composed woman in her early fifties, standing opposite her conversation partner, the large contained man with graying sandy cropped hair. The large man gestured with one of his hands, making a point to the red-haired woman who tilted her head backward slightly and then to one side. The old man on the sidewalk continued to watch, as the large man folded his arms and began rocking slowly on his heels and the balls of his feet. The woman squared herself and extended a small pale hand, which the large man grasped and shook. The figures nodded to each other and then continued in opposite directions along the connecting walkway.

"Sir, excuse me, sir?" A DC policeman, wearing a blue uniform baseball cap and heavy winter jacket approached the man. "Sir, can I help you? Do you need directions?" The policeman was smiling, but watchful. The old man gave the appearance of being suddenly startled awake.

"Oh, excuse me? Oh yes, of course. I'm sorry, officer. What was that again?" He chuckled and smiled at the policeman. His tone genial but deferential. "Quite a sight, isn't it?" The old man continued, "you know, I work not too far from here, and pretty much pass by the White House – to and from – every day." He grinned and shook his head slowly, conveying a sense of wonder. "And it's pretty amazing," he went on, "this is where the elected leader of this great country of ours – 320 million people and counting! – lives and works. Sometimes, you just gotta pause and take it in."

The policeman relaxed visibly and grinned back, taking in the smiling, warm and apparently sane expression of the older man.

"I know just what you mean," the officer replied. "It's really something to see, and easy to take for granted."

"You can sure say that again!"

"Well, everything's fine then?" the policeman was solicitous.

"Oh sure, gosh, thanks. I guess I should get going," the older man observed, mostly to himself. "Oh, and um officer, thanks for asking, and have a great day," he added. His good cheer seemed to have kicked up an additional notch.

"You the same, sir."

The older man responded with his smile and a quick wave. He turned and started to make his way down the Pennsylvania Avenue sidewalk.

CHAPTER 23

A few days had passed and Ben had not seen nor heard from Casey at all, which seemed odd to Ben – certainly from a managerial or organizational perspective. There was no steady communication, even if there was a chain of command. He was Casey's direct report. His absence didn't really bother Ben too much. As far as work went, he liked to be left pretty much to himself, anyway. And, Ben reasoned, they were a small autonomous unit, just him and Casey. There was no steady stream of deliverables to account for, no touching base with colleagues and other teams on project updates, certainly no matrix reporting. There single line to supervisory authority led only to the President and his chief diplomat. That's the way Nixon and Hoover had structured it and that's the way it's remained for the past forty years – now in train to hit the fifty-year mark. This whole thing, Ben reflected, had a ritual quality about it, perhaps even extra-legal. So, as it was from Nixon to Ford...eventually, from Bush II to Obama – and that, Ben marveled, in the midst of the global financial implosion – and now from Obama to Rasmussen. There was an Old Testament feel to it, Ben reflected further. As far as he knew, there would be no judicial review, nor would there be Congressional testimony. There was just, and would continue to be, this arrangement. What else could you call it?

Per Casey's request, Ben had penned summary notes of the kick-off meeting, and had followed the format that Casey and Oberkotter had used. He was able to knock that off pretty quickly, and hoped his rendition would be satisfactory for Casey.

The note-taking might seem to be mundane, but it was important. Aside from the memos Jim and Harold had written, the notes engendered the institutional memory of the relationship between the United States – or rather, earth – and something sentient and beyond it. Jim and Harold had been meticulous in their note-taking. Ben shifted in his ergonomic chair, and stared for a moment at the large red binders arranged with other reference materials on his desk. He resisted the impulse to riffle through the red binder pages.

Ben shifted around in his chair again, and reached for his Starbucks. He was there in the office early, as was his wont. Still situated in the bullpen, which he really didn't mind. The hallway office, just down from Jim's, still had to be refitted. The building was thick with tenants – private sector tenants – so maintenance hadn't gotten around to his work order. Ben really didn't mind, besides, he liked the proximity to former team members in the bullpen, the ambient chatter and bullshitting was agreeable. And, Ben acknowledged to himself, he did have a matrix reporting set-up, since Jim had farmed him out as well on ad-hoc projects and piece work to Timmy, who was deluged. Well, I like the analytical side and the topics, he reflected.

Ben stretched his limbs and surveyed the open floor surroundings. Timmy hadn't made it in yet, but would soon be there. The others would make their appearances in a varied pace until about 9am, depending on whether toddlers had to be dropped off, how well commuter lines were functioning, or early morning affinity. They would get there. Analytical types were often, but not always, responsible people, that was Ben's views. He enjoyed the quiet though, right now, with nobody really about. For some reason, he was in earlier today than he usually was. He had been showing up generally at an earlier margin, since he split with Mae. The quiet and the control were such nice things, he liked that. Ben unfolded a copy of the *Washington Post* and scanned the front page, which featured an article, just below the crease, on Sybylline Corporation's vending contracts with two Macao resort and entertainment companies. Ben read with interest that Sybylline would unwind its analytical services –

current management was promptly expediting steps to do so, the *Post* reported. There would be no awkward business exposures to impugn the newly installed President, Sybylline management assured. Rasmussen remained the company's single largest shareholder with holdings worth several billion dollars, all of which remained frozen in a blind trust, along with other proceeds from the President's liquidated assets. Somehow, the President managed to hold on to his Sybylline stakes, as he conferred with and stood literally head and shoulders above a feverish and intent legal team. Nestled in the article was the President's picture, showing voluntary muscles curved into that strange infectious warm grin of his – part Andy Griffith, part Siddartha. That thought and image passed through Ben's mind. The phone on his desk lit up. It gave its shrill electronic tone, startling him to pick it up.

"Stern," Ben, still startled, replied blankly.

"You're here! That's great," it was Casey. Ben was additionally surprised. Casey had been in his office all along. That was his extension. Ben had somehow missed noting any lights on in his office.

"Great man, great," Jim continued, "hey, can you pop into my office? Er, tell you what, I'll see you by the elevator. Let's take a hit." (Casey's shorthand for getting a coffee.)

–

Carrying their respective tall coffees, the two entered Casey's office for a sit down. Jim had mentioned to Ben, as Ben was ordering his coffee, that a quick debrief of the Oval Office meeting with the aliens was in order. Jim's reference, made in the middle of the coffee line, struck Ben like cold, wet snow. He gulped at first but then realized that Casey's language was generic – mentioning only "the meeting" and "going over comments", and the like. No need to be skittish in the Starbucks line.

Jim was animated and voluble, full of energy this morning. His lean frame and wizened face, stretched and tempered from decades of running and a progressive counter-culture attention to diet, was full of expression as he talked. Casey's no-gluten diet seemed to give him an alert quality, Ben observed. Copious coffee, consumed every day, also helped. Once back in the office, Casey turned to Ben, bright-eyed.

"Ben, take a load off, let's talk." He pointed to a chair by his desk, and seated himself behind his own desk. "So, a good kick-off, huh?" he opened up.

Ben grinned, was sheepish, "Jim, I have to say, it is really something – truly amazing – to work with you on this, and to participate in maybe the most important ongoing dialogue in the world. I really feel fortunate..."

Casey raised an index finger, while showing Ben a mock indignant look, "Now, don't be unctuous." He grinned back and nodded.

"Yeah, I know what you're saying, it's strange. Pretty amazing, too."

The two men fell into a momentary silence, sitting there, sipping from their coffees.

"So," Casey sucked at his teeth, "what were your impressions? What did you think of it?"

"Well, it definitely was amazing, definitely weird, but also – as it was, as we undertook our discussion – pretty conventional, too."

Jim nodded, grinning. "That's right, that's right. After all, they want to relate to us, right? They want to communicate clearly with us."

"Yeah, exactly. Obviously, no problem interacting – given the form they assumed, right?" Ben added.

"Yup, that's right. On their 'style' – in a word – did you notice anything else?"

"Well, yeah, the Callers – the two men – they looked pretty

familiar, both of them. The black guy – the African American, he looked like..."

"Don Cheadle," Jim interjected, smiling more broadly.

"Yeah, exactly," Ben felt gratified, coming full circle on this. "He really looked like Don Cheadle!"

"What about the other guy?" Jim was prompting.

"Umm, well the other one...the older white guy. Yeah, this is funny, kind of a blast from the past – you know, he was a pretty big guy." Ben was commenting in free form, continuing, "you know, I think..." he smirked slightly, showing some effort, "He reminded me of Ed McMahon, Carson's wing man."

"Exactly, he did look like Ed McMahon," Casey leaned forward from his seat, showing a grin – more of the shit-eating variety.

"Yeah, Ed McMahon, maybe a little healthier looking. I don't know – heavy, but less jowly." Ben was nodding to himself, then observed, "you know, it can't be coincidental – that they look like these celebrities. There must be a reason for this."

Casey folded his hands behind his head and leaned back in his chair. His customary Sierra sweater vest gathered pontoon-like over his torso, "It's their modus operandi."

"What do you mean?" Ben queried.

"Since we've known 'em, the Callers have been the facsimiles they produce – these holographs or projections. Indeed, as you say, they are highly sophisticated ones. They're the vehicles they've been using to communicate with us."

Ben nodded, agreeably.

Casey continued, "The Callers want their communication with us to be frictionless, effectively. They don't want to scare us. They want us to feel comfortable."

"So, they evoke familiar figures for us," Ben inferred.

"That's right, they do."

"But," Casey was emending, "not too much so – some nuance,

you see. No huge names. They draw on appealing people – people we like."

"Yeah, makes sense – Don Cheadle. Everybody loves Don Cheadle."

"You bet," Casey limned into professorial mode, "everybody does, that's right. But Don Cheadle also *blends* – he could be the UPS guy, or your accountant. Everybody likes UPS, people depend on their accountants – for safety and security."

"Yeah, hmm," Ben agreed.

"Even the name – Jonathan Winter. A name pretty close to the one of that cuddly, ursine comedian Jonathan Winters. Everybody loved Jonathan Winters. You see, it's not so current, but vaguely familiar. A little weird too, I guess," Casey reflected.

"Wow, it *is* weird," Ben replied thoughtfully. "But I guess it works!" he said, almost to himself.

"Yup, it does, it has – as I said, that's been their way, since the beginning." Casey stretched out his arms, yawned and cracked his back again. He blinked both his pebbly blue eyes and smiled at Ben. "You know, as I said earlier, they want to feel comfortable, for that matter, amenable. So, they trot out these characters – not so famous – but known well enough." Casey remained professorial, homiletic. "They want us to react positively, naturally, in our interactions with them. The familiar forms the Callers assume remove the aspect of the stranger, but subtly. It's the feeling we might have when sitting around a campfire at night," Casey gesticulated with his hands, setting the stage.

"Strangers appear, emerging from the dark, evoking anxiety. They quietly sit beside us and we turn to look more closely and then recognize them as friends. It's a feeling we experience when we see a friend emerge into lit view on a dark city street. We feel anxiety, then relief, then comfort."

"The Callers reason that our baseline reaction to them is, would be, fear – at least apprehension," Ben offered.

"That's right," Casey nodded. "They represent the unknown to us, and something powerful – being able to travel from somewhere, God knows where. They come from somewhere we have no conceivable way of reaching."

Ben nodded, seriously. Peering back at him, Casey cracked another smile and sought to break the momentary pall, "Well, I – or I guess me and Oberkotter both – we dealt with some real characters, I can tell you that."

"Huh?" Ben, asked and, seeing Casey's wide smile, broke into an accommodating one, too.

"Yeah, they seemed to go through a fair number of Western types during those first administrations. We had a Dennis Weaver guy. For a while we had Strother Martin doppelganger, actually sounded a lot like him, too," Casey chuckled with the recollection.

Ben scratched his chin, grinning at the thought of these Caller appropriations, "You know, Jim, these guys seem to have a real handle on our popular culture, but I think they might hit a few bumps from time to time – like that linebacker thing."

Casey grimaced a bit, squinted his eyes, "I know, right? It's like there's a bug in the code. I've seen other stuff like that."

"Yeah, their spiel on Operation Linebacker sort of threw Rasmussen off. Not exactly comfort-inducing."

"Yeah, Ben, I guess so. The President seemed a little weirded out," Casey mused, "but, to me, what's interesting was the interest the Callers had just in that image, so to speak. It seemed to resonate with them and their take on Rasmussen."

"I agree, it did," Ben replied, thinking about their Oval Office meeting.

Casey closed his eyes for a moment, trying to picture the meeting choreography. "You could sense it, by the way the Callers moved their forms, their expressions, how they sought to pace the conversation."

"Yeah, I think you're right," Ben replied, conjuring images of the meeting in his mind.

"Anyway!" Casey sat up straight, "we can parse this later in more detail."

Ben blinked, "Yes, probably better later."

"I liked your notes, Ben – the recap of the meeting was good," Casey had now transitioned. "I think you followed the format well, good job."

Ben shifted a little in his seat, "So, you're good with the file?"

"Yeah, that's fine. I'll encrypt and store, destroy any electronic files you have. I'll print out a copy for the binder."

"Uh great, okay," Ben remained stymied by the dissonant archival practice, but went with it. Everything anyway was just so weird.

"So, what are you working on, now?" Casey cocked his head to one side, grinning.

"Timmy has got some stuff lined up. I may be working with other colleagues on some things," Ben replied.

"Great, great, that's good," Casey said winsomely. "Hey, I note your use of the word 'colleagues' – we don't say that much here, kind of a continental of German usage, *die Kollegen*. Well, that's good. You know Ben, I noted your German fluency indicated on your CV. We work with these guys on this stuff, as you know. The Callers seem to like them," Casey smiled.

"Yeah, that's right. The Five-Eyes group and Germany. I remember you mentioning them."

"Well, anyway," Casey was now in the process of adjourning, "continue your work with Timmy. I think that's good. Keeps you involved in the local weeny ecosystem here, and in good graces."

"Uh, thanks Jim."

"You and I will be talking periodically about stuff. I'll keep you posted re the meeting schedule – I may have some miscellaneous projects developing as well."

Ben had by this time stood up from his chair and was readying his exit, "Sounds good, Jim."

"Yeah, I'll be in and out, so text me with anything. I check my emails, too."

"Yeah, sure, of course."

"Oh, very important," Casey stood up and was at Ben's elbow. "I've had some communication with our Caller colleagues, they're interested in you."

Ben slowed his pace to the door, and turned toward Jim, who now assumed an emollient but somewhat clinical tone, "One of them from the meeting, Steve Allen, will get in touch with you – they know how to reach you."

"Wow, thanks, that...is...something," Ben emphasized each word slowly, and laughed.

Casey laughed as well, "Don't worry about it – It'll be fun, and very interesting! Will be interesting to go over your meeting during a debrief," Casey inclined his head.

"Yeah, I'll be on standby for it," Ben was intrigued, but nervous – more dealings with the unknown.

"So, good, stand by for that." Casey concluded, "As I said, I'll be in and out for the rest of this week, but let's grab lunch some time over the next few days."

"Sure, that'd be good," Ben was still in a slight fugue about the upcoming one-on-one with one of the Caller reps.

"Great, I'll ping you with some times."

Casey clapped Ben on the shoulder, as Ben adjusted where he stood and caught a glimpse of the picture on Casey's desk. There clustered in the photo were Casey, his late wife and his three daughters. The family man, Ben idly thought. He found himself then outside Casey's office and in the gray carpeted hallway. He made his way back to the bullpen.

CHAPTER 24

That evening Ben was at home, asleep, in his neat, book-lined bachelor's apartment. Secure in his bed, sleeping a deep REM sleep, something suddenly prompted Ben to awake – suddenly alert, clammy from his deep slumber. He was awake but his body, from his nasal passages down, still felt lethargic, caught in a sleep-induced fugue. He listened to the timpani drum sound of the rain falling against the bedroom window in his single bedroom apartment. He cringed at the thought of the cold winter weather outside and peered harder against the darkness of his room and the faint outline of the possessions he could make out. Thunder outside made a large rapport, so weird to hear during the winter months. He reflexively pulled the covers closer up to his neck.

Buoyed from the effect of his deep sleep, Ben began to recall the dream he had awoken from. The images were clear and reflective, of gold and gold leaf, modern. There appeared his dissertation advisor, his hair white, tousled, unkempt. His advisor had on his rimless glasses, was large and stooped, and friendly, as Ben remembered. His advisor had grown up in San Mateo, Ben recalled that. He met his advisor again, in his dream. They met in a modern shiny vestibule, with the gold and the apparent gold leaf. Along the vestibule, there were several elevator banks. Ben knew he was supposed to meet his advisor there, they then walked quietly together. Ben was happy to see Professor Keith, winsome and present in his dream but now absent, with dementia, Ben knew. They approached a set of brass or gold subway turnstiles that Ben knew he had to pass through. At one of the turnstiles, a group of four or so men stood behind it. Ben could not make them out in any detail, but they were focused, Ben sensed, and seemed very intent on something. Ben remembered smiling at his advisor, who had crooked his head down toward Ben, and smiling, too. His advisor turned to the men behind the turnstile and started speaking Mandarin – or at least it seemed like Mandarin. The language was guttural and tonal. Ben didn't know Mandarin, he thought his advisor didn't know Mandarin, either. The vague men behind the turnstile backed up, then he and his advisor went through. Ben heard the turnstile chamber turn first for his advisor, then for him. That's when Ben had woken up, alert.

He snuffled to clear his sinuses and stopped thinking about his dream. Feeling the urge to pee, he stretched his limbs to revive them, pulled himself upright and made his way to the bathroom to relieve himself. Then, he went back to bed.

_ CHAPTER 25

Casey never met Ben for lunch that week. As far as Ben could tell, he hadn't been in the office either, which was fine. Doing pinch-hitting with Timmy and his old group was really okay, as far as Ben was concerned. He relished the normal, the clarity of his old routines. The meeting with the Callers, with the President and the Secretary of State, seemed now to take on a sepia tone, even though it had only been a few weeks before. Maybe the Callers – the aliens – would decamp soon, Ben often thought to himself, making life that much less complicated for the United States, the world – and him. Ben surprised himself that he actually wanted such a resolution, such closure, or that at least part of him did.

He was thrilled to be in Casey's confidence – in the Callers' confidence as well, for that matter. He was proud, even though such knowledge as he had could not be shared with anyone. Ben knew this and appreciated it. He also drew some satisfaction, deep satisfaction, that by working with Casey he was doing good work, God's work – a mitzvah, as his dad might say when commenting on good deeds done. Ben was part of a great effort – from Nixon and now to President Rasmussen – almost sacred for humanity. Ben would smile at his own grandiosity, but still felt it – the sacred satisfaction to be part of this conversation with something or someone from parts unknown. That was one side of it for Ben, but there was also something dreadful. He felt the instinctual vein of unease that ran through his consciousness and his thoughts about the Callers. It was a basic misgiving that he couldn't, and didn't want to, shake. Thoughts of the Callers closing their book on activity with humanity acted like a palliative, relieving Ben's mind, masking that unease he felt. The little human settlement would then be left alone, untouched, floating – if not, perhaps, so serenely – in the deep cosmic expanse. Part of Ben hoped for this, the other part told him to just relax about it.

–

"Man, I love time off!" cried Brenda, eyes wide and colorful.

She and Ben were seated at a café table in historic Charleston. On the spur of the moment, they'd decided to take a long weekend trip. Charleston was close by, and Brenda had managed to call in a marker or two to get some time away from Bloomberg. For Ben, there was no problem in getting away from the office. Another week had passed by and although his interactions with Casey were pleasant, everything was pretty cursory. Casey had been smiling and amenable about Ben's request, ribbed him about getting away somewhere with his "girlfriend". Of course, Timmy was ready with the green light, being the co-conspirator with Carole to cinch the Ben and Brenda union. Matrix reporting thus taken care of, Ben could go. Brenda had made all the arrangements – airfares, reservations made at a boutique hotel. Brenda was so proactive and can-do, just like Mae had been, and no doubt still was. The thought sent a chill through Ben, which he quickly shucked off.

"I love this town, so much charm," Brenda said again, leaning closer to Ben, over the table top, gravity and posture emphasizing the outline of such a pleasing bosom. Ben was so happy to be there, with Brenda. He was keeping pace.

"Yeah, I know, right?"

Brenda's smile gleamed and she squeezed Ben's hand in response, then fingered her glass of draft beer before taking a sip. Mae, Ben reminded himself, never drank any beer, unless with colleagues after work, and generally at kit pubs. It was part of his work relations modus. Alcohol for Mae was meant to be tactical, meant to facilitate things, to grease social wheels. For her, beer was imprecise, fun, caloric, often extraneous.

Ben leaned back in his chair and took all of Brenda in. She was magnetic, but warm. Confident and at ease, like a fellow sojourner who knows the road better than you and guides. Not like Mae, whose energy and confidence seemed to impel one with the need to do something. This stream of thoughts caught Ben by surprise. He blinked quickly to clear his head. An involuntary and embarrassed grin broke across his face.

"Oh, should we head back to the hotel?" Brenda arched an eyebrow and grinned back at him.

Ben laughed, flummoxed, "Oh yeah, I mean, great! But let's go for a stroll," he felt strangely demure, "take in the city a little more."

Ben reached for his wallet and laid out cash for the bill. Brenda rose from her seat and took his arm. They walked out to enjoy the harbor and the city's restored architecture.

CHAPTER 26

Back from Charleston, Ben had checked his iPhone and noticed some unanswered calls with blocked numbers. Whoever it was hadn't bothered to leave a message, so he disregarded the calls. The weekend with Brenda had been so nice – and so fun. Her energy and warmth were an emollient, kneading a relaxed comfort level into Ben. He had realized for a while that some kind of insulating, fundamental dumbness – no other word for it really, maybe something clinical, perhaps – had waylaid his desire to form any lasting romantic attachments. Ben knew that he had been more of an instrument in Mae's larger plans. His passive nature, and Mae's own winning certainty, had made it easy at first to slot him in. But now Ben realized that at some day, Mae must have just stopped and threw up her hands. He was too difficult to re-engineer. That was in spite of himself, Ben said to himself, knowing that he would have been content with a functioning, stable home life and family, even at the direction of the hyper self-actualizing and self-mobilizing Mae. He widened his eyes momentarily to clear away the reverie and picked up his Sunday *New York Times*.

He glanced over again at his iPhone and saw the digital display for a missed call and a voicemail, which he promptly checked. It was Steve. Steve Allen. Ben's face became quizzical and pensive. Casey had told him to expect one of the Callers to reach out to him, but it was still strange – to receive and hear a voicemail from something that was a human facsimile, not AI or a recording mind you, but something other than human. It wasn't telemarketing, it occurred to him. He giggled at that, but then became serious. It was something, it was some form of alien intelligence, about which he really knew nothing.

"Uh, hi Ben," the recording began, "this is Steve. Steve Allen.

I'd talked with Jim." The recording went on, "He mentioned that I should call you." Ben put the iPhone on speaker so he could listen more clearly and take notes, if need be. "Anyway," Allen went on, "it would be great if we could meet offline. Put more of a face behind the name, so to speak. How about drinks/early dinner next Thursday. Say 5:30pm? We can meet at Brasserie Beck on K Street. Great food, very good beer," Allen elaborated. "You'll like it," he appeared to sneeze on the recording, then snuffled a bit. Did he have a cold? Ben wondered, listening.

"Anyway, I'll be there at 5:30pm on Thursday," Allen was summing up, "so, enjoy the rest of your Sunday. Uh, take care." The message ended.

Ben sat back farther on his chair at the table in the neat and well-maintained kitchenette. He gazed around the apartment, then back at the small iPhone, resting beside the Sunday paper. Obviously, I am not going to miss this meeting, Ben thought. Will talk to Jim about it.

–

That work week Casey was more available – out but then in the office more. He shared some information that he was scheduled for a one-on-one meeting with Rose Levchin later in the week, which he was not looking forward to. Levchin had characterized the meeting as a "skip level" one, where she would be meeting with him, that is Casey, who was presumably one level or so junior to a State Department bureaucrat who would otherwise directly report to her – hence "skip level" meeting. Casey was really unmoored, so to speak, as a bureaucrat, so she couldn't really ascertain his position. Levchin had conveyed to Casey that she was excited about their meeting, though – thought it would allow her to communicate more informally, get into more of the gritty details. Casey grimaced at the thought.

When Ben shared that he was meeting Steve Allen for drinks that Thursday, Casey was enthusiastic. It was a great validating sign, Casey observed. The Callers were probably already comfortable with Ben, thereby confirming his presence and participation in the dialogue.

"You'll come away with a lot," Casey offered.

When Ben asked if there were any particular stratagem to follow, or questions he should pose, Casey was glib, "Just be yourself." He clapped Ben on the shoulder and reassured him that the meeting would go well. Just at that moment, Casey made a face – or contrived one – showing exasperation, as if he'd forgotten something. He had to leave the office for a bit, maybe a few days, so rationing away any further counsel for Ben regarding his upcoming Caller meeting. Casey looked to be in high spirits and confident. Ben hoped it was infectious.

–

On the scheduled evening, Ben showed up at Brasserie Beck on K Street. The décor was reminiscent of a late nineteenth-century European train station café. It evoked for Ben Gare du Nord or Leipzig's grand Bahnhoff. Old circular clocks were mounted on the dark wood walls. The clocks showed prominently, as if to allow travelers and commuters easy means to check the time. The restaurant and its foyer deceived, implying a large space for rushing clerks and bourgeois commuters, even though the restaurant stood only on a standard K-Street allotment. Ben could see a dozen or more tables set with white linen and silverware. The ceiling was much higher than usual, adding to the Central Station effect. Ben scanned the few diners there and saw a late middle-aged, silver-haired man waving to him. The man was seated at the far end of the restaurant, at a table close to the ornate wooden bar. Ben headed toward the man, who rose from the table and shook Ben's hand when he arrived.

"Hey Ben, thanks for coming, glad you had no problem finding the place."

Steve's grip was strong and his hand was much bigger, enveloping the younger man's. Steve used his other hand to clap genially Ben's corresponding shoulder. Ben mentally retrieved at that instant the observation a fellow analyst had once made, over a few beers at McGillicuddy's, a kit pub close to work.

"That's a grin-fuck," his colleague had said.

"Don't you ever notice how so many business and political leaders interact at some important signing?" rheumy-eyed from the beer consumed, his colleague stated. "They shake hands and usually one guy or the other guy uses his other hand to clasp the other guy's arm or shoulder..." his colleague paused again, his body like a full sack on the barstool. "That's the grin fuck," he smiled, closing his eyes, nodding, "that's when the other guy is going to get completely hosed."

Ben thought sometimes about that conversation and his old colleague, a smart guy – and funny. Ben recalled that his colleague had become even more thoughtful about his observations, drawing up approaches to code for the frequency of the handshake/shoulder clasp tandem and any association with foundering agreements or worsening conflict levels. The colleague hoped to be able to test for significance.

"Ben? Earth to Ben?"

"Oh, man, sorry about that Steve," Ben said, embarrassed, finding himself still standing by the table. Allen had already sat down.

He was jovial, "Lost in thought, huh? No worries."

"Yeah, I guess. Jim's got me pinch hitting some work with another group at the office," Ben simulated amiable chat, but actually found himself to be genuinely relaxed and informal around Allen, this large non-human.

"Don't worry about it," Steve waved a hand, "come on, park yourself."

"Thanks, man," Ben slid into his chair.

"Yeah, I know what you mean," Steve rested his arms, confiding, "stuff can really pile up, I know..." Steve drew out the last words for emphasis.

A waitress came by their table. She asked in a pleasant, vaguely French, accent whether they were ready to order. Allen chose the beef *carbonnade* and frites, Ben opted for the steak frites.

"Try the Belgian beer, very nice indeed," Allen suggested. "Go for the Hellas – nice and not too heavy with the steak frites."

Ben did so. The waitress left to place their orders, and promptly returned with two pints. Allen wrapped one large hand around his glass and steadied his gaze at Ben, appearing for the moment a bit solemn.

"Ben, to you and yours," Allen lifted his glass toward Ben, "thanks for coming by."

Ben was struck shy by this sudden solemnity, but reciprocated, clinking his beer mug with Allen's.

"A real pleasure, Steve, thanks for inviting me here tonight."

"By the way, you're my guest – dinner is on me," Allen bowed his head slightly and made a small open-hand gesture.

"Oh, umm, that's not necessary, but thanks. That's very nice." Ben absently scratched at one of his eyebrows, grimacing self-consciously.

Allen registered Ben's quizzical expression and so elaborated.

"Oh, not to worry, we're fine, totally covered on expense. But, how about you, you're good with this? Does this require sign-off?" Allen was solicitous.

The question broke some of the fresh ice and Ben loosened a bit, shrugging his shoulders, "Oh, that's not a problem. Jim and I, we're a small specialized team, deep in the bureaucracy, I guess.

No worries about having to declare a dinner." Ben still looked nonplussed, although was trying to be polite.

"Great, great. Umm, you know, we have developed a pretty effective little infrastructure. Nothing too intrusive or big, mind you..."

"Oh..."

"Well, let's say, we're pretty good in the market..."

"Oh, okay," Ben nodded.

"But I should add, I want to add – we pay our taxes."

"Okay, well, that's very good," Ben continued nodding.

Allen affected comfort and confidence in these revelations, "Yeah, taxes...it's a point of ethics for us, really."

"That's great, I think it's great that you guys do that," Ben affirmed.

"Well, of course, we keep a pretty low profile. We emphasize trying to stay low key," Allen stared at the amber contents of his beer.

"Yeah, I can see why that would be important..." Ben still affirmed.

Allen continued gazing at his beer, but then looked up, smiling at Ben, "But, you're new!"

The waitress materialized at table side, laden platter in hand. She began distributing its burden.

"Okay, steak frites for you..."

"And, for the distinguished silver-haired gentleman, here, the beef *carbonnade* and French fries," she said smilingly to Allen.

"Oh, marvelous, looks fantastic, thanks."

"Excuse me," the waitress was still smiling down at Allen and by immediate proximity, at Ben.

"Yes?" Allen looked up, smiling and curious.

"Did anyone ever tell you that you look just like Ed McMahon?"

"Oh gosh," Allen laughed, knowingly, "yeah, I get that sometimes."

Ben was looking on. He could only take it in.

"Yeah, I know," the waitress continued to pursue the subject. "You really do, maybe a little rosier and fitter looking than the actual guy..."

Steve appeared flattered, "Well thank you, that's nice, very nice of you to say."

The waitress smiled even more broadly, and turned toward Ben. "Doesn't he though? He really looks like Ed McMahon," she exclaimed. "Am I right?"

Ben feigned wide eyed agreement and nodded back to the waitress, "Definitely does."

His confirmation appeared to satisfy the young woman, who arrested her line of inquiry.

"Anyway, let me know if you need anything else, gentlemen. Enjoy!"

The two men thanked her in unison and, with that, she left them to themselves. More white noise had begun to build, as the bar and restaurant was starting to fill up. Dark suited drinkers and diners were standing two-deep at the bar and capturing all of the restaurant tables. There was no business-casual attire to be seen. Ben looked on, with a quizzical expression – the sight of Steve eating, not of the other diners, astonishing him.

"Oh, yes – I am eating," Allen was registering Ben's astonishment, and spoke with his mouth full. "You're wondering why I'm eating – even though you saw me order something?"

"Ah, no – umm, yes, I mean..." Ben scuttled any embarrassment, "*how* are you eating?"

Allen smiled and nodded as he chewed, then stretched his chin and neck out as if to facilitate swallowing. "Yeah, I get it, it's weird." He lowered his chin. "Well, we have the technology," Allen grinned at Ben. "So we, meaning us – or what you guys call us, 'the Callers'" Allen sat back and made a pair of air quotes, "have the ability through this form, to ingest food through the use of energy and gravity, and process it very, very finely. Long story short, it looks like I'm eating." Allen tucked again into his stew, "Great verisimilitude, right?" He then stopped again, smiling and waiting for a reaction.

"You know, you guys never cease to amaze..."

"Well," Allen sat up and crooked his head to one side, "I actually enjoy the experience of dining – I mean, me, behind this me," Allen spelled it out. "I've seen a lot of different places and cultures," he began gesticulating to emphasize larger points. "I've learned that the dining experience is really central to how one lives – how a being, *any* being really, lives."

Ben laughed a little to himself, while shaking his head, "Powerful technology, yup, understood. But you can't really taste what you're eating, right?"

Allen raised his fork, making a rhetorical point, "Yeah, that's true, I can't really taste. Not like you."

"So...?"

"But, I can still enjoy the experience – the context, the actions, the gestures," Allen had laid his silverware down and was grimaced for a moment, seeming genuinely flummoxed in that instant. "I dunno – I guess the best way to explain it is that it's like observing and being part of some performance art."

"Performance art?" Ben enjoyed Allen's off-the-cuff ruminations.

"Yeah, definitely," Allen was sitting squarely against the back of his chair, his arms folded across his chest.

"Eating, dining – this is primal essential experience. An ur-experience, if you will. In my own way, I experience dining, value it."

"I appreciate that Steve," Ben felt warm and encouraging. "Your points are interesting. Very helpful, I think – at least for me."

"Well..." sat relaxed in his chair, arms still folded, "I think it's good we understand each other somewhat – obviously within limits – remember the 'Prime Directive'." Steve adopted a mock serious tone, making again air quotes, this time for the 'Prime Directive', then raised a cautioning index finger.

"Of course, understandable, I get it," Ben smiled, enjoying the flow of commentary from Steve, before tucking again into his steak frites. On the one hand, Ben thought as he gazed at his dinner partner, what could be weirder...sitting down to a nice dinner with some highly-crafted alien construct? On the other hand, Steve's an okay guy, he reasoned to himself.

Allen caught Ben's gaze. "Everything okay? Hey, do you want another beer? I'll flag our waitress."

"Oh, uh, yeah sure. Thanks Steve."

Weird, Ben finished his thoughts, he's pretty relatable. He gets us. Ben refocused and remembered that he had just answered in the affirmative for another beer. Allen was engaging in banter with their waitress and placing an order for another round. The waitress laughed at Allen's remarks, while swaying her form slowly from leg to leg, in time with their exchange. She didn't rush the order and lingered a little longer, keeping her gaze on Allen. Ben could see that she liked him.

"Well, great, thanks so much. I agree, not such a bitter taste. We'll take two more," Allen smiled, looking appreciative.

"Okay, two it is," their waitress confirmed. She then bent forward slightly, with her hands on her knees, fixing her eyes directly on Allen, "You are so nice...and considerate! I'm making these next two on the house, on me. Just so nice!" Smiling, she turned on the ball of her foot, and made her way toward the bar.

"Thank you, that's just so nice!" Ben beamed after the waitress.

"What a nice kid!" Allen was grinning and nodding his head at Ben.

"Yeah, definitely seems very nice," Ben agreed, still bemused by the courtship dance between Allen, his non-corporeal friend, and the actual live human being who was their waitress.

"Anyway," Allen unfolded his arms to lean closer across the table, "it's good for us to get together, for me to meet you, for us to get acquainted."

Often it seemed that Allen said things in threes – the same thing, three different ways – or it seemed so to Ben.

Allen placed one of his large hands on top of the other, then rested both on the table. Ben noticed a gold wedding band on one of Allen's index fingers. Nice touch, he thought.

"Yeah definitely," Ben concurred, unconsciously tacking more toward a Rotary Club tone. He caught himself. He was being a pleaser, but this was important.

"I really appreciate the opportunity, Steve, sir, to sit down with you and have this kind of talk."

"Ben, come on, you're a pretty accomplished guy. Jim's told me a lot about you. 'Steve' is just fine." Allen was avuncular, Ben could see it was a default setting of some kind.

"Uh, sure, thanks Steve," Ben complied.

"I've worked with Jim for a little while now," Allen volunteered. "Colleagues of course had worked with him previously, for many years, as you know."

"Yeah, I know, Jim was uh present at the creation," Ben chuckled nervously at his own remark. He didn't know why.

CHAPTER 27

"That's right!" Steve stabbed the air lightly with his fork for emphasis. He had by this time finished most of his beef *carbonnade*.

"A very dependable – and insightful – guy," Steve continued, "Jim's facilitated great communication for all of us." He looked thoughtful for a moment, inserted another forkful and chewed slowly. He swallowed, coughed and nodded, affirming his own thinking. "Plus, he's helped give us a great perspective on you guys."

"I know, Jim's a great guy. I'm glad he brought me on board." Ben wanted to please.

"Damn straight. Jim is a great guy," Allen responded. "And he has a lot of confidence in you. Since he does, so do we."

"Thanks Steve, I appreciate that, am frankly honored," Ben lowered his head, he was being sincere, certainly for that moment.

Steve grinned, sank his chin to his chest, then raised it again to catch Ben's eye, "I'm glad, we need you. You're helping maintain this very important dialogue. Jim and, of course, the Presidents – God bless 'em – have all been great advocates for humanity." Steve began elaborating evenly, "We have learned a lot, are learning a lot…"

Ben was attentive, "This is a singular development for our world, for our species" Ben replied attentively.

Allen smiled at Ben, "I guess you could say that, and I agree with you." He sat upright in his chair, arching his back to crack his vertebrae and stretching his arms out, then emitted a protracted yawn. He released the tension in his body, and sat again more relaxed, looking benignly at Ben. "Ben, you're still single, right? I mean, you know, it's not really that long after the divorce."

The switch from the existential to the fundamental and personal caught Ben off guard. "Uh, yeah, uh…that's right. Single now, yeah. Divorce was a little hard, but it was a good thing, I guess. Good for both of us." He grinned stupidly, feeling a little disoriented. What the hell did that have to do with anything?

"Well, I'm glad you're able to move on," Allen, his non-human dining partner replied, pushing idly at his dinner plate.

"Um, why are you asking about it, Steve?"

"You know, Ben," Allen scrunched his shoulders closer together and lowered his chin a little, affecting personal concern, "one, we've gotta do due-diligence, of course, on whom we deal with, and two, we take an actual interest in our people, like you for instance."

"Me?"

"Yeah, you Ben. I'm glad things are moving along for you, as I said," Allen was solicitous. "In fact, word is that you've got a pretty cute new girlfriend these days," Allen smiled, seemingly happy about this turn of events. Clear-eyed and conspiratorial. Ben coughed in mid-sip of his beer, before responding.

"Uh, yeah, you're right, Steve. She's a pretty neat girl, I'm lucky."

"That's great, Ben, great! Good to hear," Allen added, jovial and endorsing.

"So, well, the rest of the family – they okay?" Allen squared his shoulders and leaned further toward Ben.

"Yeah, sure, everyone's good," Ben's voice was even but a little higher. He was nonplussed by the family question and became a little defensive.

"So, Maggie," Allen sounded casual, "she's got all her credits from CCAC? Is she trying to line up a design or marketing gig in the Bay Area?"

Hearing Maggie's name spoken by the Caller stopped Ben for a second, like the effect of drinking water more chilled than expected.

"You guys know about Maggie?"

"Sure, your sister, she's a great kid," Allen grinned. "Much better people skills than you have, my friend!" Steve playfully cuffed Ben's shoulder. Ben breathed in and gazed at Allen. They've really been doing their due diligence about me, he thought. Steve caught Ben's gaze and his blank face and shaped his own expression into a thoughtful and trusting one.

"Hey, as I said, we're always concerned about the folks we work with."

"I guess so..."

"But Ben, no worries, right? We respect people's privacy."

Ben shook his head and accepted the incongruous statement. Their waitress brought over two black coffees and the dinner tab ready for signature. Allen huddled over the bill, while putting his charge card back into his billfold, which was weird, Ben thought. Neither plastic card nor billfold might actually exist.

"So. your mom, Ben, she's doing okay?" Allen asked, while still studying the bill.

"Yeah, sure, why?" Ben felt suddenly skittish.

"Well, I'm glad. She's been a lot more active, getting healthy, not losing so much weight, staying steady..."

"Yeah, that's right..." Ben felt nervous, even a little indignant at the detail Allen apparently knew.

"Well, it's good that she's been able to taper her dosage of Minformin," Allen said knowingly. "Good to see that she nipped away at that early cancer."

Ben hadn't shared this information with anyone, hadn't discussed his mom's condition with anyone outside of his family. He was dumbfounded, but at the same time, not. This was total information awareness. Why should he be surprised that these people, these *beings*, knew all about him?

"Yeah..." Allen looked up at Ben, "It's the exercise, that's helping. She's really taking good care of herself these days." Ben could see that Allen wanted to reassure him. "And it's working, your mom's doing fine."

"You guys sure seem to know a lot," Ben smiled wanly.

"And you know," Allen began to confide in a soft, warm voice, "after doing more analysis, our guys believe your mom is doing really well. And also, it turns out she has next to negligible risk of dementia onset. I know you've all been worried about that, too, given family history."

Just listening to his family's medical situation, witnessing the depths of his family dynamics being plumbed, Ben became fatalistic. The Callers did know everything, or really could know everything, if they wanted to. He got the message. Ben glanced over at the restaurant bill and saw that Steve had scrawled in a handsome tip, even relative to the total after including tax.

"Ben," Allen fished into his pants pocket to extract what looked like a Samsung Galaxy phone, "I want you to take this."

"Really, wow, a studio parting gift?" Ben replied glibly, before catching himself again.

"Funny! No really, I think you'll see it's a useful tool," Allen grinned.

"A tool?" Ben was now agreeable.

"That's right. Correctomundo!"

At Allen's prompting, Ben picked up the Samsung phone, fingering the glossy red jacketed device. The faint plastic and metallic feel and smell were familiar. He opened it up to see if it would actually function.

"Ben, this is something we devised, it's tailored specifically to you. As its sole owner, it recognizes you and will not react – or be usable – for anyone else."

"For me – okay. What am I supposed to use it for?"

"You can contact us whenever you feel the need to. I'll generally be on the line; it could also be one of my colleagues." Allen flashed an earnest expression. "When you need to," he went on, "just key in your date of birth. That way you'll be able to reach us."

Ben continued to handle the Samsung proxy, shifting it from

one hand to the other. He ran his fingertips over the smooth red surface and then put it in his pocket.

"What if I lose it?" Ben asked – a legitimate question.

"First, I would say 'don't'. Secondly, it's no big deal – that is, if you do." Allen was being very matter of fact.

"It'll be like any other Samsung, except it won't work for anybody else. If someone steals it from you, you've lost it, whatever, they won't be able to use it. They'll probably throw it away." Steve seemed comfortable with the scenarios.

"No chance they could try to re-engineer it?" Ben, ever the analyst, continued to plumb.

"Not a chance – they won't know nothin' from nothin'," the Caller was confident.

By this time, the bill had been paid, the coffee drunk. Ben could see that Allen was ready to call it a night, as he began to show some fatigue in his face and was idly drumming his fingers. The two men oddly, spontaneously, began talking about the Redskins franchise and then Ben's favorite team, the Forty-Niners. Then, unconsciously and tacitly, they left the table and made their way outside, stopping outside the restaurant. Allen asked if Ben wanted to share a Lyft ride. Ben declined and wished Allen a pleasant evening, thanking him for very nice meal and hospitality. Ben then reflexively stopped, stood still and looked squarely for a moment at the congenial, suddenly-still Steve, from God knows where and what. He thanked him again then made his way to the closest metro entrance and home.

_ CHAPTER 28

He was old, but he was with it. Casey digitally hailed a Lyft car, which took him to Foggy Bottom and the State Department building on 21st and C Street. He loved this new app – some pleasant conversation with the driver, but everything already paid for, including tip, which meant he could just exit the car upon arriving, which he did. He emerged from the vehicle, straightening his suit, his conservative dark blue suit – another day in a suit! It bothered him, the formality and departure from his usual business casual. His face, as it almost always did, belied any trace of pique, though.

He remained, as he had been since he was a boy, a Great Plains optimist, even when he had molted into a counter cultural Berkeley faculty hippy in one of its more recondite social science departments. But then, of course, there was the deep immersion in the Nixon administration, his bureaucratic remit, and the natural mellowing effects of the passing decades. But, throughout, the core of that Plains state optimism had remained. That optimism, that baseline mood, had worn a setting on his face, and its small fine features. The small pebbly blue eyes, however, conveyed a shrewdness that could be mistaken for, and often was, amused friendliness. Casey's held a taut and pared frame, the effects of mindfulness, an East Bay holistic diet, generally-speaking, and steady running. The composite was of a wizened but vigorous senior.

A little girl, standing beside her mother at the curb, greeted Casey as he left his ride. Seeing him, she fixed her gaze on the wizened, yet vigorous old man in the conservative dark blue suit. She waved and gave a drawn out "hi". Casey turned to see her and hunched down to her level.

"Hi there!", he replied, affecting a grandfatherly tone and smiling broadly at the child. He then stood straight, still smiling and gave a small nod to the bemused mother.

Casey walked on to the Harry S. Truman Building, another neo-classical wedding cake of a structure where State resides. He had never made this trip before. The State Department, or rather all of the preceding Secretaries of State, had in some tacit way deferred to him and Harold as the de facto executor function for US inter-stellar relations. Kissinger, Vance, Jim Baker, Albright, Condee Rice, Hillary Clinton, the mournful John Kerry, all of them had adopted a passive stance in this area. As had the preceding Presidents, they had entrusted to him and Harold – the Berkeley hippies, Casey smiled ruefully at the thought – the mechanics of the relationship with the Callers, and in some sense its extent and pace. Casey was thinking, as he made his way through the Truman Building's security, that that Hooverian-Nixonian operational modus couldn't last, not indefinitely, and in fact it hadn't. There was a new sheriff in town, Casey saw that. Levchin was naturally aggressive and inquisitive. Inquisitive was fine, he thought. What all of that bundled analytical energy in the petite taut person of Secretary Levchin would mean was the source of some uncertainty. Casey felt that discomfort, just as he felt the constraints of his standard business attire.

Casey found himself in the antechamber to the Secretary's office, where an aide greeted him enthusiastically and ushered him into Levchin's office, before quickly closing the door behind. The office was more baroque than anything in the White House, which tipped its hat to a certain folksiness and ease of photo op moment. Casey studied the wainscoting and the elaborate fireplace mantel. A large blue and maroon Persian rug declared the territory, behind which rested a heavy, dark and ornate wooden desk.

"Dr. Casey..."

Casey gathered himself and saw Levchin standing beside her desk, set behind that large Persian carpet. Casey, despite himself, despite his reverence for his dead wife, despite his years, and in spite of his agnostic view on the vital and corporeal, felt a pull from Levchin's clear green eyes and generous mouth. Her glossy red hair was arranged, if precariously, on the top of her head. Casey shook his own head, hoping Levchin wouldn't notice his interest and snapped back to matters at hand.

"Secretary Levchin," Casey was jovial, "many thanks for setting aside time to meet with me today. I appreciate that, given your considerable travel schedule and notable commitments."

"Oh, of course, Dr. Casey. But I invited you..." Levchin feigned a bemused reaction.

"Well, indeed," Casey shook his head and grinned, opting for an ingratiating tone, "but, all the same, I do appreciate this chance to speak with you like this – in this subject area, our dealings with the Callers..." Casey became halting, as if catching himself beginning to share confidences that he shouldn't. Levchin caught this from his expression, and smiled, "Please, Dr. Casey."

"Please, Jim."

"Of course, Jim... there's no need to worry here. I make it a point to have my office frequently proofed against any sort of eavesdropping." She adopted a hushed tone, sharing a confidence, "I must assuage the not insignificant streak of paranoia that I have." Levchin smiled slightly and bowed her head just a bit.

"Well, can't say that I'm not relieved." Casey drawled this last sentence, affecting a rustic tone.

"Please Jim, call me Rose. That's a name I like my friends to use." The green eyes that had fascinated Casey gazed steadily at him.

Casey stood in the middle of the Persian rug, effectively in the middle of the large room, high-ceilinged and capacious, filled with objets d'art and other precious things, signs of global affection – or maybe tribute? Levchin absently ran her hand along the adjacent desk surface, and then positioned herself directly behind the desk. He could see that she was lost in thought for that moment. The warmth in her face was gone and her expression had become fixed, harder. She seemed to be deciding whether she should interact directly from the desk and chair, or if she should do otherwise.

Casey thought he might be witnessing the outward signs of the executive function in her mind weighing this encounter. He took notice of the deep, blue suit Levchin was wearing. He noticed that although her presence was small and delicate, it still conveyed a kind of force, certainly an energy. Casey studied Levchin, as Levchin studied the surface of her desk. On it were neatly-arranged files and memos, in discrete batches and piles. Casey looked from Levchin to the desk, then back to Levchin. For him – an anthropologist and a student of human war-mongering – the image of the diminutive but focused Levchin looking fixedly at her desk evoked a Soviet marshal, reviewing dispatches, contemplating a Russian counterpunch in the midst of the German advance.

Levchin suddenly raised her head, smiled and engaged with Casey.

"Please Jim, let's sit at the couch, it's more comfortable! I've got some observations I'd love to run by you. Would love to hear your feedback on these." The voice, mid-Atlantic, she wheeled quickly around the desk, and took Casey's elbow, leading him to sit with her at the nearby couch.

Levchin was bright beside Casey, while his smile was wan and faltering. A young male aide entered the office and glided toward the low coffee table, where he placed a beverage service before them. Levchin mouthed a silent thank you, then held the coffee urn, decanting first for Casey, then for herself.

"I just take my coffee black," she noted generally. "I am an inveterate coffee fiend, drink it constantly, non-stop, throughout the day."

"Well, I like mine black, too. Also drink a heckuva lot of it," Casey volunteered.

"You know," Levchin continued in an even more agreeable way, "coffee is the wooden staff I lean on. I truly need it. Always so much to do!" She sipped appreciatively at her cup and shifted in her seat, crossing one knee over the other. "I'm glad we have this opportunity to speak with each other, Jim. In a plain, uninterrupted way."

"Likewise, I'm glad to have the chance..." Casey tried smiling more openly, and nodded agreeably.

"Wonderful, I had hoped so."

Levchin gazed at Casey. She shifted her weight slightly on the couch, seeming to mark an end to the prefatory remarks.

"So, Dr. Casey, Jim, I think I need to know more. We need to know more about the Callers – who they are, what their intentions are, why they are here. I've discussed the matter with the President; he agrees, unequivocally."

Casey turned his head to meet directly the Secretary of State's gaze, which had grown harder. Her clear green eyes were directed toward him. Unconsciously, he rubbed his chin, letting this overture wash over him. He was stunned and wanted to hunker down. After decades of a passive executive branch, this was new – the summoning, the confidence. There was no wonder, no fear.

"Umm, Madame Secretary – er, Rose – the points that you, that you – and of course, the President – are making are, in many respects, highly understandable and sound."

"Yes, Jim, I think so..." Levchin leaned in closer to Casey.

"Our relationship with the Callers," Casey began gesticulating – not in an expansive way, but in a controlled way, as if he were demonstrating the workings of a small complicated machine. "Our modus, I guess, has functioned well for over forty years."

"Yes, really?"

"I believe it has," Casey replied, hoping to be congenial, but firm.

"But surely Jim, the sheer imbalance, the power imbalance

between ourselves and the Callers places us, categorically, in a precarious situation." Levchin's response was measured, but Casey sensed her patience already thinning. Her speech had become oddly accented.

"But nothing, to my knowledge, has undermined our trust in the Callers," Casey pressed on. "Their presence in our world has been minimal, negligible."

"Uhhh..." Levchin seemed suddenly to register a slight distaste towards Casey. She recoiled instinctively from his sense of trust.

"Well, that is, to-date," Levchin responded. "Nothing of aggression or alarm, as far as we know, *to-date*," she emphasized. "Which leads me to another point, another imbalance – or asymmetry, if you will. We know nothing about them; they, of course, can – and most probably do – know everything there is to know about us." Levchin appeared baleful at the thought.

"That is true," Casey conceded, nodding, "that has always been the case – part of the bargain with us, part of their value proposition, as I think the current phrase is."

"Well, I perceive it as a gross vulnerability, Jim. One which an *ally*, I emphasize the word, would happily emend."

"Yes, in most circumstances, quite right. Yes, indeed, right..." Casey sought to steady the conversation. "Allies should be forthcoming with one another, sharing is the manifestation of trust."

"So, the Callers then exhibit no real trust in us. That is not the behavior of an ally."

Casey had sought to be congenial, if only to allay his anxiety, but reverted slightly to a more formal tone.

"Madame Secretary, that was part of the arrangement – the agreement we have with them. We, in a sense, really don't get to ask much, because...umm...they don't want to interfere."

"Yes, I understand, it's about the TV show. You had mentioned that," Levchin was adamant, cut him off.

"But, more importantly, Rose," Casey felt the need to be insistent, very much wanting to repeat another point made earlier, "the Callers offer protection. They cloak us, humanity, our planet, and hide us from things we would not want to encounter."

Levchin sat back in the couch, eyed Casey, tried to get a better picture, "But Jim, how do we know this? How do we really know this?"

Casey's face puckered, and despite himself, he inclined his head, smiling, close-lipped.

"Well, we don't really know... Previous administrations, the Presidents to date, both Harold and me...we all have assumed so. We believe this to be the case."

"So, you *believe*?" Levchin continued. "I would argue that you are taking this almost as an article of religious faith?" She was becoming captious.

Casey seemed to snap to, a booster shot generated from internal chemistry. He leaned forward, placing one hand on his knee, leaving the other hand free to help him declaim.

"Rose, we of course can't say, with certainty, that there has never been anything from another world – that there is nothing, aside from the Callers themselves – here on our planet. That said, through our own SETI review processes, our findings from technical and rather arcane intelligence gathering, have found nothing – nothing since I've been doing this over the past forty years."

Levchin gazed at Casey and returned a tight, closed grin, "Okay, so it would seem there is nothing, has been nothing – so we are safe?"

"Well," Casey, ever the social scientist, couldn't help himself, "of course, there are no such absolutes..." He sat back on the couch, crossing his legs and resting one forearm absently over his lap. He began sampling from his coffee, regretting his empirical evenhandedness.

Levchin leaned closer to the Berkeley professor on the couch.

"I appreciate your perspective Jim, really I do," Levchin paused, casting her gaze downward, giving the impression of deliberation, "but, I see our current arrangement with the Callers as problematic, as being inherently flawed." Levchin opted for a sympathetic yet discerning expression, seeking to appeal to Casey now as scholar-to-scholar. Her tone and inflection, rich mid-Atlantic.

"I see," Casey was staring off, beyond the coffee table, thinking.

"You see," Levchin continued evenly, "the Callers are here, we have acknowledged that, formally. As such, we have extended them "comity" – the international legal term – or recognition. We welcome their presence and they are therefore welcome."

"Yes, that's understood..." Casey responded, trying to be agreeable while thinking about whether he could steer the conversation, or not.

"There has, of course, been no real reciprocity," Levchin was continuing, again evenly, "which makes for too much uncertainty, too much confusion."

"Rose, as we discussed, just earlier, there are limits – caveats – to our relationship with the Callers," Casey began imploring, while trying not to sound too desperate. "They really didn't have to...interact with us at all. They can act unilaterally – with us, and toward us – in any way they wish."

"That would not be the behavior of a steadfast ally. It begs the question of the relationship," Levchin replied, curt and prompt.

Jim stared at her. Her words were drawn, teeth apparently barred.

"Look, the relationship has worked. We have – to the extent that we know – enjoyed – peace and security in the greater cosmos." Casey flourished his hand toward the office ceiling to underscore the vastness of that cosmos. "The reasons for the nature of our interaction are plain. The Callers have been straightforward with us, from the beginning."

"Ah yes, their 'Prime Directive', like in the TV show," Levchin sat back in the couch, her lids half-closed, which Casey quickly interpreted as distaste.

"You know, Rose, I've been doing this a long time and each administration, Democrat or Republican, has followed the precedent. Has followed the lead on how we deal with this stuff."

"All of that precedent," Levchin grinned at Jim. She looked almost mischievous. "All that precedent, as you put it, makes it right?"

"Rose, from what I have seen, these interactions – these, oddly, quarterly meetings with the Callers – have been wholly salutary. These encounters have resonated with each of the Presidents." Unconsciously, Casey reached for Levchin's hand and began patting it, as if to reassure. She looked nonplussed and pulled her hand away.

"Dr. Casey, Jim, we have a long-standing relationship with the Callers, I understand that." Levchin clasped her hands on her lap, and paused for effect. "But the relationship has been one-sided... That one-sidedness presents too much uncertainty."

"While in certain respects, you're right, Rose, there is an information deficit, I guess you could say. They know much more about us; we know very little about them. True enough."

"Precisely," Levchin received Casey's concession and was intent on rolling forward.

"But, it's important to add," Casey looked on at Levchin, hoping to wend this small but important point through, "that our meetings – our encounters – with the Callers have given us more." Casey paused then, likewise for effect. "The fact that they're here, talking to us, after having traveled such great distances..." Casey cupped his chin and shook his head slowly, feeling actual wonder. "I think that it's given our leaders, each of our Presidents, hope. Seeing that someone had actually made it, that they hadn't destroyed themselves, but had developed." Casey became wistful and he smiled at Levchin. "I think that has been inspiring for our leaders, it's been reassuring. I think each of the Presidents came to the same view: that if the Callers were able to do it, maybe we can, too."

"Inspiring, yes. I take it you mean avoiding nuclear oblivion or some other humanity-induced extinction," Levchin said, glancing at her wrist watch. She suddenly appeared preoccupied with something else that was materializing on her day's agenda.

"Jim, I must say, I think it's been fruitful for us to meet."

"Well, yes…" Casey stuttered a response, struck a little by the abruptness, but acknowledging to himself that the State Department dynamo had other fiefdoms to attend to.

"Jim," Levchin slowed her pace, leaning closer to Casey and focusing, "let me just say, our relationship with the Callers must evolve. The President believes this. We must foster this evolution. It is, I believe, healthy, and should be natural."

"Our relationship with the Callers is an extremely important one. We should indeed nurture it as best we can," Casey agreed, grimaced upon hearing his own statement, never comfortable with this kind of diplomatic elocution. He would have to keep watching, and determine how he might steer Secretary Levchin's intentions, if possible.

"Yes, nurture, foster, evolve, I agree," Levchin nodded perfunctorily, "but we must have alignment, Dr. Casey, on our end. The President and I feel that to be crucial." She was emphatic.

Levchin stood up from the office couch, signaling Casey to do the same. She turned smiling toward him, extended her hand and grasped his.

"Jim, as I said, very fruitful discussion."

Somehow, an aide had appeared at Casey's side to show the elder anthropologist out.

"Let's bear in mind the importance of alignment on our side. We can, and must, cultivate progress in this critical relationship."

Levchin was elliptical enough so that her aide was not clued in.

Casey then found himself ushered, like an important parcel, carefully out of Levchin's office, through the confines of the State Department building and out onto the sidewalk, where he hailed a Lyft car. He had much to think about.

CHAPTER 29

The scheduled White House meeting was taking place. These early morning visits to the Oval Office had become, if not routine, familiar. Ben felt the warm glow of some small pride at the thought. He would have loved to share this with his parents. He mused for a moment – what could it be? Achievement? Status? I guess, a confidence? Yes. That was it, but he couldn't share it, of course. This was beyond the pale, except for the people and the facsimiles of people who were present in the room, and except for a very small sprinkling of political leaders and administrators around the planet. He would have to be cryptic and vague with Mom and Dad, with Brenda, with everyone.

Ben snapped out of his reverie and glanced at the President's large frame positioned on the couch to Ben's right. The President recognized Ben and gave him a sidelong wink. Ben, still young and prone to wonder, scanned the tableau before him. He and Casey were seated, as had now become habit, on the federal chairs placed next to each other and at the ends of the opposing couches. Between those two couches, the low dark coffee table rested, placed there as if to separate disputants figuratively, or broker a potential settlement. Ben looked to the chair on his left, and saw Casey smiling amiably, although looking intent. Seated on the couch to his left the two Callers sat, both in their usual dark suits, both looking winsome but also very serious, already sensing something from the President and his petite Secretary of State. Ben then looked to the other couch, taking in earth's mighty designates. The President conveyed a sense of a warm, quiet bonhomie. He seemed pleased with the occasion, and was ready to begin the discussion. Secretary Levchin sat at the other end of the couch. Her expression was neutral and serene, but she seemed sharply focused, vaguely coiled in anticipation of this latest opportunity for conversation with the Callers. President Rasmussen shifted his weight forward and rested the palms of his hands on his knees, affecting an informal manner.

"Jonathan, Steve, very nice again to see you and to continue this regular sequence of discussions, convened since President Nixon's first term in office..."

"Well Mr. President, it is truly an honor for us. We feel a strong affinity for your people – in a word, humanity. It's a great pleasure and rewarding for us to counsel, as we can, and to develop further our relationship, which is now tenured, and I think, a mutually satisfying one," Winter replied, smiling and benign, conveying an ersatz human warmth which evoked in Ben an even deeper admiration for alien technology. He wondered what was at the other end.

"Thank you, Mr. Winter or, should I say, Jonathan," the President was also warm and informal. He returned Jonathan's engaging smile and extended his arms above his head for a moment, stretching his back, communicating a relaxed atmosphere, détente. "From what I understand, the normal protocol has been for Casey to provide an update on any signs of extra-terrestrial life that we've discerned on our planet..."

The two Callers glanced at each other for a moment. "Yeah, generally we've done it that way," replied Allen, raising his hand to confirm the usual step.

"If it's okay, I'd like to shift that segment toward the end of the meeting – unless of course Jim has some new pressing information he'd like to share with us," President Rasmussen swayed his torso and glance toward Casey to prompt a response.

"Uh, no sir, nothing of any pressing nature to report," Casey absently riffled papers on the credenza, watchful and helpful. "I can provide more context later, Mr. President."

"That's great, sounds very good, thanks Jim."

"I'd like to now turn over the discussion to Secretary Levchin, who I think will introduce some interesting points for the group

186

to consider. Rose?" The President leaned toward Levchin. Both Callers turned in unison toward the Secretary of State.

Levchin smiled at the Callers and nodded respectfully toward them.

"Thank you, Mr. President, gentlemen," Levchin began. Ben noted the full mid-Atlantic vowels, the crisp enunciation. She was already coming across very credibly.

"Our relationship is now truly a tenured one," Levchin continued, "we are grateful and value this relationship as a benison to mankind, not only to the United States." Ben, watching and listening, noted her use of the archaic term 'mankind'.

"And yet, there has been an inherent asymmetry in this important friendship, throughout these past decades." Levchin elaborated, "You know much about us, and we have been forthcoming, sharing our values, weaknesses, and our fragilities with you. But we know nothing, really, about you. We do not even know your actual physical appearance." The two Callers viscerally reacted to Levchin's comments. They sank back into their couch, and began gazing at their own extremities, fidgeting, looking at different angles of their feet. "We propose," Secretary Levchin went on, "that you share with us more about who you are, where you come from, what your history is."

Winter quickly glanced at Allen, and then rustled himself into more square position on the edge of the couch, "But, if I...Madame Secretary – uh, Rose – we do not want to interfere or effect you in the least way possible. Much like your 'Prime Directive' in the *Star Trek* television show prescribes. Undue interference, we believe, would distort your development."

"Of course, Jonathan, we respect that. We respect your intentions," Levchin's returning glance was calm, the green-eyed gaze was level. "But frankly, we need to know more."

Winter and Allen remained silent, waiting for Secretary Levchin to continue.

"Secondly, our desire is to have much greater awareness regarding what our environment truly is – in terms of 'space', as it were," Levchin shifted in her position, glancing and leaning toward the President, who sat beside her. The President maintained an attentive but impassive expression.

"We need to know what threats are really out there, so to speak – if any. We need to know, in more detail, *why* we should indeed appreciate your veiling technology – something that protects us from these large, unseen threats. Why must we be implicitly afraid?" Levchin absently looked down at her lap and brushed away a small item of schmutz from her pantsuit. "And lastly, gentlemen, we feel that with the now long-tenured relationship we have with you, and in the proper spirit of our friendship," here, Levchin uncharactersitically cleared her throat of a nervous constriction, "let us initiate together, a program of technology transfer..." Allen abruptly shifted at his end of the couch, "...which envisions the sharing of constructive know-how, not only to the benefit of the United States, but to the benefit of all mankind, humanity."

Levchin sensed the providential moment and was poised to continue. Casey was tugging nervously at the lapel of his suit jacket, the kind of clothing he never got used to wearing. Seated across from Levchin, Winter turned his head to look at Allen. It was a calm movement, by all appearances, but Ben could see it was also a WTF moment. He stared at the Callers. Allen turned his head to meet Winter's gaze.

Pausing, Levchin was surprised to see that the Callers were no longer listening to her but concentrating on each other. The President remained opaque, watching. Casey shook his head and looked down – he seemed weirdly self-recriminating to Ben. The Callers both then turned to look at President Rasmussen and Secretary Levchin. Looking at the two human public figures, they did not seem angry – their expressions were calm and rather neutral. They continued to sit there quietly, beside each other, on the couch. But Levchin was still startled by their stillness and wondered whether she should continue. Suddenly Winter, closely followed by Allen, rose to stand. They levelled one last look at the President and Levchin and then turned and walked toward the door of the Oval Office. They didn't bother to acknowledge Casey or Ben. Casey leaned closer to Ben, but seemed to be talking to himself, "They're leaving the meeting...They're leaving the meeting!"

Casey's tone was hushed, but urgent and surprised. He quickly got up from his chair and walked toward the door that the Callers had just left ajar. Ben turned to watch, through the now-open door, Casey speaking in a controlled manner to the two Callers, who stood there respectfully giving him an audience. Ben couldn't hear what any of the parties were saying, but could see that Casey was desperately pitching. The President's admin darted among Casey and the Callers before fetching and returning with the virtual overcoats they had brought with them. The Callers had begun nodding intermittently, as Casey declaimed, before he then extended his arm to shake the hands of each alien in turn. The Callers then put on their overcoats and left, presumably outside to Pennsylvania Avenue. Ben really couldn't say.

_ CHAPTER 30

What could he do? He was back at his desk in the bullpen. Building maintenance was still having problems setting up his situation in the office next to Casey's. Ben had been randomly pondering this logistical detail and was still distracted by the abrupt exit of the Callers from the Oval Office. Casey was plainly distracted, too. He had made his way out alone from the meeting, exchanging only a wan smile and a stony gaze with the Commander-in-Chief and his Secretary of State. What else could *he* do? At least for now? The new policy agenda had been apparently set. The Callers had broken away from the meeting weirdly, like two marionettes. The two had turned toward each other, stared at each other, and then moved to the door. It was like they were communicating telepathically. But *Jesus*, Ben was thinking, did that really matter? They weren't even people, they were projections of people, imitations of sentient beings. Some guy – or some *thing* – controlled these facsimiles. Ben felt a sudden ambivalence, he actually liked Steve - residing as he was somewhere out there in time and space. Ben grimaced, thinking about Casey. The curdled expression he saw on Casey's face just after the meeting and before he had disappeared. The phone began buzzing at Ben's elbow. He picked up.

"Good, you're back," Casey's slight Plains twang sounded down the phone receiver. "Why don't you pop in – we should debrief, a lot has happened."

Some genuine Great Plains understatement there from Casey. The Callers' abrupt exit from the meeting marked the first formal break in US extra-terrestrial relations in over forty years. Who knew what the Callers would be deciding to do now?

Ben got up from his desk and made a quick step across the matt-gray industrial carpet toward Casey's office. He stopped at the office doorway to see his boss seated, elbows on desk, hands cradling his forehead. He looked up and motioned Ben to take a seat. The old Emeritus hippy leaned back in his chair and reached his arms up skyward to stretch. Ben noticed that Casey had removed his tie and was open-collared, absently aping the business casual look. The overall effect was rumpled.

"Jesus H. Christ!" Casey grinned, cracking the vertebrae in his back, "That's what my Dad would say. Yes, that's what he'd say!" Still grinning, he settled in his chair, appraising Ben. Then he leaned forward and rested his arms on the desk surface, "So, what's your take on this? Where are we now?"

Ben unconsciously began scratching the back of his neck; he couldn't but return Casey's grin, almost in an embarrassed way.

"Uh, well, this to me seems pretty big – an extraordinary break."

"Yup, that's right, well-said, 'an extraordinary break'," Jim was nodding. "The first such instance, I do recall, in over forty years."

Ben nodded ruefully.

The men stared at each other for a moment., before Casey grimaced and threw one of his hands forward, "Yeah man, I knew the meeting would head in that direction..."

"What? How so?"

"I met with Levchin at State, not even a week before," Casey slouched lower in his seat.

Ben saddled one leg perpendicular to the other and shifted in his chair. He was curious about the Levchin encounter. "Wow, so what did Rose say? How did she steer the meeting?"

"Levchin and Rasmussen want a more assertive stance from the Callers, as we just heard. That's what she emphasized – she ticked off a number of very novel objectives that she and the President envisioned for the relationship,"

"Man, that's assertive – and ambitious! The Callers have been pretty proprietary about what they know, what they want to do, and what they don't want to do. Am I right?"

"Spot-on, that's exactly right," Casey's grimace etched deeper, "Levchin had spelled out for me what they – she and the President – intended to do. Talked about the importance of 'alignment'," Casey made air quotes and rolled his eyes, "and having a united front."

"She sure went for it," Ben shook his head and marveled.

"Yeah, I thought I could massage, and hopefully, subvert the message. But... Rasmussen was clearly behind it. They attacked. She blitzed."

"Well, Levchin is kinda slight for a linebacker," Ben couldn't help but grin.

Casey laughed, "Okay, well, a safety blitz maybe."

Both men fell silent again.

Casey looked down for a moment and then raised his head, looking almost paternal. "Ben, let's take a step or two back for a second. What's your view on this? How do you see the Callers and their motivations?"

Ben liked these questions, he had been ruminating about them and others like them for some time, "Well, you know Jim, Levchin is right – just as you already know – the situation's pretty one-sided. The Callers do know a lot about us and we really know nothing about them. Not even what they really look like."

"Yeah, all true. That's been established," Casey was attentive, punctuating Ben's stream of delivery.

"Well, I also think Levchin is right in another way. She's right to point this out – it is an asymmetry."

"True, again."

"But why is it so? That's the question to ask," Ben glanced absently at the familiar family photo on Jim's desk. Ben was fond of it, and liked the mise-en-scène it showed of his boss, a man he respected and was growing protective of. There was Casey, a bit younger and hale, along with his handsome wife, seated together on the couch, their attractive daughters arrayed behind them. Casey, now a retiree – at least from his university job – wife, now dead, daughters, far away. Ben turned his head to see his boss still focusing on him, eager for his input. Casey was grinning, small pebble blue eyes alert, still looking healthful and winsome, but now to Ben's mind, a little desiccated around the edges, and wizened, and old.

"You know, that's a good question to ask," Casey volunteered, "and the response has been the emphasis the Callers always place on non-interference."

"That may be true, at least in part," Ben went on, "but I see the asymmetry – the knowledge deficit, so to speak – as a resource advantage. The Callers have created a mystery and in deference to that mystery – an abiding faith, one which we share with the other five-eyes countries and with the Germans, I guess."

"That's an interesting thesis, go on." Casey was encouraging.

"Think about it," Ben began explaining, "we don't really know what's out there. The Callers' intentions may still be fundamentally very good, but they themselves may be grappling with issues and problems of their own."

"Yeah," Casey rubbed his chin, grinning, eyes twinkling, "that's a natural supposition to make."

"As I said, the Callers – with their *Star Trek*/Peace Corps-style mission – may be genuine, at least in part. But there may be bigger stakes for them," Ben paused to collect his thoughts. "Think about Earth – this precious blue planet, such a valuable life-giving resource..." Ben paused again, idly massaging his temple with his index finger. "While the Callers know about us, others may know, or would like to know, about us, too."

"I think I see where you're going with this. The Callers are in a form of competition..." Casey nodded and mused, "There are possible rivalries, there may be enmities."

"Exactly," Ben moved forward in his seat, "rivalries. It could be some form of great power politics. Earth, our precious Earth, could be, or could become, the object of competing influences."

Casey, the retired academic, grinned at his evergreening, thoughtful graduate student, "I like your great powers politics concept. Harold and I never thought, weirdly, in those terms. We should have."

"But, again," Ben enjoyed the old man's praise, but wanted to temper it, "this is only really a guess, a hunch really."

Casey raised an index finger to make an addendum, "Certainly, introducing humanity to the interstellar hurly-burly would present a host of problems for the Callers. Earth would be 'in play'. Shielding us and protecting us is effective – it keeps us out of play."

"That's right," Ben nodded, "it's really efficient for them, if anything. They do end up sheltering us, but we become a planet they don't have to contest – with our agreement as well."

Casey paused and stiffened in mid-thought. He wondered alarmingly if he had just had an odd shortness of breath. He certainly hoped not.

"Well Ben," his demeanor became nostalgic, the fear of any sudden shortness of breath dissipating, "I've known these guys – I guess we can call them that – for a long time. My gut tells me they wanna help us, they don't want to screw us up." Casey made his pronouncement, then yawned, stretched and cracked his spine, as he was wont to do. Ben was fond of the sentimental side to his boss, and grinned warmly, if a little shyly, "Jim, you know – you're probably right on this. It's just good to look at all the angles."

"You bet. That's something we have to always do," Casey's expression was still warm, but the smile was close lipped, reflecting an acknowledgement that the Caller known unknowns and the unknown unknowns were altogether baleful.

"Yup," Ben stared absently at Casey's desktop, while nodding slowly, "Levchin and the Chief," the term both Casey and Ben used when referring to the contained, megalithic Rasmussen, "they may be on to the right stratagem, actually."

"Could be, but they played their hand too hard, too quickly," with that, Casey raised his hands and clenched his fists, then arched and cracked his back again. "You know, when Harold and I first started out with this thing – facilitating these conversations, one-sided I grant you –we both believed it was good to keep the Callers talking." Casey stared for a moment, then pushed the rimless glasses, which he wore inconsistently, along the bridge of his nose. He straightened in his chair, shrugged and gave Ben a hapless grin, "You know, if they do just stop talking to us – we really don't know what they'll be up to."

"Yeah, well, my gut tells me," Ben was scratching the back of his head, and then screwed his face into an expression of sympathetic concentration, "they'll wanna come back – they've devoted themselves to this strategy, whatever it truly is. Plus, the costs for them must be so low – why not revive it?"

"Good points, yup, good points," Casey smiled broadly at Ben. "Yeah, we gotta keep 'em talking. You know, the situation kind of reminds of a story or parable Lincoln would use." he went on methodically. "Well, prior to the Civil War, well Lincoln – the man – had always found slavery abhorrent, but – the antebellum Lincoln, one has to say, placed the concept and reality of Union above everything else," Casey paused, the same smile on his face, the eyes seemingly turning inward. "Anyway, Lincoln – the politician, and Lincoln – always the attorney, puzzled over what to do. The malign institution of slavery and the fate of the country, this prompted in Lincoln a story. Maybe you've heard it?"

Ben was smiling, enjoying Casey's homily and so replied, "No, can't say that I have."

"Anyway, thinking about slavery and the country, Lincoln scratched his head and cited the story of the wolf and the farmer. So, the farmer and the wolf come upon each other and engage in what was – at least for the farmer – a life threatening tussle. You've heard this one, right?"

"No, no, I don't think so," Ben averred.

"So anyway, another farmer then comes by, and sees his friend in a fight for his life, holding the wolf just back and just by its ears. The shocked farmer shouts, 'My God! What have you got there?'. The other says, 'I surely don't want to hold on, but I daren't let go!'"

Casey sank further in his seat and smiled contentedly, "That's how Lincoln summed up a paralyzing, frightening situation in which the nation found itself. And, in the case of slavery, a vile, criminal and morally-noxious one. Still, many people just didn't know what to do... forcibly abolish slavery and risk plunging the nation into civil war, or tolerate that abominable institution..." Casey grimaced at his own interpretation. "Well, I think my analogy is a little obscure, but just roughly there." He drummed his fingers on his desk and went on, "We do have a big engagement – with the Callers – and we want to keep it going. We don't want to let go."

_ CHAPTER 31

Ben loved being at 'home' – home being his parents' house. He enjoyed the space, the splendor, the solicitous doting. It was wonderful, although as a man now in his thirties, he copped guiltily to this delectation. Ben took a sip from his coffee mug and peered from his vantage point in the family manse aerie, gazing at the shades of olive green, gray and slate-blue water on the Bay and admiring from an acute angle the rust-coloured construct of the Golden Gate. He paused to take in the kitchen he found himself in, seated on a high stool, pulled up to a large marble-topped island. Ben simply enjoyed the expanse, the space, the large uninterrupted window onto the Bay. The capacious kitchen and its deluxe appointments were comforting.

Ben was often oblivious to nice things, or rather, just happy for what was there. He had liked the charming apartment he shared with Mae, but then that was gone. He liked his pleasant, but probably less charming, and certainly much smaller apartment in Arlington. But that was okay. Ben told himself it was nice and, probably, objectively, it was. He was happy with it and told himself that he liked experiences more, which in fact he did. He liked having time to himself. He liked to read, to ruminate, to idle (although he told himself he shouldn't do too much of that). Ben gazed off again, admiring the Bay. He idly ran a finger over the sleek marble surface of the island countertop. Yeah, this was home, even though it wasn't his childhood home. Ben hadn't grown up there. The house where he'd grown up was several blocks over. It was nice too, but his folks had moved into this one after he had left for college. His dad's consistent, successful litigation efforts had bought this house with the tremendous view of the Bay; his mom, an erstwhile litigator, had made the home their own. Ben nodded to himself, but now Dad was happily 'of counsel', and his mom enjoyed her different avocations.

"Hey pal," his dad ambled into the kitchen. He was dressed for the day in worn jeans, a print Oxford shirt, and broken in loafers, marking him as an attorney at rest. "Great to have you here, pal. So, you got in fine last night?"

Ben noticed his father's warm brown eyes, 'chocolate brown', as his mom liked to describe them.

"Yeah, no problems at all dad, really great to be back with you guys. There's some coffee ready."

"Super, don't mind if I do." Ben's dad poured himself a cup.

Ben looked at his father's warm open face. Here was a happy man, who had been an active, focused and utterly consumed attorney. It was a nice change, Ben could see. His dad's face, with the wire frame glasses and cropped gray hair brushed back, reminded Ben of the older Jimmy Conway character in *Goodfellas*. It was a weird association, Ben always noted to himself.

"So, how's the analysis business? Feds treatin' you well?" His dad by this time had plunked himself down on the stool beside Ben.

"Good, Dad, good," Ben turned to his father to explain, "well, I guess, I dunno, umm, I've actually gotten a promotion."

"Really? Wow! That's great!" A sturdy clap on the back followed. "Why didn't you tell me about it earlier? I would have loved to have heard."

"Oh, umm, I'm sorry, Dad. It's not really a bigee."

"Well, I think it is! Certainly, sounds like it is!"

Ben's dad was genuinely elated for him – and, from habit, protective of his sometimes oddly-quiet, thoughtful son. He was thankful Ben had never considered the law.

"So, tell me, Ben, why the sudden, wonderful elevation?" Stern senior was still merry, mirthful grin creasing and animating the old litigator's face.

"Well, it's more of a global remit – a little ad hoc."

"Really? Well that sounds a little vague, but impressive!"

Father clapped son on the back again, then affectionately rubbed Ben's shoulder.

"Oh Ben, I'm so glad you're up and you're just helping yourself." Ben's mother entered the kitchen. Like Ben's dad, she had on a pair of comfortable worn jeans and looked prepped for gardening. She glided by the kitchen island, giving the men folk kisses on cheeks. "I'm so glad you're staying with us for a few days. What a great treat to hear you wanted to come visit!" Her light blue eyes opened wide, simulating surprise, heart shaped face yielded a warm smile.

Only her coiffed silver hair rested fixed, impassive and unmoving upon his mother's head. It was the one physical characteristic reminding Ben that his mother had once been, like his father, a corporate litigator. In present circumstances, though, physical demeanor and mien were light and gentle.

"So, Ben, tell us more about this girl Brenda. I'm so happy for you!" Ben's mom's voice ended on higher trilling note, much higher than her usual mezzo tone.

"Me too, buddy," Ben's dad added, "she's very cute. Hot even!"

"Yes, very telegenic," his mother added wryly.

"Well, she's very lucky to nab you, son," Ben's dad was solicitous, happy for his son. Stern senior and his wife had taken Mae Sprinkel's divorce from their boy much harder than even Ben had. They felt deeply the loss of a relationship that was supposed to go without a hitch and with the prospect of grandchildren, yet wheezed, sputtered and came to an abrupt and premature end. Even being attorneys, they still stood agog, as Mae and the other Sprinkels methodically divested themselves of Ben. "Where's the emotion?" Stern father had muttered to Stern mother. They also saw their clipped male child feeling, it appeared, less pain and dislocation than they did. Ben seemed to them like a bedraggled, steady aquatic bird, stunned by the waves, but still planting itself upright, shaking its feathers, grooming itself quickly, and re-establishing some kind of equilibrium among the elements. This though did not assuage the elder Sterns, and they were invested in hoping a great deal for their boy.

"So, Ben, she's real cute. This girl Brenda."

"Your father likes watching her on TV," the wry tone from Ben's mom again.

"Well, she's very pretty," Ben's father affirmed, although dutifully abashed.

"You can tell she's a very intelligent young woman – so poised and well spoken." Ben's mother was pleased and nodded at her own comments. Her light blue eyes opened wide again as she reflected that her own diffident, albeit smart, son had landed such a catch.

"You are really, umm...going out with her?"

"Yes, Mom, I am, I guess. We're spending time together, we like each other." Ben's expression toward his mother was warm and indulgent. His smile was close-lipped, though.

"Well, you hold onto her Ben, she's really something. I can tell!" Mrs. Stern was hortatory.

"How did you guys meet, anyway?" Ben's dad interjected with a plain question.

"My boss, Timmy."

"You mean your *old* boss," Stern senior, habitually cross-examining, corrected his son.

"Yeah, umm, that's right. Timmy, yeah, Timmy and Carole, Timmy's wife, introduced me to her. They fixed us up."

"It's always friends..." Ben's mom's voice was even, reverential. "Timmy was such a nice boss, a nice person..."

"Actually, I think Carole had a lot more to do with it," Ben was grinning, "I think it's kind of a hobby of hers."

"Anyways, you really... benefitted," mother Stern stabbed each word with her extended index finger, smiling but staring at

Ben for emphasis. "So, hold onto Brenda," another index stab, "I think she's special."

"Yeah, Mom. I want to. I will." Ben was cheered thinking just about it. He smiled at his parents.

"I'm happy for you Ben," Stern senior clapped Ben again on the back. His mom pulled her stool closer along the island to be closer to her two men. Everyone settled in, quietly sipping their coffees. Stern senior scanned through the morning paper, while Mrs. Stern paged idly through the *New York Times* Sunday magazine and Ben began reading something in another of the Sunday papers.

CHAPTER 32

"Mr. President, I think I can put this very accurately for you. Your administration is the first to ever have to cope with a genuine and unfolding interstellar crisis."

Casey, again in an unaccustomed suit and tie, had finagled a quick meeting with the President, albeit a walking meeting. The two had been striding at the President's smooth clip along one of the West Wing corridors. Hearing Casey's words, the President suddenly stopped mid stride and stood, weirdly still, like some giant earthmover with the ignition cut. The large Buddha-like Commander-in-Chief stood beside the slight, wizened Casey and took in the old man's counsel politely, serenely. Rose Levchin had arrived and was now standing in front of the two men, quietly listening as well, but clearly ready to set-to, if the President signaled.

Casey's mind still reeled at the Caller walk-out. He glanced from the immense bulk of the President to the small, martial Levchin and suddenly felt tired. Casey practiced daily meditation, so he was more able to accept at some level the difficult, the untoward events. There is no permanence, there is only change. Should what happened really be so surprising? Casey licked at the roof of his mouth and gathered himself, focusing on intentionality. The Callers had walked out – an alien species, with indeterminate yet vast scientific power, deciding not to entreat any more with the United States and its retinue of allies. This could mean a solid diplomatic break. There could be consequences, big and unknowable ones. Casey's gaze shifted again, from the gimlet-eyed Levchin and then up to take in the President's carved features. He seemed to be in a good mood. No apparent crisis for him.

"Jim," Steve Rasmussen's voice was warm, "it's good that we're doubling back and talking about this."

"My gosh, there he is!"

A stooped old man, wearing a red windbreaker and a red baseball hat with a large black letter "N" and a rendered football stitched on its front, stood at the front of a contingent of White House tourists, each wearing at least one article of red clothing. The group of close to twenty consisted entirely of senior citizens and small children – the precious grandchildren. The group was close, now within easy eavesdrop of the policy conversation. Levchin glowered at the interruption, but just for a second; then her expression took on a neutral hue and she took small steps back toward the corridor windows and away from the interlopers. Casey instinctively followed suit, peeling away from the President to watch the spectacle.

"Holy mackerel, a whole bunch of Nebraska Cornhuskers!"

Casey saw Rasmussen's limestone features fill with energy, becoming open and inviting towards the tourist band.

"Sir, it's an honor," another of the senior males from the group offered. From them, soft mutterings of "Mr. President" and "So nice to see you Mr. President, sir" emanated. Three very small children quickly ran and seized the Presidential legs, which prompted Rasmussen to fold his frame for selfies and group photo moments, the picture taking prompting Casey and Levchin to pull back further into the background.

"Man, you guys always gave us a tough time." The President was engaging, playing up his collegiate Gopher days. The little crew beamed at the President's remark.

"You were a great ballplayer and you're being a great President!" Another of the seniors averred.

"Thanks, friend," Rasmussen said, smiling, shaking his head and raising his hands in mock disbelief, "I don't deserve such kind words."

Murmurs of disagreement with that statement, and additional Presidential affirmation poured from the group.

"Maybe I should use my blitzing more, and get some real things done here in Washington!"

This brought laughter and a round of applause from the group.

"Do you guys think we can do it?"

"You bet, sir!" Someone shouted, prompting more cheers.

"Alrighty then!" Rasmussen grinned, pinning his shoulders back. At that moment, some bemused security people came upon the Nebraskans, corralling both seniors and grandchildren. President Rasmussen smiled and laughed, shaking tiny hands playfully and making warmer two-handed handshakes with the older folks.

"Enjoy your time in Washington, folks – even with all the elected office holders here."

More general laughter and smartphone picture-taking. The President gave a conspiratorial wink to the embarrassed security detail, who coaxed and shepherded the dependable voters and grandchildren away from the President. After a few moments, the little group had left.

President Rasmussen lowered his head for a few seconds, then focused his attention back on Levchin and Casey. The warm animation that had captured the President's features suddenly leaked away. His current resting expression, now familiar to Casey, was contemplative, technical even.

"Voters, huh?"

Casey and Levchin gave an obligatory chuckle.

"So, where were we? The Callers, yes." The President said, stuffing his hands in his pockets and turning his gaze first to Levchin then to Casey. "We have a new situation on our hands, am I right? No other administration ever found itself at this particular fork in the road, just as you've said Jim," the President nodded deferentially to Casey. "What to do?" his voice was calm.

"You know, any company, as it grows..." Levchin and Casey

looked up at the President, readied themselves for a story. "... the company gets bigger, it begins to need financial backing. You meet bankers and yet more bankers," Rasmussen paused, seemed to do some internal editing, then went on. "So, of course I meet guys from B of A/Merrill – they're big underwriters, both equity and on the fixed income side. This became important, as Sybylline was growing," the President was now rocking lightly on his heels, recounting the story.

"Well, I'm talking with these Merrill guys – old timers mind you, relationship people for the bank. We're talking about different stuff, obviously about financing, about the footprint size we were seeing for the company." Rasmussen had lapsed into jargon. "So, anyway, one of the old guys, probably had been at ML for decades," the President extended a large, long arm for effect. "He'd been at Merrill when Dave Komansky was CEO. Komansky was a bright guy, but pretty tough looking – underworld figure type of guy. Very big fella but, as I said bright, polished too. As someone said, the man could be intimidating, looked like an impeccably dressed coke machine. Komansky was very hands on, too," here, the President gesticulated with both hands to illustrate the point.

"Of course, I'm with these guys, they're trying to sell product: the ability to raise liquidity, swap out of this rate or that, cost-effective capital, etc., etc.," the President whirled his hand nonchalantly, "Of course, they talk how they can protect me from risk – again – one sort or another. They talk about hedging strategies, different strategies. So, my guys and I, we listen. My hand still on my wallet." Rasmussen chuckled and feigned protecting his billfold. Levchin and Casey chuckled in response.

"Anyway, we're listening," Rasmussen, now the raconteur, continued. "They may have some insights, something valuable to say. So, one of the older guys, he trots out this story, which was funny because it was almost contrary to what they were trying to do – sell me stuff. So, this senior guy starts recounting this Komansky story, which is, I guess, one day somebody goes up to Komansky and tells him that he has this 'perfect hedge' for some toxic stuff they have on the ML books. So, Komansky turns to the guy," the President paused to hunch closer toward Levchin and Casey, "and he tells the guy, 'the only perfect hedge is when someone else fucking owns it'." Rasmussen fell quiet, but his shoulders were shaking with mirth – a strange sight to Casey and Levchin.

"Anyway," the President continued, straightening his back and smoothing the front and sleeves of his jacket, "that brings me all the way around, back to our own conversation. Thanks for indulging me."

Rasmussen stood fully straight, looming over Levchin and Casey. He lowered his head slightly and closed his eyes for a moment. He registered a small, child-like smile and absently tugged at the lower lobe of one of his ears, as if to execute an internal signal. Then he opened his eyes and looked squarely at Casey.

"So, Jim, I guess the operative phrase from that story just now is, 'when someone else fucking owns it'." the President enunciated that last phrase clearly, but not harshly. In a sense, Casey wasn't surprised by what would come next, but it was all still pretty weird.

"Sir?"

"I think you know what's coming, Jim. You're my booked hedge. You own this 'fucking' problem," the President seemed glib, but was deadly serious.

"I think, ah, I understand your view. Of course, you've just said in so many words what you want to do," Casey felt oddly hamstrung and deferential. It was weird what presidential power could still do, even after forty plus years – what with natural Plains deference for authority, and fear of FBI internment as well. The President shrugged involuntarily, then placed his hand lightly on Casey's shoulder. Levchin stood by, watching impassively. The

President was focusing on Casey and seemed poised to offer a defensive call or signal, just beyond the line of scrimmage.

"Umm, okay Jim, you own this problem. I trust you and I trust in the years of experience you have dealing with the aliens, I mean the Callers," the President paused, working to convey a warm and trusting expression. Casey was happy to hear this, eager even. He had confidence in his relationship with the Callers – he had known them, or rather their facsimiles, for so long.

"Of course, sir. There has been a long-standing and tenured relationship between our two respective sides; the United States, and the..." here Casey paused, reaching for the appropriate term, "the Caller community." There was really no other way to put it. Casey had no knowledge about how they were organized. No clear idea. He was also confident that no human being on this planet knew.

"And," Casey sought to emphasize, leaning his fit yet aging form toward the President, "I'm comfortable with the personal and institutional trust I've developed with the Callers to approach them and troubleshoot some of our current impasses."

"Good, that's very good, Jim," Rasmussen stood with his arms folded, rocking back and forth on his heels. He cupped his chin with his thumb and index finger, then began elaborating further, "I believe Secretary Levchin ably presented the objectives we envision for our relationship with the Callers. Both she and I agree that our Caller relationship must evolve. But, that said..." the President paused, and absently stuffed his hands in his pockets, "the how and the when, as to the way these objectives will be reached, are subject to flexibility and ongoing discussion."

Casey grinned and nodded in agreement with the President's point. He saw Levchin raise her hand gently, as if to request to speak, but the President raised his own hand to stay her question. He peered again at Casey.

"There has to be distance, Jim. You understand that. Your

intermediation, I guess that's the word for it, has fostered the relationship with the Callers, while also effectively delimiting that relationship.

"I guess you could characterize it that way," Casey produced a folksy grin, "as delimited."

"As Dave Komansky might say," the President's gaze was steady, "it's your fucking problem now."

"I get that, sir. No sitting President could devote much – time, no matter how subtly."

"Precisely Jim, I have to have distance. It's your 'fucking problem'," the President repeated, making air quotes. "That's the most effective and efficient approach."

Casey felt Levchin's gaze on him, but knew she was with the program. He turned to look at her and saw an expression that was not warm, but perfectly equanimous.

"Good luck, Dr. Casey. I wish you success," she spoke softly.

"Jim," the President's voice was relaxed, as he clasped Jim's shoulder and shook his hand, "let me add to Rose's good wishes. Good luck and Godspeed. Keep us posted, as you see fit."

CHAPTER 33

Ben had seated himself at the outside veranda of the Starbucks on K and 22nd. The wrought iron seat – or maybe it was hardened industrial plastic – was not, thankfully, forming a perspiration seal between the seat of his pants and his bottom. Enduring late spring weather had pushed back the humidity curtain that normally descended on Washington with the advent of summer. Ben had taken off his business-casual jacket and laid it over the back of another chair. He was surprised that no one else was sitting outside in light of the pleasant weather. Probably because of the lack of wi-fi, he thought. Ben wanted to be outside to see and greet Allen, whom he could now see making his way to their meeting. Striding quickly toward Ben so as to be truly on time, Allen would have struck Ben's parents as a very close incarnation of Ed McMahon, albeit a much healthier looking one. As he got closer, Allen raised his hand in a small wave and grinned at Ben. Ben got up from the table and stepped forward to greet the advancing McMahon avatar.

"Hey man!" Allen said, smiling and striding, and gamely seized Ben's outstretched hand, "Great to get together, I'm glad we can catch up."

"Steve! Great to see you man," Ben winced just a little and hoped Allen didn't noticed it. Ben was always a bit unnerved by the Caller's breezy entrances. He actually liked Allen, weird as that was. Allen stood in front of Ben, smiling and in apparent good spirits, but scanning different directions – first toward the interior of the Starbucks and then toward the street.

"Glad you set this up and we can meet," Allen offered.

Ben noticed a thin film of perspiration on Allen's ruddy complexion – it was in fact something one would normally expect to see on an older, slightly overweight, large white man rushing to make an appointment in a humid, tropical environment. It was a nice touch for the simulacrum, Ben noted, feeling suddenly doleful, despite Allen's bonhomie.

"We've reached quite an impasse, huh."

"You could say that," Allen grinned at Ben, "but Jim has been quick to begin working the order – communicating with our side. We're all trying to smooth waters – we want to work with you guys," Allen cleared his throat and raised his chin, "to see what we can do."

Ben shook his head, "Well, I'm glad you guys are keeping the faith on this."

"You know, really, we get it – we want to work on this," Allen was expansive, rocking back a little on his heels. "Even as we were leaving that busted meeting, I knew we could work through this." Allen shifted to one hip and placed a hand on the back of a nearby chair. "Anyway, take a load off," he pointed to where Ben had been sitting, "I'm gonna grab some coffee – do you want anything?"

Ben was now used to talking to someone who actually wasn't there, "Oh, umm, chai tea for me, thanks Steve."

Allen hastened with purpose toward the Starbucks door. Little would the barista at the counter know that they were dealing with a highly advanced form of alien intelligence. Ben stared at Allen's back. Yup, who knew?

"Oh, of course, we're good with the meetings, same format again," Allen said over his shoulder to Ben.

After a few minutes Steve came back, carrying a tray laden with a cup of chai and a black coffee and settled back into his chair.

"Of course, just as I said, wanna emphasize this from the start, we're still good with the meetings," Allen began unburdening the tray, handing the chai to Ben, "as I was saying. Jonathan and I are firmly supportive. Our bosses are good with it, their bosses are good with it, too." He took a sip from his coffee.

Ben sipped from his chai, taking it all in. It was surprising to get the meeting like this, although the Callers seemed to like these different episodic interactions. Casey reasoned that it was "more human" for them, and therefore helpful toward sharpening their verisimilitude, although Casey also admitted that he was no mind reader and so was only speculating. Still, he felt that the Callers liked what they perceived to be more of an informal setting. It was indeed "more human", more of a "water cooler interaction", especially with the "new guy", in other words Ben. The two, Steve and Ben, talked over coffee about how constructive re-starting the periodic meetings would be. When Ben asked why they, the Callers, hadn't just let Jim know over the phone about the re-start, Allen almost seemed to convey surprise at Ben's own ignorance and simply said that the Callers appreciated "having a lot of touches" about something so important. In fact, Allen indicated that Jonathan wanted to schedule a conference call near term, with all four of them participating again, at least. He referred to the two tandems – Jim and Ben, he and Jonathan, as the "advance teams". He seemed to like that phrase. It was important now more than ever that they all be aligned, so Allen emphasized. He would fill in the call details with Casey.

After explaining the Caller's position, Allen settled back into his chair, looking even more relaxed. Some silence between the two ensued, compelling Ben to make general observations about the weather and the Washington humidity. In a random way, Allen asked Ben if he managed to follow Stanford football, which Ben said he didn't. Allen lightly tapped the table with the palm of his hand, noted that things were busy and that he had to "get back". To what, Ben couldn't picture.

_ CHAPTER 34

The following week, Ben was in Casey's office with the old man sitting across from him looking happy and full of pep. Casey conveyed a sense that all was right with the world. The recent meeting between Ben and Allen had been a matter of preferred practice, if not protocol, for the Callers. They had wanted to "touch base in person". They drew comfort from that sort of thing, Casey divulged. Still, it had been an important thing to do, he explained, since one could never really know how and what the Callers thought about things. Casey averred again that he could never be a mind reader with these guys. The pending conference call would be more or less a formality too, but better not to take it for granted.

Casey had cleared more open space on his desk and stood what appeared to be a Samsung Galaxy phone on its bottom, the same kind of phone which Ben had and which he made a point not to lose. Casey had a Starbucks black coffee steaming about a ruler's length from the propped-up Samsung. Ben himself was cradling the cappuccino he had purchased during the coffee run he and Casey had done quickly before the call.

"You had a good meeting then, with Steve?" Casey face was open and smiling.

"Yeah, definitely good, I think," Ben sat up higher in his chair. "Steve seemed pretty content, and was pretty decided. Really wasn't much to discuss."

"Well, yeah, I knew it'd be pretty much a cake-walk. They've been feeling pretty conciliatory, almost from the get go." Casey nodded toward Ben. "Plus, they wanted to meet you again, get more of a feel, enlist you more explicitly in the process."

Ben smiled, shaking his head, "So, that's what Steve was telling me as well. But, I mean, Jim, you're a pretty vigorous guy." Ben was feeling genuine fealty, "You're great, you're not going anywhere."

"Hey, I know, and no worries," Casey said merrily, rubbing his hands together in anticipation of striking items off the to-do list, like the pending conference call.

"You've apparently passed all sorts of sniff tests with our friends," Casey declared. "More importantly," he went on, "at least I'd like to think, is that you have my confidence, Ben."

"Thanks Jim, that means a lot," Ben did feel grateful.

"Anyway," Casey glanced at his watch, "I think we're right on time, I'm gonna dial-in." Casey grabbed the mobile from the stand and punched in a quick sequence of numbers. "I've put it on speaker," Casey reached across and placed the Samsung again back in its cradle. The little phone vibrated, emitting the call tone. Someone picked it up at the second ring.

"Steve Allen," the voice was friendly, the acoustics oddly cavernous.

Casey leaned in, placing his forearms on his desk. "Hi Steve," he was expansive, "I have Ben here as well..."

"Hi Ben," the friendly voice chimed in.

"Hey Steve," Ben answered back, raising his hand unconsciously in greeting.

"That's great, great to have you guys on the call," the speaker phone emitted. Ben wondered who – or actually, what – they were talking to.

"I've got Jonathan here with me as well."

"Hi, gentlemen," Winter's voice was lower than Allen's, and sonorous.

"Hi Jonathan, really appreciate that you guys have set aside time for the call," Casey completed the greeting protocol.

"No problem, it's good to formalize things a bit," the tone was now a bit paternal, Ben thought.

Casey clasped his hands on the desk, "Well, shall we get started?"

"Yeah, just a second," that was Allen, then the little mobile phone presented mat silence. Ben sensed Winter and Allen had put them on mute.

"Okay," the phone sprang back to life, the Caller acoustics were still weirdly cavernous. "We're good here," it was Allen again. "I think I should preface the meeting with a few opening comments."

Preface, Ben thought to himself and nodded.

"Hi Steve, Jim again. Go ahead, that sounds fine."

"Okay, great. Of course, to put everything into context, the terms President Rasmussen and Secretary Levchin articulated were a non-starter, completely unacceptable."

"Yes, I think we can understand that," Casey was smiling, staring at the cradled Samsung.

"That said, we're, on the other hand, not going to say that there's no flexibility..."

"And, there is some understanding," that was Winter's baritone. "Our relationship with you, with your society, has by this time acquired a weathered and warm patina. We've certainly gotten to know you better, and though you may not think so, you've become more familiar with us." How, or to what extent, Ben could not plumb.

"That's right, which is to say, just to put it plainly, we like you guys. We like humanity," that was Allen again.

"We do," Winter chimed in, "but we are limited. We are limited by, ultimately, what we feel is best for you."

"Of course, sure," Allen added, the helpful interlocutor, "which is again to say that we are motivated to sustain and deepen our relationship with you, that is with humanity," his voice sounded clearer and higher than Winter's. "But we really are bound by a sense of responsibility to maintain our non-disclosure – I think that's the term-of-art."

"Gentlemen," Casey now responded, "I can say that the President has a fresh appreciation of this point."

Ben could see that Casey had shifted his gaze, was smiling, waving his hand slightly toward the door. Ben turned in his seat to look back and saw Timmy standing in front of the office window adjacent to the door. Timmy was motioning to Casey and raising his eyebrows. There was something on his mind. Ben smiled at Timmy and made a slight wave back. Ben turned back around and saw Casey smiling at Timmy. Casey raised his fist to his ear and raised his chin, making the universal hand-held phone sign to indicate that he would call Timmy later. Ben twisted his neck back again to see Timmy nod and make the thumbs up sign before walking away.

Ben's saw Casey frame visibly relax now that Timmy had left. He folded his hands together on his desk and turned back to the cradled Samsung.

"Steve, Jonathan, let me emphasize that I think everyone's again on the same page. Let me also emphasize that the President does also appreciate your point of view," Casey paused for a moment, and sank back in his chair – for effect, Ben figured. He then leaned again toward the speaker phone. "While we do feel that the points made during our last White House meeting represent goals for our relationship," Casey paused again, "the timetable, as the President emphasized to both me and Secretary Levchin, is undefined. We believe, gentlemen, that we can reach these goals when both sides see that the time is right."

"Then Dr. Casey," the melodious voice from the Samsung was Winter's, "I think we understand each other well."

"Then I can communicate to the President that the quarterly meeting format can resume?"

"Given our newly arrived-at understanding," Winter intoned, "I can say our people would be fine with that."

"Excellent," Casey leaned on one elbow and radiating enthusiasm, "so then I can begin setting up for the next quarterly?"

"Sounds good, that would be fine," Winter was warm over the phone.

"Jim?" Allen chimed in, "Can you direct the meeting details to me? As per usual protocol."

"Sure Steve, will do."

"Great, thanks."

"Jim, from our perspective – I can see Steve nodding – I think we're all set here." Winter, still warm over the Samsung, was ready to conclude.

"Oh yes, I think so, we're good here too. This has been very encouraging and helpful. Much appreciated guys." Casey directed his gaze at Ben, "Ben, do you have any comments?" Ben mildly surprised, shook his head.

"I think we're good then, nothing more to add," Casey concluded from the human side.

"Thanks Jim, Ben," Winter replied. Ben could hear a slightly fainter "thanks guys" over the speaker from Allen.

"We're looking forward to the next scheduled quarterly," it was Winter again. "All the best, gentlemen."

Casey reached over and pressed on the digital face of the phone to end the call. He sat back, relaxed and happy. Ben felt buoyed by the results – and the weirdness.

CHAPTER 35

Ben sat at the end of the bed in Brenda's apartment, hunched over and happy, preparing to get up and make his way to the galley kitchen. There was morning coffee to be had. He began mobilizing lower body and raised his frame to standing, when a pillow sailed across and hit him squarely on the back of his head. Really awake now, he stood up quickly and turned to look at Brenda, who was sitting and resting against the headboard.

"You really have problems with intimacy, Ben."

Brenda's blue eyes were fixed on him, her reddish gold hair was loose around her head and her long legs were extended and crossed at the knee, arms folded tightly at her chest.

"I'm sorry, wha'?" Ben felt flat-footed.

"I ask you about your work, your week – you just ignore it!" Brenda was firm and declarative.

"Oh, umm, I was in a little bit of a fugue..."

"That's exactly what I mean, Ben. Sometimes, it's like you have this barrier around you, this fog bank, I dunno..." Brenda was frustrated and slid quickly off the side of the bed, pulling her New England Patriots jersey – a no. 12 for Tom Brady – down to mid-thigh. She strode to the kitchen galley, pre-empting Ben and began sorting through coffee maker and filter on the counter. She silently measured out scoops of dark ground coffee in a tight, emotionally-laden way. Dark roast was, after all, Ben's preferred blend – she liked the fruitier Costa Rican. Ben walked over and rested his hands on the kitchen island's crushed-stone counter-top. He gazed across it at Brenda, who avoided his eyes, remaining focused on the compact burbling coffee maker.

"I mean, Brenda, we share a lot..."

Ben knew he was sounding plaintive. But he thought he *had* shared a lot! He had talked about his childhood, about his hyper-working, functionally alcoholic father and his at times somewhat-out-of-it mother – both of whom he loved very much. He had even talked about his own oddness, though he knew that was pretty obvious anyway. He talked about his caustic little sister – he loved her, too. Jesus, he had even opened up about Mae. That was an emotional centrifuge all by itself. Ben was awkward, he knew, but he was good at some things (not with his marriage, but he had talked about that).

Even with all that sharing, Brenda had told him, with one of her penetrating stares, that he had "trust issues".

Ben knew in his bones that he found it hard to trust. That, as much as he studied and learned, the world in its complexity was a hard place to navigate. He didn't always see it, or get it. But he actually loved sharing things with Brenda; she was kind. He knew some things about Brenda as well, but not really that much. She liked to listen to him more and made time for it. She cared, Ben realized, which softened the rancor that was gathering.

"You didn't even tell me you were visiting your folks!" Brenda looked up at Ben, her blue eyes unwavering, which unnerved him. They signaled her disappointment in him. Ben hated the disapproval.

"You know, I mean, you were busy...I was just getting away for a few days, it was just my folks. Anyway..." Ben cobbled together the rationale. Acknowledging this, Brenda made an elaborate gesture of pouring Ben a cup of coffee.

"You were incommunicado. Not even a phone call, or text..." An eyebrow arched on her heart-shaped face.

"I'm sorry," Ben said softly. He was sorry.

"Your folks probably don't even know about me, do they?"

"Oh, no. That's not true. They do know! They really like you! My folks watch you on Bloomberg – they tell me how lucky I am."

Brenda smirked and sipping her coffee, "Sure, sure they do, as if I'm supposed to know, since you never talk about your family."

This was caustic and also a case of selective memory, since Ben knew what he had revealed, or thought he had revealed, which was so much about his life and family. Funny, Mae would get incensed about the same thing. This was taking on the semblance of a pattern. Ben shook his head at the thought.

"So, there's your family and your cryptic style, and there's your work," Brenda pressed on.

"I mean, come on, I'm trying..." Ben's deep limbic caution kicked in. The work area was especially sensitive.

"Baby," Brenda skirted the kitchen island, lowered her chin and looked at him intently. She curled her index finger and gently placed it under Ben's chin, positioning his gaze with hers. "You have to learn to trust, to be open."

"Umm, yeah." Ben replied. "I know, I know babe..., I'm sorry for being – for being me – with my different hang-ups, issues..." Ben raised both of his hands up, then dropped them to his sides. He looked up to meet Brenda's gaze, hoping to placate. Brenda beamed down at Ben - any hostility now drained away from her features. She reached and drew him in close.

"Don't you know, silly," Brenda whispered in Ben's ear, "I love you."

Ben hugged Brenda back, he knew he loved her too.

_ CHAPTER 36

Ben exited from the Ballston metro stop, bushed and contrary. He had been burning the proverbial candle at both ends, seeing to projects that Timmy pushed his way – a working cover that could be strenuous – while also addressing tasks Casey was assigning. There was analysis for the mid-year quarterly to compile, data from SETI and others to parse and Casey wanted him to follow a recent "hunch". So now, Ben was scanning and sifting through all literature and available intelligence on any breaches to the Asilomar Protocol. In total, Ben found the full docket of work interesting, but just in the last weeks a little exhausting. He found it difficult to always compartmentalize the hyper-classified work with Casey and the camaraderie he continued to have with Timmy and the rest of the team. The Callers' omniscience about himself and his family had also been unnerving, exacting a kind of white-noise strain on Ben's sense of well-being.

–

Ben slipped quietly back into his apartment and shucked his business casual clothing for comfortable jeans and a polo shirt. He drew a nice helping of prepared quinoa from his refrigerator, then broke open a plastic palette of pre-cut and sliced vegetables. He took the vegetables to his electric range and reached for the skillet, adding a small dose of olive oil, then began preparing his dinner, enjoying the simple activity of turning and pushing the vegetables over the hot surface. Within a few minutes, the vegetable concoction was done. He poured the skillet contents over the waiting plate of quinoa, then sprinkled some grated parmesan on top. Good, no gluten, Ben thought idly. There seemed to be an association between gluten and the occurrence of nasal inflammation. Ben knew that his nasal issues had been a risible bête-noire for his former wife. It had been a hard lesson.

Surveying the colorful dinner he had prepared for himself, Ben felt a warm sense of reassurance. He put the plate down on the adjoining small table, then fetched some sparkling water from the refrigerator. He sat down at the dinner table and directed his chair toward the wall-mounted television, close by in the small tidy apartment. The TV flickered on, as Ben began tucking into his dinner. A CNN logo pirouetted on the screen followed by some ponderous incidental music. A CNN commentator appeared on the screen:

"The theater of operation: northeastern Syria," an even baritone voice began, "new American synthetic units deployed, securing tactical advantage with little or no loss of life for US or enemy combatants...We are now bringing live, from US Central Command at Al-Dueid Air Force Base in Qatar, General M.K Fisher-Spillane."

Behind the newscaster, the shaved head and large square frame of General Fisher-Spillane materialized on the studio screen.

"Thank you, General, for joining us," the commentator swiveled his chair toward the screen.

"It's a pleasure, Tim." The general's voice drawled (a southern accent?). His smile was agreeable. "Today represents quite a step in the evolution of US force deployment, wouldn't you say, sir?"

"Yes, that's right," the general drawled. Chin on bullet head lowered for emphasis. "Operation Open Mike was a success, with no loss of life for US forces, and minimal enemy casualties."

"Can you elaborate on that, General?"

A pair of large white hands now appeared from under the desk where the general was sitting. They were moving about, along the desk surface, as if to convey the contours and breaks in the engagement terrain.

"We deployed our new synthetics simultaneously among

select village and urban areas in the Syrian Northeast Sector, frequently under enemy control."

"Synthetics?" the commentator put the tip of his glasses toward the corner of his mouth.

"Yes, that is correct, synthetics," the general folded his hands together, resting them on the desk. Ben thought he looked professorial.

"Those deployed units," the general drawled, "are STUFs, that is Semi-Autonomous Tactical Unit Fighters. These forces are especially adept at being in harm's way." The general extended his hand, emphasizing his point and seeming to reach out directly toward the TV viewing audience.

"General Fisher-Spillane, I believe we have a tape segment we can show our audience on the deployment of the new STUFs, as you call them."

"Very good, please proceed," the military man nodded. A grave voice-over then cautioned viewers about graphic upcoming scenes and that discretion was advised.

Ben watched the screen change and reveal the image of a placid, bright blue and white day. It looked to be a stationary shot at street level for the camera. It almost seemed staged for Ben. How did they, whoever they were, manage to do that, Ben wondered. The street scene revealed bleached white stucco alabaster houses abutting each other in a jagged one- and two-story line, the daylight intensity only softened by the dust emanating, it seemed, from the stucco walls themselves and from the ground. The day looked hot. Over different entry ways and between adjoining buildings colorful textiles and sheets were suspended taut, providing shade and breaking up the monotony of light. On one side of the screen, he saw the limbs and then entire frame of a deliberating, gangly man emerging. The figure moved into full view, then stopped, crouched and extended its neck to look around. Then it moved again, stopped again. The figure was followed by others, all moving in a punctuated, recursive way, like their leader.

The long, lean men Ben saw were not people. They were elongated and much larger than human beings generally are, and they moved in such an odd way – coiled and watchful. The figures were silver and gray, showing jointed limbs and metal plate and what looked like rubbery connective tissue. A bright orb shot from offscreen, tracing and careening directly into the chest of the second man in the formation. The explosion was abrupt and loud, prompting Ben to sit back in his chair. The smoke and dust cleared and the struck-down STUF raised itself to a prayer-like kneeling position, then into a posture as if it was trying to catch its breath. It reached for its weapon and pulled itself upright, then coiled again for the reconnoiter. Another mechanical fighter had straightened quickly and appeared to focus at some farther point. In fluid motion, the STUF attached a projectile to the end of its weapon, and fired. Ben could hear the explosion and the sound of crashing rubble.

The group of STUF units started moving at a faster pace, with the camera panning in and out on the group's progress. They descended upon a white stucco structure, then Ben heard shouts and some screams coming from people not on camera, – sounds of a general melee. Soon, the STUFS started shepherding knots of confused and frightened men into the open. Some STUF units corralled the straggling men, who were furtive, looking disoriented. The scene ended to reveal General Fisher-Spillane's impassive expression. He started toying with an attachment on his lapel.

"Am I on now?" The general continued fingering at his jacket. The camera shifted to the CNN commentator who was frozen for a moment, eyeglass leg still stuck in the corner of his mouth.

"Umm, General," the newsman roused himself, "that was quite a sight."

"Yes," the general replied, becoming matter of fact, "we were able to attain the immediate objectives with minimal loss of life – on both sides."

"Umm, yes, yes that is gratifying. I'm sure to our viewers…"

"Yes, sir, it was – for the President, the informed members of Congress, and our military, I believe, as well."

"Uh yes, yes, of course," the newsman tried to rally, although still struck by the image of mechanical soldiers robotically – no other word for it – attaching bayonet blades to their weapons. That said, he gathered himself, "General Fisher-Spillane thank you for your comments and this highly relevant footage."

"Thank you, my pleasure, sir."

"We'll be back in a moment after this brief pause."

Ben pushed absently at his quinoa. An animated figure, apparently a cowboy, flashed onto the screen, hopping among a tray of dishes in an open dishwasher. Ben studied the cowboy figure who was whooping and roping recalcitrant dish stains. The dishes were left sparkling.

"This is big, this is very big," Ben mused to himself, still absently pushing at his food, staring at the wall mounted screen.

The news soon continued, with the CNN commentator turning to a panel of designated experts, military people among them as well as journalists and policy analysts. Ben watched the ensuing discussion heat up, as some speakers cited lower loss of life projections; others contested those findings. Still others questioned the morality of having mechanical men do the fighting, while discussion flared over the role of Sybylline, the President's company, in the critical software for the STUF units. The military men attempted to assuage misgivings, noting that the STUFs were "getting better", and that they were "learning". The remarks did nothing to temper unease, but catalyzed more reaction from the other panelists. A commercial break blocked more discussion. Ben had had enough and switched off the television.

CHAPTER 37

Ben felt neglected, but happy for Brenda. They didn't seem to have had much time to meet during the past weeks. Brenda had been so busy reporting on Washington developments, the STUF's advent – "STUF happens", as she merrily put it. Brenda had in fact been doing a fair amount of reporting on Sybylline. Thus far, it seemed, everything regarding Sybylline, the STUFs and military procurement was panning out, totally above board. Something that was utterly frustrating for Brenda the reporter. Dealings with the US military also appeared to be clear, which Brenda reported in different electronic missives and video segments. She was busy! And there was still the scent of a story, maybe something deeper. Brenda and her colleagues continued to rummage among people and files, odd tidbits here and there, to see if there was. Of course, the actual *product* from Sybylline was highly classified. The adaptive networking software that the company had developed could not be pried open for public view, white papers on different technical issues notwithstanding.

–

For the Rasmussen administration, the STUF issue seemed to be generating a steady but low level of political noise. The President and his Vice President – a woman and former senator from New Hampshire – went about business as usual. The two continued to canvas voters – in large gatherings, small business environments, the occasional staged dinner and other retail political events. The VP had been, like the President, a collegiate athlete: in her case, a long and rangy member of women's crew. She was a lawyer, quick-witted, an advocate/enforcer for the President and also, like the President, gay. Rasmussen's strange, non-neuro typical charisma and his VP's quick and assertive intelligence made them an effective team. She, of course, didn't know anything about the Callers. No Vice President of the United States ever did.

With the reconciliation that Casey had brokered, the quarterly meetings between the Callers and the President resumed at the end of June. To Ben, the Caller facsimiles now seemed more solicitous of the President. Probably because of the STUF issue, Ben thought, although the administration seemed to be handling the impact on the American attention span pretty well. TV segments were beginning to wane. The White House loaded the news outlets with technical experts, who worked to fill airtime with abstruse detail on the more publicly-vetted technologies about the STUF procurement. This coverage was often difficult to follow and had a numbing effect. The technical experts also managed to bring up the prospects for beneficial military/commercial synergies. This was meant to be soothing.

During the re-launched quarterly meeting, Casey and Ben had no real material items to share with the President, Secretary Levchin and the Caller folks. SETI findings were thus far nil, which was par for the course. Ben remarked to himself what an honor it was to have the President pour and serve him a black coffee from the rolled-in coffee station. It was awfully hospitable and the President had done the same for the other attendees, taking requests for black or with cream. Rasmussen was a flat-hierarchy kind of guy. Even the Callers got into it, obliging the President and requesting cups of steeped Earl Grey breakfast tea. To Ben, it was weird seeing these two apparitions sipping at physical tea, but such were the wonders of Caller physics.

The President had also seemed more mechanical than usual, his interactions were more studied and just slightly halting. "The man's in his head a lot," as Casey later observed. The meeting, though, had followed its normal rhythms, with the President and Levchin fielding various and sundry questions from the Callers. Casey interrupted from time to time; Ben was generally silent, as per protocol.

CHAPTER 38

They entered the system at below light speed, making their way through space still marked by the sun's energy, then through the belt of cosmic dust and debris toward the orbital paths of the four interior planets. They gauged direction toward the moon of the third one and then remained stationary, hidden in its shadow.

The small team slid into the upper atmosphere of the third planet. They cloaked themselves and made their way along the western coast of what its inhabitants call the United States. Still hovering high above, they descended in their craft toward the southern outskirts of the conurbation called San Francisco. They felt secure and undetected. Recent technology enhancements gave them an edge – that's what they believed, at any rate.

It was just before 4am Pacific Standard Time and they were positioned before an intersection in an industrial warehouse district, exerting a force that enveloped the gray structure. The field of energy they generated extended from above the structure and flowed uninterrupted into the earth, some measure below the structure and its seismically retro-fitted foundation. With this action, they knew their quarry was now well aware of them. It was just them and their quarry, they believed. No evidence of any human life at this time, in this place. They knew they had the upper hand. This presence, this location, had somehow evaded them. They didn't quite know how, but they had contained it now. Their analysis was also now more thorough; there were no other such places on this planet.

Overtures were made, but no response. They signaled again, and waited. Nothing. The team members looked at each other. They weren't able to establish communication, but orders were clear and orders were orders. The team lead initiated the command sequence. The energy surge catalyzed and engulfed the warehouse and immediate environs, leaving the target area flat, hard and smooth – like a pool table. Whatever had been there was no longer there. Everything else was fine, left intact. The crew of that tiny space ship had the capacity to contain and direct the massive amount of energy and heat. They took pride in that precision. No human collateral damage, either – at least as far as they could detect, but they were confident about it. Otherwise, that would have been tough to deal with back at HQ.

Their craft ascended slowly from the street corner, gaining altitude and a perspective on the city. They banked, taking a broad arc to see the upper peninsula view, the Golden Gate Bridge, and the blue ocean beyond. Beautiful. The team appreciated it. The ship picked up speed and set its course.

_ CHAPTER 39

"Hello?"

Miriam Casey had picked up her dad's trembling mobile which was lying on a small patio table, upon which were also strewn Casey's blue polo shirt and a club towel. If there was a call coming in on his mobile, it would be important, her dad had said. It would probably be his new hire, Ben. It would be about work. She held the phone to her ear and squinted, looking across the row of lounge chairs into the club TV room, where her dad stood still in front of the mounted screen. She began walking alongside the pool to hail her father, who was immobile, facing the screen.

"Uh, who is this?" It was a mild voice on the line. Miriam thought it was kind.

"Well, hello, I'm Miriam Casey, err...Dr. Casey's daughter," Miriam replied, quickening her pace toward the club lounge and TV room, "and you must be Ben! Dad, umm, Dr. Casey, said to expect your call."

"Oh, hi, great! Thanks for taking the call, umm, is your dad around?" The voice had gotten tighter, "I mean, Dr. Casey. Is he around? I'd really like to talk to him. It's very important, thanks so much."

Miriam Casey grimaced at Ben's nervous insistence. She was a handsome middle-aged woman. Naturally graceful and erect. Much older and more certain of herself than Ben was about himself. Natural good cheer prevailed, though. She remembered that Dad had spoken warmly of his young colleague. It was good that he seemed to have a nice friend like that at work – God knows what they were all up to there. A cloud coursed over her brow. She strode toward the lounge entrance. Why didn't Dad just retire and come back to live full time in Berkeley? He loves it here so much, anyway, she thought. She rallied, then allowed her facial muscles to relax.

"Hi Ben, I'm gonna hand you over to Dad." She crossed the entrance, now holding the Samsung in both hands.

"Dad?"

Casey turned to his daughter. He looked startled. She was taken aback.

"Thanks Maya," Casey said, using the family diminutive for his daughter, who handed him the phone and turned to leave.

"Hello Ben!" Casey's greeting was merry and drawn out. "You must be seeing some of the same real shit going down on TV."

"Jim, this is strange stuff. I think there is a lot of shit going down, as you were saying." Ben continued to watch the CNN coverage that Casey was watching, too.

"Yup, that's right," Casey stared at his large TV screen.

"Umm, yeah, uh Jim, have you reached out to the Callers about this?" Ben's voice sounded an octave higher.

"Already have."

Ben nodded to himself and his phone, "Where are you anyway?"

"Oh…" Casey began yawning and stretching in reaction to Ben's question, working to crack back vertebrae, still holding the phone close to his ear.

"I'm in Berkeley. I can get back to Washington – no problem at all. Can be back in a jiffee. Am here because I thought I'd be able to mellow out with the grandkids."

"Oh, that's right, you're a granddad," Ben nodded on his end of the line.

"Yeah, that's right. I'm here with my daughter Miriam and her two girls – twins, now tweens. Nice girls, but a little contrary at times." Casey grimaced, and began cradling his forehead.

"Look Ben, stand pat. I'll be back by tomorrow some time. I'm sure the President is freaking, since he's a smart guy, and probably has an inkling on what's going on."

"Is there anything you want me to do?"

"No, thanks, that's okay. I've reached out to the Callers, and I know how to get hold of the President," Casey was reassuring, and felt himself reassured.

"Okay, I'm here, just let me know if you need anything."

"Thanks Ben, I'll see you tomorrow. Let me know if you learn anything new."

"Sure thing, thanks Jim."

They hung up concurrently. Shit happens, Casey mused to himself. After forty years plus, shit's bound to happen. He needed to tell Miriam that he was leaving early.

_ CHAPTER 40

He was an old man, and heavy. It helped that he had a good tailor, who fit him into capacious, elegant dark blue suits. But with advanced age and corpulence, there were limits to be observed, as the old man realized every time he hoisted himself from the back seat of the sedan. The driver would always get out of the car to help, the old man would always refuse. Leaving the air-conditioned limousine, the old man felt the thick humidity of a mid-summer New York morning. He mopped his broad forehead and pressed the top of his cropped, wavy white hair, which was generally impervious to wind or any other external conditions. The driver bade him a nice day and then drove off, while the old man made his way to the office tower entrance. He moved at a slow, but constant pace, allowing for the overall faster flow of sidewalk traffic. No one noticed him as, like a tugboat, he drew closer to the mid-town Manhattan entrance. He was, and had been for a long time, a famous man, notorious in some circles. Much of that fame and notoriety had been planted decades ago. And he remained on the global stage, even as senescence approached. His body was bothersome and failing, but he had kept his acuity. His rumbling basso voice, accent and mannerisms had endured for so many years, ample material for talk show monologues and comic routines. He remained the same presence for many, just as he had so many years before.

The old man took the elevator to the reception area of the consultancy he had started after leaving public office. Being totemic, he retained great marketing appeal, so he continued to make appearances for the business, suffusing it with much-needed attention and cash. His own interests and analytical efforts were ongoing and he quite liked staying involved, even though his wife scolded him to slow down more. He would not, he thought. The old man approached the reception desk and asked if his sports magazine had arrived, which the young person behind the desk – they were always very deferential and diffident, which he couldn't help – busily fished for and then produced. He still loved to follow his favorite team from Fuerth, always did – even after his anxious flight from that small Bavarian town so many years ago now. Behind the desk, a CNN newscast on the screen caught his interest. The camera panned over a city industrial yard that looked like it had been milled flat and strangely uniform.

Strung across the area was some yellow police tape that seemed to demarcate a section of the sidewalk. The remaining sidewalk was unimpeded. Behind the talking CNN reporter and the vestige of limp tape, the industrial plot looked smooth and gray. It looked to be a literal tabula rasa, as if just wiped clean. The report switched to an expert from the American Geophysical Union, who looked baffled. Grimacing, screwing up his face and working his expression, he pushed his glasses along the ridge of his nose and commented that the phenomenon of uniformly-smooth and empty industrial yard was open to conjecture. The magnitude of energy must have been intense, but highly localized, the expert noted. It had to have been some anomalous phenomenon, but *what* exactly he and his colleagues couldn't yet say. The screen flashed back to the street scene and the CNN reporter.

The portly old man continued to stare at the wall-mounted TV screen. He adjusted his bifocals resting on the ridge of his nose and stood still. The receptionist behind the desk also seemed to be held in flux, looking on at the old man, and finally asking if there was anything she could do. The old man lowered his gaze from the TV and stared past her. He remained still, still staring, prompting the young receptionist to stand and lean forward toward him.

"Sir?"

"Mein Gott, sie haben es endlich geschafft..."

Casey and Ben sat at curbside from the local Starbuck's, close to the office. They chose to brave the humidity outside. Both men sat together at the little mass-produced black wrought-iron table; they were intent on playing catch-up ball. Casey revealed to Ben that the Callers had actually admitted responsibility for the Daly City "incident". "Our measure," as they also described it, but they were also taciturn. Casey had then presented the facts, as he had them, to the President who, at least momentarily, went "ape shit", according to Casey.

"First time I'd seen that mechanical golem get truly emotional about anything," Casey added. "He was bent out of shape, just for an intense moment, regained his composure – and mind you this was over a secured line with Caller tech – and tried to parse out what happened: the whys, the wherefores. Sorry to say, the Callers haven't offered up much yet."

Ben grimaced, "You know, Rasmussen's been able to handle the STUF activity and all the shit with Sybylline." Ben shook his head, "Those are still bad optics."

"Yeah, I know, the STUF really hit the fan," Casey grinned back at Ben, but then took on a sober mien.

"Now this – something highly strange, highly technical, highly potent," Ben emphasized the last quality.

"I agree – some strange, potent shit," the old man couldn't stop grinning.

Ben shook his head again, "Man, it's real grist for some conspiracy theorists."

"Like your girlfriend," Casey's grin became puckish.

"You're right," Ben smiled back, "Brenda's all over this."

Casey and Ben had both seen the news clip with Brenda offering commentary from the White House south lawn and adducing just that – a conspiracy.

"Look, I'll press on this with the Callers," Casey straightened his back against the faux-wrought-iron chair and placed his open hands behind his head – as a runner does when catching breath, or as someone might prior to execution. Ben's imagination had turned morbid.

"Ben, just as you said," Casey began tapping the table, "this is bad optics, so I'm sure the President will give the Callers – and us – an audience. Levchin will, of course, have to be there too." Jim unconsciously adjusted his brow, contemplating the volatile Secretary.

"Yeah, Brenda, the media in general, they're all over this. The scientific community wants to indicate this as a natural phenomenon, but they don't yet have an explanation for it..."

Casey nodded, "Yup, I know, the media wants to say it's man-made, much better story – even better still, if they can link it to Sybylline." He folded his hands on the table. "The only way out of this is through Jonathan and Steve. The Callers made this mess, they will have to clean this shit up."

_ CHAPTER 41

"We are definitely all over this!" Brenda yelped. She sat content and purpose-driven, smiling at Ben and then at the plate of al-dente pasta she continued to twirl with her fork. Ben was shtum, but also smiling. They sat at a new favorite, Loco Roma, a Peruvian-Italian-Chinese fusion place, close to the Ballston stop.

"I was talking to the guys who cover science. They say the earth, or more specifically, the ground there, is like freeze-dried coffee." Brenda took a forkful of her al-dente pasta and chewed.

"You mean you could drink it…?"

"No, you idiot…" Brenda half-laughed but gesticulated for emphasis, "I mean, the soil was totally transformed. Whatever coursed through it, changed it." Brenda dabbed at her mouth with a cloth napkin, "The guys told me they're going to ship a lot of it out for analysis."

"Those guys being the government?" Ben sought verification.

"Yes, *those* guys," Brenda was sour, but in overall good humor. She shifted to sit squarely in her chair. Peevishness egged her on.

"Whatever it is you do, or you guys do in your group, do you talk about this kind of stuff?" Brenda sat, holding her fork upright beside her plate. She was waiting for a response.

"Actually, not so much I guess, mostly just about things with policy ramifications…" Ben gestured loosely with his hand. It was an unsatisfactory answer. Brenda stared back, her fork still held erect.

"I guess you guys really don't delve into this kind of stuff?" Brenda was sour and resigned to leaving be her soft-spoken and evasive dinner companion. Ben, smiling now, just shrugged.

"Not really our area. Of course, I couldn't tell you anything, if it were." He shrugged once more, and took a sip of wine.

"Yeah, I understand." Brenda turned her head to the side, then returned her gaze to Ben. She smiled, still seeming disappointed.

The rational, methodical Ben felt no compunction about hiding anything he knew or did from Brenda. The warm-blooded Ben felt some sadness that he wasn't able to confide in her about this and other things

—

The sun had shone brightly in the Washington summer sky. In the Oval Office, they were meeting later, much later in the morning than they usually did. Ben blinked and looked around at the general survey. As per custom, Winter and Steve were seated on one of the federal couches, with Secretary Levchin and the President seated on the opposite one. The polished credenza separated the two sides. A new person was sitting at the end of the Caller's couch, which intrigued Ben. From the look of steady intensity on Casey's face, Ben reasoned he was intrigued, too. Levchin conveyed her usual cool reserve, hands folded on her lap. The President was quiet and dominating on the sofa, alert, ready to call a defensive audible, Ben thought.

The man seated at the end, clearly a military man, cleared his throat and began to speak. Winter quickly turned to stare at him. They all leaned in closer to listen. Casey was rubbing his chin. Clearly this new man, a Caller, hadn't been briefed on the standard protocols, Jim mused.

"Mr. President," Vance Packard, the grave military man, had begun, "I wish to convey our earnest apology. Please consider our armed intervention a single and unique action of such kind. We did this on your behalf and we are confident we will never have to do so again." Packard spoke in a clipped manner, articulate and efficient. Jim saw from the bars on his shoulders that he was a US Army colonel – or rendered as one. The 'colonel' had taken off his cap and had laid it on the credenza. He looked to be in his mid-fifties, an African American man, his hair cropped tightly at the sides – standard military. He also sported a trim mustache reminiscent of the old-time actor Adolphe Menjou. He looked taut and fit in his olive-green uniform and wore decorations highlighting different US engagements during the past twenty-five years. The Callers didn't spare any details, Casey thought.

Winter cleared his throat, nodded toward Packard and then leaned toward the President and Secretary Levchin. His voice was palliative, his gestures open.

"This is the man who led the military action – Colonel Vance Packard."

Each of the human beings in the Oval Office stared at the newly introduced chimera.

"While our action was, admittedly, abrupt, we intended it to be quick and precise," Winter went on.

"That's right," Colonel Packard sat forward on the couch, the crease in his military pants remaining unaffected. He placed one hand on his knee and gestured freely with the other. "That's right, the presence – which would have been alarming for you – was there. We sought to negotiate. When that didn't work, we removed it." Packard nodded and ran a hand unconsciously over the top of his tight crew-cut. "Fortunately, we can say no humans were harmed in any way during this operation."

"Any witnesses?" Levchin piped in.

"None ma'am."

Ben gazed at Allen, whose expression was pleasant and neutral. Winter's expression was also poised, although Ben could discern faint signs of irritation at the colonel's hands-on style.

"What was all this about?" Exasperated, the President shifted his body forward.

Winter raised his hand slightly to stay any comments from Colonel Packard.

"I must say, to our surprise, we detected a presence, a harmful presence for you in the location of Daly City, California."

"A harmful presence?" The President sought confirmation.

"Yes."

"In Daly City, California?"

"Yes."

The President sat back, resting against the couch, "Are there any other 'presences'?"

"No, Mr. President. We were surprised at finding this one," Winter was rueful, "we intensified our screening effort and found no others on the planet."

"But, you acted unilaterally?" Rose Levchin was smiling at Jonathan. With her Socratic question posed, she waited for his response.

"Time was of the essence," Winter maintained his rueful tone, "we needed to remove this real threat for you all."

"Had to be done," Steve hands on his knees and leaning closer to the credenza, chimed in. "These guys – er, this presence – it wasn't a good thing."

The President turned to look at Allen, and blinked.

Levchin cleared her throat, prompting each of the attendees to look at her.

"Of course, your action was unilateral, a complete surprise to us and an attack on US soil. It was an act of war."

Levchin had concentrated her small frame upright on the couch, her hands remained folded on her lap. The small open smile on her face was steady, as was her stare at the Callers. The Callers seemed to sway, while seated on the couch. They were processing what she just said, Ben thought to himself.

240

"Ma'am?" Colonel Packard opened from the Caller side.

"Again," Secretary Levchin began in clipped mid-Atlantic, "we bear the effects of this fundamental asymmetry in our relationship. We are transparent and available to you, you disclose nothing with us. You now act unilaterally and carry out an attack on US territory..." Levchin turned to look at President Rasmussen. Ben had Levchin's profile in view. She looked Grecian and oracular – her dark red hair, nacreous complexion, her mouth painted red from the lipstick she favored. The President sucked in air, expanding his large diaphragm and let it out in a whoosh between his teeth.

"This was a violation of our national sovereignty, gentlemen."

"Of course, we understand," Winter's tone was warm and sympathetic. He did look like Don Cheadle, Ben thought. God, how could you not like Don Cheadle? "We truly wish it hadn't been the case," Winter continued.

"But it was," the President interjected plainly, "you guys made a mess. Allegedly saving the planet, but there's details that you'll share with us."

"That's it precisely," Levchin agreed.

"Plus," the President was not through, "there has been, pardon my language," the President grimaced and gesticulated, the presidential haunches hugging the edge of the couch, "serious blow-back shit affecting me directly – and my administration."

"Yes, sir, of course," Winter was solicitous.

"The conspiracy theorists are trying to pin this on Sybylline – Jesus..." the President shook his head. "As far as I know – and I'm pretty sure I know – we've never had anything like this in Daly City, although I guess that's orthogonal to the current situation in any event." the President looked momentarily quizzical, then hardened again. "You have to clean this shit up, make it go away."

Winter gazed directly at the President, who had folded his arms across his chest.

"Sir, I think we can take care of this situation for you," Winter lobbed back.

"We'll be able to dope the data, sir," that was Allen. "It will confound your analytical types. They'll think of it as a strange but natural phenomenon."

"Good," the President had stood up from the couch and extended his hand to the three Callers. "Please take care of this, gentlemen. And no more surprises."

_ CHAPTER 42

Ben was at McShiksal's for lunch. He had decided to take a personal day – just for the hell of it, and Casey was okay with it. Was even jovial about it, "Go ahead, we're caught up," he said. "Have fun!"

Ben liked McShiksal's, yet another kit pub close to the Ballston stop. The sandwiches were really good and he felt ready and inclined to indulge his ur-need for gluten, sinus inflammation be damned. What was also nice was that he had cadged for himself a lazy Friday and a three-day weekend. Idle choice sat him at the bar, where he sat comfortably, elbows resting on the dark polished wood. He ordered a roast turkey sandwich on a Kaiser, with the works, noting to himself casually that the tryptophan effects from the turkey might be pleasant. June, the waitress who had taken his order, was warm – a nice kid, Ben thought. Funny, June's a 'kid' now. I'm thirty-plus, not so much of a kid and already divorced, already through that weird washing machine. Ben stared at his Diet Coke. Kids go through divorce; kids aren't named respondents in a divorce settlement, though. The image of Mae's business-like expression creased and folded Ben's mind. His thoughts changed rail and he began thinking about Brenda, which brightened his feelings.

Her demeanor was always merry, her body sexy and earthy, her presence so compelling for him. Ben thought about their tickling games and their kissing games. I guess I'm not *always* that analytical. Like a dashboard light, a stray thought registered that he hadn't been able to see Brenda during the last couple of weeks. They had had some quick phone chats, texting, email exchanges. All nice enough, fun and heartening for Ben. He loved Brenda's brio, her turn of phrase, wryness and humor. He liked his description – Brenda's brio – he liked the alliteration. Felt silly and guilty about that. But she was so busy. They hadn't been able to make a connection in a while. Hopefully, this will let up soon, Ben thought. She was focused on her work, seeming to try and catch at something, and Ben understood and conceded that. She was also uninterruptedly curious about what he did and was doing, so he had to deflect that too, which he did with a consistent milquetoast response, being general and vague. This would frustrate her at times, so Ben would then have to explain in a clear, solemn – but not unfriendly – tone, that his work was classified, compelling him to be very hush hush about it. Brenda would smirk and shake her head at this feint, but note that she understood, which would prompt Ben to make light and mug for the camera a bit, which lifted her mood and eased his own baseline anxiety. This generally worked.

They did generally enjoy each other's company, but she'd been elusive and Ben felt a little lonely thinking about it. June brought over Ben's sandwich, which was served on a flat cutting board and garnished with a pickle. Coleslaw and a large flute glass of French fries completed the order. Ben reasoned that if he shifted his next run from three-miles to five-miles he should neutralize the effect.

"Do you want me to top up that Diet Coke, Ben?"

"Oh great, yeah, um please, thanks June," Ben nodded appreciatively. June smiled back and poured. Ben looked along the bar and focused on the wall-mounted wide screen TV, which flickered and summoned his true heart. Brenda appeared on the TV with the Bloomberg attribution under her image. The screen flicked to the Bloomberg commentator, then back to Brenda. She was responding in an even tone, her face confident. Her voice was friendly and familiar to Ben. It was the same one she'd use when discussing where they might want to go to eat. It was also very clear and on-point. Ben watched and listened.

"Brenda, this is indeed interesting – the development you've just unearthed," the commentator leaned his body forward in a way that implied growing interest.

"That's right, Steve. Bloomberg News has learned that the military official..." An image of Colonel Packard appeared on the screen, showing him approaching the West Wing entrance. It was definitely Packard, Ben acknowledged. Ben could see in high resolution the striding Packard, name tag evident, his face, complete with trim mustache, visible. "...an apparent US Army colonel named Vance Packard who met with the President last week, is recorded in the White House log. His identity, though, has not been acknowledged in any of the branches of the US military."

"Very unusual. Brenda, can you elaborate?" The silver-haired commentator had corrected his posture and was now looking directly into the camera.

"That's right, no official acknowledgement from the US military." Brenda paused for effect, then continued. "Bloomberg News approached US branch sources for confirmation on Colonel Packard. They have no record of him, they have no idea who he is."

"Hmm...and the White House?"

"White House sources have no comment," Brenda was ever so slightly rocking back and forth on her feet, plainly enjoying this, "other than to say they believe Colonel Packard is who he says he is."

"Well...very interesting – and weird," the commentator noted.

"There's something else, Steve." Brenda raised an eyebrow. "Bloomberg News researched the name Vance Packard further. We did in fact find one entry..."

"And, anything material?"

"There actually was a Vance Packard, an author and social commentator. Packard wrote a book back in the 1950s called, *The Hidden Persuaders*."

"Interesting..." the Bloomberg man chewed thoughtfully at the end of a pen cap.

"Packard's book dealt with advertisers and their increasing

use of psychology and subliminal selling tactics. It stirred up a lot of controversy at the time..."

"Hmm, very interesting, and again, umm – weird."

"I know, isn't it?" Brenda was smiling.

Ben had taken a bite out of his sandwich, but wasn't chewing.

"Well, we have the mysterious Vance Packard, and we have a cryptic White House, and dubious new technologies, and Daly City, and Sybylline..." the Bloomberg news commentator gazed directly into the camera. "Where this all leads? It's anyone's guess."

Now hale, the commentator signed off, "Excellent reporting, Brenda. Keep us posted!"

"Sure thing, Steve."

"Fuck," Ben muttered, as he pushed himself away from the bar and headed outside to make a call.

CHAPTER 43

Ben found himself gripping the armrests of the faux-federal style armchair in which he was sitting. He was in Casey's office. It was mid-morning on Monday – a relaxed time for a conference call – not the usual 7:00am or 7:30am intensity. Oh, for some acrid coffee, a bagel, or a Danish; well, maybe afterwards. It was still a more relaxed time to have this call. Yet, Ben felt a nervous energy, generated organically, internally, but also building from his proximity to Casey, who was also nervous. Casey was a Watergate baby and sensitive to the still-new media-drawn connection between the Oval Office and Colonel Packard, a military chimera.

"These things build," Casey muttered, then related in step-wise fashion the bungled plumbers' break-in to Nixon's final helicopter ride. Casey had been able to connect with Allen on Friday, but the Callers were still blasé about it. Casey had wanted to address this quickly with "all hands, on deck", which was effectively just the four of them – Casey and Ben and the two Callers. Casey mentioned that Allen was soothing. "This can wait until Monday", he had apparently said, Steve agreed to a con-call then.

So, Ben sat there, just a little nervous, as Jim keyed in the call numbers on the little standing Samsung. The phone was set on speaker and whirred into life.

"Hi," it was Allen.

"Great, thanks Steve, thanks for joining the call," Casey was rubbing the back of his neck, while staring at the Samsung. Ben noticed Casey's white buzz cut, it seemed more bristly than usual.

"Is Jonathan there with you?"

"Oh yeah, we're both here."

"Yeah, hi Jim," that was Winter's lower, more mellifluous tone.

"Great, gentlemen, I know you are aware. We have a current pressing issue..."

"You mean the Packard thing."

Ben leaned in closer to hear Steve's tenor register.

"Yeah, it's a thing," Casey put an emphasis on "thing", he would not be put into context.

"Yeah, we've been thinking about it a lot, actually..." Allen trailed off.

"Jim, this is Jonathan. We have given this thought, as Steve mentioned," Winter conveyed control.

"So, your thoughts?"

"We spoke with some of our people, folks who specialize in you guys..." Winter's tone resonated clearly through the Samsung.

"It's a news-cycle issue," Allen chimed in.

"Well, ahem, yes, as Steve just said. Basically, it's a news-cycle issue."

"Which means...?" Casey was quizzical.

"Which means this is going to go away," Winter's voice was reassuring.

"On the face of it, the situation is pretty weird, but," Allen raised his voice for emphasis, "the White House will stand pat. All they know is that Packard was mid-level army brass – they'll stick to it. It's safer and easier. As for the US military, they can still say they have no records. It's easier for them, and the beauty part: it's truthful."

Ben perked up further and leaned forward, "But won't the two stories still conflict?"

"Not to worry, and not really," Allen began to sound overweening. "Remember, the US Army will be telling the truth. They have no records of this guy."

"So, this will be good...?"

"Sure it will, nobody needs to be caught in a lie."

"Which is good, I suppose..." Casey needed more.

"The military flacks can 'intimate' that yet-to-be-confirmed Colonel Packard is involved in classified matters..." The speaker on the Samsung's other end paused for effect. "The President *is* allowed to confer with advisors on classified matters..."

"Gentlemen?" Winter now jumped in, "The news-cycle will mature on this item – rather quickly, so our internal experts tell us... What we'd like to do now - update you on what concerns Daly City."

"Thank you." Casey sounded gravelly to Ben. "We'll take your word on it, regarding the news cycle, I guess...We're all ears about Daly City." Casey and Ben looked at each other to confirm a united listening front.

"Our people are working on this," was once again mellifluous, "we're intent on steering your scientific community's perceptions and analysis toward the conclusion of a natural phenomenon, albeit one that may be considered quite extraordinary."

"We're doping the data," it was Allen now. "They'll actually love it. It'll generate a lot of grants."

Casey smiled with his mouth closed, lowering and shaking his head. He was always amazed at Caller knowledge of human arcana.

"Indeed, we have recourse to information and data your scientists detect, record and analyze," both Ben and Casey detected some exasperation in Winter's voice. "We will be able to influence clearly the conclusions they reach. No need, really, to go into further details, Jim."

"Just stay tuned," Allen chimed in again. "We're in the process of implementing."

Casey smiled and looked at Ben, who was surprised that his own mood was lightening.

"That does relieve my mind, I'll convey that discreetly to the President," Casey responded.

"Great, great, anything else on your side?" Winter's baritone sounded lighter as well.

Casey looked at Ben, who shyly shook his head, "No, I think we covered the important items. I think we're good here."

"Great, that's good, that's good to hear. Reach out on anything else."

"Thanks guys, for setting aside time."

"No worries, our pleasure. I'm glad we could sort through this stuff together. Jim, Ben, take care," Winter signed off and the Callers dropped off the call.

Casey leaned across his desk and cradled the Samsung into his pocket. He sat back, folding his hands behind, "Well, they've begun the clean-up process."

Ben rubbed his face, was grimacing, "Can they really be that effective?"

Casey's gaze shifted from the ceiling to Ben at eye level, "I think so, I think they can, I think they can..." he began scratching his chin.

"But, I mean, tampering with the seismic – I guess – data. And the whole Packard thing. Do you believe that?"

"To answer the second question first – never underestimate the ability of a bureaucracy to obfuscate – so yes, I do share their view, and I agree: The news-cycle means the whole thing will begin to peter out..." Casey began to scratch the back of his neck, "On the data issue, well Ben, you've seen – and I've certainly seen – that they have the technology, the wherewithal, that's conducive to a lot of deus ex machina stuff. I'm sure they'll be able to do it."

Ben couldn't shake the incredulity. "Really, you think they can do this? We're talking about a lot of stuff – geophysical evidence, hard copy printouts, electronic bookmarks, files, electronic files, data dumps, data dissemination..."

Jim ran a hand over the coarse bristle of his buzz cut, "Yeah, I think they can do it."

_ CHAPTER 44

"You know, I should really call him," thigh resting against gunmetal gray desk, she leaned and thought out loud. "But, I've been so effing busy," Brenda explained to herself and her colleague, Susanne, a sympathetic and competitive woman, who was seated at the same work station. Susanne enjoyed Brenda's confidences. She looked up smiling, showing her own telegenic expression, this time fun and conspiratorial, capturing Brenda's.

"Well, Ben sounds really cute, I have to say, and sweet and focused on what he does, and cuddly."

"Like a rabbit."

"Like a rabbit? See what I mean? I'm jealous Brenda," Susanne giggled and smiled more broadly.

"He's a bit strange..." Brenda was quieter, reflecting again.

"Aren't they all?" Susanne was still smiling, coaxing.

"Yeah, you're right about that," Brenda shrugged for her friend and leaned more heavily against the desk. She kept her arms folded and breathed in deeply. She turned her torso slightly to look more squarely at Susanne then smiled, as if a pleasant, encouraging thought had crossed her mind. Susanne reflexively smiled, sensing something was very good, indeed. But Brenda's gaze then changed, her eyes seemed now opaque and without expression, startling Susanne. Brenda placed the flat of her hand on the desk top to support herself; she began gasping, her gaze now fixed beyond her colleague.

"Brenda?"

Brenda Donovan's body stood still, but began to waver on its foundational supports.

"Brenda, Brenda honey! Are you okay?"

Brenda gasped and coughed, with her free hand she snatched at her blouse collar. She coughed again, making a guttural sound, but couldn't speak. Her features began to contract and she winced, seemingly in pain. Susanne watched as Brenda's legs gave way. Her head and neck went loose and her cheek smashed against the edge of the desk surface as she fell down. She settled prone on the durable, scotch-guarded carpeting, and was still.

"Brenda!"

Heads turned from computer screens and conversation circles. "What? What's up? What happened?"

Susanne was still sitting down, but she leaned forward to peer over the front edge of her desk. She held the fingers of her right hand over her mouth and started to cry.

"Jesus, she had a seizure or something."

A small crowd gathered around the desk space.

"Did you hear that sound, when she fell?"

"That was her head hitting the desk," someone else said. More people shuffled toward the scene.

"Guys, give her room..." Susanne was now composed and stood up trying to instill order. She went round the other side of the desk to kneel by the body of her prone friend. Two male colleagues joined her.

"Let's cushion her head," one said.

"No, no, stop," the second interjected, "she may have damaged her neck, spine." He crouched and reached over to feel Brenda's forehead. Susanne knelt closer to smooth and brush away hair that had fallen over part of Brenda's face.

"Did someone call 911 yet?"

"I think so..."

"Please do it!"

Susanne gazed at Brenda's face, now more fully visible, revealing the gash she had suffered from the fall. The wound was already swelling and darkening. Brenda's eyes were shut tightly, as if she didn't want to see what was happening around her.

Her breathing had become ragged. The talking and murmuring around her and the desk space had begun to die down. Everyone was just looking at her.

—

Ben showed up early, as he always did, to the office. He loved the security of it. But the image of Timmy and Carole standing just by the office bullpen, that was weird, jarring the usual morning comfort.

"Uh, hi guys, great seeing you here, Carole." Ben was polite but confused.

"Oh Ben..." Carole took a step forward, prompting Ben to stare at her. She laced her laced her fingers together, almost as a way of preventing herself from hugging Ben until the full news had been related.

"Hey Carole, what's up?"

"Ben, have you heard? Did anyone call you?"

Ben directed his gaze to Timmy, who grimaced and looked down.

"No, I mean, why? What was I supposed to have heard?" Ben asked, worry beginning to creep in.

"Brenda passed away last night," Timmy blurted out.

"What...what are you talking about?" Ben said disbelievingly, yet automatically distancing himself and therefore remaining calm.

Timmy and his supportive wife began speaking in turn. Carole unlaced her fingers and showed the palms of her hands.

"Brenda died yesterday – late in the afternoon. I'm so sorry." Carole said, her voice cracking as she reached for Ben, giving her nonplussed friend a tight hug.

"Gosh, umm, are you sure?"

"Yes, I'm so sorry, yes," Carole nodded tearfully.

Timmy stepped up and wrapped his arm around Carole to give her a squeeze.

"Carole only found out about it at yoga last night. There were some Bloomberg people there, they told her about it. It was a complete shock, so fucking strange..." Timmy murmured, summarizing.

"This is real? Brenda's gone?" It suddenly penetrated. Ben gripped the bridge of his nose and shook his head. His own strangeness momentarily buffered the impact, as his strangeness had done with different things throughout his life. His broken marriage, among other life events, all wove their way through a membrane that protected a person like Ben, who could learn and assimilate a lot, but who could also be easily overwhelmed.

"Yeah, it's terrible, buddy," Timmy breathed in and exhaled. "The Bloomberg folks told Carole that Brenda had a sudden, fatal heart attack, something to do with her hypertrophic cardiomyopathy." Brenda's condition reeled off the tongue for Timmy, ever the analyst reading documents. "That's what the ER told them." Timmy showed a tight close-lipped smile. "That's what Brenda's friends had told Carole. I looked it up. It's congenital – simply put, the heart degrades and fails. Effects young people mostly. Totally fucked up," Timmy said, patting Ben's shoulder.

"Hi everyone! Oh man, looks pretty somber here, what happened?" It was Casey, cheerful in his Sierra Club version of business casual. He had emerged from the office hallway and was striding toward the group.

"Oh, hi, I'm Carole, Timmy's wife, we've had to bring some terrible news for Ben."

"Jesus, what happened?" His bright pebble eyes widening, Jim surveyed a visibly saddened Timmy and Ben, who looked still and quiet.

"Hi, I'm Jim, love your husband, great guy to work with...what's going on?"

Carole's voice descended to almost a whisper, "Ben's girlfriend, she was so sweet – she died yesterday! Such a shock." Carole continued, now in full whisper, "We came to check on Ben, we had to tell him."

"How?" Blue eyes wider still, Casey fished for elaboration.

Carole sighed and allowed her shoulders to relax, "Crazy heart attack, massive. She died almost in an instant." She shook her head, "Such an attractive girl – and so healthy!"

"Christ," Casey drew the corners of his mouth back. He looked down, and then moved toward Ben, reaching to touch him on the shoulder. "Ahh, man, I'm so sorry buddy," he continued patting Ben lightly, "sometimes the universe is really fucked up."

Ben rubbed an eye with the palm heel of one of his hands and returned a small smile.

"I'm still processing."

"It's okay, take some time. Take the time you need." Casey tried to be, and genuinely was, solicitous.

Carole stepped closer, genuinely caring toward the two people on earth assigned with coordinating the relationship between the US government and some kind of advanced interstellar civilization, though she didn't know that.

"Ben, I just wanna say that we are here for you. Timmy and I are here. We'll do whatever you need," Carole paused to take a short breath. "This is so tough, we're so sorry."

Ben relaxed his hand, dropped it from his face and stood smiling, as if a thought or an image had just streamed by, grabbing his attention. He had in fact been thinking – a range of thoughts. A sudden picture, the curvature of Brenda's hip and her full smile, produced an ache in him. She was gone now. He saw her laughing and happy – with him. How she loved to tease him, and laugh, and tussle and handle him. All of it washed through Ben. Carole gave him another hug.

_ CHAPTER 45

She hated humidity; it was everywhere and hanging along the entire eastern seaboard. A colleague had once suggested that it might be better to turn the entire Northeast into a national park or a reserve of some kind, given the unbearable summers. Of course, the suggestion came from someone at the far western Hoover Institution. Yet, how can anyone live here?

The woman mopped the sides and back of her neck, pushing against her dark red hair. She stopped for a second, adjusted and smoothed her navy skirt, and then plunged into the mass of air-conditioned space in the Park Avenue office building. She was alone, having told her small security detail to find a cool spot for some coffee. The striding woman in the lobby was small and slight, but directed. Clear green eyes took in the lobby's expanse as she made her way through the largely open area. Then, through security, up the elevator bank, through a succession of minders and then into a corner office kept at 65 degrees. She was let in, and stood before the doyen of American foreign policy. A bright, brown bear of a man, hailing originally form Fuerth, Bavaria, and coming onto the American scene via Washington Heights, rose from his desk, with halting effort, and extended his hand.

"Madame Secretary, a pleasure!" His small blue eyes shone behind bi-focal lenses. He stepped around his desk to get closer to Rose and gently shook her hand. Levchin smiled, felt the urge to curtsey, but did not.

"Herr Doktor," she trilled the r's, the consonants and vowels were Russian inflected.

"Come Rose, this way," the welcoming, portly man indicated an arrangement of two stuffed chairs and a small polished, circular wooden table between them, situated at the opposite corner of the office. Large windows met at that seam, providing a view of the city from that Park Avenue vantage. Someone had also brought in a coffee service, without Levchin noticing as she greeted Dr. Kissinger. It was stationed by the table. Kissinger was smiling, and looking at her with warm, if slightly rheumy eyes.

"I thought it would be nice to chat over some coffee," he offered in the famous, rumbling basso profundo.

"Thank you, Dr. Kissinger." Levchin seated herself.

"Please, Henry," Kissinger said, waving his hand forward in a self-deprecating way. He seated himself and then decanted a cup of coffee for Levchin. She eschewed his offer of milk and sugar. Kissinger poured himself a coffee, and sat back heavily in his chair, resting his hands on his knees. He was smiling fully and evenly and looked genuinely pleased to see Rose Levchin. Rose sipped her coffee, taking it black.

"Dr. Kissinger, Henry, thank you so much for setting aside time to meet on such short notice," Rose crossed and re-crossed her legs.

"I'm an old man," Kissinger rumbled, "with a large and mostly empty office. People are courteous to me, and largely ignore me these days." He waved a turned-up palm and continued smiling. "Oddly and funnily enough, I seem to have nothing but time now," he confided, hunching closer to the table.

"What can I do for you?"

"The Callers," Levchin declared, "I must discuss them with you."

Kissinger sat still in his chair, his watery blue eyes shone, smile still in place.

"Of course, I see, I expected as much. Things have been happening." Kissinger lowered his head and peered at the table top.

"Precisely, Doctor," Levchin nodded, "you were there from the start, so I've been told. I would love to hear your views, have your guidance."

"I know, the dynamic seems to have changed. Something Nixon and I feared would happen." Kissinger turned his gaze from Levchin and began surveying midtown Manhattan far below.

"So, it seems, so it seems, Herr Doktor," Levchin's gaze did not waver from Kissinger's solid presence.

"When I saw the news, saw the reporting of that incident in California, I knew it was them."

"Just so, they told us it was an attack to protect us. Of course, we have no real knowledge, no leverage..." Levchin laid her hands palms down on the little round table.

Kissinger had still been staring out the window, as Levchin was speaking. He shifted his position and his gaze. His mood had somehow brightened, maybe because of the quick recall of a memory.

"Is Jim Casey still there? I believe he is, right?"

"Dr. Casey, why yes, of course he is," Levchin nodded to Kissinger.

"Yes, that's good. I had heard Oberkotter had passed a few years ago," Kissinger mused to himself.

"This man I did not know," Levchin drawled, "Casey has a young man, a new assistant, to help him."

Kissinger nodded mutely.

The old man straightened the glasses on the bridge of his nose, so as to stare more intently at his interlocutor. "Rose, had you ever wondered why this force, these *things* – how else can one put it? – why we called them 'the Callers'?"

"I was told, and I imagine, that it was a particular fancy of President Nixon's," Levchin sounded diffident.

"Yes, you're right, it was Nixon's idea. But I don't think you know why?" Kissinger became more animated and leaned toward the table.

"No sir, I must say I do not," Rose confessed.

The intensity leached somewhat from Kissinger's face. He

smiled, mostly to himself. "Well, why indeed. You know, President Nixon came from – he grew up in – a small southern California town, one called Yorba Linda…" Kissinger seemed reflective, yet prone to expatiate. His rumbling and subdued Germanic tone was soothing. Levchin steeled herself against sleep.

"That's very interesting," she said, not knowing why. Maybe to be agreeable, something that surprised her.

"Yes, I think so, too," Kissinger continued. "So, as I was saying, our man Nixon," his voice became lighter, "was from this little town, a farming town, really. Nixon had had a hard life as a child, at least in some ways. The family ranch failed." Kissinger paused, appeared bemused, gathered his thoughts. "But, Nixon's family rallied – they were Quakers and lived by their faith. They moved to nearby Whittier, which had a large Quaker community at the time. The family managed to open a gas station and grocery, and made a go of it." Kissinger looked becalmed, and smiled. Having concluded, in Levchin's view, this baffling anecdote, Kissinger rested against the back of his chair and laced his fingers together in the form of a steeple, gazing warmly at Rose.

"Richard Nixon was a brilliant, cunning man. Of course, very paranoid, too. But then we all were – grasping and paranoid," Kissinger seemed wistful. "With all that – rather useful – animal cunning, Nixon also had a rather developed sense of propriety," Kissinger continued gazing at Levchin, now with almost a sense of wonder. "I think it all boiled down to his upbringing," Kissinger explained, "as so many things do." He took a small sip of coffee. "It certainly shaped his sense of metaphor."

Rose arched an eyebrow at Kissinger's last remark, prompting him to smile more broadly.

"You see, here was this new very powerful presence before us, this unknown and unknowable interlocutor – seemingly benevolent, but for how long? To what extent? We had no way of knowing…" Kissinger's voice trailed off and he ran his hand over coarse wavy hair, momentarily lost in thought, before continuing

"So, Nixon reasoned that this powerful new presence should be treated decorously – like someone invited to the front room or parlor of his childhood family home. We, with our beautiful blue planet, would entreat and engage with this formidable new suitor, this gentleman caller – just as any connubial woman from a fine upstanding family of Nixon's childhood would have. Careful not to spurn, but manage, such a consequential beau." Kissinger raised his eyebrows to elicit some response from the listening Levchin.

"So, this was your status quo." Levchin had taken it all in. She gazed at the old man.

"Our modus vivendi, modus *operandi*, rather," Kissinger insisted on specifics. "Yes Rose, we wanted to engage with them, entreat with them, as they seemed to wish. And obviously, we were terrified. Our hope, what Nixon and I wanted, was to engage with them, as they seemed to want, thereby precluding anything else that they might seek to do."

Levchin sighed for effect and took a breath, "But of course. Dr. Kissinger, circumstances have changed."

"They have, I know, just as we feared they might," Kissinger closed his eyes, for a moment appearing the mystic. "There's not much I can say – I can only counsel you simply." The old man breathed in and exhaled slowly through his nostrils, as he had done habitually, when he was a smoker decades ago.

"You must continue to engage, maintain dialogue with the Callers," Kissinger opened his eyes and gazed levelly at Levchin. "Such a fundamental power asymmetry between ourselves and the Callers precludes anything else, Madame Secretary."

"Although I do wonder, Dr. Kissinger," Levchin countered, "the circumstances have become much more complicated. The Caller attack marks a revelation, don't you think so?"

Kissinger returned her stare. Incongruously, Levchin thought, he glanced at his wrist watch. The old man sipped from his coffee, then paused.

"Circumstances are different, but do not cajole. Maintain the status quo."

_ CHAPTER 46

Ben sat at the Logan terminal for his fight back to Washington. He sat there with a roller board and newspaper editions piled onto the seat next to him. He liked physical papers and there, neatly re-arranged after initial reading, were the *Post*, the *WSJ*, the *FT* and the *New York Times*. Ben still subscribed online to these publications – he was on omnivore for news. But for any travel excursion, he liked to buy and handle the physical copies. It was a more immediate physical experience, more comprehensive, more associative. His eye was able to skip more easily across the open printed page, acting on an item of interest in one place, seeing how it tied in with another place on the page. That was harder to do on an iPhone and or iPad screen. He loved the indulgence of print on paper.

The papers were there stacked neatly beside him; he wasn't sure if he would take any of them on the plane. He had already consumed most of their content; having arrived so early for his flight, he had ample time to read. Ben loved arriving early; he loved the steady-state, comforting boredom of waiting for a flight. And he always loved airports, they conveyed adventure to him, providential comings and goings. He loved to wonder. Brenda's face appeared in his mind and he took a sip from his fourth cup of Starbucks that morning. She was smiling, as if she could see him now. She looked capable and impatient to Ben. Her certainty and confidence pinned him for a moment to the back of his plastic waiting area chair. He was a reader but failed to "read" things. He missed social cues, emotional depth, so Brenda would tell him, critiquing and instructing. Her patience was finite, but she loved to laugh – at, and with him..

Ben knew he could be dense, *was* dense. To mitigate, he copied and adapted, and tried. He sought to self-actualize. I'm hanging in there, Ben thought. He sighed, took another sip from his coffee, then paused and said to himself in a soft voice, barely audible, "It's crazy that I got into Stanford."

He sat his coffee down, oddly deftly, balanced precariously on the curvature of the other plastic chair beside him. The memorial service for Brenda had been strange for Ben. It had been held at her folks' home in Newton, Massachusetts. Her remains had been cremated and preserved reverently in a blue celadon vase, which now rested on the fireplace mantel of the family home. Any deep emotion, or mourning, seemed oddly absent. Maybe it was because the family was originally from Wisconsin? Maybe it was because they didn't show a lot of negative emotion there? Ben shook his head and touched his temple. No, it was just kind of strange, that's all. Her folks definitely seemed to love Brenda and they definitely fawned over him. They told Ben that he had made Brenda happy, was a blessing for her, which made him glow. Her parents were nice balanced people, as Brenda always remarked that they were. They were, if anything, happy at the change Brenda undoubtedly made in the spiritual sense. Maybe it was all a Catholic thing? Ben couldn't say, though there had been a priest there and a lot of guitar music for effect. Some friends from Tufts and Bloomberg were there and said some wonderful things about Brenda. Ben even surprised himself and shared with the group what he really loved about her – her humor, her joy (her sensuality he kept to himself). It was so good, Ben thought, that Timmy and Carole had been there, as well. They were such good friends. He smiled at the thought of them.

A shift in the mounted overhead TV screen caught Ben's attention. It was a live CNN update. On the screen, a man with thick, somewhat coarse, dark hair and a penetrating gaze framed by rimless glasses was declaring something to the interviewer. The talking man was an authority, there was a screen label indicating his affiliation with Cal-Berkeley and the American Geophysical

Union. The volume for the TV had been set low and Ben had to lean closer to listen. A few travelers walking by the gate paused to focus on the screen as well. As the Cal professor was speaking to the interviewer, the language lapsed into technical jargon, prompting apologies to the interviewer and the viewing audience. The guy really looks like Trotsky, Ben thought. Trotsky was actually a pretty good-looking guy, he mused absently. Somehow, the sound picked up from the screen. The images shifted from the professor to an abstract map of the Bay Area and to a more detailed map of Daly City and then back to the professor.

"Based on our latest findings," the professor seemed to be concluding, "and after having scrubbed, or rather checked more closely the data we have..." Ben and the people around him listened closely. "...we're making at least a provisional judgment that the Daly City incident was certainly an unusual event – even anomalous – but well within the consideration of geophysical phenomena we have analyzed from earth history."

"Does this still signal a near-term quake event for San Francisco and the Bay Area overall?" the interviewer queried.

"Ah, well, I can't really say that," the Trotsky-like professor pushed on the bridge of his glasses. "Daly City was an idiosyncratic event, umm...that is very particular, something that stands alone, by itself. We'll just have to keep a monitor on seismic conditions, Jim." Trotsky smiled and pushed again at his glasses.

"With that, let me say thank you, Dr. Hasenpfeffer, for these illuminating comments. That was Dr. Felix Hasenpfeffer with some re-assuring news, perhaps," Jim smiled and nodded to the viewing audience.

The screen cut to a commercial. Ben smiled to himself. The Callers had been able to "dope" the data. Daly City was now a natural earth phenomenon, so the experts agreed. The Caller trail had been airbrushed away. What couldn't these guys do? Ben questioned, not wholly rhetorically.

Someone from the airline announced over the loudspeaker that the shuttle would be boarding. The announcement roused Ben and he gathered his roller board and papers, dispatching the papers to recycling. He had forgotten his coffee, which stayed poised precariously in the curvature of the seat well beside where he had been sitting. Ben got into line and ambled forward, as tickets were screened. The announcement and boarding process jostled at an association in memory in his head. He had recalled to himself Brenda's funny usage, when they were traveling, whether it was to Charleston or San Francisco. Brenda would always say to Ben that they had to get going, because the plane was "loading", not boarding. "Loading." That was funny, Ben smiled to himself, and handed over his boarding pass to be processed.

_ CHAPTER 47

Running was a form of moving meditation (with due attention to traffic). The humidity was clearing and Ben had started keeping his daily regimen again. It was his routine, clocking miles before really beginning his activities. It was something he had been doing since high school, when a PE teacher and coach noted Ben's impervious constitution to pain and reasonable speed. Broadly, it was athleticism. It may have helped him get into Stanford.

Ben was gliding past the Ballston stop, then past the Methodist church, which sped by to his left. There was the feeling of autumn in the air, with Arlington now leeched of humidity and the remains of summer. Ben felt calm and moved quickly toward his apartment.

"Ben!" The voice behind him was clear.

He kept going, but slowed his pace to a shy confused trot. He could hear that someone was ambling closer to him. His senses told him that whatever it was had gotten closer. He made a diffident turn, raising his eyes to look. There was Brenda.

Ben stared, rooted to the spot. He couldn't help but beam at what definitely seemed to be Brenda. But fear held him in place.

Brenda was laughing. Wow, she looked great, Ben thought incongruously.

There must've been some gross mistake – her family and everyone thought she was gone, when she really wasn't. There were her ashes, in that vase, on the fireplace mantel at her folks' home... But here she was. Brenda walked slowly toward the immobile Ben and gave him a light kiss on the cheek.

"Ben, I'm so glad..." she sighed happily and hugged him. He felt the smooth skin of her cheek against his. He could feel her warmth against his own sweat-sodden t-shirt. She squeezed Ben. "So good to see you." Brenda rocked with Ben to and fro.

"God, you're alive?" Ben gripped her and stretched his arms out from his shoulders, holding her as if he were holding a picture and drawing perspective.

"Well, yes, I am," Brenda smiled in response, winsomely pushing her hair away from her face and smoothing the front of her pantsuit. She looked like she was be meeting Ben for a coffee during any normal work day.

"Brenda, I mean..." Ben shrugged to himself, stared absently over her shoulder, beyond her, "what *happened*?"

Brenda produced a closed-lipped smile and lowered her gaze for a moment.

"Well, Ben, we know you've been talking to some people, very special people."

The penny dropped and Ben saw that he wasn't talking to Brenda anymore, not the Brenda he thought he knew, at least.

"What do you mean? I'm not sure I understand," Ben replied automatically. Part of him was stalling for time, though the rest of him wasn't really aware of that.

"Ben, I am like them, those people. I am different, but I am like them." Brenda playfully poked at Ben's chest. She appeared cheerful, just like the old Brenda. "I have so much to tell you, Ben." An expression of wonder formed on her face. She looked friendly, not so ominous. Not like it had seemed just a moment ago.

"That's why I want to, I *need* to, meet your friends, your colleagues, I need to meet them and tell them, describe to them..."

"Whom? Whom do you need to meet?" Ben wanted specifics.

"Those who are talking to the special people," Brenda's expression was wondrous, "I would like to meet your President, Mr. Rasmussen, his very vivid female helper, and the old man who is your good friend. These people I must meet."

'Brenda' finished her declaration and smiled broadly at Ben. Her speech had oddly taken on an ESL cadence to it, Ben thought, but it was soothing and drew him in. Ben found himself feeling comfortable and agreeable.

"We have so much to offer, Ben. So much to offer to you all," Brenda leaned forward and gave Ben a small kiss on the cheek. It seemed real enough. She returned Ben's stare with an earnest look.

"Maybe I can introduce these people, I probably can. How... how would I be able to reach you?" A very matter-of-fact question.

"That's very simple Ben, very simple," Brenda grinned and tilted her head to one side. "All you have to do is say, 'Brenda, please appear', three times in succession."

"Just say, 'Brenda, please appear', three times in a row?" Ben sounded tentative.

"That's right, three times. Much like your *Wizard of Oz* movie," Brenda nodded to him.

"Then you'll come?" Ben was still dubious.

"That's right, then I'll come. I'll hear, *we'll* hear you," Brenda nodded again. "Ben, I think I have to go now," Ben's Lazarus-like 'girlfriend' reached forward and hugged him, he could smell the tea rose that she always liked to wear. "I missed you so much, I'm so glad to see you now."

Brenda squeezed him, and then pulled her head back to look plainly into Ben's eyes. Ben gazed at the same merry eyes and the same full smile. It sure did look like her. She dropped her embrace and stepped back, surveying Ben and happily taking him in.

"Wonderful boy," she said lightly, almost to herself. "When you want to reach me Ben, just say – three times, in reasonable succession, 'Brenda, please appear.'"

Ben blinked, nodded, "'Brenda, please come', three times."

"That's right, just like that," she snapped her fingers, nodding and grinning.

"OK, I've got it, I think," Ben smiled wanly.

Beholding this strange creation before him, it was still great to see her, he confessed to himself.

"Well, I have to go now. So great to see you Ben, I love you!" Brenda said in a heartfelt and earnest tone – or so it seemed. Ben didn't believe, but allowed himself to believe. It was a strange encounter with God-knows-what, but it had been so nice.

"Goodbye Ben," Brenda smiled again, but looked mournful.

"So nice to see you!" Ben found himself exclaiming.

"Remember, three times," Brenda nodded to Ben.

"Okay, I've got it, three times."

Brenda blew a kiss at Ben, turned and began walking away. Ben smiled and waved faintly, but then became slack jawed from the encounter. He watched her walk down the sidewalk, just in front of the Methodist church, then disappear.

_ CHAPTER 48

"Motherrrfuckerrrr..."

Casey had breathed slowly over the phone to Ben, when Ben explained that his apparent girlfriend had just introduced another facet regarding discussions with other worlds.

It was actually something Casey had feared all this time: the introduction of other players, the resulting complexity, more unfathomable uncertainty...

During their conversation, Casey ratcheted down, becoming more stoical, adjusting to more of a lower def-con mode, Ben thought. The President would need to be called directly, which Casey would do. They would have to let the Callers know; Casey was confident about that interaction somehow.

Later, Ben found himself slipping quietly out of his own office en route to Casey's. Ben closed his office door, turned and bumped into Timmy, who must have made his way quietly down the hallway.

"Ben..."

Timmy looked down, shaking his head and lightly touched Ben's shoulder. "How are you, man? How are ya holding up?"

Ben just looked blankly at Timmy, "It's tough, yeah, it's tough..." he mustered a response. Recent events – the death and apparent re-animation of his girlfriend (which he kept to himself) had put Ben in a dazed state.

"You know," Timmy was elaborating, sincerely, "I haven't really connected with you after the service at Brenda's folks' house."

"It was beautiful."

"Yeah, it really was," Timmy recollected, smiling, "Brenda's folks were so kind and open. Anyway," he grew solemn, "just want to let you know," he squeezed Ben's shoulder again, "anything you need, anything we can do, just let Carole and me know."

"I know, man. I know," Ben maneuvered his body just to the right of Timmy, but held his gaze. "It means a lot."

"Okay, just know that. We're here for ya."

"Thanks, man."

Timmy sighed, but smiled, "Hey, plans for lunch?"

"No man, I'm free. I can come by your desk at 12:30pm, if that's good."

"Great, see you then." Timmy gave Ben a friendly nod and turned to head down the hallway. Ben made his way to Casey's office and slipped through the door, closing it quietly behind him. He saw his boss sitting upright at his desk. Ben noticed the white stubble on his cheeks and chin. His eyes were even more pebbly and brighter than they normally were, conveying a merry but focused attention. The Samsung was already in its cradle, positioned in the middle of Casey's desk. He exhaled, and smiled at Ben, while shifting a little in his seat. Ben took a seat in the functional metal chair opposite Casey's desk.

"Okay, great. Busy morning. We're first going to talk to Jonathan and Steve, then, after that call, we're going to call the President directly."

"The President?"

"Yep, I got a hold of him and the Callers after you gave me your news."

"What was the Caller reaction?" Ben leaned forward, curious. "Were they alarmed? Were they piqued?"

"Nope. Didn't tell 'em yet. I did tell the President. He was, if anything, weirdly cool about it. Like it was a new item in a business plan, or some new coding or something. Such a weird guy..." Casey bent his head and scratched the back of his neck.

"Wow, that's, umm, interesting. But why not the Callers?"

Casey leaned back and his arms toward his desk. "I'd like to get," he began stretching the length of his back, "as much of a sense of their..." he tilted his shoulder to his ear then brought it

271

back down, "...reaction as possible. They're sociable, they engage, but it could be weird. They're alien beings."

Casey straightened again and then gave a loud sigh. Big smile, eyes even brighter, "Shall we get to this?"

Ben nodded, smiling back at him, "Let's do this."

Casey keyed in the number sequence into the Samsung display, hit speaker, and then set it back in its cradle again. Ben heard the call whirr and then connect at the other end somewhere, where its mate was.

"Steve Allen," a flat, confident tone sounded through the little Samsung.

"Steve, great," Casey smiled at the phone, "I've got Ben with me. We really appreciate the time you guys are setting aside on such short notice."

"No problem, you're piquing our interest. I've got Jonathan with me here."

"Great, hi Jonathan."

"Gentlemen," the even baritone.

Casey glanced at Ben, and then at the Samsung, "Ben says 'hi' as well."

"Great, good. Glad to convene the call with you all," Allen was matter-of-fact and ready to begin. "So, what's up?"

Casey laced his fingers and rested then on the desk surface, "We believe this is important to share with you promptly." Casey glanced at Ben, and continued, "Ben had a very recent encounter with his girlfriend, whom he – we all – had believed to be deceased. Their conversation was revealing..." Casey trailed off.

"Just to clarify," Allen began to focus, "Ben's girlfriend – we're assuming she was human – had died. But she appeared out of the blue and spoke to Ben?"

Casey leaned toward Ben, "Ben, can you provide color on this?"

Ben sat forward in his chair, leaning more directly toward the speaker phone, "My impression had been that my girlfriend was human. My encounter and conversation with her, just recently, convinced me otherwise."

"Ben?" It was Winter, his voice low and calm, "to confirm, what was your girlfriend's name?"

"Brenda Donovan, she had been – whatever *she* is – a Bloomberg reporter."

"Righhht," Winter teased out the word, sounding thoughtful.

"We knew of your relationship with her, Ben – her presence and role with you. But we were not aware of her full extent, apparently."

Paper shuffling sounded through the Samsung, and some off-mic hushed exchange and discussion ensued.

"How can I put this?" Ben looked at Casey, who nodded encouragement back at him. "I think, I mean...in fact, I *know*. Brenda is a lot like you guys. She is from another world, that I can say."

"Like us, Ben?" Winter articulated slowly.

Ben stared at the Samsung and spoke clearly, "Yes, like you, like your representations to us. So realistic, yet she was, *is*, non-corporeal."

"What's intriguing for me, guys," Casey now chimed in with rhetorical support, "is that you didn't catch it."

There was more shuffling of paper and Allen's higher timbre voice came through the speaker, "You know, it's a big universe out there. A lot going on."

Ben sensed that the phone seemed to go on mute for a moment, then resumed, "So you're right, Jim. We didn't catch it. We were snowed, just like young Ben here." Allen seemed to emphasize the point. Ben blinked. He didn't disagree.

"Well, we have a pretty good idea whose efforts these are," Winter interjected, rallying the Callers and sounding paternal. The phone seemed to go on mute again; Casey and Ben looked at each other, Casey raised his eyebrows.

"Let's just admit to ourselves that things change, things move very quickly," it was Allen, striking a confident tone. "But we have a handle on it now, I think. It's not going to present any additional problems for us," Allen's tone resonated confidence.

Casey rested his forearms on the desk, "Can you elaborate more clearly?"

"Let's just say..." Allen paused. "It's sort of like... we'll be able to put another patch on our overall system approach, so to speak."

"Which of course leaves us still with the current situation," Winter spoke, clearly and mellifluously. "You are no longer terra incognita."

"That's right, that's right," Ben leaned toward the Samsung, Casey motioned his hand in a small roll to prompt Ben further.

"Brenda, I guess, conveyed the message. This new group would like to meet all of the principals. They'd like to open up discussions." Ben sat back and rested his hands on his lap. He nodded at Casey, who then leaned closer to the cradled phone.

"Actually, guys, I think it would be a good idea..." Casey left the sentence to hang, his own mouth was slightly ajar. The two human beings in that downtown Washington office received only silence over the speaker phone. There was an occasional shuffling of paper again, the faint sound of things being moved on a desk. Ben imagined that someone was writing something down.

"Okay, very well," it was Winter's voice.

"I'm glad. I'm glad you're amenable," Casey put an upbeat glaze on his reaction.

"If that's what you feel is the right thing," Winter intoned.

"Well, I think, yes. This is a good thing. I'd like to counsel the President to that effect."

"Well, okay then," Winter sounded accommodating, *was* accommodating, "we just want to help."

"Thanks gentlemen, much appreciated here. Ben and I will be

talking to the President promptly. I'll get back to you as soon as I can with next steps."

"Very good, as I said, keep us posted," Winter said matter-of-factly.

"Thanks, thanks for your time, gentlemen,"

"Okay, we'll hear from you soon."

"Sounds good, take care."

"Take care, so long."

The call clicked off; the dial tone sounded. Casey pushed a button to switch it off. He absently caressed its carriage and then sat back, sighed, decompressed in his chair for a moment.

"Okay, go to the bathroom, get a coffee, do whatever you need to do now, then come back in five minutes. I'm gonna grab a coffee from the machine." Casey started to extricate himself from his desk.

Standing by his chair, but anticipating, wavering, Ben questioned Casey, "The President?"

"Yeah, we'll give him a call in about five, he's expecting us."

_ CHAPTER 49

The little Samsung whirred again in its cradle on the desktop. The dial tone sounded once, twice, then – conforming to some universal human sensibility – got picked up on the third ring.

"Rasmussen."

The voice – nasal, Minnesota, somewhat metallic – had a weird cavernous effect.

"Umm, Mr. President?"

Casey couldn't help but smile to himself and to Ben. He was struck by an epiphany that the President was really weird.

"Yeah, it's me," the Presidential bulk shifted audibly over the phone, "you guys caught me mid-set, I just want to finish this, won't take too long."

The Samsung emitted a grunt from the President and then the collision of metal on metal. There was a final clang.

"Sir? Mr. President?"

"Yeah, I'm here."

"Sir, are you okay? Where are you?"

"Right. I'm in the POTUS fitness room."

"Sir?" Casey was trying to process.

"Just finished a leg press set. Don't worry, this call is secure, plus I've got privacy and don't have to note our call in any diary, or anything."

The President sounded matter-of-fact, relaxed, still metallic. He began to elaborate without Casey even asking, "I've got a pretty disciplined workout regime, so not out of the ordinary for me to punctuate the week with it."

"Sir..." Casey nodded at the phone, working to comprehend.

"I can talk to you guys without me letting anyone know and without anyone taking any notice."

"Yes, of course sir, that's very good."

"I'm working out, it's official, it's explained as part of the Presidential regimen."

"Very good, sir," Casey was obliging. There ensued a rhythmic clanging of some heavy object. The President's breathing became ragged over the speakerphone.

"Sir?"

"Just got in another quick set," the President sounded winded.

"Umm, very good, sir."

"So, talk to me, what do we know now?"

Casey folded his hands on the desk, nodded to Ben for concurrence and directed himself toward the speaker phone.

"Mr. President, as you know, Ben's recent encounter with some additional intelligent alien life form changes the landscape fundamentally, as I discussed with you during our earlier call..."

"Go on, we've covered that," the President was calm, vaguely impatient, metallic.

"My counsel...my recommendation, Mr. President, is that we convene a meeting with all concerned..."

"Given alien technology, that would be everyone on this planet. We're all *concerned*," the President replied pithily.

Casey and Ben could hear the President fiddling with the setting on some sort of weight machine.

"I mean, the immediate principals, Mr. President..." Casey remained unfazed.

"And so, that would be...please confirm for me, Jim, whom you have in mind...?"

"Well, sir, that's obviously you..."

"Of course, I'll bring Levchin, too."

"That's right, yes," Casey nodded, "our Caller reps, whom I can coordinate with, plus Ben and me – and of course, this new interlocutor."

"Right, right. Jim, you mentioned earlier, this was Brenda Donovan? From Bloomberg, right?"

"That's right, deceased, but no longer so, apparently. Ben can provide some detail," Casey motioned to Ben to provide some color.

Ben leaned toward the phone, "Mr. President, I can summon – I guess that's the right word – Brenda rather easily. It's strange, but wherever they are, they're listening for my signal to them."

Ben shrugged his shoulders, being as nonplussed as the President.

"Okay, that's great," the President sounded distracted, even more metallic. Casey and Ben could hear what sounded like objects being manipulated and adjusted. Was he preparing to do another set? The President seemed to take a breath, and became more present

"Brenda Donovan, I watched her reporting from time to time. She – I guess we can't say that categorically – was very lucid." The President sounded thoughtful.

"That's right," Ben nodded glumly, "Brenda is a non-corporeal representation of some kind, much like Jonathan and Steve are."

"Behind which, there are the people – or *things* – we're negotiating with," said the President.

"That's correct, sir," Ben was respectful, also now freshly depressed that he had fallen in love with a chimera. It had seemed like love to Ben.

"Great," the President replied, accompanied by a baritone rumbling, a long sound indicating he was either yawning or stretching. "Thanks, Ben, for these comments," he resumed. "Jim, your view on next steps?"

"Sir, as discussed, we convene promptly a meeting, a physical meeting of all the principals – yourself, Secretary Levchin, the Callers – such as they appear to us in their manifest forms – Ben and myself, and this new alien facsimile, Brenda. I urge that we do this in short order, sir." Casey gripped the arms of his chair and leaned toward the phone. His small, pebbly blue eyes were intent, mirroring his single-minded recommendation.

"My sentiments exactly. I concur," the President's metallic voice was registering almost a tenor. Was he still exercising? Ben wondered. "I'd like to be a little more sub rosa in terms of meeting surroundings, etc..."

"How so, sir?" Casey queried. Plainly energy levels were up all around, Ben thought.

"Well, this novel meeting – to include two different alien interests – should be even more private and discrete, I think. I would like to hold it at Camp David. That way, we have more assured privacy."

"I like that idea, sir. I can let the Callers know about the venue. No problem in getting them on board."

"Good, let's get moving on this. I suggest we schedule this within the next two weeks. I'm not traveling any time soon. No hot decks or memos have crossed my desk. I think things will be clear near term."

"Great, sir, let me know. I'll communicate with the Callers," Casey was nodding again.

"Great, I'll send details to you offline. Thanks Jim. Ben?" The President raised his voice with the interrogative.

"Yes sir." Ben snapped to and paid attention to the cradled Samsung.

"You're sure you can...what's the word? Conjure – summon – Brenda?"

"Umm, yes sir. Brenda, er, the facsimile, seemed motivated. They would like to speak to us. To *you*, sir." Ben looked at Casey, who gave him an encouraging wink.

"Good, I'll give a rationale about needing some Steve Jobs-like time for presidential reflection, and I'll make sure to keep staffing there at a minimum. We'll have privacy."

"That sounds good, Mr. President," Casey leaned back in his chair, signaling mostly to himself that the call was concluding.

"Any questions on your end?"

"No sir, I'm fine with our direction. Ben?"

"No sir, thank you sir," Ben responded to the phone.

"Great, we'll move on this. Jim, I'll forward more details as soon as I have them. Reach out to the Callers."

"Will do, sir."

"Great, thanks guys, take care. You'll hear from me soon." The phone clicked, ending the call.

_ CHAPTER 50

Ben sat at the long dark wood table and rested his hands against its surface. He looked around the brightly-lit conference room. Absently, he craned his neck this way and that to take in the wainscoting that framed the room's ceiling against its walls. The trim was a bright white, while the room had been painted in matt gray. The overall effect was of a room for a graduate seminar. The seats were moulded wire and orange plastic, contrasting with the dark brown table. A spider-phone sat in the center of the table, but there were no other hints of technology.

"The Callers managed to get here, too."

It was Casey whispering to Ben. Ben could hear the hard Omaha "r". Casey kept on whispering, for no apparent reason other than some momentary diffidence. "Didn't you see them get out of the escalade? They parked out front, as we were walking in."

Ben mutely shook his head. He was no longer struck by Casey whispering. Now the thought that these two apparitions, Winter and Allen had driven up in a car, or in something that appeared to be a car, held sway in Ben's attention.

"They should be here any minute or so," Casey became more audible. On cue, the Callers there then appeared through the open doors and seated themselves opposite Casey and Ben. The two chimera and the two men exchanged pleasantries and some idle conversation. Allen was always more informal and maybe more adept at small talk. Winter was warm, but quieter. Ben had dressed in a nice polo and jeans for the "relaxed" off-site Camp David setting. Casey looked Sierra Club, as usual. The two Callers were in dark business suits, as usual. They looked as Nixon did when he was famously photographed walking on the beach.

The President and Levchin quickly followed the Callers, who both angled themselves toward the head of the table. They appeared as freighter and small military escort – Rasmussen's massive size and Levchin's small and taut figure. More like a carrier task force, Ben thought again. Both were dressed casually, too. They had gotten the memo, although Levchin was both casual and lacquered. The President seated himself, fingered his notes and gamely looked at the attendees. Levchin sat to his side, concentrating on the notes before her.

"Jim," the President began motioning in the air, "we'll be able to get the new person here?"

"That's right sir, that won't be a problem. Ben knows the code," Casey responded and turned in his seat to look at Ben. Levchin looked up, and the President, smiling, now looked directly at Ben.

"Sure, umm, yes sir," Ben gazed levelly at his leviathan Commander in Chief. "I can call – or summon – her. She should come, then."

Just saying that, Ben realized how ludicrous it sounded and was struck by the fact that he didn't sound – or feel – a bit nervous about it. His mother would call that self-possession. It just struck him as strange. Turning in his seat now, so that he sat looking away from the conference table, and feeling a little less self-conscious, he muttered the incantation, just as Brenda had instructed. He sounded the commands clearly, but in a low tone, almost liturgically. Almost immediately, they heard a small knock at the conference room door, which then cracked open slightly before swinging wide. A face and figure leaned in through the opening – quiet and smiling shyly. It was Brenda. She surveyed the room, looking at each person in turn, then caught Ben's gaze. Her features softened more, and she smiled even more broadly.

"Hi Ben."

The President rose from his seat at the head of the table and swayed a bit as he waited for Brenda to walk toward him. Seeing the President rise, Levchin also stood, brushing the front of her pantsuit, and waited beside the President. They formed an irregular skyline at the head of the table.

Brenda extended her hand to the President, who grasped it.

"You've come a long way," his voice was warm, orotund, sitting in place of the observant, slightly mechanical tone that was his default setting. "Welcome to the United States," the President said, still smiling, before releasing her hand and lightly touching her shoulder.

"Thank you, sir. It's an honor, Mr. President, to be here." Brenda's smile was broad and even, she glanced down for a moment, appearing demure. To Ben, she looked radiant. Brenda then turned to Levchin, who stood, with eyebrow arched, at the President's side. "Madame Secretary, it is an honor, ma'am."

Levchin grasped Brenda's hand and looked squarely at the apparition, "And you are...?"

"I'm Brenda Donovan, from Bloomberg News."

Levchin winced and nodded, "Of course."

The President relaxed his large frame and pointed to the end of the conference room, where a coffee service had been quietly wheeled in.

"Okay, everybody, umm, we have some coffee, beverages, some breakfast items. Please help yourselves and then we'll get started."

The four humans adjourned momentarily to the coffee trolley. Ben looked over to the conference table, where Brenda and the Callers were seated on opposite sides. Each looked content and impassive. None of them bothered to get up for coffee or a breakfast snack.

The humans, though, availed themselves of the coffee service. Levchin opted for black tea with a dab of honey. She paused before the trolley and chose a small red apple from the bowl of fruit. She held it, scrutinized it, then exhaled a fog on its bright polished surface and rubbed the apple against her blouse in a quick fashion. She returned to the table, as did the others. The people were sipping at coffee or tea, nibbling at items selected from the trolley. The Callers were sitting contentedly, beatific.

"Alright." the President rested his hands on the table surface, breathed in deeply, expanding his diaphragm, then exhaled. "Let's get started. As you can imagine, I've been giving this a lot of thought." The President paused and scanned at the assembled at the table. "After conferring with Secretary Levchin," the President gestured to his left, where Levchin quietly nodded, "we have decided on the following format. The decision we reach today, at this table, will either confirm or modify our policy regarding extra-terrestrial life and interstellar relations."

"We plan to arrive at this today – in sum." Rasmussen directed his gaze slowly around the table, meeting the eyes of each person – earthling and non-earthling alike. Rasmussen folded his hands into a steeple, resting flat on the table, while he began to elaborate, "Each of you will participate. Everyone in turn will provide thoughtful – but spontaneous – remarks on what direction our policy should take: Should it remain as is? Or, should we change it?"

The President paused, closing his eyes and clasping the bridge of his nose for a moment before continuing.

"I'll call each of you – Rose, Ms. Donovan, Jonathan and Steve, Jim and Ben. I expect that each of you will be incisive in your comments."

Still gazing at the President, Casey leaned toward Ben and muttered under his breath, "This could be a crap shoot."

"Good," President Rasmussen gathered himself, leaning back in his chair, "let's get started. I would like to ask Brenda Donovan to make her case for us. To speak on behalf, I guess, for this new extra-terrestrial community." The President turned his head to look squarely at Brenda. "Ms. Donovan, the floor is yours."

"Thank you, Mr. President," Brenda cleared her figurative throat, and continued. "It is a pleasure and I appreciate the opportunity to speak to you, to speak to all of you – and Ben," Brenda paused to rest her bright gaze and smile on Ben, who began to crimson, "it's just so nice to see you."

Casey turned toward Ben and grinned, the President briefly arched his eyebrows, Levchin pursed her mouth. Brenda turned her gaze to the President and, smiling, went on.

"This is a special time for humanity, a seminal time," she leaned forward in her seat and pointed at some metaphorical point in the air. "I believe humanity is ready for this moment." Brenda paused again and surveyed the group assembled around the table. "I understand – we understand – that you have a relationship in place, one that gives you comfort, a feeling of stability. We would in fact like to change that, and embolden you." Brenda was magnetic to Ben. He continued to focus on her, as she explained. "We – a gathering of different beings, different worlds – would like to make that relationship better, more expansive, more open – more fruitful, dynamic and stimulating for you."

"Mr. President," Brenda continued, a lock of chimerical hair falling across her face, "we can offer so much to your people, to all of humanity. We are prepared to do so, because we know you are ready." With that remark, Brenda turned to stare at the two Callers, who were seated at the other side of the table.

"And so, Mr. President, we invite you to end an isolation, which is no longer necessary, may never have been necessary. We invite you to join the larger universe. We are ready to help expand the scope and breadth of humanity's possibilities." With that, Brenda smiled and gave her head a demure tilt, folding her hands serenely on the table.

Rasmussen nodded his head slowly and stared for a moment at Brenda. He was processing, Ben thought.

"Thank you, Ms. Donovan," Rasmussen conveyed a small smile, and appeared engrossed.

"Looks like he's processing that input," Ben whispered to

Casey, who turned to grin at his direct report.

"Your observations are, in many ways, cogent," Rasmussen smiled, his facial muscles beginning to relax. He straightened his shoulders and posture and shifted himself to face the two Callers, who met the Presidential gaze.

"Gentlemen, I would like now to hear from you. I have known you only for a short time, but have been impressed by your candor – if not always by your transparency. I would like to hear your views regarding Ms. Donovan's proposal."

Winter and Allen looked at each other, before Winter leaned forward, clasping his hands on the table. It was a very slow, deliberate movement, very human. Allen turned slightly in his chair and leaned on its plastic structure closer to Winter, waiting for his boss to speak.

"Mr. President, thank you for this opportunity to share a perspective, however briefly, on this issue of, let's say – openness – and to address Ms. Donovan's points."

Ben studied Winter, whose mien was solemn, his head dipped slightly. For a moment, Winter shut his eyes. Ben perceived the gravitas and sincerity. Was this all for effect?

"We've been talking with humanity for a while now," Winter began elaborating. "First with your President Nixon, now with you. We have enjoyed this privilege and appreciate it," Winter shut his eyes again, for a moment.

"It has indeed been our privilege to know you, to hear you, and dare I say – to protect you – so you can grow and develop, so you can become robust and thoughtful in a much larger world, in a much larger realm of existence."

"On the face of it, very commendable," the President showed a tight but agreeable smile.

That was glib, Ben thought, but he noticed Rasmussen's fixed concentration on Winter, who returned Rasmussen's stare.

"I can say honestly, forthrightly, we do care for humanity,

but we must let you go your own way, follow your own path..." Winter's voice trailed off, he turned his head and seemed to look at the conference room door, then resumed, "We have found this to be the best way – to let you develop under your own power. We are here, Mr. President, to renew our offer of protection, if you still wish, so you can do so."

"Well, ah, thank you Jonathan." The President looked genuinely pleased.

"And one more thing..." it was Allen, sitting beside Winter. Ben noticed for the first time that Allen had been taking notes on a long yellow legal pad, which was weird. Allen raised his head and with his writing hand, held his Ticonderoga pencil upright to make a point.

"Remember, as they said more or less in the *Transformer* movies, 'You are a young race.'" With that, Allen lowered his head and scrutinized his notes.

"Right," Rasmussen looked fazed, but rallied, "it is helpful to hear from you, from all of you."

Rasmussen shifted in his seat, grimaced, and shifted again, as if to relieve pressure on his lower spine. He smiled at the Callers and then directly at Levchin, who returned in kind. Although she was smiling, she seemed more tightly wound than usual, ready to put her two cents in, it seemed to Ben.

"Rose, I'd like to hear from you next. You've shared some cogent observations with me, and I think we'd all benefit if you'd share them with the group."

It was a nice lead-in. Ben looked at Casey, whose amused, mischievous expression was duly in place and familiar to Ben. There was though, a thin terror-struck overlay to his face that Jim may not have been conscious of, but was there. It was an expression marking nature and chaos. Levchin was such an engine, unceasing. Who knew what she would say – or what she would want?

"Mr. President, thank you," she opted for a serene and thoughtful tone, "I appreciate sitting here with you to, as you say, share my thoughts."

Ben surveyed "the group" as the President put it, which counted four human beings and three alien simulacra; indeed, seven beings and facsimiles thereof in total.

Levchin continued, "Our relationship with the Callers has been an auspicious one. We should be grateful –we *are* grateful – for their care and the friendship they've shown us." she paused, resting the flat of one hand on the table, the other she kept bunched.

"This has been a special relationship for humanity, and for, specifically, the United States – a relationship now going on more than forty years. But..." Levchin steadied her gaze, looked even more thoughtful, "the only constant is change, change is constant – I believe the Buddhists say that." She looked almost bemused, then gathered herself.

"And, I know, in my bones, that humanity is moving forward. The United States is moving forward."

Ben studied the features of the Callers, of Brenda, each of whom seemed to be looking blankly back at Levchin. Their staring was unsettling; without seeming to notice, Casey and Ben by contrast were registering open, inviting expressions, encouraging Levchin to carry on.

"But change, yes," Levchin scanned the table, "the Buddhists were on to something...Why deny it? In short, we, Mr. President, must change as all else changes around us. We must revitalize this long and special relationship, make it more dynamic. And so I posit, sir, that we need to knead, mark, and reinvigorate this Caller relationship. To do so, we should extend that welcoming hand – our welcoming hand – to Ms. Donovan and her, er, people. There is so much we can learn and do from this emboldened new start."

Rasmussen straightened in his chair and seemed to loom over the entire table. His hands remained politely folded on the table top and his eyes fixed on Secretary Levchin. Jesus, how big was this guy, actually? Ben thought.

"Very bold, very decisive Rose. Why?" The President asked.

"Mr. President, as they say, I'm glad you asked," Levchin was ready to elaborate, "and it's very simple."

At the table, Brenda was beginning to look pleased at this human's perspective. Casey and Ben were uneasy about the bravura.

"Humanity is developing and progressing quickly. I believe firmly we have the capacity for this – an enhanced relationship – and now, clearly, we, humanity, could benefit from technologies and methods that the Callers and, indeed, Ms. Donovan's people could present to us, if they were allowed to. The challenges we face, collectively, are enormous, despite ingenuity. We can, as one might say, use all the help we can get," Levchin concluded.

"You think so, Rose?" the President was laconic, but focused.

"I do, sir." Levchin continued, "And I think we, the United States, are here providentially. Our institutions are robust, and our sense of pluralism is deep and long standing. We are in a position to lead humanity in this transition." Levchin paused to let her words settle among her listeners, human and alien.

"The benefits from a fruitful exchange of ideas, from technical revelations, would be enormous for our country and for humanity as a whole. We would, more than ever, count on and value our friendship with the Callers," here Levchin made an open-handed gesture toward Winter and Allen, who sat impassively. Were they morose? Ben thought.

"And, of course, we would foster new ties, new exchanges, and be the better for it." Now standing by the table, Levchin rested her folded hands in front of her, signaling a conclusion to her remarks.

The President was silent for a few seconds more, shook his

head then nodded slightly, gripping the bridge of his nose briefly with thumb and index finger.

"Thank you, Rose. Thank you for these comments. Your thoughts and energy are always so valuable. Again, many thanks."

"Thank you, Mr. President," smiling to everyone and no one in particular, Levchin sat straight in her chair. Brenda looked flushed and happy. She leaned closer over the table, and said in a mouthed, hushed tone, "Thank you so much Rose. Very thoughtful comments!" Levchin managed another smile which then degraded. Seeing a television personality that truly wasn't really there was discomfiting.

President Rasmussen rubbed his brow and tapped lightly at the table top.

"We've been gathering comments from around the table, and they are much appreciated." Rasmussen's face had suddenly become warmer and open, his smile infectious and benevolent. It was a look displayed in televised town hall discussions, in in-depth media interviews and in curated campaign imaging. It was also a fundamental and primal gesture, evocative for being a sign that someone so physically powerful and potentially threatening meant no harm. Humans and non-humans smiled back at the President. Both Casey and Ben leaned closer over the table to study him.

"Jim, I'd like to hear from you, from your team." The President opened his arms and gestured expansively. His voice was warm and soft, much less mechanical than it could be, Ben thought. "We would all benefit," the President went on, "to hear your perspective, one informed by over forty years of experience."

"Yes, sir. Thank you, sir," Casey contemplated the President.

"Please, Jim," the President sat forward and gestured toward the extent of the conference table, "the floor is yours."

Casey shrugged and rolled his shoulders as he leaned closer to the table, his smile fixed. He placed a hand on the table and turned to catch Ben's attention, then turned toward Rasmussen.

"Mr. President, I'd actually like Ben to share some of his observations with the group first. I think they'd be very helpful. I can then make a few of my own remarks, if that would be okay, sir."

Rasmussen appeared relaxed now, with his shoulders sagging forward, his expression attentive but indulgent. Ready to listen, but maybe he had already decided on what to do. The thought transited through Ben's mind.

"Okay Jim, that sounds good," the President nodded. "Ben, please share your thoughts. I'm interested in hearing them."

Ben looked quizzically at Casey, who nodded and smiled back. Ben steadied himself where he sat, although he didn't really feel that nervous. The room's plainness and decorative familiarity was also comforting. Ben placed his hands, one on top of the other, on the table and addressed the President.

"Sir, there is something we can point to with certainty," Ben paused, and stretched his arm over the table to point to the two simulacra. "We don't know much about the Callers. We don't know where they come from, we don't know what they look like, we don't know what they eat, if anything. We really don't know why they're here."

Ben paused again, seeming to collect his thoughts.

"They have, of course, given us a reason. And it's a very appealing reason." Winter and Allen moved in their seats. Allen began fingering his tie. "And, maybe it's even true." Ben, to his surprise, ended his last sentence a half-octave lower.

"But, one thing we can say, which is also evident, is that their touch, whatever it might be, or has been, is very light. There are no invading spaceships, no legions of alien soldiers, our cities still stand. We can still try to make our own way." Ben stopped again and examined the faces of President Rasmussen, stony and watchful, and Secretary Levchin, who appeared introspective.

"We also know that their technology is powerful, certainly far beyond ours. But, for whatever reason, at least as far as we can discern, we have never felt the bite of that technology," Ben continued, inadvertently exchanging glances with Brenda.

"Maybe the Callers, maybe they are really solicitous of us. Maybe they are here with us doing only what they can do, given the larger, higher, broader environment that is theirs." Ben shut his eyes for a moment and then opened them. "I recommend, sir, that we keep the status quo. It has worked. We may be better for it; we're not worse."

The President emitted a sudden, large basso yawn and stretched his shoulders and arms in opposite directions, startling the group.

"Thanks, thanks very much Ben, very thoughtful comments," the President smiled at Ben magnanimously. "Jim, I appreciate Ben's comments. I'd also like to hear yours. What's your take on where you're at with our friends, the Callers, and with our prospective new friends" The President extended an open hand toward Brenda.

"Mr. President," Casey stared directly at the President. The pebbly eyes were very bright. It occurred to Ben how much older Casey looked, just then. "Mr. President, we've been talking with the Callers now for a long time, since President Nixon's time, since I was a young man." Casey took a measured breath, continued, "Not to get too personal, but the country and I have experienced an awful lot during the intervening time. For me, life certainly went on since Mr. Nixon's day – got tenure, published a fair amount – even more noteworthy, certainly in retrospect, got to teach a lot of people, raised children, enjoyed grandchildren, savored my friends, loved my wife and still mourn her passing."

Casey stopped, his gaze now distant and directed toward nobody.

"Mr. President," he began again, "as Ben pointed out, the

technical power the Callers have is considerable, maybe in some ways beyond what we can conventionally measure. But here we are," Casey focused again on the President, "we've lived our lives, since President Nixon's time. And the Callers have been here, with us, as interlocutors – maybe even as friends." Casey paused and glanced at Winter and Allen, who shifted in their seats.

"President Rasmussen, during this time as well, since I've been at my post, so to speak," Casey gave a small grin, and looked down, "our nation and the world have seen progress in so many ways. I believe the Callers have neither influenced nor hindered this progress.

"Even now sir, this progress continues. You may not be fully aware yet, but others helping pursue long standing federal scientific efforts will surely brief you, if they haven't already. That progress to date is considerable." Ben turned more in his chair to stare at Casey, wondering at his boss's new depths. Casey went on.

"My clearances have always been high, and I've been around for a long time – with many ties over the years," Casey met the President's impassive gaze. Levchin knitted her brows, as she studied Casey and took in what he was relating.

"And we, the United States, and for that matter humanity in general, have been left alone to explore and follow new lines of inquiry – with truly no interference from our friends, as they have promised," Casey gestured toward Winter and Allen, who to Ben appeared vaguely embarrassed and diffident in that moment.

"Even now," Casey noted, "our assigned scientists and engineers are working on the technology to make operational light speed barrier circumvention real for us. They are getting closer, and making progress. This will mean that we'll be able to travel realistically to the stars." Jim became wistful.

Ben glanced at the callers to see their reaction, which he couldn't parse. He turned to see Brenda, who looked now weirdly out of character and dismissive.

"Why wait Mr. President? We can provide that technology to you now!"

"Sir, we are making progress, and we will get there," Casey continued unfazed. He straightened his back and concluded, "Mr. President, I advise you to maintain our policy with the Callers, just as it has been. It has served us well. I think they've proven to be our friends, and we've been able to move forward under our own power. And thank you, sir, for allowing me to share this view." Casey then seemed to slump toward the back of his seat. He heard, without looking, the somewhat muted, but exasperated sigh from Brenda at the other table end.

At his end of the table, the President sat quietly, smiling, with eyes closed, serene. He had steepled his fingers and now pressed his fingertips to his mouth, opened his eyes.

"Very well put, Jim. Very clarifying."

The President shifted his bulk then in his seat and returned his gaze to Casey and the others around the table.

"Jim, I really appreciate the input you've provided, as I do the comments and observations of everyone here today," the President made a solicitous scan that captured each of the others. "The comments you've all made are very helpful. They've, uh, prompted a lot of thinking on my part," the President nodded to confirm the point.

"I think now would actually be a good point for us to take break, maybe to gather our thoughts a bit. Let's push away from the table, and reassemble in a half hour or so. So, let's break for now."

With that, the President rose from his chair, smiled reflexively at the small gathering, and began making his way toward the conference room door. Casey saw that Levchin sprang with some alacrity from her seat to trail behind the President. He could see through the open doorway that she apprehended him. Although Casey couldn't make out what they were saying, he watched the small, taut figure that was Levchin making small precise gestures. The President's form, opposite Levchin, appeared large and still. Casey could see Rasmussen nod to his Secretary of State, and then turn away from her and move on. Levchin stood still for a moment, then turned to go in the opposite direction.

Casey shifted to his side to see Ben, who appeared to be idling and lost in thought. The old man began absently drumming his fingers on the table, before deciding to stretch his legs as well. He rose from his seat and tapped on Ben's shoulder, pointing to the doorway. Ben looked up and quietly nodded. Casey exited the conference room into the hallway, which was carpeted in a durable red fabric that, while still uniform and structurally sound, harkened back to some much earlier administration. The batten board walls were modest, although well maintained, clean and neat. The place maintained itself, but design was an afterthought, plainly. Casey shooed the idle impression from his mind and decided to take the President's cue to step outside for some fresh air. The old man automatically detoured to the men's room.

Walking in, Casey kept his gaze directed a few feet in front of him toward the ground. Looking up, he stutter-stepped and paused, seeing the President's large frame looming over one of the urinals. Ben walked past Casey and stopped at a urinal at the other end. Casey grimaced and noted to himself that he did have to go, so positioned himself at the urinal between Ben and the President's towering form.

"Jim." the President's voice was light, with more of a tenor aspect to it just then.

"Sir." Casey looked up toward the voice.

"Will see you back in there in a few minutes," the President noted, stopped to shake himself, then zipped, flushed, and headed toward the bathroom door. In one motion, he wavered for a moment, corrected, quickly washed and shook his hands dry, then left. While Casey couldn't see the President exit, he could hear the sequence of actions. Now, removed from the Executive presence, Casey unconsciously relaxed and passed what had been the morning's coffee, before gathering himself and turning slightly to the motionless Ben.

"See you back there in a bit."

Ben nodded. Casey strode toward the sink and washed, then made his way outside. He would stand there and pause, for just a bit.

CHAPTER 51

Casey walked back into the conference room after just a few minutes outside. He eased back into his seat and nudged Ben's shoulder, prompting a raised face and smile.

"How are things?"

"Fine, I guess. The President's not back yet." Ben motioned toward the end of the table. Casey noticed a cup of steeping tea in front of Ben then, looking across the table, he saw another cup of steeping tea. This one was placed in front of the seated Brenda, who was smiling benignly.

"You talk with Brenda at all?" Casey now whispered to Ben.

"Yeah, a little," Ben answered in a matching hushed tone. He leaned in closer toward Casey, "She admired your comments, said she liked what I'd mentioned, too." Ben paused and looked down. "But she hopes that we, rather the President, comes to an 'enlightened' decision."

"Which means...?" Casey provided the Socratic coaxing.

"That, of course," Ben gesticulated softly in the air, "humanity opens up to the universe, that sort of thing."

"Did you say anything?"

"Not really," Ben continued to whisper, "we have our view, which is more or less contrary to that, at this juncture... I just said it was nice to see her again," he added.

Casey nodded and sighed. He looked across the table and saw Brenda, looking winsome, sipping at her hot tea. What was she, *it*, thinking? Casey scanned the table further and saw Winter sitting very still, eyes closed, face arranged in a beatific expression. Sitting next to him was Allen, who caught Casey's glance and returned a smile. He was sitting upright, looking alert and was, weirdly, sipping at a coffee. Casey shook his head to himself and folded his hands, resting them on the table.

The small figure of Levchin bustled through the doorway and into the room. She headed for her place at the table, close to the President, while sticking her cell phone back into her handbag. Levchin stood before her seat to smile at the other attendees, "Nice to have a break." She spoke in her Russian-tinged lilt.

"Yup," Ben smiled and nodded toward Levchin.

"President should be back pretty soon," Casey whispered to Ben, then sat back in his chair and studied the wainscoting.

Strange, Casey thought to himself, this was like a break in a seminar session. He smiled to himself at the thought. When the President returned, Casey noticed a refreshed Chief of State, more relaxed. Rasmussen conveyed a warm grin to all around the table before taking a seat at its head. With the President smiling, everyone smiled back. The President's warmth was infectious. Everyone seemingly wanted to be agreeable. Rasmussen extended his arms over his head, stretched them a bit, reaching for the conference room ceiling and yawned. He then brought his arms back down to his sides and adjusted his chair. Everyone was still smiling, waiting. Rasmussen's expression remained amiable, but somehow now, just a little intense. He rested his elbows on the table.

"You know, it's important to be deliberative. I get that," the President nodded, suddenly interjecting, it seemed to Ben. "I do like deliberation, but I also like efficiency, for lack of a better term. I see the value in clear transmission, without so many oscillating efforts. I'm struggling for a metaphor, I guess..."

President Rasmussen idly waved a hand in the air. The rapt audience, both human and non-human, were quiet and still, sensing a judgment coming. Ben could see that the President – a systems person, an electrical engineer – sought the value of a clear signal.

"So, this is a freighted issue, a freighted issue," the President continued. "It's fundamental to us – humanity. This issue entails our relationship, really, with the cosmos. It may actually entail our survival…"

President Rasmussen now seemed distracted; his eyes were distant. Ben looked around the room to see everyone staring at the President. Casey's brow was furrowed, his expression intent as he faced the President. Rasmussen's developing homily and the steady attention of his listeners evoked an image in Ben's head. It was as if the President were the leader of a small group, a band, a wandering Mesolithic party. It was as if he were their shaman, albeit a very large, imposing one. They needed to know what to do. He would tell them.

"Like I was saying," the President snapped out of the momentary fugue, "I think it's best to deal effectively, efficiently. You've provided me information and views in the best way possible. That's why I convened this meeting. I'm grateful to be able to digest, to process, what you've all said."

Ben looked across the table to see an impatient cast start to rise over Levchin's expression. Down from Levchin he saw Brenda, who was smiling and slightly nodding at the President, as if to please and coax him along. Ben looked to the other side to see the two Callers sitting silent and impassive. Steeling themselves?

"So, I've found that taking information in, insofar as I can, as reasonably as I can, and then moving forward…being able to "satisfice", as the great systems-thinker Herbert Simon might have put it, but I'm getting off topic…" The President precluded further rambling and for a moment looked pensive.

The air, Ben noticed, seemed to be chalky, dusty. Camp David was pretty old. This conference room was in order, sure, but a little neglected maybe. Such thoughts had a brief footing in Ben's mind. He absently rubbed at his temple and tried to listen.

"The main point I want to make, from the very helpful input you've all provided, and from what I can observe…" Ben stared and could see the Presidential eyes were now calm and level, clear and steady, pebbly, like Casey's, which he had never noticed before. "...and analyze," the President said, looking warmly at the group, "and weigh and even intuit, is that I must conclude that our present tenured relationship with our Caller friends should be maintained."

Ben heard Casey's noticeable gasp and felt his playful punch on the shoulder. He turned to see Casey still seated, but smiling, working to contain himself. Ben looked across the table to see Levchin register a mildly frustrated expression and shake her head. Both Winter and Allen seemed to brighten, but were contained. Brenda looked nonplussed, but remained silent, a vestigial grin still in place. Rasmussen, looked a little wistful, rueful even, and directed himself toward Brenda.

"Ms. Donovan, I want to thank you, I want to thank you very much for opening up this new line of communication," the President paused. "It's made all of us think." Rasmussen made an open-handed gesture. "It has certainly made me think," he looked down at his lap, then back up.

"Brenda, I have to say, though, that things have to stay, stay as they are. We'll keep them, as they are. We're not ready for any changes..." President Rasmussen gave a tight-lipped smile and shook his head slightly.

"GREAT!" It was Casey, now he couldn't contain himself. "Yes!" His pebbly blue eyes were sparkling, his expression giddy. Casey grabbed and punched at Ben's proximate shoulder.

Rasmussen appeared startled at Jim's sudden outburst and shifted in his chair. Rose looked on exasperated, but maybe already reconciled to the policy confirmation.

"Yes, well..." Levchin's voice, slightly Cyrillic to Ben's ear, was accepting, "we must have certainty."

"You're making the right decision, sir," Casey was emphatic.

The President rose from his chair and walked toward Brenda,

towering over the simulacrum. Ben looked on sympathetically, also feeling nostalgia and pangs for Brenda, despite an inclination not to. Sitting beside him, Casey could see that.

"Don't worry too much about it, pal. Such an interesting..." Casey searched for the word, "...figure."

"There are plenty of fish in the sea," he went on, fatherly, "you'll meet someone else, even human."

"Uh, yeah, right," abashed just a bit, Ben turned to smile at Casey.

"Ms. Donovan," President Rasmussen took Brenda's hand, while she emerged from her seat, "the best of luck to you in your different efforts."

"Umm, thank you, sir," Brenda smiled but looked pensive, as Winter and Allen clearly focused their attention on her. She let go of the President's grasp.

"Perhaps we'll meet again one day."

"Yes, well, maybe, maybe so," Rasmussen was halting, but accommodating.

Brenda stood before the table, facing everyone, "It was a pleasure working with all of you." She smiled demurely, while Winter and Allen continued to stare. Focused but impassive.

"Goodbye everyone!" Brenda turned on her heel, and began walking toward the conference room door, but then stopped. "Good bye, Ben." She smiled with what seemed genuine affection. Ben blushed, but smiled back, and then she was gone.

"Yeahhh!" Casey was still exuberant.

Ben focused on the space where Brenda had last been. So many good times, such fun – the thoughts flitted through his brain and were gone.

"Sir," Casey continued, "you made the right decision, sir."

"Yes, I think so," Rasmussen sat with fingers clasped and resting on the bridge of his nose. Levchin sat quietly, as if to conserve energy.

"I think I did. I think I made the right decision," the President concluded again.

The Callers had by this time gotten up from their seats. They stood, rather respectfully, to the side of the conference table, beside Levchin and the President. In their dark suits side-by-side, they looked funereal.

"Sir," Winter began, at that moment seeming more empathic to Ben, "I understand this was probably a tough decision for you, but it was the right one."

"Yes, yes, President Rasmussen, I agree," Allen began, becoming more voluble and less stately than Winter, "I have to agree with Jonathan, you've certainly done the right thing. Damn straight."

President Rasmussen looked first at one Caller and then at the other. He began studying the two in his own analytical way, prompting Allen to continue talking and elucidating.

"The woman, er, envoy, you've been speaking with – well, not necessarily so bad, as these things go..."

"No, not necessarily bad, that is correct," Winter added solemnly.

"But, they are...they, and others, are..."

"Mischievous." Winter punctuated Allen's sentence.

"That's right," Allen smiled, "Very. They are indeed mischievous."

"As Steve has intimated," Winter continued, "we know who and what they are... And we've bolstered and updated the screens and defenses for your planet."

"That's correct, Mr. President. We have," Allen reiterated Winter's declaration, in a supportive tone.

Winter's gaze was level with the President's.

"They won't be bothering you again."

While listening, Rasmussen unclasped his fingers and briefly rubbed the flat of a palm over his face. "That's very good, gentlemen. I appreciate the enhancement of our defenses, so to speak."

"Thank you, sir," Winter smiled warmly, but continued staring at the President.

"But," the President hadn't finished, "I need to know more, I think *we* need to know more..."

Winter's smile broadened, showing his even teeth.

"Given, sir, this current juncture – what you've just experienced, how tenured our relationship is – I think we can arrange that."

_ CHAPTER 52

A couple of weeks later, Casey and Ben were back at Camp David, at the President's invitation. They were both dressed casually, with Casey looking ready for a leisurely hike in the Berkeley hills. He wore a deep blue Cal baseball hat with the cursive gold lettering, which brought out the ruddiness in his face. Ben stood with his arms folded, rocking back and forth on his trainer-clad feet. Beside them stood President Rasmussen, wearing a blue business-casual blazer that was somehow tailored to accommodate his shoulders and Secretary Levchin. Neither made small talk with each other or with Ben and Casey. Levchin stole a quick look at her watch. Both Ben and Casey had brought with them small carry-on luggage items, which were parked right beside their feet. In front of the President, his Secretary of State and their stationary luggage stood two young men with roller boards, also dressed comfortably and casually, but carrying automatic pistols. The little group looked attentively toward the compound entrance and security emplacement. Casey looked at the security detail and gently shook his head, chuckling.

"Having the guys here was my idea," offered the President, noticing Casey's reaction. "Rose and I looked into it," he added.

"They are Special Forces," Levchin's Russian lilt announced, "and completely trustworthy. They know nothing about it and will say nothing about it," Levchin finished, looking to Ben like the perfect Soviet: stolid and impassive.

"A big day, sir," Casey added just to fill the space.

The sound of two black escalades drawing up to the sentry focused the group. They looked on as the vehicles passed through clearance and drove up, slowing and then parking beside them. Winter and Allen emerged from the SUVs, car doors closed with a solid report. Both simulacra were dressed neatly and casually – like Casey, ready for an enjoyable hike amidst exurban nature.

Of the two Callers, Winter strode first toward the President.

"President Rasmussen, I see you're ready," he gestured expansively. "I'm glad. This is a big day in our evolving relationship. Glad to see you, too, Secretary Levchin. I think you'll find our upcoming trip informative, indeed."

Winter appeared courtly – and handsome, Ben couldn't help but notice. His manner was cosmopolitan for the little gathering. He reminded Ben of some university administrator at a well-positioned place and Ben couldn't help but smile.

"We have security as well, Mr. Winter," Levchin helpfully intoned, looking for a reaction.

"Oh yes, um, I see," Winter studied the two Special Ops men for a moment. "I thought you might."

"Glad we brought two vehicles, makes it much easier," Winter smiled at Levchin and the President.

"Hey Jim, Ben," Allen smiled, also animated by the occasion.

"Wow, this is really something," Casey stepped forward to shake hands with the two Callers.

"I know, right?" Allen nodded, smiling.

"One thing, guys – umm, Jim, do you have the Samsung with you?"

"Yeah, sure," Casey fumbled in his pocket and retrieved the cell phone, handing it to Allen.

"Great." Steve took the device and began touching different symbols on the display, "Super, that's it. It's set now."

"Oh, uh, what?" Casey and Ben looked more closely at the phone face, which showed two adjacent blinking green lights on a map schematic.

–

"My boss is gonna explain in a second," Allen grinned at the two. "See the two blinking lights on the phone? They are saying to the two escalades that 'you are here'." He was jovial and Ed McMahon-like.

"Okay, everyone, please draw in a little bit closer," Winter said, still smiling, getting down to business. "Mr. President, you and Secretary Levchin – and your security detail," Winter paused, allowing a small ripple of frustration to pass over his face.

"So, yes, right. We will, together," Winter resumed, "embark upon our trip, during which you will be briefed and interact with the two of us – that is, Steve and myself." Winter pointed to himself and Allen, who waved, "as well as with a few of our colleagues."

"Luckily, we have two vehicles – had anticipated the security contingency," Steve was winsome, and interjected helpfully.

"Yes, right," Jonathan's mild pique seemed to improve.

"Oh, one thing," Steve chimed in again, "a quick show of hands on this – does anyone have any internal medical devices? Anything like a pacemaker, something like that? Show of hands, please." Allen scanned the semi-circle as Levchin, the President and the security team looked nervously at one another.

"Okay, great, looks like we're all set."

Rasmussen turned to Casey, "Jim, the White House press team knows that I'm at Camp David again for a 'deep retreat'." Rasmussen gestured the air quotes to embellish.

"The Vice President is covering – obviously, she doesn't know the specifics." The President widened then narrowed his eyes. "If anything happens, work directly with her."

For a moment, Casey looked gob-smacked, but then rallied.

"I'm sure the trip will go very well, sir. No reason not to think so. This is historic."

Winter stepped closer to coordinate.

"Mr. President, you and Secretary Levchin will ride with me in the nearby vehicle. The security detail will be with Steve in the other car."

Allen waved to the two special forces men.

"Guys, come with me, but first let's park your pistols and

luggage in the back." Allen opened the hatch of the escalade.

"Also, I want you to unstrap. Anything metallic – other guns, knives, wristwatches – small stuff, like wedding bands are okay – phones, let's put it all in the back." The two men put the designated items in the box Allen proffered. He set it in the back and closed the hatch door.

"Oh, one thing!" Allen raised his index finger in the air and turned from the back of the escalade. He trotted over to Casey and Ben.

"Guys, watch the two green dots on the Samsung screen," he pointed at the screen face Casey was holding. "The dots – that's us, these two vehicles," Allen clarified. "You'll be able to track us, as we begin driving. Just keep a tab on the green dots."

"Well," Casey chuckled, "I suspected as much."

"Great, buddy," Allen clapped him on the shoulder.

"You'll see us – that is, the green dots moving along a path rendered on the screen," Allen explained. "After a bit, not too long after we get started, you'll see the two green dots vanish," he concluded smiling and stood there, for a moment weirdly satisfied.

"But, don't worry," he opened his palms for emphasis, "everything is good. When the green dots disappear, that means we'll be starting the next phase of our trip, okay? It's gonna be okay, really." Allen smiled again at Casey's nervous expression and touched his shoulder.

"I have no doubt, my friend." Casey replied cheerily and shook the hand of someone who wasn't really there.

"Alright, we've got to get going. Thanks guys. Remember, watch the phone."

Allen gave a final short wave and trotted to the second escalade.

"Godspeed!" Casey called, waving and looking on as the escalades started.

Allen in the second car flashed his headlights for Winter in the first escalade. Both vehicles pulled forward slowly, tires crunching over the pavement, heading toward the sentry and exit. Casey held up his mobile, so he and Ben could track the movements of the two green blinking dots. The little caravan stopped briefly at the exit check point, and then moved on.

"Well chief, they're on their way."

"It certainly looks like it." Casey sounded fatalistic.

The two men continued to study the small phone screen. Two green lights moved steadily along a line on the schematic, then corrected course at a right angle to travel along another line, continuing along the screen path for about a minute, then two, then three. Then the dots vanished.

_ CHAPTER 53

It was mid-morning on a Saturday in the Oval Office. There they were, or here we are, Ben thought. All of us in our not even business-casual, just casual-casual. Ben picked at the sleeve of his Nordstrom's smart-care shirt, then absently rubbed the heel of his palm against his jeans. Casey turned to look at him, the boss's pebbly blue eyes were happy and expectant. Ben smiled a quiet response.

They were both seated and accounted for in simple federal style armchairs, which, for some aesthetic reason or for reasons of protocol, were positioned off opposite corners of the Resolute Desk. Casey sat easily in his chair, comfortable in his Sierra Club olive green vest and worn khakis. He placed a hand on the Resolute Desk, which seemed to Ben a very familiar thing to do. Altogether, this was a very different meeting. There they were, sitting in the Oval Office on a quiet Saturday morning, to talk to the President of the United States, putatively to discuss "Global Cultural Trends". Something innocuous, diverting, and even fun for those interested, who might check the day's calendar. And there, behind the ramparts of the Resolute Desk, sat President Rasmussen himself, wearing a worn and extremely large Stanford sweatshirt, the distinctive red lettering stenciled across his chest.

"Nice shirt," Casey was playful, and sarcastic, staking his ground as a Cal Emeritus faculty member.

"I note the sarcasm," the President grinned, raising an index finger.

"Anyway, thanks guys for coming in this morning – later and a little easier, right? We'll get some coffee in here in a minute."

"Sir, Ben and I are very excited to hear about your trip – your journey. How was it?" Emeritus or not, the old man was genuinely enthused.

"Well, Levchin and I have been back for two weeks now and I've wanted to debrief you both, of course," the President's expression was nonchalant as he idly rubbed his hands together.

"I thought this venue and time to be nice and relaxed – not so crypto," Rasmussen smiled broadly. "This would be the right way to share impressions."

From their chairs, Casey and Ben leaned in closer.

"What were your impressions, Mr. President?" Casey asked.

"How did you get to where you were going, sir?" Ben added.

"Well," Rasmussen rubbed at his chin, "I guess, from the start, it was pretty strange." He managed a tight smile. "We drove on those country roads outside of Camp David. All very ordinary, really. I seem to remember Jonathan making small talk, Rose's upper arm resting against mine..." Pausing a little for effect, the President continued, "The next thing I noticed is that the car – our car – and the car carrying the security detail were stationary, just parked in a spot."

"Man, I mean *sir*, that's pretty disorienting," Ben noted. Both he and Casey were intrigued.

"Yeah, it was..." The President absently massaged his temple. "The whole area looked like a hangar bay, what looked to be different kinds of ships stationed in there – some small, some bigger. Had a kind of *Battlestar Galactica* feel to it..." Rasmussen mused, then trailed off, recollecting.

"The first contact, sir, I must say, with an alien place," small blue eyes opened at the thought as Casey took it all in.

"Did someone actually, meet you there...?" Ben asked tentatively but to the point.

"Yes, indeed. You remember Colonel Packard, Vance Packard – from our meeting here? He was there, he was there to meet us." Rasmussen nodding at this, mostly to himself. "Yup," he continued, "so all of us decamped from the cars. Colonel Packard – who was actually in dress blues – was with a small detail of personnel. They actually piped-in *Hail to the Chief.*"

"Funny thing," the President said quizzically. "I couldn't really make out the faces of the others – the other Callers, that is." He pondered at his desk for a moment. "No, I couldn't, Levchin couldn't either. Damnedest thing."

The President's face then brightened again. "We weren't alone..." he said cryptically.

"Who else was there?" Casey smiled and coaxed.

"What I mean to say," the President began elaborating, "the Callers had reached out to the Germans. The other country we include in Caller related matters, in addition to the 'Five Eyes' partners."

"Oh, well that makes sense, as things go, I guess," Casey said, pulling at his chin.

"Who were they, specifically, sir?" Ben interjected.

"They brought on board Dr. Ursula von der Leyen, the German defense minister. She had two security men with her."

"Ah, *die Kriegsministerin*," Casey responded promptly.

"Umm, yeah, that's right."

At that moment, a uniformed person from the White House staff wheeled in a serving trolley with coffee and refreshments. The President fell silent, as did Casey and Ben. They sat impassively while the White House staff member put finishing touches on the coffee service.

"Thank you so much, much appreciated," the President said cheerfully.

"Of course, sir. Please let us know if there's anything else you need."

"Many thanks, I think we're fine here."

The President grinned and nodded at the man. The three continued to stare until the staff member, now bemused, closed the door behind him.

"Well, it's here. We should grab some coffee, right guys?" The President smiled matter-of-factly at the other two. All three rose from their chairs and ambled to the coffee service, helping themselves to its offerings. Standing next to President Rasmussen, whose iceberg-like dimensions made him surreally large relative to the smaller and slighter figures of Casey and Ben, creating an almost spatial distortion.

"So, Mr. President, tell us more. How did your stay unfold there? Have you any idea where you were?" Casey was cheerful, the coffee further priming the occasion.

"Yeah, location. Funny enough, I actually have an idea of where we were…" The President rocked back on his heels for a moment. "Jonathan and Steve were open and very hospitable to us. The ship we were on, which I think was pretty immense, was situated, or cruising, or whatever, quite close to our nearest neighbor, Alpha Centauri."

"How d'ya know that?" Casey scrutinized the President.

"Steve mentioned it," the President replied nonchalantly. "Let me say, guys, the hospitality was pretty nice." Rasmussen waved an index finger between the two for emphasis.

"We of course had meetings, briefings, but the setting, I have to say, was really pleasant, very agreeable."

"How do you mean, sir?" Ben wanted the President to follow through with his train of thought.

"Well…" Rasmussen paused for a moment, shifted his weight from one foot to the other, "the facilities – I guess that would be the word – were pretty nice. We had comfortable conference rooms, sitting areas – everything very well done."

"Wow, that's great," Ben acknowledged.

"Yeah, they always had coffee, snacks, soft drinks – that sort of thing – always available," the President explained.

"Wow, human stuff," Ben noted, impressed.

The President nodded warmly at the recollection.

"Yup, so as I said, we had meetings – very revealing meetings," Rasmussen lowered his voice a half-octave.

"I'm glad to hear it, Mr. President. Ben and I would like to provide our counsel, inasmuch as it would be helpful," Casey was courtly and expressed himself thoughtfully.

"Thank you, Jim. I really appreciate that. That's, of course, why I brought you guys here today – just to touch initially on a few things." The President smiled warmly at the two of them.

"Sir?" It was Ben.

"Oh yes, Ben. Question? Ah, let me just say, let's be informal here. As I said, this is pretty much an informal meeting. Just call me Steve," President Rasmussen lightly gesticulated to add to the point.

"Uh, thanks, Steve."

"Your question?"

"How did you know, again, that you were close to Alpha Centauri?"

"Well," the President was smiling, "I, in fact, really don't know for sure, but that's what Steve told me." The President finished his sentence and looked at the expectant expressions on the faces of Casey and Ben, so elaborated.

"It was actually during our break, after meetings concluded during the first day, it seems – so hard to get a fix on the day and time, you know," the President wrinkled his brow and scratched at the back of his neck.

"Well, as I said, we had a break or free time, before they set up the dinner buffet."

"Dinner buffet?" Ben again.

"That's right. The food was fantastic, if I say so. First night was basically a Tex-Mex theme. Second night was Oktoberfest-style. The German guys said it was pretty authentic. Rose and von der Leyen are both pretty much vegan, so they were able to accommodate that, too."

Ben and Casey nodded mutely, encouraging the President to continue.

"Anyways, during this break, Steve stood before this large bay window, and gave a nice presentation on the different star clusters and nebulae we could see. Truly beautiful. But it was kind of weird – it was like watching Ed McMahon narrate a *Nova* episode." The President smiled more broadly at the memory.

"Here, I've got some pics," the Commander-in-Chief pulled out his iPhone, and showed the screen to the other two. "See, here's Steve during his presentation."

Ben could see a hale and avuncular Allen gesturing toward a star cluster.

"...and here's Rose with Minister von der Leyen," the President toggled to another photo.

"Those two got on like a house on fire. Look like sisters, don't they?" The President asked rhetorically, gazing at the petite, attractive, manicured and smiling women on the screen.

"And here's another one, kind of a team photo."

There, the US and German delegations stood together smiling. To Ben, the neatly-arrayed figures, smiling and casually dressed, gave the impression of a standard photo from some corporate or departmental off-site.

"Nice pic," Ben added.

"Thanks," Rasmussen put the phone back in his pocket, suppressed a yawn and refilled his coffee cup.

"So, sir, I mean Steve, what else can you tell us?" Casey pushed the discussion forward.

"Well," the President took a sip from his coffee, "Rose and I are preparing a guidance memorandum, given the many things we were able to learn."

"Sort of like Kennan's *Long Telegram*..." Ben nodded, looking thoughtful.

"Well..." the President grimaced, as he tried to seize the historical reference.

"Of course, that's a great idea, sir, er...Steve. You and Secretary

Levchin are putting that together now?" Casey added helpfully.

"That's right, and I want you, Jim, and Ben to look it over after we've drafted it." The President squared his shoulders at the declaration.

"Of course, Steve, that's what we're primed to do," Casey clapped Ben on the shoulder.

"Good."

"Steve, just one more question," Casey's small, bright eyes locked onto the President, "can you share, generally, what you've learned?"

The President stood quietly and looked steadily at Casey and Ben.

"Well, I guess I can say," the President stopped, reflected a bit more. His face broke into a small grin. "I guess you could say that although the distances are vast, space is still crowded..."

Casey nodded, smiling. "That makes sense."

"Guys, let's sit down, I can share a few more things with you," the President winked at his advisors on interstellar policy.

Coffee cup in hand, President Rasmussen ambled toward the Resolute Desk. Casey and Ben followed to take their seats.

FIN

ABOUT THE AUTHOR

Michael ("Mike") McDonnell has had a professional career in financial risk management, namely in country risk, market and credit risk management. He has had a life-long interest in global politics and history. His fiction will interweave themes that combine science fiction with elements from history and politics, and evolving society. Mike received his BA in International Relations from Macalester College, and has an MA in International Relations from the University of Chicago. Mike also holds an MA in Applied Statistics from Columbia University. Mike grew up in Omaha, Nebraska, but has lived and worked in New York, in Munich, Germany, and in the Bay Area of Northern California, where he currently resides. "The Callers" is his first novel.